The Ghosts of Amalgam:

The Linking Tome

JUSTIN ARTHUR FREEMAN

Outskirts Press, Inc.
Denver, Colorado

This is a work of fiction. The events and characters described here are imaginary and are not intended to refer to specific places or living persons. The opinions expressed in this manuscript are solely the opinions of the author and do not represent the opinions or thoughts of the publisher.

The Ghosts of Amalgam: The Linking Tome

All Rights Reserved.
Copyright © 2007 Justin Arthur Freeman
V 4.0

This book may not be reproduced, transmitted, or stored in whole or in part by any means, including graphic, electronic, or mechanical without the express written consent of the publisher except in the case of brief quotations embodied in critical articles and reviews.

Outskirts Press, Inc.
http://www.outskirtspress.com

ISBN: 978-1-4327-1376-8

Outskirts Press and the "OP" logo are trademarks belonging to Outskirts Press, Inc.

PRINTED IN THE UNITED STATES OF AMERICA

PROLOGUE
RAZIEL AND ETIENNE

In fifteen hundred Paris, France, a young man named Etienne Robert began a new life. He has a dashing face with slim blue eyes, trimmed brows, thick curly brown hair, an aquiline nose, and thin lips. His stature is imposing at six feet, with a medium build, strict posture, and stern face because of his introspective nature. At age twenty-three, Etienne was grieving over the sudden deaths of his father and, just yesterday, his mother.

Walking down the Parisian street, his mother's dying words fill his head: *Etienne, don't be a peasant forever. Find some way to make the world remember you and our family's name.* He yearned to fulfill his mother's wish. Etienne entered a pub and drank well. The wine went down bitterly as he watched drunken men laugh gaily and spill beer in their delight. The happy patrons gorged on meat, stew, and bread, flushing it down with beer or wine. Others gambled in large groups or told tall tales, but they were all joyfully inebriated. The packed bar seemed ripe to burst like a full keg seeping beer out the wood.

Etienne saw no one sullen like himself until he glimpsed an odd beggar in the corner. Though he wasn't upset, the beggar appeared worried and contemplative. While trying to place his emotion, Etienne noticed the beggar's unnatural beauty. His face was radiant and perfectly symmetrical. His eyes were fine ovals with purple pupils, his plush lips were almond-shaped, his nostrils were wide and dark, his cheekbones were centered and prominent, and his skin was moist and unblemished. He was dressed in torn clothes and his clean, smooth hands snuggled a dirty cape for warmth. By his smooth skin, Etienne believed the beggar probably had not been poor for long or that he was in disguise and held close to his cape to conceal his identity.

The beggar's eyes focused on a chipped cup he was sliding back and forth between his fingers. Its castle designs were faded and had two bowls, one smaller for holding the cup Etienne thought, and the other for drinking. The beggar gazed at him and Etienne felt a sensation in his mind, a throbbing like a light headache.

The beggar aroused an unsettling feeling within Etienne and he stood to exit the bar. However, the pleasant mood of the pub turned as the gregarious crowd exploded in violence. A gambler felt he'd been cheated and a brawl ensued. Cups flew, liquor spilled, and shots rang, splintering wood, breaking bottles, and ripping Etienne's back in several spots. He fell, paralyzed and bleeding, growing cold as he watched his blood creeping into his vision.

The bar blurred into a white haze and suddenly he found himself in an expansive snow-covered field with numerous small hills. Etienne stood and looked at his hands; they appeared normal but slightly transparent, and he could see his feet through them. He rubbed his skin; it felt like gelatin and his clothes were the same as in the pub down to the bullet holes. Mystified, Etienne walked around hoping to find someone that would explain what was happening to him and discovered a single figure in the distance, slightly transparent.

"Hello!" he shouted. It turned to him.

"A ghost!" said Etienne.

He was afraid and turned to run but saw more ghosts behind him. Snow exploded in small columns along the ground as if cannon fire barraged the field. Ghosts appeared in the wake of these columns. The sky changed from gray to maroon as if ink blotted its surface. A tower rose in the distance. Its multiple windows issued orbs of yellow light that swarmed about it like bees around their hive. As Etienne tried to grasp the moment, it disappeared instantly.

He was back in the pub, propped against the beggar's knee. He wet Etienne's lips with water from his cup.

"Easy," said the beggar.

"Wha—what happened?" asked Etienne.

"You were shot by that man." Cup in hand, the beggar pointed a finger to a slain man hunched over in a chair, the gun slipping out of his loosing grip. "It took me a while to revive you."

"Revive me?"

"Yes. You died."

"Wh—Where'd I go?"

"Depends, what did you see?" Etienne looked into the man's eyes and saw genuine concern.

"I saw a field covered in snow and people but they looked like…"

"Ghosts. They were the spirits of deceased men and women who, unlike you, weren't able to be brought back to life."

"H—how did you bring me back?"

The beggar raised his cup to Etienne's eyes. He opened Etienne's shirt and poured water onto his wounds. They healed instantly and all the water absorbed into his skin. The beggar placed the cup into Etienne's hands and helped him up. He stood as tall as Etienne did at six feet.

"Is he alright?" asked the bartender returning into his disheveled pub with police.

"Yes," said the beggar.

"Thank God," the bartender sighed.

"*God had nothing to do with it*!" the beggar screamed alarming the bartender, the police, and Etienne.

"Can you walk?" the beggar asked. Spite lingered in his voice.

"Yes. Who are you?"

"Raziel. I'm an angel."

"An angel as in a servant of God?"

"Don't mention that name! Give me that favor as I've given you back your life and more."

"What was that place and how did this cup revive me?" asked Etienne anxiously.

"That place is Amalgam and that cup has granted you eternal life."

"Eternal life?" Etienne looked at the cup in his hands, its gold trimmings and blue and white castle design now shone bright in the dim pub. "Where did this cup come from?"

"A cathedral in Amalgam's angel province of Messina and from this day, tell no one of how you came by it. You'll want to stay clear of ghosts from now on, especially those working for the barons if you wish to stay immortal," said Raziel. He moved swiftly towards the pub entrance and looked to his right and left.

"I must go, Etienne, come here." Etienne didn't remember telling the angel his name, yet having been saved by Raziel he felt compelled to obey. He stood next to the angel and saw the police blocking entry to the pub. Parisians moved cautiously as the quelled gunfight had spilled into the streets and disrupted normal business activity.

"Do you see them?" asked Raziel.

Etienne saw a few ghosts searching along the crowd, invisible to the mortal host. They carried ethereal weapons: swords, staffs, ball-shaped crystals, and some household items like pitchforks, axes, or shovels.

"Yes, I do. Who are they?"

"They're Morrigan Guards. Avoid them at all costs and never acknowledge their presence."

"Who are they looking for?"

"Me."

"What did you do?"

"A great sin for a just cause so that God won't be the only one to give out infinite justice. I stole that cup to give to the Phoenix who will save us all when he's entered Heaven. The Phoenix and I are trying to save souls from Hell and I ask you to help us in this task."

"Why me?"

"Many reasons, your personality and aspirations, but also because you're alone. You have the power to give immortality; be responsible with it. You'll want to save loved ones, friends and people who'll draw your sympathy but DON'T. You don't know what they'll do with their immortality."

"I read your mind and I saw into your soul. I know that what you will do with your longevity might aid the Phoenix, but what can you tell about a person just by looking at them? Can you distinguish a murderer from a peacekeeper, a lover from a rapist, or a saint from a sinner? No."

"For your own protection use good judgment and save only the estranged. The fewer people you help, the less you'll interfere with the Judgment and the Judge." Raziel moved closer and said, "A*nd we are not yet strong enough to resist Him or his* *barons*. The cup is called the djemsheed; it's a magical chalice that can grant immortality and take it from those who drink from it. When you decide to bless someone with this gift, have them drink water from your cup, and only water, because it's the one element that can activate the cup's magic. If someone's immortality must be removed, place some of their blood in the second and smaller bowl; three drops should do."

"Magic exists? Didn't God forbid it?"

The angel twitched at the mention of His name.

"Yes, but seek out the Amalgam Realm and the Phoenix within it and he'll teach you why it exists."

"Who is the Phoenix?" asked Etienne.

"A man blessed with the Creator's powers. He's our last hope for Cedric, Marcela, and me to re-enter paradise. Nevertheless, we must be cautious even of him. Men often abuse their power and as a precaution, I taught the second and third secrets of the Phoenix mark to two others in case of the Phoenix's corruption. You work for us now, an associate of the angels and I'll pass on the first secret to you through which you can undo the Phoenix's immortality."

The angel whispered the secret in Etienne's ear. Etienne listened with keen interest, not missing a single detail. Raziel returned his gaze upon the crowd and the ghosts lurking within.

"I have two more requests of you, Etienne. First, head to a restaurant called the Hammel; ask for Duncan or Pierre. I've told them their new master will carry the djemsheed. Show it to them and they'll be your eternal servants. Secondly, find your way into Amalgam. If you can accomplish this, you'll be the first man to prove the existence of life after death and obtain the fame and fortune your heart desires. When you reach Amalgam, find our prison, and free us if the Phoenix hasn't done so and your reward will be an unconditional pass into Heaven. Farewell, Etienne."

Raziel de-materialized from mortal sight but Etienne could see him as he flew past the crowd. The Morrigan Guards all chased after him turning into orbs of light like those in the wintry field. Etienne later discovered that those guards captured Raziel. His imprisonment sparked a massive celebration in the Amalgam realm. A celebration sullied by panic and chaos with the brilliant and frightening rise of the Dark Phoenix in a towering column of blue flame.

CHAPTER ONE
LAUREN WALSTON AND THE POOL PARTY

Baker's Creek is a small coastal town that is growing at a particularly swift pace. Geographically, the town is fertile and vibrant with its lush green trees, multiple streams emptying into a lake, barrier islands, and numerous hills but none larger than one giant incline in the center of town. It's populated by many wealthy families and has a particularly youthful demographic. Aside from the occasional malicious rumor about supernatural phenomena, many residents consider Baker's Creek the ideal suburban society. This progressive community has taken great care to mesh its development with the landscape, forging a town that appears to have grown with the natural environment.

One such area is that of Evelyn Lane. This street

lies upon a low hill with tiny yards containing trees and big bushes at the foundation of the colorful two-story brick houses and a view of the water a few blocks away. In one particular house, number twenty-five thirty-seven, a warm yellow glow emanates from the second floor bedroom. Within the room are posters of popular young male entertainers, teddy bears, and numerous photographs some of which depict cardinals, lilacs, and starfish. A telephone, a melted jasmine-scented candle, a diary, and a Bible open to the Book of Job lay on a bedside table stand.

Inside is Lauren Walston, a rising high school sophomore relaxing during her summer vacation. She is a black girl with brown skin and eyes whose short black hair falls barely to the bottom of her ears. Lauren has sickle-cell anemia, a genetic blood disorder that can cause excoriating pain episodes, yet she has been remarkably, and inexplicably, healthy for a majority of her life. She is a petite five-foot-five when standing but now she sits upon her bed, watching channel seven on a small television.

The channel broadcasts the fledging news station of her father Willem Walston's growing media network. Lauren watched carefully as she hoped to see Willem, who left on a business trip a few weeks ago. He anchors in the studio occasionally and, lately, has arrived in town and gone to work instead of stopping by the house. Her mother, Anita, has made scant mention of him other than how hard he is working.

A commercial for the news program preceded the broadcast. In it Willem was standing straight, strong arms crossed, dressed in a white shirt and blue tie. His thick black hair shined in the studio light and his brown eyes were determined as he delivered his station's commitment to the news. Reporting is Mr. Stroud informing his audience that the top story tonight on August fifteenth, two-thousand three concerns the opposition against raising the body in the unmarked grave at Baker's Creek Memorial Cemetery. He proceeded to describe the cemetery's history as a graveyard of shipwrecked sailors, washed inland and recovered from Sailor Lake, identified, and then buried. Local families want to raise the grave to prove the sailor as a genetic ancestor. Mr. Stroud continued:

"City councilman and excavation opponent Dr. Stephen Knowles continues to petition the courts and the mayor to halt the excavation. Dr. Knowles cites unnecessary expense and irreverence to the dead in order to solve 'a trivial mystery.' Nearly a hundred citizens have joined him in opposition to the excavation. However, the court sided with the families and set the excavation for September tenth."

Without a glimpse of her father, Lauren's thoughts turned to her friend Amy Thompson's birthday party. She tried to remember some of the expected attendees and could only recall her friend Renee, Amy's pal Peter, a loathsome boy who Lauren believes Amy fancies, and her crush Jason Birch. She pulled a photo of him from her dresser drawer taken during a biology class field trip to a greenhouse and gazed at it fondly. Lauren carried her camera everywhere, honing her skills so that she could become a photographer at her father's paper and was doubly grateful she brought it along that day because she captured her favorite picture of him.

Jason is five-foot-seven, slim build, innocent eyes, mocha skin, and a nice close trimmed haircut with small waves in his hair. He willingly posed for her, and she asked him to sniff a bouquet of roses during a class field trip. His brown eyes rose slightly above the red flower leaves, sending chills down her spine, and warming her very spirit. She poorly hid her enthusiasm around him and realized most people probably knew she was attracted to him. Lauren's head filled with lovely memories of them dancing at last year's homecoming ball and she was swaying in his arms again.

She daydreams often when thinking of him and felt like indulging in one now so Lauren moved Amy's birthday present, a bracelet, to her table stand and pushed aside her clothes for the party so that she could stretch out on her bed. She put on her favorite music and listened through her portable CD player. As the songstress sang a love ballad, her eyes closed and in the darkness stars sparkled, the ocean roared, and she and Jason sat atop the hood of his car on the grounds of the Baker's Creek Lighthouse.

She gazed deep into Jason's eyes with a big smile as they discussed their dreams. Lauren had wanted to ask him out when they were alone in that rose garden but she was too shy and resorted to fingering her hair, smiling, and laughing at his jokes, which were funny. The wind picked up, Jason took off his jacket and threw it around her shoulders. He used this moment to get close and tried for a kiss. She closed her eyes and he said to her, "Are you going to Amy's party tonight?"

"Huh?" asked Lauren looking around. Jason and his jacket dissipated into thin air and she felt cold once again. She fell to the ground as his car vanished from under her; the lot melted away to her mother standing in the doorway of her bedroom. Lauren saw her mother, Anita Walston looking curiously at her with a grin and odd sadness about her. Anita is five-foot-six; a slim body despite gaining a few pounds around her stomach and waist, black hair like Lauren's, brown eyes, and slim chin. Lauren quickly turned to her clock, the time was six thirty, and replied, "It doesn't start until eight."

"Shouldn't you start getting ready?"

"I have an hour and thirty minutes, Mom!"

"It takes thirty minutes to get to their house on Crow Island so stop daydreaming and get ready," said Anita approaching to sit on her bed. Lauren could tell something was on her mind and moved her headphones and compact discs from the bed to make room.

"Your father's here," said Anita silently.

"He is! Did he just get back from his business trip?" asked Lauren swinging her legs around to get up.

"No, Lauren, listen for a moment." Anita stopped her from standing up by placing her arm across her stomach. "He didn't go on a business trip. He left me." Lauren's eyes narrowed, she was confused and tried to understand.

"*He left you*, as in…"

"Your father and I are getting a divorce. I—I wanted to tell you earlier but, I didn't know we were going to go through with it. Willem and I have been having problems for a while and…we couldn't see ourselves working through them…together."

Lauren placed her hand on her chest in hopes of easing the sharp pain she felt there and the soothing the tensing muscles.

"Do you remember when you heard your father and me arguing in the middle of the night three days after our wedding anniversary in July? The next morning you asked me about it and I said it was about an unpaid bill. The truth is that night he told me he was leaving me for Natalie, a photographer at his paper. He left home and went to his office where he told me the next day he wanted a divorce. He wanted to speak with you but we knew that if he were to show his face around here, we'd end up arguing so we agreed to spend a few days apart. It turned out to be weeks, but at least we've calmed down a bit."

Lauren's eyes welled up with tears and she wondered if she was still dreaming. She trembled with anger and sadness. Anita pulled her close, Lauren put her head on Anita's shoulder and thought about the times she spent with her father, and how happy they were as a family. How Willem taught her to ride a bicycle, how the three of them went to the theater to see her favorite plays, how they supported her during cheerleading tryouts even though she didn't make the team. Were they lying all this time and for how long?

"I'm sorry I had to tell you tonight. I know how important this party is to you but Willem didn't want me to put it off any longer. He wants to ask if you would like to stay with him at his apartment for a few days so he could explain. I don't want you to come down to speak with him until you're ready." Anita moved Lauren's hair back so that she could see her face; her eyes were becoming red so Anita tried a more optimistic approach. "Lauren, you'll still have two parents that love you."

"Do you still love him, Mom?"

"Yes, Lauren, I do," said Anita sincerely. "It's not the end of the world honey so please cheer up. If you want to talk to him tell me now, I'm sure he'll understand if you need more time."

Lauren didn't know what to say nor did she respond to her mother. She lay on her bed and hid her face. Anita stood; Lauren could feel her hovering around her for moment before she left the room. Lauren continued crying, when her parent's voices seeped through the walls.

"Why can't I see her? What did you say? You placed the blame on me didn't you?" asked her father.

"Who walked out first, Willem?"

"This isn't my fault, Anita, you know that."

Lauren stopped crying to listen. For the first time she understood why they were divorcing. Thinking back, she remembered how they no longer kissed at breakfast, never talked about meeting each other for lunch, and never went out for dinner anymore. Was she unaware to the whole situation because of her infatuation for Jason? Lauren thought her ignorance wasn't completely her fault. She only heard one of their previous arguments because she had to use the bathroom in the middle of the night.

"Now she's going to think the worst of me. I'm going up there to talk with my daughter," said Willem.

"I just told her, give her some time. Don't go barging up there you might frighten her."

"What's frightening is that until tonight she thought we still loved each other."

Willem's cutting words pierced Lauren's heart. How could her father be so cold to her mother? Lauren heard his footsteps loudly as he approached so Lauren got up and rushed to lock the door. The knob turned as soon as her fingers left the handle. He knocked and turned the knob again before he spoke.

"LAUREN, OPEN UP!" said Willem. Lauren was scared; she never heard her father this angry. He knocked forcibly against the door and it shook inward. Lauren moved back and got in the bed in case her father opened the door. He continued pounding on the door, taking out his frustration on it.

"*WILLEM STOP IT! Are you insane?*" asked Anita.

"Why are you *making* me do this Anita? Be honest with her, she's no longer a child, she'll understand!" said Willem.

"What makes you so certain she'll understand her father breaking her door down to tell her you're walking out on us?"

It was silent for a moment; Lauren listened for voices, noise, anything. Then she heard footsteps going down below; she got up and pressed her ear to the door.

"You want to be difficult, I'll show you how difficult things can get," said Willem and the front door slammed shut.

Lauren went to her window and peeked out. She could see her father moving around the front of his car, a new one, with a pretty woman in the passenger seat. He started the engine and sped away; Lauren unlocked the door and went downstairs. She looked for Anita and found her sitting in the living room, hands covering her face. She was crying silently, Lauren had never seen her mother cry and felt sick at the sight. She ran to her mother's bathroom to vomit.

Lauren threw up dinner and let go of disbelief; her parent's marriage was over. Ever since she took an interest in dating, Lauren wished to find a boyfriend with whom she could experience a similar relationship. Now her parent's marriage, her model of the ideal relationship, destroyed much of her hope. She flushed the toilet and leaned her back against the tub, thinking of happier days, until she felt a hand touch her shoulder. Anita was standing over her, sullen-faced handing her some tissue; Lauren took it.

"You've got to get ready for Amy's party," said Anita.

"I don't want to go, Mom," said Lauren, drying her eyes with the tissue.

Anita crouched down, "I promised myself I wouldn't ruin this night for you and I hadn't planned on it. I didn't tell you while you were in school because you had finals and I didn't want our problems to affect your schoolwork. I hadn't planned on telling you tonight either because I knew you wanted to see Jason. He'll be at the party right?" Lauren nodded yes. "So try to have fun and when you come back I'll tell you what's likely to happen over the next few months. Go for me okay?"

Lauren didn't understand why her mother wanted her to go to this now insignificant party but she obeyed. She took a bath and dressed herself in the black skirt and red blouse she excitedly laid out earlier. Lauren left her room, forgetting Amy's present, and crept to the top of the stairs wondering if Anita was crying in private. She found her waiting by the door rummaging through her purse to find her car keys. She watched as Anita hesitantly removed her wedding ring before placing it into her purse. The sadness was present behind the smile she gave her daughter as Lauren walked down the steps. Lauren forced a smile; she didn't want her mother to start crying again.

"You look wonderful."

"Thanks."

"Oh, wait a moment." Anita moved to the den and opened her purse, spilled its contents on a small table and closed it. She handed the purse to Lauren; it was red with a gold fastening buckle. "Take this, it matches your outfit."

"Thank you."

They walked to Anita's brown sedan, pulled out the drive, rode silently to the Thompson's residence.

* * * *

Anita pulled into wealthy subdivision that was usually quiet but music and bright lights were pouring from one large house crowded with cars. Anita parked a short walk away and turned off the car. She sat for a moment with her hand still on the key in the ignition. Lauren knew her mother had something on her mind, but whatever she was going to say came out as, "Good luck tonight. I'll be back for you in three hours."

Lauren got out and when she closed the door she peered through the window to see tears rolling down her mother's cheek as she started the car. Lauren walked solemnly to the three-story brick house. She rang the doorbell and waited, not thinking to walk around to the back because her thoughts dwelled on father's words, "This isn't my fault Anita, you know that." She wondered what he meant but at this moment, she couldn't fathom any wrongdoing by Anita when Willem was the catalyst of her misery.

Luckily, someone was in the house to open the door, her best friend, Renee Dupree. She is a black girl with dark skin, straight black hair that cuts off at her neck covering her small ears, and beautiful arched eyebrows. Her babyish face holds wise eyes that are black and sharp, her lips are full, and her nose is orb-like at the tip. Tonight she dressed in a violet skirt that approached her knees and a black blouse. Lauren and Renee had been friends since sixth grade and Lauren could always trust her with her most private secrets. She wasn't the type of girl through whom many rumors flowed or was the subject.

Lauren well remembers the day she met Renee; she had come in class late and smelled heavily of cinnamon and a mixture of other scents she couldn't place. Peter noticed it and immediately set to teasing her about the odor and her bizarre collection of books, all dealing with theories on the afterlife. He accused her being a witch among other things, but Lauren realized in Peter's taunts that he was attracted to her. Lauren embarrassed him in this way saying he paid careful attention to her and could only express his feelings by mocking her. Peter blushed and stuttered refuting Lauren's claim prompting laughter from the class. Renee was extremely appreciative and they've best friends ever since.

"Hey, Lauren!"

"Hi, Renee," said Lauren with a melancholy drawl.

"What's wrong? You look upset."

"I am upset," said Lauren.

"Oh well, come in and tell me about it."

Lauren entered and Renee took her to the Thompson's living room which was in the rear center of the house. Inside was a round glass table set before a stylish curved suede couch and a huge wall-mounted television. Directly past the living room, Lauren could glimpse part of the Thompson's magnificent kitchen, which was now softly illuminated but no one was inside. Between the living room and kitchen was a flight of stairs that led up to the second level. To Lauren's left was a glass wall with a sliding door to the backyard where she could watch the party unfolding.

"Why weren't you outside?" asked Lauren.

"I wasn't in the partying mood. You know, with my mother's death and all."

"Yeah, I was really depressed when I heard about it. She died from cancer?"

"Yes, it was in remission for a while then it spread fast, throughout her entire body. She was trying to cope with her fear of death and she was in so much pain. She was telling us how…how much she loved us while fading in and out of consciousness then she didn't wake up. I didn't even have a chance to take in the fact she was going to die before she was gone," said Renee silently tearing midway through.

"She let out this awful yell while in pain I can't get it out of my head…"

Lauren gave her a hug and as she held her she whispered, "My parents are getting divorced."

"No! Willem and Anita? They were so happy whenever I was over." The news was a total shock to Renee and she held Lauren at arms length to see the truth in her face.

"They're good at hiding their problems. Mom hasn't told me much about it except that Dad was leaving her for a photographer at the paper. Before that they were arguing late at night when I was sleep."

Lauren sat on the couch. She felt comfortable confiding in Renee. She had lost a loved one permanently and Lauren reasoned she knew exactly how she felt. She placed her mother's purse on the glass table in front of the couch.

"Before I came here they got in another argument. Dad was so angry he almost broke down my door."

"Was he going to hurt you?"

"No, he thought Mom was blaming him for the divorce. He thought she was withholding the truth from me."

"Was she?"

"I don't know. Mom said she was going to tell me sooner but didn't because I had final exams and it got pushed back until tonight."

"I can understand that. I could hardly concentrate on my finals because I was so depressed about my mom's death. I spent much of my time staring of into space wondering where Mom was, if she was in Heaven, if there was a Heaven. I barely passed."

"How's your father handling it?" asked Lauren.

"He's managing. He had planned on growing old with her but 'till death do us part' doesn't mean in a good fifty years. He can't imagine a family trip without Teresa and with the loss of her income he has to work two jobs to pay for my college education. I told him I'd stay in-state but he said he would get the money to go where I originally wanted. After Mom died I realized how selfish I was and how I spent time arguing about things not worth fighting over."

"I know, before I came here all I could think about was how much I liked Jason."

"Oh," said Renee gravely.

The glass door slid open and in came a wet Amy Thompson. She was wearing a red bikini with big white polka dots. Amy has long black hair, glamorous eyes, and a voluptuous figure after having lost weight from a stomach virus. Lately Amy has been the subject of much contempt at school. Aside from being the prettiest girl at Royce High, many girls hate her because they teased Amy when she was fat and now she's been stealing their boyfriends for revenge. She also spread rumors about them, true or untrue it didn't matter, and claimed their ex-boyfriends had said it. Lauren learned of Amy's behavior from girls in the bathroom cursing her in frustration after losing their sweetheart.

They met in the seventh grade when Amy was unpopular with her classmates and Lauren was extremely shy. They became friends and got along well, and then in eighth grade, because of class schedules, Lauren rarely saw her except for the few moments when Amy was being humiliated. As freshmen, Amy and Lauren had only one class together but Lauren, in poor health due to sickle-cell, fell ill and then Amy with her stomach virus. However, the days when they were together Amy and Lauren shared their secret crushes, gossiped about teachers, and studied together.

"Hey Lauren, when did you get here and why aren't you outside?"

"I just arrived then I started talking to Renee," said Lauren standing up with Renee rising also.

"Hope you brought a swimsuit otherwise you might want to sit this party out and where's my present?" asked Amy disappointedly looking at Lauren's inappropriate attire and her empty hands. Lauren forgot all about Amy's present and that the birthday party was a pool party.

"Sorry, I forgot it at home. Is everyone in the pool?" asked Lauren.

"Just about, we're having a blast. I'm going back out to join them after I get a couple of towels for everyone. Come with me," said Amy. She took Lauren by the arm and up the stairs; Lauren said to Renee she would be back as she left.

"I know you've heard the rumors about me and just so you know the rumors are true," said Amy, no longer holding Lauren's hand, skipping a couple steps at a time. She entered the bathroom directly in front of the stairwell. The towels were in a small closest behind the bathroom door that swung outward so Amy's voice was muffled occasionally during the conversation. "But I'm changing, Lauren—" she closed the bathroom door to get a few towels then pulled it open to talk.

"I think I've found—" the door closed, "the one I love."

"Really? A little premature to say you love him."

"You think it's just another crush?"

"No. Just not *love*-love."

Lauren questioned the meaning of true love after witnessing her parent's marriage fall apart tonight. The door swung open with towels stacked on the bathroom sink. She also wondered how Amy could have fallen so hard for Peter; the obnoxious boy who's only redeeming qualities is that he's smart and good-looking.

"We've been dating for a month now. I haven't told anyone about him; didn't want rumors to start flying around and this time the guy is single."

Amy handed Lauren half the towels and Lauren stepped back under their soft weight. "I wanted to make sure he felt the same way about me before we started claiming each other as boyfriend–girlfriend."

"That's interesting, you said you hated labels. You said it was like being considered property."

"That was the excuse I gave guys when I wanted to break it off with them. I don't see anything wrong with being considered property, especially when it's a guy that makes you feel like his most treasured possession." Amy was standing in the bathroom with her right hand on the sink, her left on her waist and her weight shifted on her left leg.

"Have you ever seen guys with something they value above anything else like a pet or I know…a comic book they're certain will be worth thousand's of dollars twenty years down the line? They wrap it up in plastic and won't let anyone with dirty hands touch it if they let them hold it at all. It's not the best example but you see where I'm going don't you?"

"I think so," said Lauren close to laughing. Lauren stepped aside to let Amy out of the bathroom. She had to give Amy her credit, she was an honest person, and not many would proudly admit truth to such an ignominious reputation.

"For a while I thought only fools would get married and change their names to their husband's," Amy said as they went down the stairs, "but when I see how many men have such respect to their name it's an honor to say you're his wife."

They passed Renee, who was expecting Lauren to return and continue their conversation but was insulted she forgot about her as they headed to the pool area. Amy slid the door open, the music and shouting voices overwhelmed Lauren. As they walked around the pool, Lauren saw first-hand how exquisite it was. The pool was an irregular shape, almost as if the designers took inspiration from the splatter of a water droplet. The three hot tubs formed the stray particles and connected to the main pool. Marble stones outlined the pool and held large lamps that softly illuminated the area.

Lauren absorbed the activity; people played volleyball in the pool and tossed each other around, others lounged in pool chairs or chased each other with water guns. Four ice sculptures, all of which captured Amy at different ages, formed a square perimeter about the pool. Many of Amy's friends were taking pictures next to them. A long table with red cloth held gifts for Amy with pizza boxes, fruit punch, and red plastic cutlery. Lauren saw a three-tier vanilla cake that looked more appropriate for a wedding than at a birthday party. Giant red balloons were everywhere and had this been February any stranger could have mistaken this party for a Valentine's Day celebration.

Amy led Lauren to a smaller table to the far right of the pool area where they placed the towels down. In the moonlight, Lauren could see a couple of guys playing football but with such little light she couldn't make out their faces. She wondered how in the world they could see to whom they were throwing the ball.

"Amy this place is *incredible*," said Lauren smiling.

"Well it's my parent's house, but thanks. I'll be back in a second. Try and have fun!" said Amy as she ran towards the boys playing football.

Lauren walked around the edge of the pool, wishing she had brought her bathing suit to jump in and play with the cute guys in the water. She heard someone whistling and turning around Lauren saw a shirt-less Peter wearing blue swim trunks and sitting up in a pool chair waving and blowing kisses at her. He is a black boy with very seductive eyes and a strong physique, light-brown skin, and his hair is neatly trimmed, high and dark. He wears a thin moustache and goatee. Lauren often remarked how his appearance is the only thing he has going for him because his attitude is anything but attractive. She rolled her eyes before looking back to the people in the pool. Lauren heard Peter remark to his friend as he reclined, "That's the kind of girl I want, classy like Amy and a hot body too."

"Hour glass girls, huh?" asked his companion causally, stretched out next to Peter.

"That's right. Don't want it any other way either."

Lauren was appalled; she knew Peter only sought girls to fool around with them before dumping them and knew he wanted to do the same with her friends. She tried to ignore him but his conversation drew her attention.

"Before I came here I met this girl—" Peter whispered to his friend.

"Who?"

"Some nerdy artist chick, anyway she was painting the lighthouse on Coral Street and my boys and I were eating at the pizzeria. We come out and I'm first to see her, so I'm thinking, 'she's kind of cute.' I approach her and she looks up, rolls her eyes, and then continues painting. Now you *know* when you see that, she wants you right?"

"Of course," said his friend.

"So I'm like, 'Hi my name is Peter Townsend and I was just wondering if I can see your work, blah, blah, blah."

"Yeah, yeah, give me the short version."

"She was completely put off. I talked to my friends and they agreed that girls could be more polite when a guy asks for a date. *So we decided to play a prank on her,*" whispered Peter, his voice was hard to hear over the party noise.

"We got some monster masks from the Costume Shoppe, changed our clothes in the store, and left out around back. We came up behind her and scared her silly. She picked up her stuff and ran but here's the kicker; we followed her for about two blocks when she took off running. Do you know that grassy hill area down near the end of Coral Street? Well she ended up taking a little spill."

"What happened to her?"

"She's all right...I guess. I was afraid she was hurt but I think she deserved it—" Peter broke off his conversation and sat up quickly when Renee walked in front of him. He whistled at her and said "Hey cutie! Still reading about ghosts and goblins?" Renee rolled her eyes and Lauren heard him tell his friend "see, that's the type of girl I'm talking about! She's so fine!" Peter whistled again and called Renee's name but she ignored him.

"I hate Peter," said Lauren.

"Your not alone, nobody likes him, not even the guy he's talking to," said Renee matter-of-factly.

"Did you hear what they were talking about?" asked Lauren shocked.

"Tell me later! Lauren, I think I should—"

"Lauren!" said Amy coming back, turning Lauren's attention from Renee. Amy gaily waved her forward when Lauren felt a rush of anxiety. Jason Birch, her crush was standing next to Amy holding her hand; Lauren approached slowly feeling lightheaded with every step.

"Lauren, this is my boyfriend Jason," said Amy proudly.

Lauren was devastated. Her only anchor of

happiness in the worst day of her life had sunk into a sea of sorrow and pain.

"*What did you say?*" asked Lauren angrily; startling Amy whose smile disappeared.

"I…I said Jason asked me out. We're dating now," said Amy moving closer to Jason.

"I…I can't…I don't understand." Lauren was growing hot with anger, she was shaking, her lips began to tremble, and her voice broke.

"What do you mean? What don't you understand about Jason and me?"

"Jason—and—and you?" asked Lauren looking Amy up and down with profound disbelief.

Renee hung her head down, she knew Lauren liked Jason and Amy's recent activity in the dating scene was not going to convince Lauren that her interest in Jason was genuine. Some of the guests also took interest in what was going on with Lauren and Amy, mostly those around the pool. Amy excused herself from Jason, took Lauren aside, and spoke with her out of his earshot.

"Does it bother you that I'm dating him?"

Lauren did not answer; she stood looking confused at Amy. She was absorbing her friend's statement becoming increasingly angry.

"I…I don't understand why you would do this to me," said Lauren, her eyes beginning to well up with tears.

"*Do what?*" Amy pleaded to understand what Lauren was feeling.

"WHAT! You *know* WHAT! You stole Jason

from me!"

"He wasn't yours to steal, Lauren!" Amy whispered trying to get Lauren to understand and lower her voice.

"Neither were all those other guys you've been stealing at school. What have I ever done to you?"

"Listen, Lauren, I like Jason. He never mentioned you nor did you tell me that you were interested in him. I'm sorry but I'm not trying to hurt you—"

"Don't try to play the innocent role, Amy. You could tell I liked him, everyone can. I never teased you so why would you take him from me? I can't believe you! You're such a bit—"

"Watch it, Lauren! Watch what you say to me, I swear you'll regret it if you make the mistake of calling me out my name," said Amy strongly. She began to walk away when she returned back to her and said, "I had my suspicions that you liked him but he wasn't with you. It seems like I got to him first and you're just going to have to *deal* with it. After all, look at you," Amy gave her a disgusted glare. "What could you offer him? You're nothing compared to m—"

Lauren didn't let her finish as her right palm slammed into Amy's left cheek, leaving a red handprint in its wake with gasps reverberating from the onlookers. Amy covered her cheek with her left hand, her face hurt badly. Lauren started to walk off but Amy responded by pushing her into the table with her presents and cake. It succumbed to the pressure of Lauren's weight and broke in two. Cake and red punch spilled on dress, the presents were crushed under her as the crowd converged on the two shouting, cheering the fight on. Lauren stood and grabbed Amy's hair, pulling it; Amy grabbed Lauren's hands, digging her nails into her skin trying to get Lauren off when her hands lifted.

Peter left his companion to pull Lauren off Amy, grabbing her breasts in doing so, and Jason got Amy as the two shouted obscenities at each other. Lauren wrestled herself from Peter and shouted, *"DON'T YOU EVER TOUCH ME!"* She kicked him in the groin. Peter cupped his privates and fell screaming as Lauren walked away furious knocking off one of Amy's ice sculptures as she passed. It fell into a hot tub and the guests in it scrambled out before the ice landed and melted. Peter's friend helped him up, asking him if the feel was worth it; he replied, "I'll let you know if my children come out retarded."

Renee followed her as Lauren left the pool area. She slid open the glass door and stormed through the house leaving Anita's purse behind. Renee entered the house after her and shouted, "Lauren, wait!" but Lauren kept moving. She ran faster as Lauren made for the front door before Renee came up to her and pulled her arm to stop.

"Get off me, Renee! You knew didn't you?"

"I found out when I got here. Amy asked me if you liked him and I said you did, but I didn't think she'd tell you like this."

"Ugh!" Lauren said disgustedly as she continued moving.

"*Wait!* Where are you going?"

"I can't believe this is happening! It's the worst night of my life, my dad walked out, Jason's with that whore, and I'm…I—I'm pissed off!"

Renee followed her out onto the porch as a blue pickup truck was speeding around a curve. Alcohol clouded the driver's mind and evil intentions controlled his body forcing him to propel his car down the road. At that speed, he was unable to react in time…

"I won't let it go, Jason! She ruined my party!" said Amy furiously entering the house. "*Where's that bitch?*"

Jason followed her trying to convince Amy not to keeping fighting, but Amy brushed him off and pushed Renee aside as she searched for Lauren. Lauren, consumed by hate for her father, Jason and Amy, and life itself continued to walk down the street venting her frustrations when suddenly a shove came from behind as Amy resumed her attack. Renee ran to break them up when a blinding light stunned them all and a great jolt of pain and force plowed them all to the ground. The truck swirled around and stopped; the driver suddenly regained his sanity and sobriety and fled the accident once he realized what he'd done. Lauren felt little pain as her senses ebbed. Life became as dark as starless space and only a chill endured.

CHAPTER TWO
GATHERING OF THE NEW CITY

Jason screamed in horror as the driver sped off leaving three girls unconscious and dying in his wake. The house filled with cries for an ambulance as partygoers came running out of the house to help. Lauren rolled a few feet away from Amy and Renee; all were bleeding profusely. Lauren felt calm and rested when she opened her eyes. She saw Jason screaming over her and was puzzled as to why. He was looking down on her with a sickened expression. Her memories rushed back, 'daddy left us, I've never seen my mother cry, Jason is dating Amy, Amy and I fought, we got hit by a car. I got hit by a car!'

"I'm okay," said Lauren to Jason. He didn't respond; he was screaming for help.

"Jason I'm fine, help me up," said Lauren but as

she placed her hand on his shoulder she knew something was terribly wrong. Her hand was transparent! She raised the other and then rubbed them together. They felt like tight jelly, she rubbed them on her face, same thing.

Frightened, she stood quickly, all too easily; she didn't feel the weight of her body. She surveyed her ethereal form and it was identical to her old physical self. Her ghostly garments matched their material counterpart, stained with blood and torn similarly. A subtle pink glow emanated from her brown-skinned body. Inside her stomach was a white light, amplifying her pink glow.

Lauren moved her hands back to her face and ran them through her hair. The strands felt tactile like her skin until she turned her fingers where it became misty as if it was made out of steam. She panicked as she stood among a gathering of Amy's guests, none of them looking at her but down at the ground.

Lauren stepped away and saw her body lying in their midst. Her arms extended above her head and blood was running from her nose and mouth. Her legs were together but heavily scarred and appeared broken. Frantic people in her peripheral view turned her attention to the second and third mass of huddled kids.

Renee emerged from one mass and stood surveying her body much like Lauren then looked dreadfully frightened at her. She could only mutter, "Lauren!" which sounded like equal portions shock and a plea for help.

"You bitch!" said a voice and Lauren found Amy standing over the kids looking down on her body. "Look what you did to my face!"

"Amy?" Lauren saw Amy looking at her with the same angry expression when they were fighting.

"Who else would it be? Damn it, look at me! I'm horrible!" she angrily sobbed.

She too was glowing pink and Lauren could see through Amy's abdomen but not clearly, the white light blurred her vision. Nevertheless, Amy was easily identifiable, still in her bathing suit and bruised similarly to her body. Lauren didn't know how to react, she was overwhelmed. She didn't think they were dead because there they were still alive in spirit, everything was happening too fast.

"Is she dead?" asked some of the young women inquiring about Lauren.

"Ambulance is on its way," said Peter to Amy's parents coming out of the house.

"Oh my God! Amy? Amy?" asked Amy's mother pushing her way through the guests.

"Someone call Lauren parents. Mr. Thompson! Help me please," said Jason.

Lauren turned to see Jason calling for help from Amy's father, who was trying to get the children away from his daughter. Amy ran towards Lauren with her fists clinched.

"Look at my parents, they're going crazy, and it's all because of you. And Jason, why is he over there next to you? You did this to get his attention, didn't you? Do you realize what you've done? My life is over!" said Amy.

Amy renewed her attack and they grappled among the crowd surrounding their bodies. Lauren tried to fight back but she was surprised that Amy's attacks actually hurt; her punches were just as potent. Renee instinctively ran to break them up when a brilliant light blinded them ending their feud. Coming from the curve where the truck had blazed through moments before the light got stronger and then dimmed.

Lauren could see two unicorns drawn to a black carriage with a black cloaked figure at the reigns. The unicorn's skin glowed in the moonlight. Lauren had only seen such a beast on posters and cartoons. Its white mane flipped wispily even though its head rocked back and forth violently. Lauren could see the driver's form from underneath his heavy garments. The hands on the reigns were skeletal, its wings were black and worn, his face was decaying with one functioning eye and the other it's bony, empty socket and its neck was part flesh, sinew, and bone.

Amy hid behind Lauren terrified. The carriage door swung open and a ghost stepped out. It was a black female, her face heart-shaped, young and unblemished, her eyes were slim and brown, and her eyebrows perfectly lined. Her hair was black and shiny, straight at the top but curly towards the ends and it reached past her upper back. She wore a full-length skirt, a collarless blouse and a cloak all radiantly white; at the bottom of her cloak raged an animated blue fire.

The girls thought she was the prettiest woman they'd ever seen. The cloak design on the ghost's back that Lauren couldn't see just yet, was of three framed doors, the middle taller than its two tightly packed neighbors. The door's cracks filled with lines of light and occasionally a particular door would swing open, displaying earthly scenes, a fiery Hell, or pure radiance. Outlined slightly white was a castle upon a floating plateau that would disappear occasionally. The ghost smiled and outstretched her hand beckoning them forward. Lauren noticed that only her hands were pink, the rest of her visible brown skin gave off a slight blue hue.

"Its alright, you're a little shocked; death can do that, but we must hurry, we have others to pick up tonight," spoke the ghost.

They didn't move so the ghost approached them slowly.

"My name is Nasra Rallens, district purveyor of the New City and your guide for tonight. What's yours?" she asked gently.

"I'm Lauren and this is Renee and Amy," said Lauren pointing to her friends as she identified them. Nasra simply nodded at Renee but turned her attention to Amy who was trembling behind Lauren and spoke directly to her.

"Amy there's nothing to fear not even my decrepit driver," said Nasra.

"*No!* I don't ride with strangers. And where would you take us?" asked Amy.

"Where you will be safe and under the Judge's protection and if you come with me, I promise you might return to mortal life. Come," Nasra outstretched her hand again. Lauren took it and Renee pushed Amy along. Nasra turned slowly and they made their way to the carriage. Lauren drew back as they approached the driver but Nasra pulled her on.

"Don't be afraid, he's more friendly and talkative than you'd think. His name's Grimsley," said Nasra. She introduced the girls to the cloak-clad driver who tugged his hood towards them as if he was tipping a hat.

"I hope not everyone we pick up tonight is as apprehensive," said Grimsley to Nasra in a breezy voice as the girls boarded.

They sat on the left as far away from the driver as possible and Nasra sat on the right. Lauren watched the site of their demise from the windows. Apparently, the crowd could not see them, the unicorn's brilliance, or the carriage. They began moving.

"Where are we going?" asked Lauren nervously.

"Amalgam, but first we have to make a few stops," said Nasra as the carriage picked up more speed and rocked its riders from side to side as if they were traveling up a mountain pass.

"What's Amalgam?" asked Renee.

"It's the spirit realm; you're in it right now. This district is what we call the New City, its as much Amalgam as it is Mortalland and don't worry you won't be alone," said Nasra as she pointed out the window. They were crossing the bridge over Arthur Sound and in the moonlit night, they could see more unicorn driven carriages carrying passengers across. Their wings outstretched, shining like stars in the distance followed by deathly black-hooded wraiths and black coaches full with equally confused ghosts. Lauren, Renee, and Amy looked out their windows. Lauren saw eight carriages flying swiftly about the mainland and Outer Banks. Their dark shapes and unicorns ghastly neighs struck fear in her heart and she sat back up inside.

"Is Grimsley a ghost?" asked Lauren.

"He's a reaper. Reapers are fallen angels whose glorious bodies have starved to their present state. Since they didn't fully turn away from God, their current manifestation and the pain they suffered to reach this state is meant to humble them. Only by faithfully serving the Lord will they regain all the power and splendor of their former selves."

"Reapers aid the Court in the Gathering of the New City, which is what we're doing tonight. They scare off cold spirits and demons in order to usher spirits into the purgation or infernal realms. Angels are the most powerful beings in Amalgam, and reapers, being weakened angels aren't too inferior so it's not wise to anger them. Their unbearable hunger is temporarily satiated after they've returned from a successful gathering. Ghosts that refuse to cooperate, or stall them in anyway, really upset them."

"What's the Gathering?" asked Renee.

"Every soul in the New City gets trapped here due to the Mortalland Seal. We have to search for each spirit individually and transport them to the Gathering Plains of New Elysian. The reapers vision see only the ethereal realm and can find a spirit anywhere in the New City."

"Oh God! None of this makes any sense," said Amy. "Reapers, ghosts...what happened to the bright lights and the tunnel; the simple stuff people said they saw when they died. Wait, are we dead?"

"No, not yet anyway, but don't worry about that and concerning the bright light, I don't know, maybe that happens elsewhere. I died here just the same as you three some three hundred years back. Grimsley picked me up along with another purveyor."

Lauren looked at Nasra and saw a bright-light emanating from her belly and inquired about it.

"What's this light in our stomachs?" asked Lauren pointing to her own radiance.

"Bioluminescence, our light source brought out during the night by a liquid sustenance we call spectroplasm. Trees, animals, natives, nearly anything which uses this substance will light up the night after feeding," said Nasra.

Lauren listened intently and watched fearfully as she saw the reapers about the mainland. They dove into Baker's Creek like scavenging vultures picking up the dead. She worried about her mother who would soon get the news of her death. Anita would start crying again and Lauren hated that she and Willem were putting her through so much stress. She wondered if her death would help Willem and Anita reconcile or drive them further apart.

They arrived on the mainland and passed by Sailor Lake where they halted briefly. Nasra and Grimsley looked outside towards the cliff underneath the lighthouse where another carriage looked strangely idle. They didn't see the reaper, unicorns, the purveyor or any passengers and a black mist filled the scene.

"Who drives that carriage, Grimsley?" asked Nasra.

"Uriel," he said. "They must've had a battle with a Phoenix loyalist. There's necrosidium everywhere."

"I hope they hadn't gathered many spirits before they got into it. Let's take a look!"

Nasra and Grimsley left the carriage and strode into the lake towards the abandoned coach. The girls looked out the window as they waded through the water. Nasra and the reaper walked about the coach looking for any passengers and called out for Uriel and the purveyor. They returned minutes later and Grimsley said he'd inform his boss, the death angel Azrael, about this incident.

They were off again, leaving Kell Road to Kepchar Street. They were so close to Evelyn Lane that Lauren wished for the driver to take her home. She would run upstairs and into her bed, awake from this nightmare, where she'd still be alive, her parents would still be together, and Jason would be single. As if Grimsley could read her mind, he turned onto her street. Ecstatic, Lauren prepared to run as soon as the carriage stopped. However, she didn't move a muscle once she saw why they were on Evelyn Lane.

Kevin Vasteck, her next-door neighbor and family friend was sitting on his porch amazed as the carriage's brilliant lights covered his face. He appeared differently, Vasteck was eighty-years old, but this man was young, possibly in his thirties. He was a Caucasian man, with blue eyes, a long nose, bulging biceps, and his hair was shaved close on the sides but the top was longer and trimmed flat. Vasteck appeared like Lauren had seen in many of his older photographs when he was young during the fifties. However, when he caught sight of Nasra, he smiled and his hair grew longer and took on a greasy texture slicking back on the sides forming the cooler ducktail look. Lauren saw her animated cloak as she invited him aboard.

While walking back, Vasteck flirted with her. Nasra blushed but not because she was attracted to him; after many years of gathering spirits, they still surprised her. Vasteck approached the carriage door and jerked back with surprise when he saw Lauren. He sat across from Renee before he spoke to her.

"What happened to you, Lauren?" asked Vasteck. Lauren glared at Amy.

"It wasn't my fault," said Amy angrily and crossing her arms.

"Car accident, you?" asked Lauren.

"Old age," said Vasteck with a sigh. Lauren smiled and nodded her head.

"Why do you look different?" Lauren asked as he sat in the carriage. Vasteck shrugged his shoulders.

"Anyone who dies above the age of thirty-three, reverts to that age upon their death," said Nasra. "However, some can still choose to represent themselves as older or younger and many do in Amalgam."

"Why thirty-three?"

"It's the age of our Savior's death," said Nasra.

"Jesus?"

"Yes," said Nasra.

"I've never been religious but at least it's good to be young again," said Vasteck smiling, stretching back.

"That's probably why you'll be in Amalgam for a while, Vasteck," said Nasra. Vasteck asked Nasra what Amalgam was and she informed him just as she did with the girls. After her explanation, Mr. Vasteck spoke with Lauren again.

"I haven't seen you in a while, Lauren, is school going alright?" Lauren's brow rose in disbelief as did Vasteck's when he noticed her surprise. "Sorry, I guess I've already become comfortable with death. I've certainly been expecting it for the past five months. Does your mother know what happened to you?" asked Vasteck.

"I don't know," said Lauren.

"Hmm," he said but then he gazed out the window and spoke, "Well, she does now."

Lauren looked out the window, she saw Anita running down the porch, jiggling the handle of her car and then fumbling quickly through her purse to find her keys. They were moving again, drawing closer to Anita and Lauren saw the she was scared, arousing that unsettling feeling in her.

"Mom! I'm fine, really I am. Don't be frightened, MOM!" shouted Lauren although she didn't even know she was leaning out the carriage window screaming for her mother. Nasra covered her mouth and pulled her back inside.

"Don't scare her!" said Nasra.

"She didn't even see me, how can I scare her if she isn't aware of me?" asked Lauren looking as her mother got into the car and pulled out swiftly in reverse and headed to the Outer Banks.

"There are ways, Lauren, and your emotions will bring them out. The only thing you might do to her is scare her to death."

"You mean we can still be seen and heard?"

"Yes. Mortals can feel, see, and hear us if the conditions are right, even fear us if we're up to no good. You don't want to kill your mother to let her know you're dying do you?"

"No," said Lauren as she sat back.

"Dying?" asked Vasteck.

"Yes, dying. Just wait, it'll all be explained," said Nasra.

They left Evelyn Lane and made several other stops. After Vasteck filled the carriage, every subsequent stop stretched the interior; a torch materialized on the right wall and an aisle between the seats and the door. The carriage had gone from comfortably seating five to twenty-five and it appeared more like a stretched hearse. It also became quite unruly with passengers complaining that they weren't ready to die.

"Who's going to feed my cat?" asked a middle age woman who had half her hair in rollers and wore a wet nightgown. The rest of her hair stood up on her head; even in death the electric shock she received while taking a bath carried its mark into the afterlife.

"Damn! I forgot to write my will. Now my cokehead sister's going to get all my money," said an elderly man.

"When's this ride going to park me at my body? I want to get back to living. This dead thing isn't working, now, Nasra, you promised," said Amy as bargained with the exhausted purveyor. "I just want you to let me out. I'll find a way back into my body and forget this ever happened."

"It's not going to happen until we reach Amalgam, Amy," said Nasra.

"But it may happen, right?" asked Amy.

"Yes," said Nasra.

"WHAT!" A young male ghost cried out. A bullet scarred his head, the hole was still smoking, and blood covered his shirt. He was a gas station attendant and looked as if he'd been harassed by his killer. "Why does she get a second chance? I got shot on the job and I'm only seventeen."

"You'll find out why but you're not getting a second chance no matter what happens so get used to being dead," said Nasra who shifted her weight and stood. She pulled from her garments a rolled piece of glowing yellow parchment, unfastened its seal, and unfurled the sheet.

"Roll call. Mr. Kevin Vasteck?"

"Here," said Vasteck.

"Ms. Gloria Dunley?"

"Present," said the electrocuted woman.

Nasra called out name after name, everyone replied in their various ways, everyone except for three.

"Excuse me," said Renee. "You didn't call our names?"

"I wasn't supposed to," said Nasra. "You weren't called tonight, you just happened to enter the spirit world."

Renee looked worried but Nasra stilled her fears saying, "Just relax."

The ride became extremely rough, they were jerking back and forth, up and down. Nasra had to sit back down and some of the ghosts were getting dizzy and begged to be put out, but Nasra didn't listen or try to comfort them.

"We're here," said Grimsley.

Lauren grabbed the windowsill and looked out. She saw the mansion called Monroe's Manor by townspeople but never knew why. Its impressive French-Renaissance design drew hundreds of tourists to the gates of this private property but no one had been inside to her knowledge or met the elusive Monroe.

On guard at the gates were two previously invisible spectral coats of armor but tonight they stood evident to spectral eyes. Their visors lifted as if they were talking, they shifted their spears, and their helmets followed the first carriage as it approached the gate. Also invisible to mortal eyes, a giant shield on the gate that read "The Amalgam House," the mansion's true name. The shield split in half as the gate opened; the carriages entered.

Lauren's carriage was in the lead. She looked to the left and saw eight carriages filing in behind from various streets, the sky above and through the trees below. The road they were on was winding and though the wheels on the carriages turned, they made no friction with the ground. Lauren wondered why the ride was so rough but gave up trying to figure it out.

She looked right at the house and thought it appeared dense. Three stories, a multitude of windows, doors, and balconies for each level that stretched alongside the entire house. It had a smooth beige color with no cement lines, and with no overgrown vegetation or visible deterioration, the house appear quite immaculate given its ancient age. Vasteck eagerly leaned forward and observed the house with Lauren.

"Ever since I was a little boy, I wondered what was inside this house. I never would have guessed it's filled with ghosts," said Vasteck. "I always thought it belonged to some elusive millionaire. I hope we'll get to go inside."

"Not tonight, Vasteck, but if you wish to see inside Amalgam House then you'll have to apply with the New City district representative."

"And is that you?" asked Vasteck with a charming smile.

"No, an elderly woman and the best oracle in Mortalland, she's in the employ of the Court."

"Again with the names, what's Mortalland?" asked Amy frustrated.

"It's what we called the land of the living," said Nasra.

"What are oracles?" asked Renee.

"Oracles are humans or shades who have been allowed by the Judge to speak with spirits. They serve a particularly useful position here because of the deceptions cold spirits play on the living. Oracles can speak directly to the Court's communication devices and interpret dreams among other things." Renee smiled when Nasra mentioned these functions and her eyes widened with intrigue. She was going to speak but withheld her comments after hearing Nasra's response to Vasteck's question.

"What's the Court?" asked Vasteck.

"That will be explained at the Procession, Vasteck. Please be patient," said Nasra.

The carriages rode past a fountain in the middle of the front lawn; it held a statue of three doors that ran water from the cracks of its frames. Grimsley was driving the carriage around the back showing Lauren more of the Amalgam House exterior. The back lawn was an extensive vegetable garden and fruit orchard; the crops glowed like small stars. On the roof, gargoyles rested on their haunches and growled at any carriage passenger who gave them an odd look.

There was a gazebo with a fountain inside of it where cherubim danced about the bowl and expelled water as they played like children. Next to it was an immense pond with what appeared to be spectral ducks wading through the water. She saw a couple of towers with mirrors at their tops that projected illusions of trees to deceive curious spectral residents of Baker's Creek. Far in the distance, beyond the garden was a small chapel.

Grimsley drove towards a gloomy garage-like construction around the back. No light left its door and as they entered even the light of their unicorns ebbed to darkness. In the gloom, they approached a twelve-foot high, ten-foot wide steel oval ring where a black and white mist issued into the hole like water from sprinklers and mixed into a grayish spray. The carriage entered the ring, everyone felt their stomachs tighten and pull; they felt as if they were moving at various speeds. As fast as light one moment and slower than turtle's walk the next until a white haze blinded them. A blistering chill overcame the carriage; Lauren and the passengers bodies were freezing and everyone except Nasra and Grimsley wailed in pain.

CHAPTER THREE
BARON CITY PROCESSION

"*It's so cold!*" Amy screamed as she held her arms tight across her bosom and closed her legs together.

"You're taking us to Hell aren't you?" asked Gloria as she snuggled with a passenger for warmth.

Everyone embraced someone in the carriage. Wound tightly with Renee, Lauren felt the extreme cold and prayed to God for it to stop. Not a single part of her body was devoid of needle-pricked pain injecting shards of ice. They entered the snowy fields and the ride became smooth. This was the natural ground the carriage wheel's sought. They rode forward for a mile to give ample space for the trail behind them. Finally, the carriage stopped and Nasra stood and opened the door. A gust seized the riders and they flinched again.

"Ladies and gentlemen, please exit swiftly. A Mr. Dillion and a Mrs. Venus, please remain seated, everyone else follow me," said Nasra.

Everyone embraced a fellow passenger before exiting. Lauren saw Nasra roll up the parchment and tilt it over a bag Grimsley held in his hand telling him everyone was accounted for. Out of the folded paper rolled several silver tokens that swelled the bag and the roll disintegrated when they stopped falling. The bag seemed to meld into Grimsley cloak and on his hand grew thin strands of muscle.

Lauren and Renee struggled to exit; their legs were quivering so hard they could barely stand. They strained to lift their heads as chilling winds tore at their faces, their lips cracked and became tight, their eyes felt as if razors were cutting them. Despite the pain, Lauren let go of Renee, who stood comforting herself and surveyed the vast landscape before them.

"Ama-Amalg-g-gam s-s-sucks," said Amy as she struggled out of the carriage, holding onto Mr. Vasteck's waist. "It's fr-fre-freezing and it's too wha-white; I can barely s-see."

"C-Complain, c-complain Amy," said Renee as they exited the carriage.

"Wh-why aren't you c-com-complaining? We cou-could be par-tying right now if it wasn't for Lau-Lauren."

Lauren didn't reply; she was enthralled by her surroundings. They were in a field of numerous small hills rolling slowly as if the wind was pushing them along like tides of water. Snow fell lightly; the sky was gray and cloudy. Hidden behind the gray clouds was a light source, trying to seep its radiance through dim, depressing shade. She saw snow-covered mountains with a city embedded in the rock to the north and green trees to the east that were larger than the California Redwoods swathe in a snowy enchanting haze at their base. To the south was an ocean and in the distant west were thick violet clouds that moved like volcanic ash.

The reaper carriages prepared to leave. The unicorns and carriages grew silver wings to take flight and the carriages shrank in size. Mr. Dillion and Mrs. Venus shouted out to Nasra, "Wait! Where are we going?" Other ghosts that remained onboard their carriages pleaded to stay with the gathering. Lauren watched them beg for release as the carriages took to the air and rocketed off in a flash of silver light.

"Lauren! Over here," said Nasra as all the spirits from the New City were amassing into a large group.

She had drifted away. Lauren rejoined the group but was curious as to why the ghosts had to remain in the carriages. She asked Nasra who replied, "Their fates are sealed in Hell forever, Lauren. Thankfully, yours and the rest of this gathering are not." Nasra distanced herself from the crowd and used her small crystal ball to raise the snow below her. She grew higher and then sprayed mist from this crystal into her mouth like breath-freshener.

"Please stay close," her voice amplified as if by

a megaphone, "Do not move out of this perimeter. It's for your protection."

She shot four small clouds of mist from her crystal that landed on the snow in a perfect square. The purple globs shot four thick columns up to a height of ten feet then translucent purple steam connect each pillar, forming a barrier for Amalgam's new arrivals. Nasra leapt off her snow pillar and, in the air, transformed into a golden orb, drawing gasps of awe from the gathered. She floated to join some previously unseen ghosts near another rising hilltop.

Suddenly, a multitude of explosions filled the snowy plain, thousands, as far as the eye could see. Ghosts emerged from these flurry eruptions as if white sepulchers dug themselves from the ground before bursting, releasing their dead. Then, a flash of white light shot quickly in the Amalgam heavens. The sky turned blood red and black clouds formed in the atmosphere. Small star-like blue lights rained from the sky and slammed into the ground, tossing up snow. When the snow cleared, ghosts lie on the ground; some writhed with pain while others shook with fear.

This went on for an hour and Lauren realized why Nasra said it was for their protection. Many ghosts were frightened after they entered Amalgam and ran, colliding with emerging ghosts or launched high into the air when the ground exploded beneath them. It looked like doomsday with a terrible sky, bodies flying, and screams of fear and pain as the ghosts felt the bitter chill.

Some ghosts ran towards the gathering's perimeter and pounded on the misty barrier screaming for sanctuary. With their deathly appearance and terrified look, Lauren was frightened and held close to Renee, Vasteck, and Amy.

"Oh my God, we are in Hell!" said Gloria. "I didn't do anything wrong!"

Lauren searched the hilltop for Nasra, where several ghosts didn't appear at all excited but hard at work. She saw them walking up a winding flight of stairs along the stone platform. It had many openings, windows it seemed with lights moving about inside. The tower rose higher yet its foundation sank and Lauren realized the plain itself was depressing into an expansive pit. Ghosts tried to run out the expanding hole but tumbled down as the slope became too steep yet the moving hills stopped their fall.

The pit sank to an indeterminable depth allowing all in the gathering plains an adequate view of the tower. Along the walls of this pit rose flat snow slabs for seats and to Lauren's surprise, the pit became a giant amphitheater. Four smaller towers rose about the circumference of the pit populated by armed ghosts dressed like Nasra. They carried weapons like swords and staffs, but some used odd tools like shovels and ice picks as their armaments. Guards they seemed to Lauren, but she wondered why security and even weapons were necessary in the land of the dead? From these smaller towers came a white cloth that sheltered the amphitheater from the harsh weather.

Lauren watched as the rolling hills formed four circular lanes between the rows spiraling from the bottom to the top of the amphitheater. The lanes took four different colors, blue, orange, green, and white, and exited the amphitheater under an archway, leveling out at the surface and extending to the city at the mountain base. Under this archway sat four ghosts, one for each lane. One ghost was dressed like Nasra and the guards about the perimeter. The other three had different color schemes and styles to their clothing matching the lane where they stood.

One was showing more "skin" than the other ghosts were. She was in autumn orange and brown dress and white shirt with her hair wrapped about her head. Another was dressed in green; he wore slacks, a tunic, and a cape designed like a leaf and wore a leaf crown on his head. The last was ragged and peasant looking, dressed in a torn blue coverall who sat on a raised square block of snow.

Turning her attention back to the pillar, Lauren saw a bevy of ghost orbs stream from the windows of the tower all of them different colors. They were hundreds, swarming about the tower in one direction, their color switched in unison to white. A ghost arrived at a podium on top of the tower; the white sheet of ghost orbs visualized the ghost's face. He also sprayed a misty substance in his mouth and his voice rang out like Nasra's but louder so that everyone could hear.

"If everyone would please take a seat we can begin the Procession," spoke the ghost. The barrier Nasra formed dissipated and all two hundred and thirty that passed in the New City were free to take their seats. Lauren and her friends all sat on the same row, near the top. The excitement quelled among the ghosts though Lauren could still hear a few cries and when the ghosts settled down the announcer spoke again.

"Ladies and gentlemen, welcome to Amalgam here in the gathering plain of New Elysian. I am the Ghost of Names and Graves and the master of ceremony of the Baron City Procession. First, as you all are undoubtedly aware you have passed away from your mortal life and entered the spirit realm. Surely, this is a grave announcement but as you see, life continues. Many of you may wonder just what Amalgam is, and I'll tell you; it's the land of purgation."

Lauren listened and observed Names and Graves as he spoke. He looked very intelligent even with his unkempt appearance. His hair was uncombed, his clothing disheveled, and he wore large spectacles that made Lauren wonder if ghost's vision could deteriorate. Names carried an elaborate tome that he placed on his podium, gestured often as he spoke, and was an excellent orator to the expansive audience.

Names continued, "The axis of all three realms;

Mortalland, Paradise, and Hell, Amalgam incorporates elements of each in order to save the spirits of its inhabitants from their sins. Here you will work to purge yourself of sin before your Judgment. Some of you have lead very positive lives and for that your stay shall be short, others have lived violent and destructive lives yet have been spared the inferno due to some redeeming quality. A few of you are castaways from the Paradise realm and its here where you'll purge your pride and envy."

"Lastly are the very small remainder who will leave Amalgam and return to mortal life, but you will never speak of this land or be guilty of the Mortalland Rule."

Lauren listened as Names spoke the rule that had several conditions included within it. It began that no being in Amalgam or Mortalland whether angelic, demonic, human, spirit, animal or native shall bring to knowledge the existence of Amalgam or its purpose exposed to uninformed inhabitants of Mortalland. The rule concluded that the aforementioned inhabitants should not open access to Amalgam for those prohibited from entering.

"Those of you who will return to life are clearly visible as slightly pink whereas everyone else radiates blue," said Names.

Lauren was thrilled she'll be going home. Renee appeared slightly amused and Amy let out a loud "Yes!" which drew spiteful looks from many blue spirits who sat around her.

"Call the hospital, Lauren, and my son. Have them get my body out of the house before I start to stink. I'm in the bathroom on the john," said Vasteck. Lauren nodded with the smile.

"This rule was drawn up by the four barons and the angel Messina, our government leaders collectively called the Court. The Court is dedicated to the purgation process and ushering souls to meet the Most High Judge. You'll be mandated to rigorous, immensely painful tasks in order to erase the sins on your guilty souls. You will then be summoned to stand before God for your Judgment, either admittance or denial to enter the Paradise Realm."

Many ghosts including Lauren were shocked at Names' description of their expected duties in Amalgam and were anxious about meeting the Creator.

"While you have been given the chance to obtain a clean slate in Amalgam a few laws carry the weight of an unpardonable sin. Therefore, you are advised for your sakes not to break our laws or face a most disagreeable punishment," said Names.

"Now, this event is called the Baron City Procession because you will proceed to one of four baron cities to purge your sins. First is Castle Everlasting here in New Elysian, the capital city of the ghost nation, Morrigan, and home of Baron Lord Catherine," said Names.

The image of Names and Graves turned into a visual of a floating castle the same one on Nasra's cloak completely encapsulated by a golden circular barrier amongst a sun setting sky and moving clouds. It truly was a city, much like New York or Chicago complete with skyscrapers, four gargantuan towers connected via a wall and three mansions in the distance.

"Floating above the Amalgam landscape, its classical architectural design is fused with contemporary interior design replete with all the amenities ghosts require." As he talked the images changed to show various sections of Castle Everlasting such as a train station, a beautiful lake and its mountainous surroundings, and a burning field that Lauren thought didn't seem to fit.

Next, Names described the City of Ages in the Arcadia province. The image changed to a gigantic coastal city that extended to an elevated peninsula and appeared to be a major port judging from the mass of large ships docked. He described it as the largest city in Amalgam governed by Baroness Samina. The expansive city was seemingly constructed entirely of sand and appeared stable yet a few of the buildings were shown to voluntarily collapse and reform into larger, new dwellings. Its architecture was Persian in design and interspersed with lush greenery and was also protected by a golden barrier.

"The City of Ages heavily utilizes time and space manipulation, shrinking everyone that enters its gate thus allowing for a more dense population. Its buildings are kept in proportion but the rest of the surroundings are unchanged, allowing those who reside in the city a new perspective on life," said Names.

Next, a city stood atop a soaring rectangular stone block tightly enclosed in a valley of mountains and waterfalls. The city was encased in a golden orb and only accessible by three bridges connected to towers extending from the surrounding mountains. Mist from the waterfalls rose high out of the chasm and a rainbow stretched over the city. Names described the Gorge of Genesis as the "Eden of Amalgam" where the Judge first created the realm.

"Located in the Empyrean province, the Gorge of Genesis is the source of endless spectroplasm, our form of nourishment. It's governed by Baron Donovan and has the honor of being the most beautiful city in Amalgam."

Shown last was a smashed castle described as Ruin Everlasting in the province of Zion governed by Baron Jonah. To Lauren it looked like Amalgam's junkyard but designed so cleverly that it appeared like a child's playground. A slew of wrecked cruise ships appeared to be the "city" for ghosts to rest while the broken castle was where the fire arose. A partially collapsed stadium was also present.

"Unlike the other cities, the purgation process takes place in Ruin Everlasting's castle, its official building being the clock tower. Baron Jonah describes his designs as a love for the magnificence of ruin and decay," said Names. Voices rose throughout the amphitheater as the ghosts discussed each city.

"I like the City of Ages. What do you think, Vasteck?" asked Gloria.

"I'll explore a bit, I'm leaning towards the capital though."

"What do you think, Lauren? Where do you want to go?" asked Renee.

Lauren told her she was leaning towards Ruin Everlasting because she liked the artistic quality of city. Renee offered up the Gorge of Genesis saying it looked the closest to paradise. They didn't bother to ask Amy.

"If your spirit is pink, however, you must reside at Castle Everlasting as every Mortalland Shade in New Elysian is required to stay in the House of Shades," said Names. Lauren and Renee were disappointed.

"Everyone else, please keep the cities in mind when we begin to form our throngs to Baronsward Citadel where you'll be transported to your desired city. If you're undecided the cities are connected by a teleportation network called the Amalgam Portal and relocation is simple should you change your mind. Now, Amalgam isn't all bad news. The benefits of being a ghost, and there are benefits, include the power of flight, transformation and the ability to use magic for self-defense."

The crowd was audibly amazed as the Skycasting Group formed the image of a ghost that turned to an orb as Names spoke of flight. The orb turned to mist, vortexes, old age and youth as Names spoke of transformation. Finally, as Names spoke of magic, the orb returned to a ghost holding a sword that created fireworks and showered the audience in confetti.

"On the back of your right hand are small graphical icons, symbols of your magical abilities. These marks are gifts originating from the Paradise Realm and they symbolize several things. For some they represent all the knowledge a person accumulated in their life, for others they explain the function the Judge has for them in Amalgam, or they embody the desires in one's heart," Names continued. The girls looked at their hands. Lauren looked at her right hand but didn't see a mark. She checked her left and saw that she had a mark of a cup filled with blood yet had no idea what it meant.

"Why is mine on the left hand?" asked Lauren to Renee. Renee shrugged without looking and said, "I got a caduceus!"

"What's that?" asked Lauren. She looked at Renee's mark; it was a pole with wings extending from it and two snakes wound around it.

"It represents healing and medicine. I guess I'm a doctor or something like that. It's interesting, I was considering going to med school," said Renee.

"Mine shows a finger pressed against someone's lips. Am I supposed to keep a secret?" asked Amy.

"My mark shows different kinds of animals!" said Gloria.

"I got a face card! A Jack," said Vasteck.

"In your free time, it's advised that you learn to use this gift from God to entertain, aid, and protect yourself and fellow ghosts when in trouble. Protective measures in the realm of the dead may seem contrary but I'll tell you, there are many things to fear here. In fact, the threat is so great that you must stay close to your cities and not wander from the ghost provinces."

"Death in this realm is as perilous as in Mortalland. Although the spirit can never die, your husks can which is what we call the gelatinous skin covering your spirit. Your husks retain your vital organs and a circulatory system to deliver necroplasm, our blood, throughout the body. They are every bit as fragile as your human form in Mortalland. If your husk is destroyed, your spirit will leave Amalgam and appear before the Judge with or without sins purged and if you've been slack in purgation, this is very bad news."

Anxiety ripped through the gathering and as they learned that mortality still played heavily in Amalgam.

"This is a negative side effect of the Mortalland Realm's influence. What may cause death relate to the dangers of Amalgam that range from demon and animal attacks to violence among ghosts. Native Amalgam creatures contain the demon threat. The animals can be avoided by not entering their borders called the Wild district, which is considered any land outside our provincial territories such as the forests to the east of us."

Lauren looked aside to the forests she observed upon her arrival. The tall, thick green trees and hazy snow billowing by the trunks was now more foreboding than mystifying as dangerous animals lurked inside.

"The most serious threat however is the Dark Phoenix, Amalgam's Great Sinner, and his Ghosts of the Snow. There are many evils in our world, but only one assumed divine power through a Great Sin, one so terrible it changed the very fabric of our world."

The ghost orbs created a montage of Amalgam's landscape showing lush forests, pleasant animal and ghost relations, pristine castles and cities along the landscape, and calm weather.

"Centuries ago, Amalgam was a peaceful and pleasant world save for the purgation fields. All was in balance and there the ghosts of Amalgam practiced their creation arts with their marks, conversed in joy, and pondered a life of incomparable pleasure promised by the Paradise realm. The Kingdom of God, Amalgam magnified infinite times over without pain or suffering, was a dream many worked feverishly for as salvation was only a purged sin away. The journey to Paradise, however, would become more treacherous after the Great Sin and the great sinners," said Names.

The orbs changed to show a ghost wearing Crusader armor and backed by three angels stealthily approaching a huge figure sitting in a chair.

The Ghosts of Amalgam: The Linking Tome

"The Holy Vessel, the body the Judge used to form our world has remained in Messina since Amalgam's creation. The Judge left his Spirit inside as a seal to separate the furies of the realms before returning to Paradise. Unbeknownst to us, was the shameful plot being hatched by three renegade angels and one ambitious ghost."

The knight floated up to the sitting colossus, stood on its legs and pulled out a wand before moving to the right arm of the Vessel and plunging it into the hand. Black smoke issued from the mark as dark mist shrouded the scene and the whole amphitheater shook, alarming the ghosts. The image became pitch black before lighting again depicting the ruined body of the Vessel whose organs were all visible.

"The Vessel of the Judge lay molested in his wake. With the removal of the Vessel's mark, the Judge's Spirit fled Amalgam, sealing access to the Amalgam Tower of Paradise and the Creator ceased summoning spirits for a year."

The orbs showed the former Amalgam landscapes beset by fierce weather. Buildings were ruined in the wake of terrible storms and the ghosts in these images were enshrouded in gelatin, and as they sought refuge from the perilous climate. Massive riots broke out over small pools of gray fluid as ghosts fought to lap from them like vicious, starving dogs.

"Thus the Drastic Change of Amalgam; no longer could ghosts live without nourishment. No longer could we travel by thinking and arrive in that instant. No longer were the seasons gentle and the world of Amalgam peaceful as before. Though we retained our ghostly powers to stave off an untimely second death, we feared for our lives once more."

"Firestorms, deluges, and blizzards became the new seasons, the infernal realm's influence on our dominion. Ghosts needed to feed on spectroplasm, a substance found in pits we called dead pools that were appearing about the landscape. The Judge instilled new leadership, our barons to replace the governing angels who left because Amalgam could not chance their corruption."

The image darkened again. Shown on the left, was Earth and other planets on the same rank stretching infinitely into darkness like a mirror reflection. Letters above the planets described them as Mortalland. To the right of the planets were towers that followed them into infinity, a valley that read Amalgam and beside this vale were two cones. One pointing up read "Paradise" the other facing down beneath Paradise read "Inferno" and to the right, connected to those cones, was the Boundless Realm. Paradise's cone crumbled as Names began anew.

"The spirit responsible never surfaced for more than three hundred years. When he finally rose, his purpose was entry into Paradise, his name, the Dark Phoenix. Immediately his followers set to war, attacking branding groups, and unlocking the seals to the mortal and the infernal realms. This second despicable sin brought mortals and ghosts closer than the Judge ever intended when Amalgam splintered into invisible continents among Earths four oceans. Demons and shades entered into our realm and a New City was formed, a place where the ethereal and material worlds meshed and is ever expanding further defying God's commandments."

The crystal in earth's tower moved into the planet and the valley wrapped around the Mortalland. Earth magnified, the globe showed five continents floating on the oceans Lauren knew weren't physical landmasses, but was now aware of their existence. They had strange names; in the Pacific Ocean was Dongabi, in the North Atlantic was Morrigan, in the south Jaheri, the Indian Ocean held Nimien, and the Artic claimed Messina.

Names described the dark purple clouds covering Earth's continents as forbidden areas, the cloud being a life-sucking plume. Names said that the only fogless land within these clouds was an area in North America called the New City. He continued, "Our realm was now smaller in size but the population remained high. The barons readjusted their cities to accommodate the more congested nature of their provinces. We've formed a military to stop the Dark Phoenix's destruction but as his name suggests, he continues to rise, and with his loyalists, cause ruin to our realm."

"The Ghosts of the Snow is what the Phoenix calls his most powerful sect of warriors whose magical skills are comparable to our barons. Amalgam snow is one of the coldest substances in our world and the name symbolizes their unrepentant disintegration into evil spirits who stand wholly against the Judge."

"The Phoenix and his witches will tempt you with the promise of an easy way into the Paradise Realm and give you power beyond the limits of your marks as an incentive. Should you give into temptation, your soul will be against the Judge forever unless you seek His forgiveness. *You have been warned.*"

Names concluded the Procession by indicating the lane colors blue, orange, green, and white would lead to Ruin Everlasting, the City of Ages, the Gorge of Genesis, and Castle Everlasting respectively. The bottom of the pit rose and the tower recessed as the orbs flew back inside its windows. The seats merged with the rising level ground restoring the gathering plain. Ghosts converged onto the four lanes of the amphitheater. As the ground settled, the ghosts from the New City began to sort with the rest of the gathering into the processional throngs.

"I'm going to the City of Ages. Are you going to Castle Everlasting?" Gloria asked Vasteck looking at him with inviting eyes.

"I guess I could tour the City of Ages first," said Vasteck as he took Gloria by the arm and led her to that lane. Lauren wanted to follow Vasteck, but Renee reminded her of their obligation.

"We have to go to the capital remember!"

"Yeah, we're going home!" said Amy excited.

CHAPTER FOUR
THE TREE RIDER'S RAID

Lauren followed Renee and Amy into the Castle Everlasting line and walked steadily towards Baronsward Citadel. Lauren looked ahead and saw the line stretched for possibly two miles in front and even more behind but moved uninterrupted the entire time. As they moved closer, Lauren realized the throngs wouldn't be entering the city but into four tunnels dug into the mountainside to the left. The guards were moving about the lanes keeping order.

Lauren saw Nasra up ahead engaged in a light conversation with a male guard dressed like a Conquistador. She smiled and waved at Lauren as they approached her. A ghost appeared in a flash of light beside Nasra. He was a young and fairly hip-looking black male wearing modern clothing and fashionable eyewear, carrying a bag slung from his shoulder. He wore a loose tie with his causal collared shirt and unbuttoned blazer which also sported an animated castle design on the back like Nasra's cloak. In his hands were a notepad and pen, which he sporadically read from while he spoke. Lauren could clearly hear their discussion and didn't mind eavesdropping.

"Nasra, I have a high priority message from Mina. Will you receive it?" asked the ghost.

"Yes, Sigpos."

"Was there a stray carriage during the gathering?"

"Yes, it was abandoned by the Baker's Creek Lighthouse."

"Apparently the reaper and purveyor returned and finished gathering. They are requesting entry from Amalgam House. Mina was curious; a reaper carriage has never arrived late to the gathering plains unless the Phoenix was involved. I was told to check with you before allowing it entry."

"Is there anything suspicious about the carriage, the passengers, or the driver?"

"No." Nasra contemplated for a moment.

"Have Mina give them permission and I'll be there to inspect it myself. Confidentiality medium, Sigpos," said Nasra.

The ghost bowed and vanished as instantly as he appeared. Nasra and her companion, walked south, intersecting through the line in front of Lauren.

"Come, Alexander," said Nasra to her companion and she told a couple more guards to follow her.

A few moments passed and Lauren could see

the portal opening some miles away from where Lauren stood. The carriage entered Amalgam, but Lauren could tell something was wrong by the commotion in the crowd. The unicorn lost all its silver color and became black as coal with red eyes that flamed up above its mane. The reaper screeched and stood up wildly flinging its arms and scythe as its body burned with blue fire and crumbled to dust. The passengers, previously calm and sedate, stammered out the carriage like drunks and appeared mad, shaking their heads as if ants were scurrying about inside and they desperately wanted them out.

"*It's been possessed,*" said Nasra as she ran towards it with a few guards following.

"The passenger's psyches have been scarred," said Alexander.

The unicorn fell to the ground and decayed so swiftly it was a pile of dust by the time Nasra got close. The fire flew off the reaper's ashes and turned to electric bolts. The bolt splintered into several hundred forming a massive tower of forty ovals, five facing the cardinal, and inter-cardinal directions at varying heights from the ground to the sky. The stray bolts condensed to solidify the tower and to create pupils for the ovals.

The pillar of eyes saw three hundred and sixty degrees in Amalgam within their unknown visual range. Yet the pillar did not remain forty strong for long, as thirty-six condensed into four large eyes. One eye turned back into a bolt and wrapped about the portal keeping it open. The other three focused on Nasra and the reaper carriage, Baronsward Citadel, and an area in the mountains to the left. Lauren followed that eye to the northwest and saw an incredible but troubling sight.

A large tree trunk was barreling towards them, running horizontal to the ground. The tree's numerous roots lifted it up, and reached around the trunk carrying it along like a spider, moving with many more legs than eight. The crown appeared to have fallen off as if struck by lighting, as the trunk was not smooth but jagged and elevated higher on the left. The crown-less tree exposed the hollowness of the trunk and from this void sprang several large gray wolves that headed directly for the ghosts.

Along the trunk sat its rider, dressed in a green and white form-fitted suit that had designs of branches and leaves all about it and wore a finely crafted three-headed mask. The head in the center was that of a young boy with tiny teeth, dirty, unmanaged hair, and debonair eyes. The left head was that of a demonic man with blue flames for eyes, decaying ears and skin that looked like ashes pieced together. Smoke rose from the face as if an extinguished flame had just scorched the head. The right face was of a featureless man with a slit where the mouth should be and the small pupil-less eyes drug lighting through them.

"What is that?" asked Renee coming closer to Lauren with Amy following, also intrigued.

"I don't know," said Lauren filling with dread.

The rider held up a staff, a thick twisted tree branch painted white. A ball of white light formed at the staff's tip and the rider shot it into the sky above the processional lines. Amazed and confused at the sight, the crowd stood transfixed. The ball settled into the sky and became brilliant white like a star then burst into red flames that rained on the spirits below. The snowy fields were set ablaze, catching many ghosts on fire. Their husk disintegrated to blue embers, sending flashes of blue light, their spirits, flying to the Judge.

The crowd erupted into frenzy and ran east as more ghosts caught sight of the tree rider and its wolves that tore into the crowd and began mauling people. Nasra saw the ghosts dashing eastward and looking west found the rider. She surveyed the field and saw that the guards from the procession were overwhelmed trying to keep order. Some of the guards were chasing off the wolves that now numbered a hundred in the fields.

"Siggy!" said Nasra and the ghost reappeared instantly. "Emergency! Tell Catherine to send reinforcements."

"Yes," said Sigpos and he flashed away.

Nasra organized the few guards around her to protect the carriage passengers. The tree rider arrived by the open portal and Nasra's guards, the tree's roots wrapped around and flung many of the guards far away into the fields. A gray disc sped through the plains kicking up snow as it moved. It stopped a good distance from the carriage, widened to sixty feet, and collapsed creating a chasm that brought up a host of guards, over fifty. The rider and its wolves converged on this group and engaged the guards of New Elysian in a bitter magic battle.

"What's going on?" asked Amy, frightened, trying to fight off the rushing mob when a ghost pushed her to the ground.

"Amy!" said Lauren as she bent down to pick her up. Lauren felt an arm on her shoulder, Renee once again, but she looked past her, a wolf was coming their way. Lauren glimpsed the gray beast; a red circular mark was square between its eyes.

"RUN!" said Renee.

They sprinted; Lauren looked behind to judge her distance from the wolf. It was coming for her, separating her from Renee and Amy towards the pillar of electric eyes. Lauren ran into it, the lightning singed her husk for a brief moment before she felt cool, serene, and peaceful. The electric tower erupted into blue flame that stretched to the sky and Lauren rose up in it. She didn't burn to death; she grew knowledgeable, powerful, and divine. She floated up the column of flame to its narrowest point and absorbed the secrets of the universe from the most holy source in Amalgam, the Mark of the Phoenix.

She could hear a child, who screamed, "NO! MY MARK!"

The child was inside the column of flame looking up from the ground at Lauren floating in the air stealing his powers. The fire was forming his body creating sinew and flesh about his skeleton. Lauren also heard a woman's voice belonging to a distant oracle who simply spoke, "Come to Messina, Lauren. Bring the mark to me!"

Lauren fell to the ground; the fiery pillar formed a white bird that flew into the child's husk. He jumped on Lauren throttling her.

"*WHAT HAVE YOU DONE?*" he screamed before teleporting away. The child's face, the mask covering the rider's head spoke to her, "*FORGET THE PORTAL! GET THE GIRL!*" The rider turned to see Lauren lying on the ground, on Lauren's right hand was an icon of a baby bird forming from ashes, the Phoenix Mark. Renee and Amy raced to her side and tried to rouse her.

"Lauren, can you hear me?" asked Renee as she shook her. Amy knelt down, "Pick her up, or these people will trample her." Suddenly the mob dispersed and before Amy and Renee came the rider's treacherous tree. The roots picked them up by the arms and cast them both deep into the riot amassing by the Skyscraping Forest. The roots completely wrapped around Lauren's body like a mummy and sat her behind the rider.

Lauren regained her consciousness and saw the enchanted mask. The faces spoke as the mask rotated to give each head a glimpse of the captive. Lauren could hear the rider talking to the mask.

"Is this the one?" asked the rider.

"Yes!" its voice echoed, "*TAKE HER TO THE MEADOW!*"

The rider and its wolves left the plains. The tree's roots stabbed any ghosts in its path as it rocketed towards the forest.

* * * *

Guards stood at the forest's edge as the chaos ensued. They constructed a wall of dew magic that barred ghosts from moving into the woods as they congregated about this barrier. The wall stretched for miles and the panicked ghosts were trying to find its end. Amy and Renee fell in the midst of the mob dazed from their flight. Ghosts shoved Amy as she tried to stand.

"LAUREN? RENEE? SOMEONE PLEASE HELP ME!" said Amy; she covered her head with her arms as dozens of hands fell on her face like hail. "GET OFF ME!" Renee said as she kicked ghosts in the knees. Renee stood, extended her arms, and ran knocking people down in her path and stepping on them without remorse. Amy and Renee collided and fell. As they sat up, they saw each other and screamed.

"RENEE!"

"AMY!"

"Help me up," said Amy. Renee stood and pulled Amy up.

"GET BACK!" Amy yelled at the crowd and they cleared a small hole.

"Nice!" said Renee relieved.

"Thanks," said Amy exasperated. "How are we

going to get out of here Renee?"

"We won't," said Renee as terror seized her face. She and Amy saw the tree rider approaching again, coming fast shouting, *"Brilzen diktat invodimi!"*

Lighting struck the barrier and it spread out along the wall breaking it apart allowing the frightened ghosts to push past the guards into the forests.

"STOP! YOU MUSTN'T GO INTO THE FORESTS!" said the guards.

Amy and Renee were the first inside, running quickly along the untamed and snow-covered floor. They leapt across the roots, the ground rose higher and became difficult to transverse without using their hands. The tree rider and wolves were menacing the ghosts from behind, pushing the gathering inward. Panicked spirits overtook Amy and Renee. In their multitude, the girls began to lose sight of each other; Amy didn't want to get lost so she ran close to Renee.

"We have to find some place to hide, at least until that tree thing rides by."

"But it's got Lauren; shouldn't we at least try to stop it?"

"How? It's moving like a train. WATCH OUT!"

Renee and Amy dived for cover as the tree rushed past. The rider made a rough turn and her tree collided against a large trunk sending splinters flying like missiles that killed two nearby ghosts. The wolves only attacked ghosts that would slow the rider; they never killed anyone in their escape. Renee and Amy stood; the forest was a mess in the wake of the rushing tree leaving a sporadic trail if the rider continued such a wild trek.

"Come on, Amy, we can follow the markings on the trees to get to Lauren," said Renee.

"I say we head back," said Amy exhausted. "There's nothing we can do for her! That tree's moving so fast by the time we get there it'll be too late."

"We should at least try!" said Renee; she could still see the tree in the distance. The many ghosts the rider passed were coming to a similar conclusion as Amy, the danger had past and it was time to turn back.

"Wait, isn't this the forest they warned us about?" asked Amy. This stopped Renee who was going on.

"They said something about the animals, didn't they?" asked Amy.

A lion's roar shook the forest; it was so loud the ground vibrated and all the ghosts covered their ears in pain. This roar hurt, it was powerful and terrifying. Amy and Renee realized they were both deaf. They tried to speak but were confounded at the total silence in which they found themselves.

Renee saw a large creature moving to her right and had Amy look as she pointed to the north, between the bushes. They saw a giant lion, eight feet tall and blistering fast followed close by a massive pride of great lionesses. There was no question that this giant beast was responsible for the roar. A multitude of white dots spotted the lion's body. Its mate, a similarly giant lioness, was six feet tall and spoke to the lion.

"Estoc, can we eat the ghosts?"

"Not yet, I must speak with Catherine and discover the nature of this intrusion to our forests," said Estoc, his voice was so deep it seemed to echo and push the air with great force. "I want you and the other lionesses in prime shape to help me deal with Catherine in case this is an act of war. Let the other animals deal with the ghosts, we'll wait for her here."

The lions sat in a large group and waited. In the few moments of perplexity after Estoc's roar, animals rushed in from all angles even the sky. The spirits of cheetahs, leopards, bears, giant snakes, bulls, hyenas and massive elephants pounced, clawed, stomped, bit, and impaled their victims. Renee and Amy ran as fowls of all kinds flew in above them, snatching ghosts and taking them high in to the air then dropping them, the fall destroyed their husks. Guards arrived from the fields to protect the overwhelming number of helpless new ghosts beset by the cold animal spirits. Fire plumes, icicles, blinding lights, concussive blasts filled the forest surface.

Little by little, Amy and Renee's hearing returned. They heard the guards shouting spells and the animals growling which made the girls feel like they were in the midst of a revolution at the zoo. A giant eagle screeched above and Renee and Amy looked up then ducked as its beak clasped shut; its bite narrowly missed them both. Its wing snagged a large branch that fell atop Amy's leg pinning her to the ground. It flew around for a second strike, its body glistening with numerous small white orbs.

"Run, Amy!" Renee shouted.

"I can't! I'm stuck! Help me, Renee!" Amy tried to move the massive branch but she couldn't. Renee rushed to her aid but the branch was too heavy to lift. The eagle swooped for a death strike on either one when a thick shell of ice encased its head and the bird fell with a large thud, shaking the ground like a minor earthquake. Behind them, a young guardsman smiled before pointing his wand at the large branch.

"Ascentate!" said the ghost and the branch lifted. "Reterium," he added and the branch spun off.

"Thanks," said Amy. She tried to stand but collapsed; her leg was broken.

"Oh my God," said Renee. "You're bleeding!"

Amy grasped her leg, bluish necroplasm streaked down her calf.

"It hurts like hell," said Amy.

"Wait here, I'll get help," said the guardsman.

"No wait!" Renee said to the guardsman. "I think I can fix this."

"You?" asked Amy disbelievingly.

Renee took Amy's leg into her hand and squeezed it. Her mark glowed and then she spoke,

"*Trilen Asten!*" The wound healed instantly and Amy no longer felt pain.

"Wow!" said Amy.

"How's that feel?" asked Renee.

"Fine," said Amy frustrated but truly appreciative. "How'd you do that?"

"She must be a caduceus mark or an oracle," said the guardsman. "Healing magic comes naturally to those ghosts."

"What's happening to me?" asked Amy. "Ghosts, blood, magic, this is crazy."

"It's the nature of Amalgam, although a raid has never happened before at the Procession," said the guardsman.

A woman screamed not far from where they were and the guardsman left to help. He turned and said, "Stay here. I'll be back to help you."

"Look out!" Renee shouted at the guard.

A large snake slithered from above and bit the guard's torso, ejecting his spirit, before swallowing his husk whole. The serpent turned its hungry eyes towards the girls with deadly swiftness. It crept along the ground slowly, turning its gaze from Renee to Amy as if deciding which one it would eat and that would be whoever ran first. The snake's reflexes were quick; it leapt swiftly at a brilliant flash between Renee and Amy crushing its head into a door that materialized from the light.

The door was hinged on a strong, thick, and elaborate wood frame with a sturdy base that held three steps and a gold-handle containing an emblem of three doors. It swung open throwing aside the unconscious snake. Out stepped the baron lord and leader of the ghost nation, Baroness Catherine of Castle Everlasting.

A black woman with brown eyes and a stern gaze, her face exuded maturity and wisdom. Her body was strong with lean muscles, her nose was large as was her lips, and her presence demanded respect. Her large brimmed white hat and robes were lined with gold inside and her five-foot-ten stature gave the baroness a commanding presence. She stepped out and surveyed the mess that was the Procession. She moved with such charisma that walking seemed hypnotic.

Amy and Renee wanted to follow her, but the snake regained its consciousness and immediately lunged for the woman, its fanged mouth stretched wide. The baroness didn't seem to care, her concerns for the welfare of the arrivals was more important than her safety. In the moment death seemed imminent, Catherine, back turned to lethal creature, spoke, "Cinzeré enferris!" The snake erupted in flames and collapsed to ashes.

"Amy, Renee, enter that door. It'll take you to the House of Shades. Wait for me to return with Lauren," said Catherine.

Renee and Amy didn't know how she knew their names or about Lauren but they didn't have any reason to question this woman or stay in harm's way. They entered the door and it sealed behind them disappearing instantly. Catherine moved into the fields and the animals seemed completely aware of her status. No other animal dared attack her.

She saw a few of her guard commanders trying to organize a way out of the forest but animals surrounded them giving them no hope of getting every ghost to safety. Each ghost they saved they told to stay close so multiple small crowds had formed. Catherine approached one crowd and used the power of her mark to create another door. This door planted itself right behind the ghosts.

"Get to the castle," said Catherine; the ghosts entered with haste.

"It's Catherine," said the guards and they cheered as the animals in the immediate area stopped their attacks and left in fear.

"Your orders!" shouted one ghost.

"Find all the ghosts and direct them to these doors to take them to the castle."

She materialized doors at four distant locations creating a hundred-mile square perimeter. The guards did their jobs well defending ghosts from the animals and leading them to the doors. It took an hour after Catherine's arrival for all the ghosts to make it to the castle. The animals realized that the baroness was now among the ghosts and decided to retreat with the exception of Estoc's pride. They heard of Catherine's arrival and surrounded the baroness once they found her.

"Baron Catherine," said Estoc bowing his head. "Surely you've come to explain your decision to go to war with us."

"We are not here for war, Estoc. You know I respect your territory and I've remained true to our separation agreement as stated in the Animal War treaty."

"THEN WHY ARE YOUR GHOSTS IN OUR LAND?" asked Estoc.

"An intruder raided the Procession frightening my ghosts and they fled into the forests."

"A pitiful excuse, it seems like you've reneged on your promise."

"Our agreement was that we would stay away from your territory and your animals would not harm my ghosts in case of an intrusion until you spoke with me. Your purpose in this realm is to protect us from the demons but you chose to fight us because of old grudges from your mortal lives. I tell you, Estoc, you've always been one step from a cold soul like your old lord Masden."

"I've changed! I'm nothing like him," said Estoc shamefully.

"Oh no! Do you realize what you and your animals have done to those slain ghosts? *Some of them are damned forever!* Be assured, Estoc, if your animals ever attack my ghosts again they'll never hear the end of the Horn of Olives."

The pride shuddered at the thought of Catherine's threat. They backed away as she began her search for Lauren.

"Catherine!" Estoc ran after her and consulted her privately. "If not you who made the ghosts enter our domain?"

Catherine turned and answered, "It was a Ghost of the Snow."

Estoc hung his head low in disgrace and led his lioness into the deeper parts of the Wilds.

* * * *

Lauren saw the trees move by as if her mother was driving seventy miles an hour. Her hearing was returning after the roar and she wondered what great beast produced such a howl. The rider's wolves jumped in front of the broken hollow and shrunk in size, returning inside the trunk. The rider had taken Lauren deep inside the Skyscraping Forest. The rider had its tree's roots wrap about the skyscraping tree trunks and lifted them from the ground to avoid creating a trail.

They stopped at what appeared to be the end of the tall forest but Lauren looked below and saw a normal size forest. Lauren could see deep into this smaller woodland and noticed a circular clearing. The trees in this field held in their crowns what Lauren could only make out as white balls and ropes. She got a better view when her captor's tree slingshot from the tall forest to the smaller one. The tree was flying high and fast but they landed gently in the middle of this meadow. Lauren took a gander at her surroundings; the white balls were captured ghosts hanging by their feet all of them appeared unconscious.

The roots unwound from her body and dropped while the others provided a platform for its master that lowered her to the ground. Lauren watched as her masked captor walked to the middle of the meadow. Emerging from the adjacent meadow edge Lauren could see a small ghost riding atop a centaur with a female one to his right. He looked no older than ten years of age and pleased to see them arriving. The child thanked, Inez, the centaur he was riding as he dismounted, and told him and Ariel, the female, to summon the other centaurs to await a meeting with him. They said they'll be gathered within the hour and left promptly to carry out his orders.

The child smiled; Lauren could see his tiny teeth with a small gap in between them. He had a pronounced forehead covered by dark, dirty hair, a thin nose, and slim cheeks that narrowed at his small chin. His eyelids encroached upon his brown pupils giving him an alluring appearance that aided him in acquiring followers. He wore a bloused tattered gray wool shirt with frayed sleeves held snugly at the waist with a black belt. A thin rope secured a gray hood at the neck and a phoenix bird brooch fastened a rugged mantle to the right shoulder. Leg bands secured his brown breeches tucked into his black leather boots.

While the rider was talking with the child, Lauren seized this opportunity to find sanctuary in the forest. As she ran, the tree's roots seized her feet and wrapped tightly around her arms. She freed herself and reached the meadow edge when the tree wrapped a large root about her neck and flung her back into the field. She hit the ground in front of the child ghost. He looked down at her and said, "You must ask for permission if you wish to leave the meadow and the answer is always no. You are my prisoner now and here you'll stay forever," the child smiled.

CHAPTER FIVE
THE DARK PHOENIX

"Let's have your name!" the child asked politely. His voice cracked occasionally as if he was going through puberty giving him a menacing tone whenever angry or authoritative when commanding. Lauren was dismayed that she'll never leave the company of a masked freak and wicked kid. She stood up, glanced back at her masked captor before speaking.

"I'll give you my name *from Mortalland*."

"I doubt you'll ever see that place again," said the child.

"Why did you want me to snare this little brat?" asked the tree rider angrily. The voice was muddled but female.

"She's taken my mark!" said the child.

The rider approached her and took her right hand, staring in wonder at the phoenix mark.

"How?" asked the rider.

"While we were fighting the guards in the mountains I was slain. The portal to the New City was active so I sent my watchtower to keep it open. She ran into my column as I materialized," said the child.

"Why didn't she die? Your column should have vaporized her."

"I'm sure there's a suitable explanation but since she's the first to live I'm guessing there's something different about her."

"Have you lost your powers?"

"She's taken the lion's share of powers but it doesn't matter as I intend to take it back now. Thankfully, the loss of the mark didn't sever my connection with your Triquetra mask. If she had taken my Tri-sentience, she could have intimate and dangerous knowledge of me."

The child approached Lauren smiling and she leaned back cautiously.

"This is my compatriot Jasmine, Great Witch in the Ghosts of the Snow ranks. I'll explain who we are during your stay as I could always use another solider to wage my war against the Court."

"And what's your name?" asked Lauren.

"I have many names though I'm infamously known as the *Dark Phoenix*. I'd really like the pleasure of your name before I learn it the hard way," said the child. Lauren was surprised that this child clamed to be the Great Sinner Names mentioned.

"Lauren…Lauren Walston."

"Thank you, Lauren, I'll see you to your prison built especially for Mortalland Shades, your sort," the Phoenix extended his arm behind him. A monstrous stem-less tulip bud came waddling towards them from the meadow edge walking on its large mutated leaves. Lauren backed away and she bumped into Jasmine who pushed her forward. Lauren raised her fist to hit her but noticed her hand was becoming blue like the ghosts and the pink glow receding past her wrist.

"You're turning blue! Soon your body will die in Mortalland," said Jasmine with amusement in her voice. The tulip opened wide and out stretched a thick tongue like a frogs that reeled her in imprisoning her within its leaves. Lauren didn't care for her prison, it was stuffy, sticky, and on the leaves were irritating thorns that scratched her body. Though the tulip held her captive, Lauren could see the Phoenix and Jasmine talking through the leaves crevices and watched assiduously.

"I'm sorry, Phoenix. If I'd known this would happen I'd have found a different way into the New City."

"Forget it, Jasmine; besides your plan was brilliant and would have succeeded had it not been for the girl. We've been setback several times tonight, the truck driver was derailed, the reaper and purveyor put up a stronger fight than I anticipated, and Lauren foils my regeneration. Yet even in our failure today there is opportunity. I was worried I wouldn't have enough soldiers to pull Castle

Everlasting from the sky, but seeing the animals rage at the ghosts I don't think we'll need soldiers at all. The animals still haven't moved on from their mortal grudges and we can channel this rage properly to align the animals to our cause."

"Estoc would never allow an alliance with us," said Jasmine.

"No, but leaderless animals would definitely respond to me especially if they believe Estoc's been abducted by the Court. Snatch the gestalt lord from his pride and imprison him in your tree. I'll leave a message for the animals so they'll get the impression the baroness ordered a raid and I'll be there to persuade them to go to war against the ghosts."

"Yes sir, I'll return within the hour. What do you want me to do with her?" Jasmine asked of Lauren.

"She'll remain here like the other ghosts. Once I take my mark back, she'll be scarred and helpless. After that, we'll see to your entry to the New City once again. We need your mark and if we fail to retrieve it from the Book of Marks we'll have to find its linking tome and you know the trouble Devon can cause."

Jasmine rolled her eyes at the mention of his name.

"And what of Etienne? He's causing too much trouble in the graveyard."

"Don't worry I have my eye on him. We must keep him alive for now even if it pains you to see him breathe."

"I want to see him suffer in the worst way, Phoenix, and anyone associated him. He's lived for centuries in Mortalland and cut my life short two decades in."

"You'll have your vengeance when the time's right. Now go, bring Estoc to me."

Jasmine bowed as her tree swooped behind her; she climbed on the trunk and sped off into the Skyscraping forest. Phoenix turned to the tulip; Lauren sat up, hoping he didn't see her eavesdropping. She looked again for the child when he appeared before her.

"Don't concern yourself with what you've seen, Lauren. You won't remember anyway when I'm done with you."

Phoenix waved his hands and the leaves opened a bit more.

"Please let me go. They said I might have a second chance at life." Lauren poked her hands on the thorny leaves as she pleaded for release.

"That's why I'm keeping you here. When your spirit leaves the body for too long your body will die. This is your punishment for foiling our plans but there is one way to avoid this fate, you can join me. I'll give you unconditional acceptance as a Phoenix loyalist and possibly a Ghost of the Snow depending on how powerful you become. All I ask is that you listen to what I'm trying to accomplish here in Amalgam."

"And what's that?" asked Lauren.

"I want entry to the Paradise Realm bar the purgation fields and the entire process. My goal is the ultimate reconciliation of all souls; do you know what that means?"

Due to the mark, Lauren was very knowledgeable and though she never heard of the concept before the answer came to her like a stroke of genius.

"It's a belief that every wicked person, demon, and even the Devil will one day be released from Hell and given forgiveness by God. Why would you want this?"

"In our mortal lives we are influenced by our societies to commit crimes we're being punished eternally for. I was one such person, a killer, swindler, and a thief; poor and ignorant trying to live day to day in my town of Toulouse, France. Then a holy man taught me the Word of God. He told me that confessing my sins would absolve me of my transgressions. However I couldn't believe it, a weakness of the human mind."

"Soon I learned of the Crusades to free the Holy Lands from the Muslims. The leaders sold us on the idea that whether we lived or died during the Crusades, God would forgive our sins. I took up the sword under Raymond the Fourth and marched to Jerusalem but my experiences during the quest made me realize that Pope Urban was a liar and the Crusades were nothing more than timely politics. The rage I felt at this deception culminated in my self-immolation which I used to protest the final affront to God about to be committed by the Crusade leaders."

"When I arrived here the Court said that salvation was guaranteed if I worked in the purgation fields, but I couldn't trust them. I died believing a false doctrine of salvation and I would not be deceived again. I would save myself only I didn't know how. The answer came by God's Will in the form of three angels who led me to Messina and the Mark of the Phoenix. After I received it I became Amalgam's Savior."

"During my wars with the Court I removed the Amalgam seals and entered the realm of Boundless Hell. There I saw for myself the tortured, mutilated, and the God shunned; it's a land without hope, happiness, or heart. Upon my arrival, the gates of Hell shook to the point that they almost collapsed. Everyone including Lucifer thought I was the Phoenix of Light returned but I'm much different. He only saved a select few from Hell whereas I would recover them all, saint and sinner alike."

"I spoke to Lucifer, his disgusting face was the most spiteful thing I've ever seen done to a creation of God, but our dialogue was not positive. I offered to take him from the pit so he could make amends with the Lord but I felt his tremendous anger, power, and selfishness. He tried to take my mark for himself thinking it would give him the power to overthrow God but I defeated him. I realized his desires would cause unneeded tension in our war. He still wants to supplant God but I could only offer the possibility for his forgiveness."

"I'm interested in saving souls and though those who stand before me must be vanquished from Mortalland and Amalgam they will be saved when I reconcile them to the Judge. Either you can stand against me or beside me, but I will enter the Paradise Door and tell God I had to take personal responsibility for my salvation. So I ask you, will you stand behind or between me and the Three Doors?"

Lauren sat in her prison and said nothing. Though she completely comprehended every word, she knew that he was wrong in every way and wondered what grandiose fantasy he concocted that made him think he was capable of doing God's work.

"Phoenix, I can't. This is your war, I just want to go home," said Lauren.

"This is everyone's war yours, mine, God's, Lucifer's, we're all real fighting for souls and salvation. Join me and I promise you power and glory or you can die in Mortalland!"

"Then no, Phoenix," said Lauren fearing her for mortal life. "I can't go against God. Though your power is vast it's not enough."

"Don't underestimate my connection with God. That's why He fears my entry to the Paradise Realm; I'll fully become his Son, in truth Him!"

"No," said Lauren. "I can't."

The Dark Phoenix sighed, "Your faith is strong but blinding you to the truth. I am God and since you have refused me you are of no use to me," he said as the flower began to close.

Lauren's screams were silenced by the encroaching leaves. She sat in total darkness for moments and then the bud leaves pressed tightly against her; her body felt as if it was going to explode. She felt drained, physically and mentally; her intelligence left her. Finally, it stopped and though she wasn't dead she was just a shell, nothing more.

Phoenix sat with his eyes closed in front of the flower. Out of the top the tulip spit out the powers Lauren had assumed. As the divine mark returned to the Phoenix a bird grew from a pile of ashes and fire into a mature phoenix on his hand. Once again, the Phoenix became attuned to the happenings of Amalgam. He knew Jasmine was returning as she burst into the meadow dragging Estoc with her tree's roots to tell Phoenix what he already knew, that Catherine was on her way.

"Phoenix! Catherine's..." said Jasmine.

He raised his hand to silence her. He opened his eyes and the tulip left for the trees encircling the meadow. From the bud issued thin white strands of silk that wound about Lauren and outstretched to hang her from a tree. The flower rapidly decayed until nothing remained of it. Estoc roared aloud but the roots of Jasmine's tree wound around his mouth and about its legs. Estoc was immobile and at the will of his captors.

Jasmine approached Phoenix and spoke, "I've

captured Estoc. I remained out of sight controlling my tree from afar; they have no idea who's responsible."

"Excellent, Jasmine, using your mind instead of muscle. Preserve our deception and never ride that tree again in the animal's presence."

"Yes, Phoenix," said Jasmine.

"Now its time to lead them to me," said Phoenix. He stood and raised his mark hand. Out from his mark shot a streak of light that reached above the trees, arched by the heavens, and dropped into the leaderless pride. The magic was an image of Catherine and to the enraged lionesses it appeared as if she was physically present but they attacked and discovered it was only an illusion.

"I've declared war on the animal race, to rescind the lands I bestowed to you for the ghost nation. It is highly advised for each of your kind to move deeper into the Wilds or face destruction in our path. I have captured your lord Estoc to eliminate any major threats to our new policy regarding animal-ghost relations. Leave swiftly or die, *you have been warned.*"

As the message vaporized the lionesses roared in anger. They cursed her for deceiving them earlier. They screamed that Catherine lied because she feared they could have killed her and how foolish they were for trusting her. Their roars carried for miles up to where the real Catherine was trudging through the great forest. She turned to the sound in wonder before going on. Their roars even reached the meadow where Phoenix and Jasmine moved closer to the king. Estoc's eyes pierced Phoenix as if he was mortal again hunting pray along the African savannah. Phoenix bowed to the lion in genuine respect before speaking.

"Estoc, lord of gestalt beasts; haven't seen you so angry since the Animal War. You were second in command after Masden right?" He waved his hand and the roots left his mouth. Estoc was going to roar to his lionesses' but Phoenix inhibited him with a spell.

"So you're responsible for this?" asked Estoc.

"In a roundabout way, yes; the ghosts fled Jasmine into your forests. I didn't expect your animals to react so aggressively to them, although I should have. The animals that follow you and Masden are beastly cold souls. Jasmine and I intend to use this hatred for ghosts to advance my cause like the first Animal War; an animal army will destroy the Everlasting Guard when the castle is grounded."

Jasmine smiled as Phoenix's plan became clearer.

"Catherine will figure it out, she'll free me, and then I'll lead my animals to crush you—"

"When your animals find you the castle will lie in ruin. You never had the pure hatred for ghosts Lord Masden had to continue his ghost eradication movement or the wisdom of the siren Selene to see the error in warring with ghosts. We are your superiors in this world and the former; it's only by Catherine's good graces that you even have a domain. A forest is no place for a lion's pride; Catherine gave it to you in order to restrain your aggressiveness hoping that you would find peace with ghosts yet you never strayed from Masden's teachings. It's this ignorance you preach that will lead your lionesses to me and beg for my help and I'll give it to them. Take him to the spectral tree Jasmine and place him in a special cell where he'll have ample space to move about, one fit for a king."

Jasmine came from behind Phoenix, focused her mind, and the tree took Estoc further east.

"Where is the girl?" asked Jasmine. Phoenix pointed to Lauren hanging upside down from a tree.

"I think we should take her to the spectral tree as well," said Jasmine. "We should make Catherine's search in vain and take the girl's mortal life. The pink color is leaving her; it'll only be a few more hours."

"Do what you wish."

"Where did you send Inez and Ariel?"

"Off to gather the centaurs for an attack to retrieve your mark. My plan will require the use of all our forces at the spectral tree so hide Estoc well. Take your wolves to the Elysian fields where you'll rendezvous with the centaurs and wait for me."

"Where are you going?"

"I'm going to deliver a message for the animals to meet me in the spectral tree's valley; there I'll convince them to follow me."

Jasmine bowed to her master and moved toward Lauren.

"What were her reasons for not joining us?"

"She underestimated my connection with the Judge. At least her faith in God is strong."

Phoenix waited until Jasmine cut Lauren down then teleported away. His body morphed to a flaming red Phoenix bird, it flapped its wings and flew east. Jasmine raised her staff and cast a Phantom Charm that emitted a visible clone of herself far down the trail of her tree and instantly she was there. In this way, Jasmine could travel great distances faster than most ghost orbs. She followed the Phoenix to her tree fortress.

* * * *

After being thrown aside in the Gathering Plains, Nasra orbed and flew into the animal forest to help salvage the Procession debacle. When a giant door materialized near her position, Nasra knew Catherine had arrived thus making her difficult task easier. When Nasra finished, she began her search for Lauren. She caught a glimpse of Jasmine returning to capture Estoc and attempted to follow her but her tree was too fast. Following the marks on the trunks left by Jasmine's tree, Nasra was able to trudge a path towards the meadow where she intersected Catherine. The baroness found her flying in orb form up a high barricade of tangled roots and in a single bound, landed at the top before Nasra and spoke to her.

"Nasra, what are you doing this deep into

animal territory?"

Nasra turned to human form and addressed her superior.

"Catherine, the Phoenix and his witch have taken a girl into the forests. Her name's Lauren Walston, a Mortalland shade. She's been in Amalgam too long, we don't have much time."

"I know. I received word there was a raid and I met her friends earlier," said Catherine turning to continue the search, Nasra orbed to keep pace with the swift baroness who could run faster than most ghosts could fly.

"Do you have an idea why they took Lauren?" asked Catherine.

"Somehow she entered the Phoenix column and *didn't die*! Something bad must've happened because the Phoenix was very worried. They were trying to enter Mortalland but when Lauren stepped into the column they took her and fled."

"Um...," said Catherine as she moved faster. She saw Nasra having trouble keeping up so she whistled a sweet melody that summoned a ghost-friendly horse nearby.

"Take the horse, Nasra, save your energy in case we have to fight again."

Nasra transformed from orb to ghost form onto the horse and turned her around as Catherine breezed by. Nasra guided the horse and rode along with Catherine continuing the conversation.

"What do you think they'll do to her?" asked Nasra.

"Probably kill her if she's taken any of his power. Knowing the Phoenix, he'll try and persuade her to join him. If she has, Nasra, I want you to knock her out and take her to the castle. I'll keep the Phoenix and this witch off your back."

They reached the meadow in short time; it was empty except for the numerous ghosts hanging from the trees.

"My God!" said Nasra. "I heard Phoenix was taking marks from ghosts but I never would have thought he'd leave them here like this."

Catherine approached a ghost and forced an arm from the bonds. Instead of a mark only a blue scar remained.

"Phoenix scars, no wonder they registered as loyalists instead of missing. These ghosts needed to be judged a long time ago but they'll never be summoned in this state."

"All of their marks are gone. Think they were looking for a particular one?"

"Possibly," said Catherine.

"Some of these lost souls look too far gone," said Nasra touching one beside her.

"We'll restore them but first we have to get them to the castle."

Catherine raised her hand and created yet another door linking to the foyer of Castle Everlasting's Guard House where the soldiers were finally relaxing after a long day of combat. A ghost was sitting at the reception desk looking into the newly materialized door without surprise.

"I need a company dispatched to cut down these ghosts, take them to the Record House, and have Names and Graves try to identify them," said Catherine. The ghost looked to his right, snapped his fingers, and relayed Catherine's orders to an unseen ghost.

"Come, Nasra," said Catherine as ghosts issued forth from the door to begin the arduous work. They searched the trees for an indication of scratches Jasmine's tree may have left, found some, and followed them. The trail ended at a cliff where Nasra and Catherine surveyed an expansive clearing dotted with hundreds of tree stumps and in the middle, one incredibly large tree.

Easily larger than any of the skyscraping trees it remained hidden because of its lower elevation. Its large green crown cast a shadow in the valley. Every few moments the leaves would become very opaque, showing the twisted branches underneath. The trunk had numerous rectangular carvings, windows giving a total view of the trees surroundings. On the flare were three treacherous openings for a mouth and two eyes. Large roots ran from the trunk, along the flare, and up to the crown. Carved into them were steps and ramps.

"We'll be exposed on approach, be ready for anything," said Catherine.

Nasra dismounted and together they orbed and flew towards the tree. Catherine's orb was larger than Nasra's. It was swath in golden strands and beads of light like an atom and had a long golden trail of light. Inside her orb were three doors floating amongst the mist that is her soul yet she dimmed this extravagant radiance to allow for a stealthier approach.

At the tree, Catherine dispelled a powerful edict charm and entered one of the windows on the flare. They stepped into a vacated sapwood prison cell with roots for the cell bars and a smoothly carved room. Spectroplasm dripped from the ceiling into a small recess on the floor, a dead pool.

"Interesting," said Catherine as she carefully scanned the strong spells inside the room.

"Dampening spells to drown out sound, edict charms, sticky sap cells, and vine bars to prevent escape, and a dead pool for food. Take note of the inventiveness of our enemy, Nasra."

Catherine bent the roots open with her spell-enchanted hands and stepped out into the large landing. The heartwood interior was wide and multi-tiered with many levels of prison cells. In the middle of the room was a pillar that stretched from top to bottom of the prison. Bridges extended to each level and the pillar had a continuous stair winding along it with a large gap between the pillar and the landings. They searched each floor; inside the cells were more scarred ghosts. Catherine passed a window and saw a massive cloud approaching the tree. She knew exactly what it was.

"What should we do with the lost souls, Catherine?" Nasra yelled up to the baroness from a floor below.

"Leave them; I can't bring guards here with the animals coming. We'll get them out another day."

Nasra also looked out a window where she saw the dust cloud blowing in the wind. Birds, elephants, bears, and all kinds of animals tossed up the sand. From above they could hear the Phoenix's voice.

"Come, come all animals for your master needs your help and war is inevitable," his voice so swelled the valley it was almost tactile.

Catherine listened while she continued looking; she was a cell away from Lauren as the Phoenix began his speech. Nasra was growing worried as every window she looked out she saw a multitude of enraged animals.

"Catherine…," said Nasra becoming extremely fearful.

"Found her!" said Catherine. Nasra orbed and flew up to her landing. Lauren was lying on the floor unconscious.

"Your loyal servant the Dark Phoenix has a plan that will teach the Court to respect your lands and we'll deliver that message posthaste to their cities," the Phoenix shouted to his beastly audience.

"Pick her up," said Catherine with a hushed voice as she created another door to her quarters at Castle Everlasting. She too was worried; Catherine could match the Phoenix in strength, but against the animal mass they would surely be destroyed. Nasra slung Lauren across her shoulder; her pink glow was all but gone except for a mask-like residue about her eyes, which allowed Nasra to carry her. The door swung open and they passed through making a discreet exit from a dangerous situation.

CHAPTER SIX
MESSINA, THE MARK, AND OSBORN HOSPITAL

The baroness and Nasra stepped into Catherine's chamber at Baronsguard, the headquarters of Castle Everlasting. It was a personal room but looked like a study filled with numerous bookshelves, a globe displaying the Earth but also the Amalgam realm and a bed. A large desk was in the center stacked with papers and three chairs were placed before it. Torches and a chandelier lit the room; the massive fireplace against the wall was shut out. A curtained archway in the middle of the room was the door to a corridor, Catherine's private entrance to the courtroom.

"I'll take her," said Catherine. "Find Amy and Renee at the House of Shades, tell them Lauren is safe and get them back to Mortalland immediately."

Nasra bowed and exited the chamber, closing its

door silently. Catherine shut the door she materialized and opened it again entering to stand before two towering angels, in the angel province of Messina. The heavenly guards knelt in shameful, silent prayer. They had white, feathered tails that formed the walls of the city that stretched for miles and the only untarnished parts of their figure. Their bodies were blackened from fierce burns, their faces covered by their boiled hands and their torn, battered wings. Two giant shields were buried in the ground, the Gate of Messina, barring entry.

Waves crashed upon the shores behind Catherine's door, the foam sparkled as if lustrous diamonds glinted in fine white fur. The twilight sky was a bright, soothing pink with traces of purple visible in the clouds that were thick, white and foreboding. Despite the city beyond the gates, there is a residual beauty and warmth upon the continent, the source of the Paradise Realm's influence in Amalgam. Catherine knows of the calamity that's fallen upon the angel city, having entered soon after its destruction. She never saw the city in its pristine state.

"I wish to speak with Messina; I'm Baroness Catherine of New Elysian."

The angels picked up their shields, their wings hid their faces until they could cover it with the armor. A brilliant white light flowed forth from the city. The light emanated from her lord, an angel, female, and inhumanly beautiful. She took many forms, even male, but she chose to appear with curly brown hair, caramel skin and purple eyes with three pairs of wings. Her white robes draped from her wrists, shoulders and waist, her legs and arms were exposed and she walked barefooted.

"Catherine, welcome!" she said, her voice gave Catherine comfort.

"This is the girl you sent me to find, but she's been scarred by the Phoenix. Hopefully you can restore whatever it is that you needed from her," said Catherine.

"Phoenix's scar can't damage what we need from her! More has happened to this girl than you know Catherine, and it's fortunate that neither you nor Phoenix could have seen it." Messina touched her head, restoring Lauren's memories, and she screamed as if she was still imprisoned in the tulip. Her pink glow refilled about her entire body, extending her time in Mortalland and Amalgam.

"Calm yourself girl, you're safe!" Catherine struggled to put her down and then held her steady so she wouldn't run off. Lauren fought against her, believing she was Jasmine until she caught sight of Messina's face whose tender gaze stilled her fears.

"Who are you?" asked Lauren.

"I'm Messina, this is Baroness Catherine and you're in the angel city of Messina."

"How'd I get here?"

"Catherine saved you from the spectral tree where Phoenix and Jasmine imprisoned you."

"Barons are leaders of the cities right?"

"Yes."

"Then who are you?"

"I am the angel Metatron."

"What's a Metatron?"

"*The* Metatron," said Catherine. "Messina is an angel that bears the Lord's credentials and acts as the voice of God."

"Before Christ came to Earth, God spoke to men in visions and occasionally requested a physical presence through which to relay a message personally. I was that presence," said Messina. "When Christ was born, I was no longer needed to speak to men. The Holy Spirit guides them now. After the Great Sin, the Judge could no longer speak to spirits in this world since your husks are so fragile. Once again I was called by God to be his oracle and lead the barons in restoring Amalgam."

"Your voice sounds familiar, Messina," said Lauren.

"It was my voice you heard in the Phoenix Column. You've made it here but sadly without the mark!"

Lauren didn't feel guilt or regret; she was still trying to get a grasp on reality. Messina led them through the gates, they were in a city that was charred to ruin.

"What happened here?" asked Lauren.

"I burned this city on orders from the Judge to shame the angels who stole the mark of the Phoenix and all those who stood by and did nothing."

They approached a cathedral, the only structure that wasn't burned but was simply spectacular.

Forged out of a material that radiated like sunbathed water and was stronger than diamond, the cathedral was as brilliant as a rainbow in this blackened wasteland. The inside, however, wasn't similarly breathtaking. The cathedral was mostly dark and a filthy, broken shamble. Cobwebs hung thick like draped curtains and little light seeped in through dust-covered windows.

Screams reverberated through the chapel. The pews were in disarray and as Lauren looked between the rows, she could see several angels lying on the floor wriggling as if they were insane or in terrible pain. They screamed for God's forgiveness. Lauren remembered what Nasra told her in the carriage about angels and reapers and she saw a few angels that looked well on their way to becoming reapers.

"How are the angels starving?" asked Lauren.

"They lack the Touch of God. There were two kinds of angels in Amalgam before the Great Sin, outcast and servants. Servants were in God's graces and most have returned to Heaven. All outcast angels remained and due to their nature and Mortalland's influence, they required God's presence, or Touch, to sustain them. The Vessel carried the Judge's Spirit and His Touch and over the centuries, they've diminished without it. I can only provide them with temporary comfort when they've completed their mandates. Until the Judge reconciles them they'll suffer, such is the fate of renegades."

Catherine drew Lauren's attention to the vault in the back of the throne. A massive, immaculately designed door painted of various angelic figures flying around a Holy Presence in the clouds.

"That's the cathedral's treasury. Inside are some of the most important artifacts of Mortalland and Amalgam."

"Like what?" Lauren asked; the massive black curtains draping a raised throne obstructed her view.

"The most important are items from the Crucifixion like the Crown of Thorns and the Shroud. They were found after Jesus' ascension, dematerialized, and stored here. I asked once why weren't they taken to the Paradise realm but Messina has never let me or any of the other barons in on that secret. Other stored items are from Amalgam's creation era like the djemsheed, Telasdod, and the Cyclonus Phalanges."

They continued on, the interior of the cathedral was arranged like a cross. The congregation of the church faced the center where the throne stood. Messina, with a wave of her hand, pulled back the black curtains and Lauren gasped in horror. There sat a giant decaying body the colossus shown at the Procession. Its flesh was rotting and its skeleton clearly visible with tattered clothing hanging off the bones. Its heart was inside, black and beating slowly and the throbbing brain was visible through cracks in the cranium. It had life but its vitals were almost gone.

"This is all that remains of the Holy Vessel of the Judge. Dishonored by the Phoenix and three angels Raziel, Cedric, and Marcela it's been decaying for over a thousand years. Its Amalgam's most important clock, for when its heart stops beating the Judge will return to reclaim his mark from the Phoenix by force. If that happens, Amalgam, its connected realms, and inhabitants will experience the full force of the Judge's wrath. My job is to ensure that my agents will reclaim the mark before that time."

"It's decayed so much since I've last seen it," said Catherine.

"Yes, it's almost dead. I give it another five to ten years," said Messina. "Do you think you can stop the Phoenix before then, Catherine?"

Catherine looked intimidated but knew Messina wouldn't take any other answer.

"Yes. But…"

"But what?"

"It's hard, Messina. Between summoning, searching for the seals, battling the Phoenix and his loyalists, running the castle, and incidents like today, I can't commit myself fully to this task. I'm stretched too thin. I don't have the ability to be everywhere at once."

"Are your barons contributing to the cause?"

"They have their own problems. Donovan's having trouble with the demons, Samina has the largest population of ghosts and Jonah's city is overrun with a closet network of cold souls. We would need another baron to take the burden off of us."

Messina was sympathetic as she left the throne

and approached the baroness.

"I know you're overworked but it's what the job requires. The only thing I can do for you is take some of the responsibility of the Phoenix off your mind. Let me see your left-hand mark."

Catherine outstretched her left hand and gave it to Messina.

"Catherine is one of the few people in Amalgam granted two marks," Messina addressed Lauren. "Her power is vast, yet she wields it with humbleness. The most loyal are always given the greatest responsibilities and two marks is a true testament of God's faith in her."

She gripped Catherine's hand and squeezed it hard. Catherine yelled in pain, falling to her knees.

"But now, she's been relieved of such a heavy burden," said Messina.

Lauren stepped away frightened by yet another brutal act in this realm. Catherine stopped wailing as soon as Messina let go of Catherine's hand. She stood calmly as if there was never any pain. Messina looked towards Lauren and beckoned her forward. Lauren shook her head no.

"I want you take this task from Catherine, Lauren. With the mark of the Phoenix cage, you're sole job will be to reclaim the Phoenix mark," said Messina. She raised her hand to make it visible to Lauren. It was that of a birdcage with blue flames for bars.

"No! I just want to get back home, this is your problem."

"This is everyone's problem. It's as much Catherine's and mine as it is Amy's, Renee's, your mother Anita, anyone. We are God's servants, Lauren, and with this mark and the defeat of the Phoenix you'll prove yourself worthy of the highest rewards in Heaven."

"*I can't fight the Phoenix!* I've got to go home and fix my life."

"Ah yes, but what can you do about your parents' divorce? What can you do about Jason now that he's dating Amy? What will you do if the Phoenix enters Heaven with the Amalgam seals removed? The Judge's fury will spill over to Mortalland, erasing all life in every realm with the Fire of Judgment."

Lauren wasn't surprised that every stranger in this realm knew her business as if they had been invisibly watching her like ghosts.

"I...I don't know, I just want to go home," she said desperately.

"She's only a child, Messina," said Catherine.

"You can't see the strength in this girl's spirit, Catherine. I expect her to regain some of the Phoenix's strength and being a Mortalland shade, she'll be able to shift between the material and ethereal worlds. There's also something special about her which I will tell you later. But you asked for a new baron and here she is."

"You intend to give her the mark of the Phoenix Cage and instill her as a baron?" asked Catherine skeptically.

"If she accepts it," said Messina.

"What province will she govern?" asked Catherine.

"The New City, long has it been its own province and in need of a baron. Although I don't think establishing a full court there will be necessary. Lauren's presence and dedication to the job should suffice."

Lauren listened anxiously as they talked aloud in front of her.

"Lauren, as baron of the New City your mandate is to stop the Dark Phoenix by reclaiming the Judge's mark. This will not be an easy task but it's one you must accomplish. You'll be able to use your gifts to achieve something positive instead of the vain pursuits of most humans."

"Catherine's right," said Lauren. "I'm not strong enough for this. I have a disease and my body can't stand extreme changes in temperatures because of it. I'm going to be really sick when I get back. My life is in shambles and I have to fix it somehow. I can't take on any other responsibilities until I do."

"So, home it is then?" asked Messina.

"Yes! Please!"

* * * *

Lauren vanished from Amalgam and gazed upon the lights in her hospital room. She heard the beeps of the electrocardiogram racing at its highest pitch, startling the doctors trying to revive her. The sickle red blood cells ravaged her veins and sent searing pain throughout her body. Lauren was correct about her disease; her body was freezing because her cold spirit had just returned from the frigid Amalgam realm. She soon fell unconscious with the doctors working diligently over her.

She regained consciousness several days later. Her father was sitting next to her in a chair reading a business magazine. He was dressed causally in a blue shirt and black slacks and appeared wide-awake. He was sipping steaming coffee from a thin paper cup with his legs propped up on another chair. She turned to him and muttered, "Daaad…"

Willem spilled his coffee on himself cursing as he sat up in surprise as if lighting had scorched his bottom.

"Lauren, thank God. I'm so glad you're awake. How are you feeling?"

"Okay, a little cold," said Lauren silently.

"I've got to call your mother, tell her you're awake," said Willem as he moved over to a closet and retrieved an extra blanket that he gently laid on Lauren. He dialed the number on the room phone and spoke, "Anita, this is Willem no…no it's not about us. Lauren's awake. Yes, she's fine. You're already on your way up? Okay, hurry while she's still talking," said Willem as he brushed the hair from Lauren's eyes. He hung up the phone.

"Thank God; we thought you were dead. I thought my life was over when Anita called that night and I know she felt the same way. I thought

I'd have to hospitalize Anita, she had gotten so upset. Imagine our surprise when the doctor said you were going to be okay. We've been waiting here ever since for you to wake up."

He sat on the bed next to her and asked, "How did this happen? I heard you and Amy got into a fight and then hit by a car?"

Lauren nodded yes.

"I hope we can find that drunk driver and throw him in jail. Jason managed to get a good look at the vehicle; police are out there right now looking for that blue truck. What were you two fighting about?"

"It's not important daddy." She was ashamed to have nearly died fighting over a boy.

Willem nodded, "You're right. I'm just glad you're alright. Your friends took a similar hit but they woke up two days ago. While you are up, I want to explain why I was so angry a few days ago. I was going to call you after the party but when the car hit you, I wasn't sure I'd ever get to talk to you again. So now that I have the chance here goes."

"The night of the accident I know I was a little irate but it's just because I was tired of your mother lying to me and I lying to you. We had been having some problems for a few months when your mother went out with her girlfriends for a night on the town," Willem bared teeth; his anger was still fresh. "That was the worst night of my life, Lauren, that's when I discovered Anita…"

The door opened and Anita rushed in. Willem disappointedly moved out of the way so Anita could sit next to her. Anita leaned over her and gave her a big hug. "My baby, I'm so glad you're awake. I was so frightened," Anita started crying tears of joy. She wept over her and stroked her gently, never moving from her side for an hour. Lauren wondered what Willem was saying, but Anita was smothering her with hugs and kisses. Then she noticed another person in the doorway.

"Who's that?" Lauren asked silently. The woman entered and stood next to Willem. Lauren remembered her as the passenger in Willem's car the night of the accident.

"Oh, Lauren this is um…this is Natalie, a photographer at my paper," Willem said blushing. Anita shook her head and continued to hold her daughter.

"Hi," said Natalie. "I'm glad you're feeling better!"

Lauren sized up Natalie, who had a slender but firm body, youthful face, brown skin and clothes so form fitting that the dress looked uncomfortable. She had a pleasant smile, narrow brown eyes, and dark brown hair; though Lauren thought something was a bit off. She was sexy, but Lauren guessed correctly that Natalie wasn't confident about her appeal.

"I hear you're quite the photographer yourself. Keep it up, maybe it will pay off some day like it did…for…me," Natalie finished silently when Anita gave her an enraged look.

"I will," said Lauren. "What were you saying, Dad?"

"I—I'll tell you later. Hey, would you like to have a talk at the grave excavation. It's not the ideal situation but it's the only free time I have with my busy schedule."

"Sure."

"I'll call you with the time and date."

They continued to talk about everything but their problems like the arriving school year until Lauren felt weary again and closed her eyes. Though her father dropped by almost everyday he never continued their conversation because Anita was always around. Lauren slept less through the next couple of days. Though she thought about the realm she had visited, Lauren believed it was only part of an awkward dream nothing more. Lauren didn't believe this, the dream was too real, but deceiving herself felt better than admitting a terrible truth. One day, when she was feeling stronger she decided to use the bathroom instead of the bedpans.

After she relieved herself, Lauren gazed into the mirror to assess the damage. Her face was horrible filled with a series of scars and patches of gauze where underneath deep bruises still bled. Her forehead had a large stitched gash through her hair and her arms were bandaged tight to keep the bones steady. While becoming depressed about her physical appearance someone entered her room almost cautiously as not to harm her anymore.

"Hello? Lauren? You home?" asked a friendly voice. Lauren leaned out to see Renee calling her. She too was in a hospital gown wheeling in an IV machine and carrying a small plastic bag.

"There you are," she said happily. "How are you?"

Lauren smiled and decided to elaborate about all her physical ailments since she had routinely answered "okay."

"My back hurts and my hips feel like they have arthritis…and my head hurt like a migraine, but I'm fine. Oh and my butt feels swollen for some reason."

"I guess we're in the right place after all."

"You look great, hardly a scar on you," said Lauren. She surveyed Renee's body, and found only one or two scars yet she was moving about very well and appeared strong.

"Yeah, the doctors were startled by my recovery. I actually think they were a bit frightened."

"Why?"

"They said when I came in the ambulance I looked as bad as you and Amy, but my wounds healed so fast they called it a miracle. I'm starting to think what they really meant was *unnatural*. One of the nurses sent in to clean my dressings gave me the oddest look when she saw the cuts had healed. She called the doctor in and they just looked at me before leaving, didn't offer an explanation or anything. I heard them talking in the hallway and the nurse was saying how she'd never seen a person heal so fast but the doctor wasn't too surprise."

"Why not?" asked Lauren.

"He made a strange remark, 'In Baker's Creek, you'll see some strange things. Don't question it or pay any attention to it, just do your job. It'll keep you sane," said Renee quoting the doctor using her deep voice.

"Weird," said Lauren thoughtfully.

"Actually it explains a bunch of the old rumors around town. I've always thought urban legends were fairly common from place to place, but some of the stories I've heard about Baker's Creek are pretty unique. Now they make more sense. I had the worst dream while I was out," said Renee. "You, Amy, and I were in this ghost world that was like purgatory or something, but it felt like Hell especially after that column of eyes came from the sky. It was the most horrible experience I've ever had but it felt too real to have been a dream."

Renee's comments unsettled Lauren so she didn't respond to her until she asked Lauren if she had a similar dream.

"I didn't see anything, Renee. I remember being bandaged and my dad spilling coffee when I woke up."

"Oh...well...that's comforting...I thought for a moment it could have been true. Maybe it would explain my *awesome recovery*."

"I bet your dad was happy you pulled through! I couldn't imagine how he'd manage if something happened to you as well."

"He probably wouldn't have made it; we'd have gone to Amalgam together."

"What?" Lauren feigned ignorance.

"Nothing," said Renee begrudgingly. She sat looking confused and disappointed before she brightened once again and sang, "Guess what you forgot at the Thompson's?"

Lauren moved to the bed and tried to think but she couldn't remember leaving anything. Renee took out of her bag Anita's red purse and handed it to her.

"Thanks," said Lauren.

"No problem. Amy's mom thought it was either yours or mine. Have you seen Amy?"

"Not yet. Did you?"

"I stopped in. She looks a mess but she's healing fine. Jason was there, they looked like they were having a serious conversation. She told me to tell you that she's not mad at you. "

"Oh yeah," said Lauren indifferently but she was curious. "Is that all she said, she's not mad at me?"

"Pretty much, I think Jason and her were talking about what happened at the party. He did say he liked you."

Lauren's heart leaped before she dismissed it. "Then why is he with Amy?"

"I'm sure he has his reasons. You never know, they could be breaking up. Be encouraged."

Lauren smiled, "I need to stretch my legs, let's take a walk." Lauren unplugged her IV machine and they strolled causally down the hall. Lauren and Renee passed by Amy's room, where Jason was still talking to Amy. Lauren wanted to speak to Jason but decided to say something to Amy first, careful not to draw her angst.

"How are you, Amy?"

Jason and Amy looked at Lauren. Amy didn't reply, she turned her head away but Jason smiled and approached her.

"How are you is the question?" asked Jason.

Lauren blushed, "I'm great."

"Good! Man, I lost it when you three got hit."

Lauren remembered that Jason was standing over her body rather than Amy's when they were lying in the street.

"I thought you handled yourself well."

"What?" Jason asked confused.

"Nevermind," Lauren smiled. "What have you been doing since the accident?"

"Waitin' on word from you three and talkin' with the cops as an eyewitness to the crime. The Thompson's, Mr. Dupree, and your parents have really been putting pressure on the police to find that guy. I got his plate number 3XHP16; I'll never forget it until they find him."

"Yeah, he needs to be thrown in jail," said Renee.

"Or beaten 'til he looks like he's been run over," said Jason seriously, "Anyway, glad to see you up and about. I'll come by and check on you two!"

Jason pushed the door; it closed slowly as he rejoined Amy who looked furious before it sealed.

"See, I told you!" said Renee as they continued walking.

CHAPTER SEVEN
DREAMS AND PSYCHOMETRY

Jason came to Lauren and Renee's rooms as promised but didn't stay long or talk much, Lauren suspected, because of a strong warning from Amy. Lauren left Osborn Hospital two days later with Anita. The dream of Amalgam she shared with Renee stuck in her mind like a bad jingle and Lauren continued to deny she'd actually ventured into such a place. Anita cooked Lauren's favorite dish, spaghetti bolognese, for dinner but Lauren couldn't eat much as her stomach was still sensitive. After dinner, Lauren went upstairs to her room. She forgot about the mess she left.

She laid down exhausted after having walked up the flight of stairs. Her room was a bit stuffy so she opened the window by her bed to let in some air. She saw Mr. Vasteck's house through her window and remembered that he had died in her "dream" and claimed his body was on the toilet. Lauren saw this as the perfect opportunity to rid herself of that silly ghost world when Anita finds Vasteck alive and well watching television in his recliner. She called downstairs to her mother.

"Yes, Lauren," said Anita from below.

"How's Mr. Vasteck? I haven't seen or heard from him in a while."

"Neither have I. It's been a few months since I've seen Kevin. I'll stop by today. I'm sure he'll want to know how you're doing. What made you think about him all of sudden?"

"Just curious."

Lauren returned to bed and was soon asleep but her dreams were much different from before. It was as if she was watching the mental images of someone envisioning scene. She was on a ship during a calm night although a storm was looming a few miles away. Two men, one was black whose face was defined, his name Lauren somehow knew was Devon Knight, the other an undefined white man whose name was Duncan were looking portside at the sea.

They looked northeast and Lauren saw the great pirate ship known as the Baker's Bane. Lauren watched as the pirates swung from the Bane and landed on the merchant ship christened the Evelyn. The sailors defended themselves well but were outnumbered. Every face was indistinguishably blank except for some of the pirates and Devon. The scene shifted quickly, Lauren was still on the ship and Devon stood next to an injured Duncan. Duncan held out a book with an opaque cover, it had an enchanted picture of a floating castle and it was radiating cool vapors.

"Wait!" said Duncan. "I can't die but I don't want them to get this book. Should I get captured and if you escape, find a man in Baker's Creek known as Etienne Robert and give it to him. Tell him what happened to me—tell him you're *alone* and he'll reward you with everlasting life!"

The scene shifted, Lauren was now walking behind Devon held at gunpoint by two pirates. They led him to the shore of a dark and uninhabited island. Suddenly, Lauren was in a rowboat facing Devon who sat quite bravely tied to two chests as the pirates rowed towards their ship. A bright warm glow and a thunderous blast turned Lauren's attention behind her where she saw the pirate ship aflame with the Evelyn.

Stranded, the pirates in Devon's boat called to their captain for orders who was approaching the island in a boat and similarly distraught by the Bane's destruction. Lauren listened as the captain replied; when quiet abruptly her boat capsized and they all tumbled into the sea. She felt the bitter chill and the sting of the water as it rushed in her nose and lungs. With her face down in the water, Lauren watched as Devon sank helplessly into the abyss struggling to free his wrists from the heavy chests.

The dream changed to Amalgam drenched in a

deluge and Devon was riding a brown horse fast and hard across the soaked plains. His heart was racing at this breathtaking speed Lauren knew this because her heart was pounding. Jasmine and her wolves were pursuing him as he made for sanctuary in a dense forest. In this woodland, the trees could move swiftly as the roots crawled along and dug into the ground.

The trees had small hollow arches in the flare and the roots rose from the ground with suction holes in their feeder roots to siphon the collected rainwater. The arches swallowed the liquid forcibly inside, so fast they created a swift current. If the trees had been a bit larger and the water level higher, the trees would have sucked Devon and his horse inside. Lauren was flying along with Devon and could see that he wore a jeweled necklace. The jewel blinked quickly and as he neared the forest edge, the trees situated and a dirt path appeared.

He dashed into the forest and Jasmine followed but the trees began to move again after Devon's entry. The rider was being slung forcibly around as its roots slipped and collided with the trunks as she struggled to catch her prey. Jasmine's tree crashed into a trunk sending her flying in the air but the largest of her wolves, the only one still in pursuit, ran underneath her airborne body and she landed on its back. She rode into an eight-lane crossroad where she paused to decide which way to go, selecting the northwest lane only to end up back at the forest edge. The dream darkened and ended with

Lauren breathing rapidly and her body trembling. The darkness turned to light as she awoke. It was morning; Lauren had dreamed for over twelve hours and was wet from sweat, drained and weak.

The suspenseful nightmare terrorized her even more because the dream appeared to show successive events in the Amalgam realm. Lauren realized it was becoming harder to deny the existence of the ghost world. Her conversation with Renee was proof enough, but she hoped it wouldn't be true. Yet hope was fleeting and for Lauren the truth was too awesome to believe all at once. If her "dream" had once again been of unicorn-drawn carriages and a convertible amphitheater field, she'd have thought it was a reoccurring nightmare. As it were, her dream included similar elements from her previous experience and that couldn't have been a coincidence.

Lauren struggled to the bathroom; her mother followed the doctor's orders and installed a chair in the shower so she could sit to bathe. She put on her nightgown and went downstairs to watch television, thinking it would get her mind off the dream. Lauren wanted to ask her mother about it, but Anita was gone and the dream probably wouldn't make much sense to her. She remembered that Names and Graves said they would be guilty of breaking the Mortalland Rule in doing so.

The only people she could contact would be Amy and Renee. Lauren considered calling Renee, though she didn't want to confirm Renee's belief having denied it so stubbornly in the hospital. She also sensed a desire within Renee for Amalgam to be real. Lauren reasoned this wishful thinking probably had to do with her mother's death which is why she didn't want to encourage Renee just yet. After all, Vasteck could still wind up in his house as alive, though not as young, as he was in that carriage. Her only option was Amy and they weren't on the best of terms. Therefore, Lauren resolved to ignore the vision as a simple dream, a very vivid one.

When her mother returned, she brought Lauren a bag of new school clothes. Inside was an array of blouses, skirts, dress pants, and jewelry yet Lauren was more accustomed to jeans and t-shirts.

"I've bought these new clothes so you can dress more like a girl. You want to make a good first impression going to a new school."

"I don't like any of these clothes, Mom, they're not my style."

"Let's make a deal, Lauren. You wear these clothes for the first three weeks and if the boys aren't giving you more attention, you can go back to your old clothes. I was hoping you'd meet someone new at school and maybe that would help you get over Jason."

"Don't worry, I'm over him," Lauren lied.

"I hope so; no one is worth losing your life over and I'm sure your father would agree if I'd told him why you two were fighting. Now I'm going to cook dinner. I'll just stick to veggies and a piece of jerky black but many strands where turning silver and white. She was dressed in a black cloak and a black and purple form-fitted suit similar to Jasmine's suit but with golden emblems of phoenixes and triquetras and a silver veil covered her hair. In her hands she carried her mask that looked very similar to Jasmine's but with a color scheme that matched her outfit.

"Although, I usually take talking conversationally alone and aloud as insanity, I assume someone besides us must have been listening. Who is this Kradleman?" asked the woman searching through the nearby trees. Heather looked at the giant tree then back at the woman.

"Kradleman is friend, but you scared him off. Who are you?"

"My name is Gretchen Reis and if I heard you correctly, you want to return to mortal life. There is one who can grant you this wish so that you can avenge yourself."

"Don't listen to her, Heather!" said Kradleman.

Gretchen moved forward apparently unable to hear the tree. Lauren could sense Heather's anxiety as Gretchen approached.

"I—I just want to see that they're dead and I want that book. Whatever it was, it belonged to my husband and I want it back."

"A book? What did look like?" asked Gretchen, her tongue nearly slid out of her lips as if she was hissing.

"I'd never seen anything like that book; it was

nearly transparent. When my husband first opened it, the book grew in size and I saw all these pictures and some writing. What was it?" asked Heather.

"A linking tome to the Book of Marks in Castle Lasting's Castigarum. The Phoenix and I materialized it long ago in hopes that he would find a mark that would give him access to the Amalgam Portal. It was lost in Mortalland upon its materialization without a trace until now. *Now that I've met you!*" Gretchen moved around Heather slowly as she spoke.

"I'll make you a deal. I'll provide for you a way into Mortalland so you can take your revenge but first you must find that book. However, in order for you to enter into Mortalland again, you must take an oath."

"Give it too me and I'll say it here and now," Heather said impatiently.

"Don't be hasty! This oath has a profound effect on your immortal soul. It's the Phoenix Oath, speaking its words will turn you into an enemy of the Court."

"THEN LET ME SPEAK IT!"

Gretchen was surprised and delighted, her eyebrows raised and she smiled.

"Wait here and I'll have the Phoenix speak with you. Stay with her!" Gretchen ordered her soldiers.

The dream shifted, to a later scene as Kradleman tried to convince Heather not to take the Phoenix Oath but she stubbornly said she would. The Loyalists thought she was crazy as Heather seemingly spoke to herself. The Phoenix arrived shortly, a fiery bird that swooped down and transformed into the child from the meadow with Gretchen slinking from behind him. The dream instantly became more detailed with his arrival, switching to a first-person perspective and Lauren realized she was watching the Phoenix imagine the scenes when he wasn't present.

"Hello, Heather, my name is Henri Dak, but you may know me as the Dark Phoenix," he bowed lowly, eyes to the ground. "Gretchen tells me you wish to pledge yourself to our cause."

"Yes! Yes! Yes!" said Heather jumping up from the rock she sat on.

"Then listen carefully," said the Child Phoenix.

The Dark Phoenix explained his purpose as he did with Lauren in the meadow. Though it appeared as if Heather was listening, it's a question if she understood. When he finished he offered the oath and Heather took it. He gripped her right hand and altered her tree mark with more power and a phoenix symbol indicating her new allegiance.

"Now you must choose a name, one that your enemies will fear and hate the mere mention of it."

"You're a Frenchman, tell me what this means," said Heather and she slowly recited a phrase in French, careful to get it right.

"It means I hate these damn jasmine flowers," said Phoenix.

"Then I shall be called Jasmine."

"What do you intend to do upon entry to

Mortalland?" asked the Phoenix.

"I'll track down the book as you requested. The thieves said they were going to the docks. I'll start there. How do I get back to Mortalland and become flesh?"

"We'll find a way and when you return we'll assess the extent of your talents; hopefully they'll prove useful. To become flesh take this." Phoenix produced a token. Again, Lauren knew this was a flesh-crafting magic token, a device of Phoenix's creation.

The dream disappeared instantly and Lauren stared sleepily at her white ceiling. She awoke on the couch and sat up thinking about what she witnessed. Most interesting was that Jasmine alluded to an apparent relationship with Nasra. Lauren realized she missed dinner as her stomach was still growling; Anita probably couldn't wake her. It was August twenty-second, a week and two days since the accident, and ten days from the first day of school.

She went to the bathroom and immediately realized that climbing up the stairs was much easier than just a few hours ago. Her energy soared and she ran up the steps. She turned on the bathroom light and gazed in the mirror at the wonder of her face. It was no longer as bruised and her legs weren't stiff. The long scar, however, remained under her hair.

"What's happening to me," she said aloud to her smiling reflection. She thought maybe the deep sleep was the cause but she knew not even sleep could heal her so fast. She went to the kitchen and found leftovers from dinner, which she devoured in minutes. Lauren then cleaned her room, den, and even the bathroom. Anita found her cleaning and asked how she went from barely walking to buzzing about like a bee.

"I can't explain it but it's better than pain," Lauren replied happily.

"Would you like to go for a walk?"

"Yes!" smiled Lauren.

They put on some sweatpants and walked down Evelyn Lane in comfortable silence for a while until Anita broke it.

"I stopped by Mr. Vasteck's house yesterday. As soon as I went in I smelled it."

"What?" Lauren asked with anticipation.

"Death! He died, Lauren. I found him in the bathroom on his toilet," said Anita and Lauren's heart fluttered. "I called an ambulance and his son. He's staying there now getting the funeral business straight."

"That's so sad," Lauren didn't have to pretend to be upset as she nearly cried. The Amalgam realm was real and she could no longer deny it. She felt the same as when she stood up over the crowd of sobbing teenagers without her body. Lauren grasped her chest, the stress pained her. Anita looked at her grimacing and asked if she was experiencing any chest pain. Lauren said no and realized why the doctor told the nurse what he did. She proceeded to ask about Vasteck to keep her sanity. "When's the funeral?"

"A week from today."

She thought of attending, since he was alive in spirit, Lauren figured that Vasteck might be interested in how his funeral turned out. Thinking in this way, Lauren was able to absorb the shock and Anita's questions helped take her mind off Amalgam.

"Old Kevin," Anita chuckled, "I remember when we first moved here, nothing in our house worked and he helped Willem fix just about everything. He'd worked as a plumber, electrician, locksmith, landscaper, God knows what else, and he was always looking for another skill to take up and someone to help." Anita smiled as she recalled her fond memories of their neighbor before switching topics.

"So what did you think of Natalie?" asked Anita.

"I don't see why Dad is with her."

"Natalie's very smart and talented. I hate that your father is leaving me but I guess she's his type. She's like me, only prettier."

"No way! And how is she anything like you?"

"She's what I used to be. Young, ambitious, gorgeous, able to fit in a miniskirt…"

"All style, Mom! You've got what most men dream of personality, humor, honesty, and loyalty…"

Anita raised her brow weighing Lauren's words.

"I was wondering if you wanted to spend some time with your father, maybe towards the middle of the school year. He's moving to a nice apartment complex in Farmington Wells called Orchard Walk."

"I like it here with you. Is this what he was trying to tell me at the hospital?"

"No, he called last night to remind you the grave excavation is September tenth. What was he trying to tell you?"

"He said it was the reason you two were divorcing," said Lauren sarcastically. "It seems pretty clear after Natalie walked in. He claims he want to explain his behavior the night of the accident."

"If that's the case then I suggest you go. He owes you that after almost breaking in your door."

"Who do they believe is in the grave?"

"No one knows; it's the mystery of Baker's Creek graveyard. There's also an urban legend that it's haunted by a ghost."

More ghosts! Lauren thought. She shook her head and sighed aloud which made Anita stop and ask if she was feeling well enough to continue walking. Lauren assured her she was fine and asked her to finish the story.

"Well, people say if you are around it at certain times you can hear voices coming from underground," Anita continued. "Lately, however, visitors have been staying away from the graveyard."

Lauren wondered if this particular legend was one of the tales Renee was referring to as she had never heard of it. Rationalizing was doing Lauren much good. She thought about other legends she'd heard, like the drifter of Barnsbury Road and the dying woman of Bouchard Museum's attic, and realized like Renee that they made much more sense. After walking for three blocks, Lauren felt more exhausted than the walk should have taxed her.

"Lauren? Are you okay?" Anita observed her walking slowly then Lauren fell, her eyes closed and she dreamed yet again.

This time she was standing before a giant crater, miles long in diameter, with a deep pit. It appeared that the ground and the mountains that stood there previously had been ripped from the surface. In the center stood a giant tree, the same one Jasmine was talking to except its crown was broken. Near the broken top the sky warped and Lauren looked higher to see the lost ground, floating high above was Castle Everlasting.

It was pulling the castle from the sky, eroding the golden shield, breaking huge shards of it that shattered on the ground. The impaling trunk speared the foundation, destroying buildings with explosive force. As the tree leveled the island into the crater, its roots beset Castle Everlasting and held it steadfast to the surface. Then a pleasant feeling came about her, like when she and Jason were dancing at homecoming, a deep sensation of happiness and joy.

She woke up at home with paramedics over her shining a light in her eye. Anita was pacing back and forth behind them, biting her nails nervously. She told them Lauren had been in an accident a week earlier but the medics said they couldn't find anything wrong with her. They advised her to consult a doctor, cleared out and left. Anita called their family physician for an emergency appointment an hour later that provided no answers.

After coming back home, Lauren went upstairs and sat up trying to force away her fatigue. She was tired of sleeping but her head was feeling dizzy and her body drained. Now that she finally admitted they were real, Lauren desperately wanted to talk to Catherine, Messina, or even Nasra hoping they could offer some explanation. She saw her hospital personal effects bag in the corner and emptied it wanting something inside to be interesting enough to stave off sleep. She poured out its contents: lotion, tissues, shampoo, and her mother's red purse. Lauren picked up the purse. It was open and Anita's gold wedding ring slipped into her hand. Lauren remembered Anita placing the ring in the purse before emptying it, yet it stubbornly remained inside. She stroked it gently then her head felt heavy as if she was remembering something long forgotten. Like sand blowing in the wind, her room changed to her mother's bedroom. Her mother's bed, which was much larger than Lauren's room, with four posts and a grand headboard sat where her dressers usually stood. The room brightened lit from her mother's four-bulb ceiling fan as opposed to her usually dim room.

Anita burst through the door, engaged in a passionate kiss with a man she couldn't see but Lauren assumed was her father. They were taking off each other's clothes and moving closer to the bed. Lauren moved back, the vision was so real she wasn't sure if they'd knock her over. As they passed, Lauren realized Anita wasn't kissing Willem but a man Lauren had never seen. They got under the covers and made love.

Willem entered the vision by the bedroom door, returning from work briefcase in hand when he caught his wife in bed. He dropped his briefcase and left clutching his chest. Lauren tried to follow him but the vision wouldn't allow her. She wanted the vision to end; Lauren couldn't believe her beloved mother was responsible for the divorce.

She didn't think to drop the ring as she gripped it tight in her fist while tears ran down her eyes. Then she heard Anita speak, "No, no, stop! I can't! Not to Willem." Lauren didn't want to see but she looked anyway. Anita forced him off her and hurriedly covered herself. She searched the floor for her clothes but stopped at the sight of Willem's briefcase. She covered her mouth and began crying.

"Thanks for nothing, Anita!" said the man as he buttoned his shirt and left, stepping on the briefcase Willem dropped. Lauren could hear the man and Willem yelling but the walls muddled their argument. Anita hurriedly put on her clothes and rushed out. The vision switched to an intense argument downstairs in their den. Willem was yelling at Anita.

"HOW COULD YOU DO THIS TO ME?"

"Willem, I'm sorry, I'm so sorry!" said Anita choking on tears.

"I TRIED TO GIVE YOU EVERYTHING! WHY DO YOU THINK I WORK ALL THE TIME?"

Lauren started to sob aloud and Anita who was on the second level heard her.

"Lauren!" said Anita. The vision disappeared, Lauren's room returned, and she rushed to close and lock the door. Her mother knocked a few times before she jiggled the handle.

"Lauren! Are you okay?" asked Anita.

"I'm fine, Mom. What is it?" asked Lauren, barely holding her angst.

"I—uh—wanted to check on you. Could you open the door?"

"I'm sort of tired…I'll talk to you in the morning, I just want to get some rest."

"What's the matter, Lauren?"

"NOTHING!" Lauren yelled. Her mother was becoming a nuisance as her rage swelled.

"Fine, I—I'll leave you alone," said Anita confused.

She heard her mother turn the door handle loose and moved downstairs. Lauren sat on her bed contemplating what her relationship with her parents had become. It was obvious Willem left for

Natalie because of Anita's unfaithfulness. Her rage turned from Willem to Anita, she'd been deceived and was devastated. She cursed and screamed in her pillow, its material muffled her cries so Anita heard nothing.

Lauren cried for a long time and in her confusion and pain, Lauren blamed Amalgam. She figured that that evil realm was responsible for showing her such a distressing scene. How else would she see something so real by touching a ring? That's when she resolved at that moment never to return to Amalgam. Her life had been threatened there, she'd seen nothing but brutality and death, and now, its horror had spilled over into her world, into her life.

Lauren was soon asleep, she didn't dream and the smell of breakfast woke her in the morning. She wondered how she could look into her mother's eyes after what she'd seen. Lauren went downstairs and her mother appeared quite at peace cooking. Lauren knew an argument would not be the best way to start the day but she had to get answers.

"Good morning, Mom!" Lauren forced pleasantries. Anita turned and smiled.

"Feeling better?" asked Anita amiably. She didn't seem at all bothered by Lauren's outburst last night.

"Yes."

"I thought you were out of it for a while there. Want some eggs?"

"Um…sure."

Anita scraped the eggs onto her plate and sat down beside her at the kitchen table. Lauren observed her mother eating with proper manners. She looked into her face as if she was trying to find the innocent mother she knew yesterday evening. She couldn't and they ate in silence. When they finished breakfast, Anita sat back with a satiated belly and smiled at her daughter. Lauren tried to evade her glance but she could feel it.

"So, Lauren, are you looking forward to school?"

"I haven't thought about it. I'm looking forward to the grave excavation though."

"Why?"

"I thought about Dad leaving and all, and I was wondering why he left." Lauren played ignorance for now to gauge Anita's reaction. She turned her eyes away and rubbing her stomach.

"I'm hoping *he'll* tell *the truth*," said Lauren.

"So am I," said Anita. She lifted her glass for a drink.

CHAPTER EIGHT
ROYCE HIGH AND THE EXCAVATION

Lauren didn't press Anita any further. She spent the last week before school relaxing her mind of all troubling thoughts like her parents and that dreaded Amalgam Realm. She was fully healed when school began September first. She woke early, ate breakfast, took a shower, and dressed, opting for the caramel brown blouse and black skirt.

She paid careful attention to how she styled her hair, as the scar on her head was deep and hadn't healed yet. She managed to hide it well except for a small bit that shown from the shadow of her bangs. She made various poses in front of the mirror and didn't notice her mother open the door.

"I see you like the clothes I bought you."

"O—oh yeah! I like them," said Lauren embarrassed.

"Be outside in five minutes."

Anita was smiling ear-to-ear as she shut the door. Lauren grabbed her backpack and headed out the house. She opened the passenger side door and threw her backpack in the back seat. She sat down and saw her mother coming out the house rummaging through her purse. Lauren thought she was looking for her keys but when she got in the car, Anita asked if she saw a prescription in the house, a refill of Hydroxyurea, Lauren's medication for sickle cell. Lauren said no and helped her search for it. They found it inside and returned to the car.

Anita started the car and backed out the driveway, rounded the corner, and sped off for school. Lauren looked out the window staring blankly until they rode past the graveyard. She didn't see anything of note, hoping to find a tent or some equipment for the excavation. Through all the headstones, she could see the lake and lighthouse in the distance. Anita pulled into a drugstore parking lot, parked, and immediately looked through her purse.

"Mom we're never going to get to the school on time."

"Yes we are. It's right there."

Anita pointed out the window with one finger, the rest clutched the prescription. She left the car and headed into the store. Lauren surveyed Royce High campus. The school is three floors high and the grounds had a small fountain with benches next to it where students sat under the cool shade of trees. She saw kids hanging around the front of the building, stepping out of cars and bidding their drivers' goodbye.

A little later Lauren saw a row of yellow school buses filing into the parking lot. The buses were packed and this told Lauren that if Anita didn't hurry, she'd be late for school. As if on command, Anita returned to the car and closed the door with her package of pills rattling. She drove out the drugstore lot and headed for the school. They stopped at a red light.

"So, do you want me to drop you off in front of the school?"

"How about behind that last bus?" The last bus was nearly a half a block from the school.

"Why don't you want to be dropped off in front?"

"No reason, I mean its only school."

"Then it shouldn't matter where you get dropped off. Remember we are going for a more extroverted Lauren. If you don't let people know who you are, you're short-changing yourself."

The car moved forward after the light changed.

"Beauty is only a fraction of attraction. Confidence and personality go a long way and one thing about confident people is that they aren't afraid to get out at the front of the school."

The car came to a halt at the front of Royce High School. Lauren got out, retrieved her backpack and bid her mother farewell. Anita waved goodbye as she drove off slowly. Lauren watched her mother leave the lot and failed to notice many of the boys getting of the buses trying to make eye contact with her.

Lauren headed in the school through the heavy doors with large steel handles. The school was well lit with brown lockers and taupe-colored hallways populated with ecstatic students meeting friends they hadn't seen all summer. Some freshmen were standing in a corner quiet and a tad nervous. Lauren passed them and came to an intersection clear of the confusion where she decided to look at her schedule. Her first class was algebra but the room number didn't print.

"Excuse me please, excuse me. Watch out!" A voice came out down the hall.

A student was pushing through the crowds. Lauren was visible after she shoved two people to the side but the student was on so much inertia that she bumped forcibly into Lauren, pushing her back and almost made her fall.

"SORRY, so-sorry" said Renee. "Oh, it's you, Lauren!"

"Hey! In a hurry?" asked Lauren.

"No, those girls walk in file down the halls forcing everyone out their way like living squeegees! Then they get mad when you push them aside, it's aggravating! Ugh!" After Renee calmed down, she saw Lauren's face had healed considerably.

"You look great, new clothes too, huh?"

"Yeah, a gift from Mom! She thought I needed

to update my style. Can you believe it, *Mom* said that about *me*!"

"Yeah, I can," said Renee laughing.

"*Renee!*"

"You'd dress like a tomboy wherever you'd go. Amy's party was the first time I've seen you in girl's clothes," Renee laughed aloud. Lauren used this moment of levity to apologize to Renee. She asked her to come into a classroom with few students and began a hushed conversation.

"I'm sorry Renee; I do remember Amalgam."

Renee stopped laughing and beamed as Lauren finally admitted the truth. Then she began to ask a multitude of questions.

"What made you change your mind?"

"I started having these dreams and then my neighbor Mr. Vasteck was found dead in his house, exactly as he said at the Procession."

"How'd you get back from there?"

"Oh, Catherine and Messina."

"The lady with the big hat?"

"Yeah."

"I don't know the other one. Where'd that tree rider take you?"

Lauren quickly recounted her tale, skipping the details but giving her the gist.

"Amazing, and you just wound up in the hospital after Messina spoke it?" asked Renee. Lauren said yes.

"And these dreams are they of the future?"

"They seem to be of the past."

"Weird. And you just picked up her ring and could see her with that guy?"

"That I wish I didn't see," said Lauren sadly.

"Oh, I'm sorry. What classes do you have this year? Here let me see," said Renee as Lauren slipped her class schedule.

"WOW! We're in two of the same classes! We even have lunch together although I usually eat in the library."

"The library?"

"Yes, there's a lounge area where the audio visual equipment is kept and my video production class is right after lunch. I'll show you."

"Which classes do we have together?" asked Lauren.

"History and studio art."

"How do you think our bodies healed so quickly?"

"I was hoping you'd know," said Renee, she smiled then gazed past her.

"The hall's clearing I've got to get going. I'll see you in history," said Renee waving as she headed out the classroom.

"Wait Renee, do you know where my math class is?"

Renee took a second look at her schedule, then at hers, "Three hundred and two. I have the same instructor but at a different time. See ya!"

Renee headed to the other side of the school. Lauren went upstairs to the third floor looking for her classroom. The bell rang and she hurried as she saw the door closing and slid in before it shut. The instructor Mr. Brubaker turned around and looked at her. Lauren froze in place when the teacher saw her and waited breathlessly for him to discipline her yet Brubaker gave a slight smile.

"Sorry I'm late."

"Not a problem on the first day. Sit down so we can begin," he said.

Lauren looked around for an empty seat and found one in the front row. Everyone looked at Lauren as she took her seat, but the focus shifted to Mr. Brubaker when he began taking roll and asked Ms. Neilson to pass out the course syllabus. A short girl stood up and took the stack of papers when Lauren saw Peter sitting behind her. He surveyed her, obviously looking for any scars and was perplexed when he found none, before settling his eyes at her chest, smirking as he dreamily recalled their softness.

After Brubaker dismissed class, Peter tried to talk to her but she avoided him by asking the teacher about the assignment. Lauren overheard Peter talking to a friend who asked him if Jason and Amy were still having problems and that he wanted to date Amy if they broke up. Lauren quickly ended her discussion with Brubaker, hoping to hear the fate of their relationship, but missed Peter's reply. While Peter and his friend were rounding the stairs, Amy was coming up.

"Hey, I just saw Lauren, Amy. She was trying to be all friendly with me as if she didn't almost *kill*

The Ghosts of Amalgam: The Linking Tome

you this summer. She throws a fit because you're dating Jason. What a childish brat!" he said.

"Maybe it's not her all fault. I didn't know she liked him that much," said Amy. Lauren was happy her friend was standing up for her.

"But yeah, it was childish," Amy continued.

"And what did it prove? You're still with Jason and completely healed."

"Hi Amy," said a familiar voice then she heard sucking noises. Lauren peeked around the corner to see Jason kissing Amy. Their smothered faces dashed her hopes of their breakup and she quickly turned around. She wished Jason had dumped Amy after Renee's encouragement at the hospital. Lauren watched them go downstairs before moving on with a hollow feeling in her chest. Renee was still pressing her for more information as they sat in history class.

"So are you going to go back to see Catherine about your fainting?"

"I'd rather not think about that place much less go back there and besides I'm more concerned about my parents than Amalgam," Lauren said.

At that moment, Jason and Amy entered the room and sat to the far right, Lauren's eyes followed Amy with envy. She made sure to hug and kiss Jason before class started. Amy leaned back quickly to peek at Lauren, smiled smugly and faced forward.

"Ugh! She makes me so sick," said Lauren.

"You're not the only one. Everyone at the

House of Shades had to hear over and over again about her relationship with Jason."

Lauren remembered the House of Shades was where all shades stay at Castle Everlasting.

"Amy was causing so much trouble while we were waiting that she was placed as a door steward. I want to ask her how she's been getting back to Amalgam."

"Why? Why would you want to go back?" asked Lauren appalled.

"Well…it has to do with my mom."

"You're hoping she'd be there? It's not the best place to be after your dead," said Lauren.

"It's better than where she is now," said Renee seriously.

Just as Lauren was about to ask what she was talking about a loud boy came in, a football player, and gave Jason a high five. Lauren didn't realize Jason was becoming popular with the "cool kids" but when the boy acknowledged Amy as well she knew why. The teacher came after him and began the day's lesson. As class ended, Lauren and Renee headed to the cafeteria to pick up their lunch.

They were careful not to get cumbersome items since they'd have to carry their food to the library. Lauren saw Amy and Jason sitting with the upperclassmen and varsity football players. She also saw Peter among them, harassing the freshmen students, stealing food off their trays, and drinking their beverages for them. Lauren desperately wanted to switch places with Amy; she'd love to be sitting with the jocks than going to the library to eat. She and Renee cleared off their trays and headed into the lounge Renee mentioned earlier. They ate in silence for a while, then Lauren asked Renee to finish the story she started in class.

"I was thinking about your ability to see things when touching objects. It's called psychometry, some psychic's claim to have it. From what I've read about it, psychics are only supposed to receive simple impressions of a person's past life, but what you described goes far beyond that. It got me thinking about what they were talking about at the Procession, you know, magic and all. And I was wondering if that's why I was able to see and hear what I have…" said Renee as she lowered her voice to a whisper.

"What's that?" asked Lauren. Renee saw this as a chance to confide in her friend and Lauren thought this was the reason why Renee was so interested in Amalgam at the hospital.

"You might think I'm crazy, but I've been hearing voices, m*y mother's*. I know it's her and she's in pain."

"Does she say anything?" asked Lauren seriously.

"I only hear her in the graveyard screaming that she can't escape. Something won't let her leave. She's frightened because she's claustrophobic and now that her spirit can't move she's stuck in her casket. Dad thinks I hear her voice because I miss her but that's not the case. This is real," said Renee.

"But Mom said several people hear voices in the graveyard, maybe you just think it's hers."

"I *know* my mom's voice! And if other people are hearing voices out there than it further proves my mom needs help along with the spirits."

"Can you talk to her?"

"No, I've been trying with these books to see if I can reach her but so far I've been unsuccessful, although I did reach other spirits," said Renee as she spilled out a host of books from her backpack. Lauren looked at Renee's books on the table. All were dealing with supernatural phenomena with titles like Communicating with the Beyond, Reaching the Realms, and Strengthening the Medium.

"I believe I'm an oracle. I thought I was a medium but after hearing Nasra describe oracles in the carriage I realized I'm not that. Nasra never finished describing what oracles could do and that's why I wanted to go back to Amalgam. This might sound odd but I could see, hear, and talk to spirits *before* entering Amalgam. When my Mom died, I tried to help her and find out what's going on out there. She keeps saying she can't tell what's happening or else *he'll* know she's been talking to me. I've got to find out who this man is and how he's keeping Mom in such pain."

"Sounds horrible," said Lauren.

"I also notice things about the living, like auras."

"Auras?" asked Lauren.

"They're lights that hang about the physical body. Auras can identify people better than fingerprints and give information about a person's health."

"Interesting! Did you get these books from this library?" asked Lauren browsing through her selection.

"Some of 'em, I've been looking around town for the rest. Whenever I go out with Dad I see if I can find a new one," said Renee.

Lauren thought for a moment in silence. She wanted to hear her mother's voice for herself, maybe being in Amalgam would grant her that as well.

"I want to hear it for myself," said Lauren when Renee gave her a sharp look.

"What you don't believe me? I thought you might understand seeing as how you're my best friend and after being in Amalgam—"

"Its not that I don't believe you," Lauren interjected, "I do, but maybe we can find someone who'll believe *us* and see to it like a priest or, I know, the oracle at Amalgam House!"

Renee remembered Nasra mentioning an oracle there.

"They might be able to help us. In fact, I'm going there on the tenth for the excavation and we'll try to figure out something," said Lauren.

"You mean the excavation of the unknown sailor at the Memorial Graveyard?"

"Yeah, how'd you know?"

"I read the papers religiously. I'm curious as to who's in it actually. You know of the old legend that surrounds the grave, don't you?" asked Renee.

"I heard it was haunted," said Lauren.

"Legend has it that the sailor in the grave was killed when his ship ran aground in the seventeen hundreds, a common occurrence back then until the lighthouse was built. Anyway, the sailor's widow was waiting for his return and when it was discovered that her beau's ship sunk she tossed herself from the cliffs where the lighthouse now stands. When the body of the sailor was recovered from the lake, the widow didn't claim the remains so his grave went unmarked. It's believed the woman cannot rest because she didn't give her husband a proper burial and for her punishment she is bound to the grave. Some claim to have seen the widow chiseling her lovers name on the tombstone at night."

"Some story," said Lauren.

"But now that we know of Amalgam, it's probably just some romantic rubbish made up to explain a ghost sighting."

"So you comin'?" asked Lauren. "Maybe we can catch sight of her at the excavation," she added jokingly.

"Sure! She might just pop up to take a picture with her lover's bones," said Renee smiling before she turned somber again. Lauren asked what was wrong.

"It's just that, every time I go out there, I hear

her voice and she's screaming for help. It hurts and I don't know how I'll handle it when I get out there."

"Don't worry, I'm positive we can help her," said Lauren assuredly.

After lunch, Lauren went to the rest of her classes and soon the day was over. For the next week, Lauren talked with Renee about their homework, teachers, and all things school. Lauren didn't have anymore dreams and her thoughts never returned to Amalgam except when Renee could occasionally be seen moping about her mother.

* * * *

On the morning of September tenth, Lauren spent the day pacing in her room. She was determined to get the truth from Willem and the thought was frightening. She didn't want him to reveal a side of Anita that would make Lauren love her less. Though she didn't think that was possible as learning of the affair didn't change her opinion, but Lauren wondered if there was more to the story. The plan was for Renee to meet at her house and walk to the graveyard.

Renee arrived half an hour late due to a massive traffic accident on Coral Street. They walked swiftly, trying to recover lost time, by now the excavation had already begun. When they turned on Kepchar Street they found an excited crowd, news vans, police cars, and ambulances.

"What's with the police?" asked Renee.

"Maybe a lot of people showed up and they're trying to block off the area," said Lauren, curious initially then became nervous as they drew closer and saw the crime scene tape. The first thing that came to her mind was her father. She ran to the crowd to ask someone what happened. One of the more subdued reporters stood outside the mob, looking in as if he wanted answers but didn't want to die for them.

"Excuse me sir," said Lauren. "What happened?"

"Chaos that's what, it's been a crazy hour. Most of the stations were covering the Coral Street crash when I get a call from the boss saying there was a crime scene at the excavation. We been trying to get answers from the police but they're not talking. From what I could gather, Baker's Creek finest get a call from a passerby saying there were strange lights in the graveyard. Police respond and four people are D.O.A. Cops seal off the area and voilá, mass media event!"

"Who are the four?" asked Lauren nervously.

"Two excavators, a cameraman, and oh, Willem Walston, from the Daily Watch."

"WHAT!" Lauren plowed through the crowd leaving Renee to catch up. She dug through the crowd and reached the police barricade holding the media back. The police cordoned off a pass to the ambulances where paramedics wheeled out the covered victims on gurneys. Lauren leaned over the barricade as far as she could when she saw him. Willem was lying by a tombstone, arms and legs outstretched, eyes open, his body immobile.

"*NO! NOOOO!*" Lauren screamed. "*DADDY!*"

Lauren didn't know how she got around the cops but she did and was tackled before she could reach Willem's body. Renee told the police she was Willem's daughter and watched as paramedics tried to calm her. They sat her on one of the folded chairs strewn across the lot as the police covered Willem's body. Renee looked at Willem's shroud with a heavy heart when she heard her mother crying for help. Renee covered her ears to shut out her mother's voice because there was nothing she could do for her.

The police took Lauren home and broke the news of Willem's death to Anita. She fainted, and when the police revived her, Anita sat frozen in a chair. After some time Lauren and Anita were functioning as best as any grief-stricken human being. The night was very similar to that of the pool party where Willem was the source of their sadness only this time it wasn't anger but grief.

* * * *

The days after Willem's death were marked by long periods of blank stares, spontaneous weeping, and a few comforting phone calls from family and friends. A week later, the police returned to inform Anita on the status of the investigation into

Willem's death and Lauren was present in the room. The police had made no progress in determining who killed them, or how they managed to leave no physical wounds or solid evidence. Toxic fumes and poisoning had been ruled out and any other logical lethal substances. They were still as bewildered on the seventeenth as the tenth but added that autopsies on the victims revealed hypothermia as the cause of death.

"In the fall?" asked Anita disbelievingly. "Wasn't it seventy degrees that day?"

"Yes, it's bizarre to say the least. Try telling it to the other families we've spoke to," said the officer.

"The crime scene yielded no clues and the camera's videotapes only showed them shivering, all of them were screaming that they were cold. It's like some super ninja or ghost killed them," said one of officers.

Lauren trembled when she heard the officer's comment before going to her room to call Renee. She told her everything the police said.

"I don't care how we get inside but I'm going to Amalgam House to speak with Catherine. Can you get us a ride?" asked Lauren.

"I'll try, Dad's not doing anything. But…"

"But what?"

"They don't know we're coming. Do we just drive up to the gate and ask to be let in?"

"Maybe, but I have to try," said Lauren.

Renee arrived with her father Barry later that

evening. He drove them to house quietly although he did ask how they got involved with people from the manor on the hill as he called it. They arrived at Amalgam House thirty minutes later. Lauren wondered if they'd get in remembering Vasteck's comments about its strict access.

The house looked quite different from last time. The gargoyle statues, the illusion creators, the suits of armor, and the shield that read Amalgam House were all missing. With some hesitation, Lauren and Renee approached the steel gate. As they moved closer, Lauren could see a man approaching across the lawn. He was a middle-aged heavy-set black man of average height, clean-shaven, and bald. In his thick hands, he carried the keys, unlocked the bars, and opened the gate.

"Turn away your driver and tell him to return in an hour," he said to Renee. He looked sympathetically at Lauren and said, "Catherine's been expecting you."

After a brief discussion, Renee convinced Barry to leave and that she and Lauren would be safe. They followed the man across the hilly lawn. Lauren saw the fountain was no longer of three doors but of five cherub sculptures in different poses joyously expelling water. The man knocked three times on the front door; it opened promptly. They entered the rectangular lobby where ghosts and mortals were moving about.

A glass chandelier hung from the ceiling. Its draping crystals emitted a soft yellow light above a large willow tree. The tree's crown stretched to the second floor. As the chandelier changed color so did the tree's leaves to purple, green, blue, yellow, and red. Glimpsing in the various rooms Lauren saw either offices or waiting rooms and lounges where spirits were talking gaily, sitting patiently or steadfast at work.

The man led them past the tree where they approached a dual staircase separated by a wall with a fireplace. This lounge area contained an elaborate rug, mahogany tables and chairs, a harp and a grand piano. At the piano, a female ghost teacher was giving lessons to a ghost boy. The boy supplied soothing music for the Amalgam House employees. Lauren and Renee took the left stairs to the second floor and took another left. They walked down a long hall until the man stopped and knocked on the door to his right. The glass door to the office held black letters that read: Nasra Rallens District Purveyor.

"Come in!"

Lauren and Renee entered behind their guide. Nasra's office was quite basic; a desk, two chairs for her guests, and two real potted plants on her desk. Also on top of her desk was a brass holder where her purple orb was placed.

"Hello, Lauren, Renee. Follow us up, Mr. Hitchen," said Nasra, rising immediately. Mr. Hitchen bowed and waited in the hall leaving the door open.

"You look strong, the both of you. You'll need

your strength when entering Amalgam and don't concern yourself about getting home. Mr. Hitchen will take care of that."

Nasra walked around her desk, picking up her purple orb and led them outside into the hallway. Mr. Hitchen followed in silence.

"We were wondering how we've been healing so fast?" asked Renee.

"You're connected to both realms. Ghosts have the ability to heal themselves over time like humans. When you entered Amalgam, the realm activated your spiritual healing. This trait carries over to the New City; your spirit and body are nursing your wounds together. If a ghost has a healing mark such as the caduceus they'll recover even faster."

"What about this scar here?" Lauren pointed to the deep gash that hadn't fully healed yet. "It hasn't gone away and it doesn't look like it will."

"It's called a fatal scar, the death mark. Everyone that's entered Amalgam has them at one point. Catherine says it's the best indication if a soul has moved on. If the scar is still visible, the soul continues to linger on their death, but if it's gone, they've made much progress towards the Judge. For shades, it'll linger until the spirit has completed their Amalgam duties."

"Nasra, I was wondering what other things oracles can do besides interpret dreams and speak to spirits?" asked Renee.

"Oracles can identify auras, see future events,

detect Phoenix loyalists, and tend to be exceptionally good at healing magic."

"Shouldn't I have an oracle mark instead of a caduceus?"

"Shades have secondary abilities like psychometry and receiving oracles to help them in their tasks though most of these abilities are meant for protection to preserve the shade's life until they can complete their tasks. But the mark usually describes the Judge's function for you."

Nasra led them to another stairway down the hall. They took a left to the rear of Amalgam House where another stairwell reached all three floors but traffic was limited by locked blue doors. Nasra pulled from her dress a key and turned the lock. The key dispelled the magic on it; the door lost its color and opened inward. A blast of icy wind caught them, Lauren and Renee shivered as they followed Nasra up.

The third floor was a wooden attic. In the center, was one large square room; its door emanating a blue light and from the cracks seeped a bright white light. Nasra led them into a room on the right filled with numerous beds and bodies lying on them. All of them appeared asleep. Their chests were rising but they couldn't be roused like Lauren in her deep slumber.

"These shades serve the Court. Shades separate their spirits from bodies here to enter Amalgam. Unfortunately you didn't learn this skill while you were in Amalgam so I'll have to do it for you," said Nasra.

"How long can we stay in Amalgam and at Amalgam House? My Dad should be coming back soon," said Renee.

"A shade's spirit usually has three days away before the body starts to whither. What we'll have to do is have one of our indwellers inhabit your body until your spirit returns. Indwellers have special skills to possess a body and assume their host's personality traits. We try to get ghosts from your generation to reside in our Mortalland shades but sometimes it's not a perfect match. Your family and friends may think you've been acting a little weird."

Lauren stepped in front of Nasra, Mr. Hitchen stood behind her. Nasra raised her orb to Lauren's nose and the clouds in her orb swirled like a hurricane. Lauren's body trembled as her spirit seeped through her nose, eyes, and mouth. She stood as a ghost yet her body dropped, dead weight, into the arms of Mr. Hitchen. He picked up her body and laid her gently on an empty bed covering her with blankets. Renee was next and when they finished Nasra dismissed Mr. Hitchen and led the girls to the center room.

Using another key, she turned the lock and led them inside. Lauren saw another Amalgam portal like the one for the carriages although this one was a smaller, personal transport. Inside this chamber was a ghost, the portal's operator, on his hand was the portal guard mark.

"Are you the special transport?" asked the

guard. Nasra replied affirmatively.

"We'll arrive in Catherine's chamber instead of the embassy tower," said Nasra aloud so the girls could hear as the portal sounded like a thunderstorm. She walked in first, Lauren and Renee followed and felt a familiar tug.

CHAPTER NINE
CASTLE EVERLASTING

Catherine stood arms behind her back in front of the door she materialized for Nasra, Lauren, and Renee, who promptly stepped out. It closed and de-materialized. Nasra moved aside so the baroness could extend her hand to Lauren. She became overwhelmed with sadness and tears streamed from her eyes but managed to maintain her composure in Catherine's presence.

"Welcome back," said Catherine, she gave her a comforting hug.

"Do you know why I'm here?" asked Lauren standing back and wiping her eyes.

"I've been expecting you. When your father arrived I assumed you'd be coming back."

"Is he here?"

"He was for three days, but was summoned for Judgment two days ago," said Catherine compassionately.

Lauren's heart skipped a beat as she asked, "Was he sent to Heaven?"

"I just see that souls are sent to the Judge; their damning or salvation is up to Him. He did leave you an anamnesis, a ghost memory explaining his problems with your mother."

"Let me have it," said Lauren moving closer to Catherine and extending her hand.

"Its magically closed and I can't undo it unless you unlock the message's seal."

"And how do I do that?" asked Lauren annoyed.

Immediately a phantom of Willem appeared next to her, fainter then most ghosts. He looked like he was preparing to speak in front of a camera instead of at her, and he composed himself to speak clearly and compassionately.

"Hello, Lauren. I hope you're not too upset over my passing but since you've been to Amalgam before I guess you know that life continues. It's unfortunate and sad that I cannot speak to you in person but its all part of the Judge's plan." Willem struggled to hold back his tears and Lauren felt hollow like when she saw Anita cry.

"Messina informed me of the Court's predicament with the Phoenix and I'm honored that you've been asked to complete such a significant and holy undertaking. Amalgam and the barons need your help. If you decide to take the Phoenix Cage mark and stop the Dark Phoenix this once, you'll break the seal on my anamnesis and your questions will be answered. Whether you wish to continue serving the Court will be a choice you'll have to make. I believe in and love you, Lauren. Make wise decisions," Willem finished and the message disappeared.

"This isn't fair!" said Lauren tearfully.

"It's true we are forcing your hand somewhat but you must understand how valuable you are to us."

"*I told you no!* It's my right to have that message!"

"*And you'll have it once you've broken its seal.* Otherwise it's just another ghost memory locked away forever in the Record House. That's the condition your father placed on the message, not me or Messina."

With a flick of her finger, Catherine magically pulled two chairs over from her desk. They both sat, Lauren was sulking while Catherine leaned forward. The baroness opened her hand, the Phoenix Cage mark twirled in her palm. Renee stood next to Lauren and Nasra next to Catherine.

"Don't let other families be split. Don't let other sons and daughters experience what you're feeling now!"

"I don't want a silly magic mark. I want to know who killed my father!"

"We don't know."

"Then why should I have to fight the Phoenix? It won't bring my dad back from the dead, or wherever he is. It won't solve a thing, so why don't you deal with the Phoenix and I'll try to grow up without my dad."

"You're wrong, Lauren; it will solve the answer to your question. You asked who killed your father, but you should have asked how the ghost was capable of killing your father! The answer is the Phoenix. Who ever killed Willem has been empowered by the Great Sinner to commit the crime. In order to stomp out any future incidents you must start at the source."

"I want to know who's responsible for my father's incident!"

Lauren leaned back into her chair frustrated and angry. Catherine hung her head and revealed, "Messina has the utmost confidence that you'll encounter your father's killer. But remember, God has the final say for vengeance is His. Your assignment is the Dark Phoenix not personal fulfillment. Do your job and your father will be avenged through infinite justice."

Lauren thought for a moment. Messina, the Metatron, said that she would encounter Willem's murderer. This affirmation guaranteed that Lauren would find out who took her father from her. Yet Lauren wondered what good would this discovery do if she could not have her revenge? She could always break the rules, kill Willem's murderer then purge her sins and live content. Only by taking the mark could she accomplish this. She looked at the flaming Phoenix cage mark and then asked, "What does this mark do?"

"The Phoenix mark cannot be placed back on

the Vessel in part but in whole. You must reclaim the Phoenix mark in its entirety and this mark will contain its parts until it's reunited."

"Isn't it whole now?"

"The mark is splintered between the Dark Phoenix's three entities. Upon receiving the Phoenix Mark, the Dark Phoenix's spirit split like the three forms of the Judge: the Father, the Son, and the Holy Spirit. Luckily, the mark regenerates him each time he dies, preventing him from entering Heaven through death or suicide, but the Phoenix remains immortal. The only way to wholly reclaim the mark is to learn the secret of the Phoenix, the clandestine knowledge that will destroy him forever."

"The guards, barons, and I have labored for years to discover the secret, but we've come up empty. If you can succeed where we have failed and defeat him, you'll return the mark to the Vessel before the Judge returns from the Boundless Realm and receive the highest of God's rewards."

"No pressure right, Lauren," said Renee with all seriousness.

Lauren nodded dejectedly and considered her options. She'd learned much of what she wanted to know of the divorce in the visions she received from Anita's ring. She wondered if what her father had to tell her in the anamnesis could explain anymore than what she already knew. She desired the identity of her father's killer, but that would mean taking on such great responsibility. Yet her father's words won out as he himself believed she could accomplish this task.

With great visible hesitation Lauren reached for the mark. She grasped it firmly and the power surged through her spirit. She rubbed the flaming cage on her hand as it materialized and warmed her skin.

"One more thing, how am I going to protect myself from the weather? When I left here last time, I was in so much pain."

"Nasra," said Catherine. Nasra silently moved to the desk in Catherine's chamber and removed what appeared to be a small necklace and handed to Lauren. Lauren looked at the jewelry; it was a small red, sickle-shaped vial with a fluid inside that could be unlocked and bended at the top to access the liquid. Nasra told Lauren to open it and take a small sip, which she did before attaching the necklace around her neck.

"This is a potion that'll keep your husk at a stable temperature when in the realm, but it won't protect you from magic spells, so be careful not to get hit with any freezing magic if the cold bothers you. It'll materialize around your neck when you return, and I'll have Nasra refill before you leave again. That amount should be good for four visits to our realm. Take the girls to their quarters at the House of Shades, Nasra, and have their friend the door steward join them."

Lauren stood, her physical strength swelled, her arms and legs were firm and she breathed deep and calm. The potion warmed her body well enough for Lauren not to fear pain when she returned. She'd do what was she'd have to in order to find the answers she sought. Nasra took Renee and Lauren's hands and guided them underneath the chandelier in Catherine's room.

"The House of Shades," said Nasra to the chandelier. The light fixture twirled in circles, its candle's flames shut out and began cracking lightning as Nasra orbed with Renee and Lauren in hand, rising up with them. Their vision blurred, Catherine's chamber swirled around until it was a blot before the eyes.

* * * *

The baroness' chamber swished into a three-story rotunda full of mirrors and five arched doorway passages at the west, northwest, north, north-east, and east. The southern door was the main entrance but they had no use for it now. Below was a reception desk in the center of the room with a female ghost seated behind it who simply smiled as Nasra and the girls descended from the ceiling chandelier with a soft tap. Both Lauren and Renee watched the House of Shades chandelier slowly stop spinning in awe that these elegant fixtures were also modes of transportation. Nasra called out to them, beckoning them forward toward the north door. Several ghosts were watching these mirrors intently, which showed various shades about

Amalgam, and Lauren wondered why the ghosts observed them so closely. As Lauren walked after Nasra, someone grabbed her arm. Amy, garbed in New Elysian wear, was looking quite displeased to see her again.

"So they found a way to drag you back here," said Amy. "I was hoping you had discovered a way of avoiding these ghosts. I thought maybe you'd share that information with me but I see that I had too much faith in you. I hate that you continue to disappoint me, Lauren."

"It's your fault you were placed as a door steward," said Lauren.

"Catherine's aide falsely accused me of being a brat, but I thought I was behaving well considering a snake and an eagle tried to eat me. They just wanted to punish me. I've had to come to Amalgam ever since the accident to work thanks to you. In my opinion the job would better suit you but I can understand if you lack the qualifications for the job," said Amy.

"Seeing as how you've met them I'll leave you to it," said Lauren as she moved on.

"This is all your—"

"I know! It's my fault!"

"Don't walk away from me!" Amy ran and got in front of her as Nasra and Renee moved toward the northern door.

"I'm going to find a way to get away from these ghosts so I won't have to be their little slave. I suggest that if you want to get back in my good graces you'll help me. After all, you owe me for nearly getting me killed."

"I got *you* killed? You pushed *me* into the car!"

Nasra turned Amy around to stop her from stalling Lauren.

"She doesn't owe you anything and you don't owe her. You're Lauren's friend from the New City aren't you?"

"I don't know about *friend*," said Amy.

"Um…you might be of some use to Lauren as well."

"What are you talking about…use to Lauren? Who is *she* that I have to be of some use to *her*?"

"How would you like to no longer be a door steward? Instead of standing at the entrance making our residents uncomfortable, you can throw aside your trifle feud and do some honest work for someone other than yourself. What do you say?"

Amy glanced back at the door before answering. "Anything's better than swinging open a damn door all day."

"So what goes on in this place, Nasra?" asked Lauren. Amy accompanied them and Nasra led them on through the northern door.

"It's a house solely for Mortalland Shades. Every mirror you see here is showing various shades about the Amalgam realm carrying out their mandates. Shades require close supervision in Amalgam to preserve their human life and if they get into trouble we send guards to their aid."

They passed through a hallway filled with doors

where at the end was a small circular room where a pillar stood extending to the third floor. They all filed in behind Nasra when stairs lifted up counterclockwise about the pillar, taking them higher until they reached their destination. She took them down a similar hallway numbered in the current year where they finally came to a door labeled August. She entered through more doors, thirty-one in all, they stopped at number fifteen. Written on the door were their names: LAUREN WALSTON, AMY THOMPSON, RENEE DUPREE, AND NAOMI HAWKINS.

"These doors certainly let you know who stays where," said Renee.

"It's a nice way to keep record," said Nasra. "Now, of all the people that died during your gathering night, you four were the only shades. Therefore you have the privilege of sharing a small room."

"Four? Who's Naomi?" asked Lauren looking at the name on the door.

"We don't know. Catherine believes she was to be picked up in that empty carriage we found by the cliffs, but she wasn't onboard when it arrived in the gathering plains and her name wasn't on the reaper's list," said Nasra.

"Naomi..." said Amy despairingly. Nasra, Renee, and Lauren looked at Amy who appeared troubled like she had just heard of a death in her family.

"Do you know her?" asked Nasra. Amy didn't

answer, her eyes focused on the letters spelling out the girl's name until Nasra asked her a second time. Her countenance changed, Amy appeared irritated by Nasra's question, "I've heard that name before but I can't remember where." Then her face expressed the same haughtiness she shows in school when Amy caught her company staring at her, awaiting an answer. She quickly dashed their hopes by saying, "But I'm so popular I couldn't possibly keep up with all of my many friends."

"Well, we'll find her," said Nasra opening the door and they moved in. They stood in a white room entirely empty aside from four small mirrors on the farthest wall.

"This certainly is premium hospitality," said Amy.

Though Lauren hated to agree with her, Amy was right to be disappointed. How did Catherine expect them to work in Amalgam with such poor accommodations in return? No bathroom, of course, she thought, but there wasn't a kitchen or even a bed, just a room.

"It can be if you use your mind," said Nasra. "If you could be anywhere you wanted where would it be?"

"I'd like to be at home in my bedroom," said Amy.

The room widening to accommodate a queen size bed, closet, drawers and a bathroom. Lauren saw pictures of Amy all on her wall, many of them with her new boyfriend Jason that made Lauren burn anew with jealousy. Her clothes lay upon the floor, stuffed animals lined the shelves, and a fish tank was in the corner.

"Wow," said Amy.

"Your turn, Lauren!" said Nasra. "Think of anything you'd like to have in your ideal home but it has to fit within our space limits for four shades, which is usually five hundred square feet. Enough space for four rooms of privacy and a living room. We don't have a need for kitchens because food is available in the city or the castle dining hall. Most people use their rooms for entertaining and rest. All other necessities and leisure activities can be found in the city."

"Doesn't sound like there's much fun to be had in this world," said Amy.

"Complain, complain, Amy," said Renee who was anxious to add her input into the room.

"It's true we do spend a lot of time working but we have fun. Rest season is a season-long festival without the torturous weather and purgation mandates. If you're in Amalgam during that time I promise you'll enjoy yourself. Wait here until Catherine arrives and fix up the place in the meantime," said Nasra as she left.

After the girls decided to have a large living room and small personal rooms, they furnished their apartment with a more exotic flair than their Mortalland bedrooms. When Catherine and Nasra entered the apartment an hour later they stepped onto a hardwood floor with a huge animal print rug that held pillow seats and a low rising table. A concave glass lantern on the ceiling with fanciful designs illuminated the room and projected shadows on the walls of a colorful parrot, a panther, and a green snake. Lauren was resting in a hammock stretched between two poles jutting from the wall. Amy sat in a beanbag chair while an animated statue fanned her and Renee was sitting cross-legged on the rug playing solitaire.

"Nice, real nice," said Nasra observing the room and Catherine was impressed too. The girls stood as they entered.

"Thanks. I'd say we did very well except for these silver framed mirrors. We tried to move them and give them a different frame but we couldn't adjust it. What are they for?" asked Renee.

"Yeah, and why's Naomi's all cloudy?" asked Amy.

"It's your window into Mortalland," said Catherine. "If you stand before it you'll see where you bodies are and what's happening to them. Usually when mist clouds the mirror someone has cast a spell on the spirit to conceal their whereabouts and I pray that we can find Naomi soon. You've already been occupied by a spirit, Amy, so you'll see your indweller moving about in your body. Renee, you and Lauren should still be at Amalgam House so you two will see yourselves sleeping peacefully. When your parents arrive, your bodies will be indwelt. See for yourself."

The girls all looked into their mirrors. Their

reflections swirled and the image blended into the attic of Amalgam House their bodies laid on the bed where Mr. Hitchen placed them and Amy's indweller was out on a date with Jason. They backed away and all filed after Catherine.

* * * *

The baroness took them back down the spiraling staircase and out onto the porch of the House of Shades. It was still day and the clouds were a radiant gray, but warmth was non-existent. Before them were a large courtyard where another mansion stood across from them, a massive wooden gate on the left, and an imposing mansion to the right, easily larger than Amalgam House and the others in the courtyard. That house had four towers surrounding it that could be reached only its connected bridge.

"Pay attention ladies, I'm going to give you a tour of my city. There are three mansions behind Baronsguard Gate to your left. The House of Natives across from us is where our resident natives stay who aid our ghosts and the House of Shades. To your right is my residence, Baronsguard, where all the official business of Castle Everlasting is handled."

Catherine led them towards Baronsgaurd Gate. They entered a garden and followed a roundabout dirt path circumventing a fountain.

"The garden is a safeguard of my castle. When Castle Everlasting is under siege, it becomes a hedge maze and the guardian manticore is unleashed to prevent trespassers from entering."

"A manticore!" said Renee who was curious to see the mythical beast. Catherine pointed down a lane to her right as she moved. The three girls looked down to see the animal cocktail that is a manticore, with the head of a man, the body of a lion, and the tail of a scorpion, devouring an eviscerated demon bull. Renee sped up to get out of its sight before it decided to eat her.

As they approached Baronsguard Gate, Lauren heard swords clashing and saw two guards on the gate walkway sword fighting. Suddenly an odd question came to Lauren.

"Catherine, can God Himself interact with Amalgam without his angel Metatron?"

"God can do anything, Lauren, but He has sent up certain rules and doesn't break them. He's limited Himself to giving ideas and dreams to his servants, and He'll punish the occasional ghost for irreverent expressions that vex Him."

Lauren heard a ghost wail in pain, she looked at the gate. One of the guards had been injured sparring and clutched his wrist. The ghost screamed "GODDAMN IT!" loud enough for Lauren and her friends to hear. A lighting bolt stretched from the sky and wriggled down to the man's head sending a painful electric surge through his body. He yelled louder than before.

Baronsguard Gate opened to reveal Brigsendale Boulevard. They traveled down a slight slope and passed the Skycasting Theater, official buildings like the Record, Barrier, and Guard Houses, and shops such as The Guard's Shield and Dress Makers.

"Over here is Dress Makers," said Catherine before Lauren interrupted, "What do ghosts need with clothes?"

"Ghosts appear in Amalgam wearing what they had on at the time of their death either in formal burial outfits, bloody torn clothes, or nothing at all. Death rags aren't fashionable because it reminds ghosts of their deaths making it harder to move on. Dress Makers has a catalog of attire from every particular age that can give ghosts a reference for what they want to wear."

"Of course, our city's garments are available as well. Many of the cold souls love their death rags; it makes it easier for them to hold to their grudges. We always support an immediate visit to Dress Makers. They have a particular interest in Mortalland Shades because they de-materialize clothing catalogs for them to supply our ghosts with more modern fashion."

Catherine drew their attention to four tall towers before them describing them as the embassy towers and the border of the castle district. The baroness said the towers handle commerce and ghost transportation between the baron cities and all the distant towns in the Morrigan provinces via the Amalgam portal. They stood at the edge of the mountain pass with a wall connecting each of them. Catherine labeled them from right to left as the

Embassy Towers of Ages, Genesis, Ruin, and Everlasting. They arrived at The Guard's Shield, a building with an enchanted sign of a ghost fighting off many spells flying at him with his weaponry.

"This is where we're headed. The Guard's Shield has a wide selection of weapons from ages past and some uniquely Amalgam designs. I want you all to pick a weapon for your training."

"Wait!" said Renee. "Can we see more of the castle? What's behind the Embassy Towers?"

"The city. It's mostly residences, restaurants, and stores," said Catherine indifferently.

"I was just wondering if we could take a look," said Renee.

"LAUREN!" said a familiar voice. It was Kevin Vasteck running towards her followed slowly by Gloria. Vasteck gave her a big hug then held her out at arms length while speaking to her, "Thank God you're alright. After I saw that tree rider take you away I thought you were dead. I was so worried."

"You should have been. It was horrible Mr. Vasteck," said Lauren.

"What did they want with you?"

"That's Court business," said Catherine.

"Baron Catherine! What an honor!" said Vasteck. He took her hand and shook it firmly and swiftly. "I'd never thought I'd get to meet a baron up close and personal."

"Thank you, but I wonder what you are doing in the castle district. How did you get behind the castle guards?"

"Oh, I have my ways," said Vasteck. He continued shaking Catherine's hand so the baroness held his hand still and turned it to see his mark.

"A Jack mark. I should have known. Never sneak past the castle gates again, Vasteck, and you'll have to tell me how you got by my guards."

"Yes, Catherine," said Vasteck. He turned to Lauren and said, "Did you do what I asked?"

"Yes, your family has made arrangements for your funeral."

"Good, don't bother attending! Gloria and I decided to stick together after the Procession raid. We've been exploring the baron cities, smaller towns, and we're working on getting back to the New City. You've got to have dinner with us so we can tell you of our sight-seeing and I'm definitely curious as to how you escaped the rider."

"Dinner?" asked Lauren.

"That information is sensitive, Vasteck, but you'll have your chance to catch up with Lauren. We'll head to the city district to find a restaurant. Will that give you an adequate tour, Renee?"

"Yes," said Renee.

They passed through the city gate. Renee and her friends saw a dense city filled with numerous skyscrapers that rose to a hundred plus stories, shops, roads and carriages drawn by mandated ghosts, hippogriffs, griffins and a few horses. They drove their passengers down the busy streets or up in the air where city guards directed traffic. On the street level were numerous restaurants, entertainment houses, and a great deal of shops dedicated to city living.

Renee caught the names of the stores and read some of their slogans like Residential Edicts, "The Best in Domestic Protection," Byraghoul Staffs, "Specialized Weapons for Specific Mandates," and the ghost hospital Husk Mold. The buildings and their crafting, brick foundations with glass-like windows got Lauren thinking about what materials they used to create their abodes and the natural resources of Amalgam.

"What's Amalgam made of Catherine?" asked Lauren.

"Amalgam's continents are composed of the same elements and minerals as Earth's crust. The Judge de-materialized the land so that it would be invisible and immaterial to humans but also tactile and usable for ghosts. We have the same natural resources including ethereal resources such as necrosidium, biosidium, spectroplasm, dew, and control over the elements of fire and water."

"So if the buildings are made out earth elements, why can't we just phase through them?"

"We use the dew element to protect our houses and enforce our laws through Edict Charms. Dew is a cleansing element that can destroy all traces of impurities and inhibit ghost's ethereal abilities. If I attempted to violate any Court law, the dew would not allow me to continue in such a course of action. Observe."

Catherine stopped the group then raised her fist

as if to strike Lauren. Her hand stopped before it could fully extend, written in front of her fist was gold letters: *Rule 5: No spirit, animal, native or angel shall harm said inhabitants of Mortalland, Paradise or Amalgam with exception to purgation rites and instruction in the baron cities.*

"Interesting," said Lauren.

"Surrounding the city is one giant dew barrier," said Catherine pointing up. They looked to the sky and saw the golden shield encapsulating the whole city.

"So long as the barrier's structural integrity is preserved the city is safe from violence with exception to Guard School, the purgation fields, and a daily thirty minute period when the Barrier House staff has to shut down the shield to do a little maintenance. Directive dew barriers limit access to domestic and private areas and dispelled only by the owner's permission or key destructs. Residential Edicts makes the best directive barriers for citizen use. The smaller towns often don't utilize these protective measures, offering more freedom but exposing ghosts to more harm. We recommend ghosts to stay in our cities until they've completed their purgation mandates."

They arrived before a restaurant called the Banshee Banquet. The building had a sign of a misty specter with greedy eyes holding a fork and knife, digging into a plate overflowing with food. Vasteck stood before his companions and said, "This is where Gloria and I were headed. I hope it'll do for our regal guests."

"Of course it will, Vasteck," said Catherine.

The Banshee Banquet restaurant was more accurately a mess hall with eight long tables for patrons and a banquet bar filled with food. Catherine led her entourage to a private room in case confidential information was to slip in conversation. Lauren sat across from Vasteck; Gloria and Amy flanked him. Renee sat next to Lauren while Catherine sat at the table's head and Nasra at the foot.

"So what do ghosts eat?" asked Renee.

"Some of the same foods as humans do, only our bodies react differently. We don't eat for nourishment just pleasure. We'll never put on weight, create waste, or get sick if we over eat. This is a gift from the Paradise realm. We will bring on ourselves extra mandates in the purgation fields if we fall into the sin of gluttony."

Catherine waived over a few waiters in the room and had them bring in a few dishes and portions of the food for their private banquet.

"But the animals are all spirits, do ghosts still eat them?" asked Renee.

"No, we're provided for by God. Like manna for the Israelites in the desert, the Judge gave us monnics, lassiberries, nanseos and other native Amalgam creatures for our meat. Fruits and vegetables grow naturally in Amalgam and we plant some in the castle garden."

"Monnics, nanseos, doesn't sound appetizing,"

said Amy under her breath.

"I wouldn't want to eat those animals anyway. They'd probably give you indigestion for months with all that stomping and roaring in the forest," said Vasteck.

The waiters brought in the strange meats for them and they began dining. One resembled a pig but mutated slightly with another unknown creature. The other looked like a normal ham but tasted far sweeter and its texture was soft as pasta. One meat, the nanseo, looked like a white oblong ball but when cut its meat was orange and tasted unlike anything mortals have ever eaten and more delicious. Lauren delighted in the delicious nanseo but its alien appearance frightened Amy. She ordered a veggie pizza instead.

"I'd never eat any animal. It's cruel and disgusting," said Gloria slurping down a spoonful of vegetable soup.

"Why were they so violent, Catherine?" asked Lauren.

"They haven't let go of their mortal grudges. Many of the New Elysian animals follow Estoc's leadership. His hatred against ghosts was fueled by the ideology of the first gestalt lord Masden," said Catherine.

"Gestalt lord?" asked Renee.

"The number of birds and beasts ever brought into existence far outreach the expanse of Amalgam Realm," said Nasra. "To fix this problem, the Judge instilled an instinct within animals to combine their mind and spirit into stronger similar-minded beasts of their kind. You may have noticed some of the animals spotted with small white dots, those are the number of spirits that have joined the gestalt lord. The more spirits amassed into one gestalt lord the larger it becomes and the more respect the lord garners from the other animals."

"Masden was the greatest of these gestalt lords," said Catherine. "He was killed by humans in his mortal life and hated ghosts ever since. Animals are in Amalgam solely to let go of their grudges towards humans after which they'll be let into Paradise. However, Masden would deny Heaven, make Amalgam his kingdom because he so desired ghosts to pay for their transgressions."

"Masden sought our total eradication from Amalgam. He started the first Animal war when he discovered ghosts could die whereas animals could not. The war lasted for a year and divided the animal community between Masden's ghost-eaters or the ghost-kind led by the peace-seeking siren Selene; however, Selene disappeared some time into the conflict. After her loss, most of the animals rallied to Masden and Estoc became his best solider and successor after his death."

"Masden believed the animals were unstoppable until he met the Phoenix and realized, as we did, the problem Phoenix's immortality presented to his cause. Masden couldn't realized his dream of a ghost-less Amalgam until Phoenix was either destroyed or allowed to leave the realm and I'm sure the Phoenix could careless because he wants ghosts to live in Paradise anyway. So they reached an accord, the Phoenix needed my castle for the Tower of Summons to lead ghosts to Heaven. Masden was to secure the castle and force every ghost in their path to follow Phoenix into Heaven or die."

"I'm guessing there's a 'but' coming," said Renee.

"But Masden was destroyed," said Catherine. "Originally my first castle resided on the surface and the Phoenix ordered him to carry it to his archipelago. Masden used nearly all of Amalgam fowls to swell large enough to carry my castle away. The Phoenix moved on the Chamber of Three Doors in the Tower of Summons unhindered because I was incapacitated in a dream."

"Who stopped the Phoenix?" asked Lauren.

"Messina. In battle, she forced the Dark Phoenix to regenerate and then vanquished Masden. The castle crashed in Jaheri adding Ruin Everlasting to Jonah's city. I awoke from the dream where I learned how to create the Horn of Olives that ended the war."

"A dream?" asked Lauren thinking of her dreams.

"Yes, the Judge brought it upon me. He spoke directly to me, told me how to craft the horn, every dimension, material, and details to be crafted. Ghosts don't dream or fall asleep, we only need to rest. The only ghosts that do dream are lost souls or those suffering from a rare ghost disease or spell of some sort."

"I've also been having dreams, Catherine, but I don't think God is responsible for them. They've been so vivid that I can feel the heat from fires in the dreams, it's like I'm actually there!"

"Yes, Messina told me you may have absorbed some of the Phoenix's thoughts and memories. The column regenerates him, mind, spirit, and powers and you received a good deal of them. That's why you're so important to us. We'll examine your dreams after we return from The Guard's Shield to see if they provide any information to his plans."

Gloria heaved deeply and Catherine asked her what was wrong.

"The war sounds so horrible. But I understand how they could hate humans after the way we treat them in Mortalland."

"They didn't have much hatred for you in the forests. Here I am runnin' for my life from the most ferocious Rottweiler I've ever seen and she's surrounded by lynxes, raccoons, even bears that want her to cuddle them."

"Show me your mark, Gloria," said Catherine and Gloria raised her hand. "The mark of the animal, they respect ghosts with that mark. It tells them you were kind to them in Mortalland. Some of the coldest of animals wouldn't dare attack an animal mark. You and anyone accompanying animal marks have almost total freedom in the Wilds, not to mention the animals may let you ride them.

"How about my Jack mark?" asked Vasteck. "What can it do aside from slipping past castle gates and pilfer weapons from The Guard's Shield?" Vasteck let this last part slip, which drew a curious look from Baron Catherine.

"You're skilled in numerous magic trades, but you might want to be careful how you use your multiple talents. Stealing in my city can earn you a purgation mandate for greed or a more rigorous punishment in the Wilds I'm certain you don't want to experience," said Catherine assuredly.

"Come to think of it, Kevin, you did learn a lot of dew magic in a very short amount of time," said Gloria.

"We should stop at a magic school so you can learn everything quickly then teach us so we won't have to sit through the boring lecture," said Renee.

"Trust me," said Catherine, "Learning magic is anything but boring. Maybe you two will be of some use to Lauren in her quest."

"And what quest is that?" asked Vasteck.

"Confidential, Vasteck, but if Lauren requests your help please give it to her."

* * * *

Soon, Lauren was finishing her dinner and learning more of Amalgam and ghost society while enjoying the camaraderie of her friends. Vasteck was teaching a trio of spells he learned to unlock doors to Lauren when he was interrupted by several yellow light rays that fell from all directions through the ceiling and gently warmed the marks on their hands. They asked Catherine about them and she replied the ghosts at the Barrier House are shutting down the shield for repairs. She said the light beams were dew rays making sure there are no cold marks in the city. Moments after they disappeared, Lauren heard a loud commotion outside.

Ghosts were screaming and a brilliant blue light filled the city. The patrons in the Banshee Banquet dropped their plates and left the restaurant. Three guards rushed into the private room and whispered to Catherine. Lauren only caught "Baronsward" and "siege" before Catherine stood and left the private room with them. Lauren and the others followed and she heard a few segments more.

"Ghosts are falling out of the Elysian embassy tower as we speak," said a guard.

They exited the Banshee Banquet to see the city in chaos. Calmer spirits helped the panic-stricken and guards carried their staffs and truss shackles towards the New Elysian embassy tower. That tower streamed ghost orbs that fell from the tower like sparks off a live wire. They were landing in all parts of the city, the boulevard, the purgation fields, even the mountain in terror.

Above the skyscraping towers, high in the sky was an enormous flaming projection of a phoenix bird carrying the Child Phoenix's head in its talons. The child's eyes and mouth were filled with lightning and out of his electric pupils sprang numerous winged centaurs and, from the mouth, one large eagle with Jasmine and the Child Phoenix riding in a basket fitted on the bird's neck towards the castle.

"Catherine, should I take the girls to the House of Shades?" asked Nasra.

"No! They're headed for the castle district. Wait here and protect the girls, Nasra. Kevin, Gloria, return to your home," said the baroness and she orbed and flew off for Baronsguard.

"My God," said Gloria at the projection.

"Come now, Gloria," said Vasteck pushing her along. "Lauren," Vasteck turned to her. "Be careful! Call on us if you need anything." They transformed into orbs and disappeared into the mass of ghosts returning to their homes.

CHAPTER TEN
THE DARK PHOENIX ATTACKS

"Come inside," said Nasra.

The girls retreated into the restaurant. Nasra looked out a window to make sure the Phoenix Loyalists weren't coming close to their location. The girls sat down in the chairs surrounding a table nearest to Nasra.

"I thought Catherine said that no animal could reach this height!" said Renee.

"The Phoenix has several tricks that we don't know about until he springs it on us. The eyes and mouth of that face have lightning in it and that element can transport ghost orbs across Amalgam. The Phoenix must be using a great deal of his magic casting that charm to bring so many of his centaurs along with him so he might not be at full power. He is very brazen as you can see, attacking this fully guarded city with only a thirty minute window. I wonder what they're after at the castle?" asked Nasra thoughtfully. She looked outside a bit longer before turning to them abruptly.

"GET DOWN!" screamed Nasra as she ducked by the window. The girls hid under the table before the whole restaurant shook due to a violent explosion very close by. Nasra stood up and looked back out the window; the girls came slowly from underneath the table. A shadow over took the restaurant and dust filled the street.

"WE'VE GOT TO GET OUT OF HERE!" Nasra screamed. The girls followed close as Nasra ran outside. Outside they saw a tall building adjacent to the Banshee Banquet collapsing towards them. Nasra led them to the right, toward the castle as the building demolished the restaurant. They ran fast and hard until a tremor forced them to the ground. The smoke filled the street; Lauren choked on the ash and coughed as she stood up.

She couldn't see through the dusty haze, but heard Nasra gagging not far from her. She could see a small ball of white light and slim brown fingers gripping it. Nasra called out to them and Lauren could see her silhouette; her right hand was feeling the dust for her companions. Nasra blew gently in her orb and the dust scattered a bit more clearing away the smoke.

"Over here," said a shadowy Renee, coming into view, struggling to approach Nasra.

"EWW! I think I stepped in something," said

Amy, her form trailing behind Renee.

"I'm coming," said Lauren as she moved closer. Suddenly, a large dark shape barreled through the dust behind Amy. The dark form of a man-horse with wings raised a spear to stab Amy.

"AMY DIVE RIGHT!" Nasra shouted.

"What?" Amy asked. Nasra threw her orb at the beast and blew forcibly; the orb amplified her breath and pushed Amy to the side and the centaur into a wall. The centaur fell to the ground dazed as more came over the rubble running down the street. Nasra took Renee to the side where Amy was and Lauren headed towards them when she heard a familiar whinnying voice saying, "To the castle!"

Lauren was trying to get out of the way when Inez spotted her. He threw a staff with a ball attached to one end that exploded into a net. Lauren fell tangled in its mesh. He stopped while the others ran on towards the castle gate. He raised his right hand and spoke into a mark, "I ran into the shade girl that entered your column."

Lauren managed to free herself while Inez continued his conversation, "They must have freed her. Yes sir, I'll fly back to the emblem with her now!" He called to three nearby centaurs to aid him, one of them was Ariel.

"SEIZE HER!" said Inez, pointing at Lauren. The centaurs lunged for her when Nasra leapt unseen from the dust and carried her off. The centaurs toppled over each other while Inez gave chase as Nasra and Lauren ran away down the street. Nasra took a left turn unto a street and Lauren followed. Renee and Amy were running past at the other end when Renee stopped Amy.

"There she is!" said Renee.

"*Run the other way girls!*" said Nasra. Renee and Amy saw them fleeing the centaurs and entered the intersection to continue down the street. Lauren trailed Nasra as Inez and his centaurs gained on them. In the intersection, Lauren glanced to her right and saw Baronsguard gate thrown wide open and the guards combating more centaurs trying to enter. She saw the garden hedges towering a hundred feet in the air to prevent fly-bys and on the mountain were massive batteries shooting down centaurs that attempted to.

"Where are we going?" asked Lauren.

"Anywhere as long as we're away from them!" said Nasra. She was thinking quickly, how to get away from the centaurs and keep the girls safe. Her foot hit a drain in the intersection, "The sewers!" Nasra exclaimed. She spoke into her orb "Exeratract manhole!" and threw her orb ahead of Renee and Amy. The orb attached to the drain cover and Nasra shouted, "Ascentate!" The orb lifted the cover.

"AMY, RENEE, INSIDE!" shouted Nasra. The girls stopped before the manhole.

"No way! I'm not swimming in ectoplasm!" said Amy.

"Would you rather die?" asked Renee.

"No!"

"Then, *get in!*" said Renee as she pushed Amy

in. Amy tumbled down, her screams mixed with the depth and the liquid below. Renee lowered herself in, looking towards Lauren and Nasra as they moved closer. When they were within safe distance of the manhole, Renee let herself fall in. As they neared, a frightened ghost exited a nearby shop and surprised Lauren. His ghostly form phased right through her body. The cold blast stunned Lauren and she tumbled to the ground.

"Nasra!" screamed Lauren.

Nasra turned to see her lying on the ground. Her fall was enough for Inez to spear her hand and Lauren screamed in pain. Nasra retracted her orb, carrying the manhole cover with it.

Ariel, behind Inez, aimed an arrow with a ball for a spearhead at Nasra's orb. The ball formed a vicious mouth that swallowed the orb sending it into the distance. The cover fell next to Nasra's foot. She pulled another arrow with an electric spearhead and shot it at the manhole. It struck the metal and created an impassible lightning barrier. She notched a regular arrow and shouted, "Don't move!"

"Get her!" Inez commanded a centaur behind him.

Lauren removed the arrow from her hand as the centaur knelt down to pick her up. Lauren turned quickly and jabbed him in the eye, he reeled back cursing and Lauren stood quickly and ran towards Nasra. Ariel aimed at Lauren, but Inez knocked the bow and arrow away saying, "We need her alive!" as he charged for her. Nasra picked up the manhole cover and tossed it into the shop's display window. The heavy cover didn't fly very far, but it was enough to break the thin glass.

Lauren jumped into the store and Nasra moved in after her. They were in a toyshop; Nasra lobbed a heavy wooden rocking horse at the centaurs as they struggled to get their awkward frames inside the square window. It struck Inez hard in the chest and he fell onto the street. Ariel aimed her arrow at Nasra. Lauren picked up a bat, her arm strengthened as she threw it. The bat struck the centaur in the head rendering her unconscious.

"Come, Lauren," said Nasra and they exited the shop around the back. In the alley, they saw more centaurs flying off and the eagle, its wings battered and struggling to fly, with the Dark Phoenix and Jasmine atop all in retreat. They flew back into the mouth and eyes of the Phoenix projection and it dissipated. The barrier re-encapsulated the city and they were now safe inside. They walked around to the storefront; Nasra found her orb along the way and arrived to see Inez and his companions struggling to stand.

"Well now, aren't you in a pickle!" said Nasra pointing up to the barrier. They looked above to see the golden shield shining above. Nasra smiled at them and they hung their heads in defeat. Lauren saw several thin rays of dew stretch from the barrier that evaporated their cold magical marks. They were powerless and trapped inside. Sigpos appeared next to Nasra.

"Nasra, Baron Catherine orders you to take the girls to the courtroom to await an immediate briefing."

"Tell her we're coming," said Nasra. "I have to get Lauren's friends from the sewers."

* * * *

Nasra and Lauren headed to the Barrier House, a square block of a building with an arched roof that held at its apex what appeared to Lauren as a garden hose nozzle. Fluid dew streamed from the nozzle replenishing the golden barrier. They found Renee and Amy shackled to a pole, part of the intricate plumbing connecting the nozzle to the dew reserves underneath the house that drained into the sewers. Yellow slime covered the girls; it was a more viscous form of the golden water-like dew.

"*I told you we're not with the Phoenix!* We're friends of Nasra Rallens and what is this sticky goop? Ghost shit?" asked Amy. The guards mistook them for Phoenix Loyalists infiltrating the city through the sewers. Nasra freed the girls and left the Barrier House.

"Thank God you found us, Nasra. I thought the guard's were going to kill us. And thank you Amy for keeping me from drowning," said Renee.

"You're welcome," said Amy grumbling, Nasra simply smiled in reply.

They emerged onto Brigensdale Boulevard, passing through Baronsguard gate that now hung off its hinges. They had to be careful to avoid the long line of captured centaurs, fifty in all. Lauren noticed their arms were tied behind their backs and their wings bound by leather straps to their bodies. They entered Baronsguard and Lauren was finally able to see the expansive royal foyer.

Immediately visibly were four huge statues of Amalgam's barons and one giant statue of Messina against the back wall that stretched to the upper levels. A silk purple carpet, which magically never wrinkled or became dirty, wound from the entrance, between the baron statues, and split as it covered the diamond-shaped staircase in the distance. Lauren gazed upon the largest chandelier she had seen since entering Amalgam and it brilliantly lit the mansion. It was spinning fast and ghosts were using it to transport them around the city.

Decorating the walls were enchanted portraits depicting scenes in Amalgam and steady religious paintings, mirrors depicting ghosts about their tasks, and heavy draped cloth and ornamental weaponry. However, the halls were in total disarray after the attack. The cloth was torn, the decorative weapons the guards used to combat the centaurs littered the floor, and several busts, mirrors, and paintings were damaged.

They traveled in ghost form up the levels to the courtroom, arriving on the third floor, restricted to all by an edict charm. Nasra cast upon them a destruct spell to allow them entry. They traveled down a large corridor where at the far end; Lauren saw a wall with a giant representation of the Three Doors.

"Is that the Chamber of Three Doors, Nasra?" asked Lauren.

"It's the pass to the Tower of Summons, the chamber lies within," said Nasra and she led them inside.

The courtroom was dark with no windows to supply lighting due to the sensitivity of the conversations held within. They walked on a hardwood aisle that split the audience pews down the middle. They sat to the left and the girls rested. The bar consisted of a swinging wooden gate between two pillars that stretched from the floor to the ceiling and railings extended from them to the walls.

Past the bar, the jury box stood against the right wall and four podiums positioned at inter-cardinal positions facing a large circular stone pit in the center. A blue light emanating from this pit failed to illuminate the room sufficiently. Behind the podiums and the pit was the bench where Catherine sat and a curtained archway that lead to the baroness' personal quarters. The seal of the Morrigan nation depicting the angel Messina flanked by the four barons adorned the wall above the archway.

"How was that ghost able to run through me?" asked Lauren.

"Shades are more solid, heavier, and less permissible then ghosts because of your connection to the living realm. Even ghosts have trouble physically touching shades, though our magic is just as effective on you. We can only touch a shade if they've been in Amalgam for a while and their pink glow is leaving them or with a complex spell that gives a ghost a temporary connection to the living. Other than ghosts, very few creatures can carry shades and many buildings outside of our cities don't make concessions for your kind."

"Is that why you have stairs in this place even though ghosts can fly?" asked Amy.

"Yes, but also for ghosts who may not have enough spectroplasm to fly, say after a battle or working mandates, so they use the stairs. Shades tire more quickly than ghosts because your husks prevent you from exerting too much energy to protect your mortal body. You'll want to conserve your strength whenever possible."

They waited so long for Catherine that the girls started exploring the room. Amy and Renee were surveying the podiums as Lauren approached the strand of blue light emerging from the pit. She stood on the stone circle, an impression that caved in towards the center from the hardwood floor. The blue light retracted into its hole as Lauren ran her hand through it. Suddenly the room brightened, torches and the chandelier lit as Lauren felt a dip.

The floor sank into a chasm and Lauren almost fell in when she grabbed hold of the hardwood. Her legs lifted due to a rising platform and her body became level. She turned around to see Catherine standing there with a tall ghost, her second-in-command.

"Take a seat, Lauren," said Catherine.

The doors to the courtroom opened wide and a host of ghosts poured inside. They took their seats in the jury box and in the audience. Catherine took the bench where an animated symbol of the Three Doors blazed on front and floated in a seated position. Three other ghosts stood or floated at the podiums, each had a symbol to appear on the stand.

Names and Graves floated behind his podium that displayed an open book with a feathered pen. A heavily built, bushy-haired, bearded ghost with large belly stood with an intimidating countenance and his podium displayed a roaring lion head. Catherine's companion on the platform was a tall, slender, bald-headed man to the northeast bench whose symbol was that of astral bodies featuring most prominently a ghostly comet that left a huge trail of gas and multi-colored dust.

"Who are these people at the podium, Nasra?" asked Lauren.

"They're the district representatives of Castle Everlasting. They're some of the most powerful ghosts in Amalgam and see to one of four districts in the castle. The bearded man called Lion Face handles the city, the Ghost of Names and Graves oversees the gathering plains, and the tall bald-headed man named Densen manages the castle district. The fourth district, the Wilds, is vacant at this moment. The ghost who presided over it was killed by one of the Phoenix's witches so Catherine's been handling that district."

She drew Lauren close and whispered, "They say she's been waiting for someone special to take over that district." Lauren wondered if Nasra was talking about her, thinking Catherine intended her to share more responsibility than she thought.

"Castle Everlasting is the only city that governs more than four districts. The New City is also Catherine's territory and soon you'll be its baron. Under the representatives are the district judges, councilpersons, and purveyors, who carry out the representative's orders. They are sitting in the juror seats along with a few guards who occasionally are brought in as witnesses."

"What's with the names like Densen? Don't you have names from Mortalland?"

"Those names remind ghosts of their past. Some ghosts had very traumatic pasts and in order to help them move on, they gave themselves new identities, including names. Some ghosts keep their Mortalland names if they passed peacefully while others use their new names as a title like animal mark Gloria or to describe their function like Names and Graves. The Phoenix loyalists create names to dwell on their pasts."

Lauren thought about that as she surveyed the ghosts allowed access to the courtroom. Among the invited, Lauren could see the messenger Sigpos. He stood, drew everyone's attention to him, and reminded the audience he was a gossiper mark filling in for Baronsguard courier Harold, which sparked numerous grumblings amongst the crowd. A ghost near Lauren remarked to his companion, "I can't stand those ghosts. Never trust a gossiper mark." Catherine struck her gavel three times and began speaking aloud.

"This court session is convened. As many of you know, the Dark Phoenix and the animals have destroyed Baronsward Citadel. The animals claim we have imprisoned their lord Estoc and they want him freed or else this city is next. We interrogated the captured centaurs and they said this raid was a rescue attempt, but the Dark Phoenix never neared our prison. He was heading for the Chamber of Three Doors and his witch was trying to break into the Castigarium."

"Why do the animals think we have Estoc?" asked Densen.

"I can answer that," said a guardsman. He was a Baronsward soldier and stated the animals captured him to relay this message. "They claim the Procession raid was an act of war to repossess their lands. They think you ordered the ghosts into their land to capture Estoc."

"I did no such thing," said Catherine.

"How'd you come by this information?" asked Lion Face.

"It's pretty clear they wanted to send a message first and prove they were serious by destroying the citadel. The animals freed us just to relay this message," said the guardsman.

"Did they say why they think we want their lands back?" asked Catherine.

"I have a theory," said a guardswoman who appeared injured. "One of the animals mentioned the lost souls in their realm specifically those in the Phoenix meadow." This garnered a moment of silence; many of the guards knew Catherine ordered this action.

"I did arrange for the ghosts in the meadow to be taken to the castle. The animals know I must send every spirit to the Judge and they agreed in the war treaty to allow me total freedom in carrying out my divine mandate. I did nothing wrong during the Procession raid. Their reasons for war don't match," said Catherine.

"Then let's tell them the truth. The ghosts fled the gathering plains in fear of that tree rider and not on our order," said Densen. Lauren listened with keen interest when Densen mentioned Jasmine.

"The animals don't know that. They probably think the tree rider was Catherine. I believe the Phoenix is forcing them into action and making us their scapegoat. That tree rider at the Procession caused all of this. Why was he in the gathering plains to begin with?" asked Lion Face.

"Yes the tree rider. Everyone, I'd like to introduce to you a girl in the audience. Lauren, step forward," said Catherine.

Lauren stood and walked slowly intimidated by the mass of people gathered. She stood on the stone portal with hands held together. She shook nervously and intertwined her fingers.

"This is Lauren Walston, a Mortalland shade. She's here with her friend's gossiper mark Amy Thompson and caduceus mark Renee Dupree, also shades sitting in the back. Lauren arrived in Amalgam the same night of the Procession raid. Fearing for her life she ran into the Phoenix's column and took the mark of the Phoenix from the Great Sinner."

The audience was stunned; some ghosts were afraid, shouting "Is she the Phoenix?" Others said mysteriously the rumors about the shade girl were true, some ghosts wondered why she didn't die in the column, and the rest were shocked the Phoenix lost his mark.

"How can that be?" asked a ghost in the audience.

"So does she have all of his power?" asked Lion Face bewildered.

"She's retained some of his powers," said Catherine. The baroness recounted the events in the skyscraping forests to Lauren receiving the Phoenix Cage Mark.

"Messina mandated Lauren to become a baron of the New City but first she has to grow in strength and experience. As my rank equal, Lauren is our new agent of Mortalland."

The audience was abuzz at the revelation of a new baron before Catherine silenced the crowd by turning the conversation back to the animal attack.

"Since the Phoenix and his witch have deceived

the animals, hopefully we can quell the animal's rage by eliminating the instigators. For those of you who don't know, the tree rider is a Phoenix witch named Jasmine. Names and Graves, read her history for the record," said Catherine and the more silent court official began flipping through a large tome and read for a short while before speaking aloud.

"Jasmine, real name, Heather Watlington, suspected accomplice of the Dark Phoenix and possible Ghost of the Snow. A branding unit removed her mark of the tree for the deaths of the Evelyn crew. The guards were bringing her to the castle to try her for this crime but Jasmine escaped and disappeared. Numerous investigative units were sent to find the book, but the linking tome could never be found," said Names as he clasped the book shut.

"I remember this case; it's still open and a high priority one. Why haven't we been able to recover the book?" asked Densen. Catherine started to answer but Lauren spoke first.

"It's lost."

"How did you know?" asked Catherine shocked.

"My dreams. In one, Jasmine is talking to a woman named Gretchen and the Phoenix. She wanted to return to Mortalland for the linking tome and to kill the thieves who stole it and murdered her. But in another dream its being hidden on an island by a sailor named Devon Knight."

"Devon, I know him. He was quite disturbed about why he hasn't been summoned for Judgment.

Find Devon, Names, read his history for the record. Continue Lauren," said Catherine as Names flipped through his book.

"Well, in that dream Devon was being told to hide the book and seek out a man named Etienne Robert for everlasting life."

The audience erupted in chatter again; some asked how Lauren could know so much, others wondered what Etienne had to do with this plot. Catherine silenced them again.

"So, the djemsheed's been found by Amalgam's oldest shade, no surprise there. He's remained so elusive we've never been able to find him, even the mirror dedicated to him remains clouded," said Densen.

"Oldest shade?" asked Lauren.

"Yes, I'll fill you in on him later, Lauren," said Catherine.

"Etienne has been gathering quite a following. Numerous doors in the House of Shades register tenants with longer than natural lives," said Lion Face.

"What should we do about him and his followers?" asked Densen.

"Nothing for now. The guards have been on his trail for some time and the incidents in Lauren's dreams took place some three hundred years ago. Etienne's interests may have changed since then; hopefully he no longer desires the linking tome or considers it lost. We'll deal with him in due time. Maybe eliminating Etienne can be the next mission of our new baron here."

Lauren stood up straight at Catherine's pronouncement. She sensed that Catherine was a bit thrilled to be sharing her workload. "Tell us more about these dreams," said the baroness. Lauren paused slightly before beginning again.

"One dream was of the Evelyn's destruction, another was of Jasmine taking the Phoenix Oath, and the last one was of a giant tree that pulled this castle into a crater on the ground."

"The Lanise crater right below us…great," said Catherine exhaustedly.

"They plan to use a tree to suck the castle from the sky?" asked Lion Face incredulously.

"The vacuums from their roots have been known to suck ghosts inside if they stand to close. If this tree is as big as Catherine says it is, it might be possible," said Densen.

"But the tree's suction only works during the dew season and with the seasons changing so randomly that could be weeks away," said Lion Face.

"Or a few hours," said Densen.

"Well the tree isn't in the crater now so let's not worry about that. Names, you said Jasmine had the mark of the tree. What does it do?" asked Catherine.

"It's one of the rarer marks in Amalgam. The only known ability is that it allows the bearer to hear the voices of trees, but it's rumored to grant limited control over them. Ah! Here he is; Devondre Knight, born in Jamaica, orphaned at eighteen, drowned at age twenty-six, and was a sailor on the Evelyn the night of its sinking. He had a few sins he worked off in the purgation fields and is awaiting Judgment."

"Step back, Lauren, I'll search for him," said Catherine as she closed her eyes. Lauren moved off the stone circle as it collapsed into void and the room fell silent. After minutes of waiting the stones returned, sealing shut without a ghost in tow.

"The portal was denied access," said Catherine, opening her eyes. The crowd sighed as Catherine proclaimed more bad news.

"What does that mean?" asked Lauren who was disappointed she couldn't see the ghost in her dreams.

"He's in a smaller town somewhere, a city that the portal cannot enter unless authorized. The problem is these towns don't bar the portal access unless threatened by outside aggression," said Catherine.

"In other words, Jasmine and the Phoenix know where he is," Lion Face said to Lauren.

"That was fast! The Phoenix doesn't like to waste time," said Densen gloomily.

"Catherine, I suggest we send a combative unit to retrieve him. If he gets captured, it'll only be a matter of time before the Dark Phoenix gets the linking tome!" said Lion Face.

"And where do we start? My portal can only retrieve ghosts, not tell me where they are. There are hundreds of towns in the Wild's district."

"Catherine, in my dream Devon was being chased into a forest, one where the trees move," said Lauren.

"There's only one of those in Amalgam. It has to be the Illusionist Forest," said Densen becoming enthusiastic and smiling. "It's east of the Elysian Fields and governed by Magician Vincent Vengrass. He's performed some of the best illusionary magic shows I've ever seen. I remember he floated a hydra right over my head during rest season…"

"Densen, please," said Catherine. "If he's in the forest he'll be at Vincent's Hobby. It's the only town in that forest."

"I recommend we send the guards immediately," said Lion Face.

"I'm going to send Lauren. With her knowledge about the Phoenix and her dreams of Devon she might be able to gain his trust."

"But guards would do the job—" said Lion Face.

"Yes, their job will be to find and eliminate whatever has beset the Hobby. If it's Jasmine hopefully they can arrest her and stop this plot before it escalates."

"Do you believe Lauren can handle this?" asked Densen.

"We'll see, but she'll not go alone or untrained. Her friends are going as well. I'll instruct them in ghost combat at Guard School and Nasra will join them to the Hobby along with a combative guard unit," said Catherine standing.

Amy frowned and said, "How is she going to volunteer me without asking?"

"Meanwhile, Names, search throughout the baron cities and smaller towns. Find anyone who might have the mark of the tree and inform me immediately so we can examine its full potential. Densen," she said turning to him. "See that the castle defenses are up to withstanding an animal onslaught. Prep and clean the Horn of Olives, make sure its in working order. Lion Face, prepare your guards for war and order a company to the Hobby. Court's adjourned."

Catherine struck her gavel and the ghosts filed out. Some of the ghosts shied away from Lauren while others walked up and shook her hand, "Its great Catherine has help. Messina must have immense faith in you."

"Wait till the Amalgam Times get word of this, a new baron!" said Sigpos. Lauren watched him spring from the audience to spread the news when a guardswoman placed the highest confidentiality on him.

Catherine came down from her podium and approached Lauren. She summoned Nasra, Renee, and Amy to join her. Catherine led them out of the courtroom. Catherine took them to the second level and into another large chamber that occupied half of the floor. The engraving above the door read CASTIGARIUM. Catherine grasped the ornate gold handles and pushed the door inward.

Immediately visible down the hallway was a wide room where an extremely large book with innumerable pages lay open low to the ground. A large and very short wooden holder held the tome at a sixty-degree angle. This book was the centerpiece of the room taking up over half of the space. Its pages contained the marks of ghosts. Written underneath were the names of their former bearers.

Catherine began, "This is what Jasmine was after today, the Book of Marks. I want you three to know how serious the linking tome Devon hid to this book is and why we've been searching for it for centuries. This book contains confiscated marks from ghosts who have inappropriately used their magic. It's the only object in Amalgam that can store removed marks and safely contain their power."

"We made nearly a thousand smaller books from the pages of this one to expedite the disciplinary process. Our branding units could remove and return ghost's marks all over Amalgam without them having to come here. These books were openly linked to the original so that when a mark was sequestered and placed in the linking tomes it would appear instantly into this one."

"However, when the Dark Phoenix discovered this connection he sought a linking tome so he could have access to all these marks. The Phoenix managed to ambush a branding unit and materialize a tome in Mortalland. We destroyed the rest with the exception of three linking tomes in the

Castigarium's of the other baron cities, but one remains and only Devon knows its location. Jasmine must need her tree mark in order to carry out the Phoenix plans."

"We can't let her or the Phoenix gets their hands on that book. If they do, not only will Jasmine have reacquired her mark, but the Phoenix would have a variety of powers at his disposal. You can ensure that this doesn't happen by getting to Devon first and have him divulge the location of that book. I can't use my portal to teleport you to the Hobby; you could wind up in the animal mass and the forest illusions could scar my mind. Nasra, you'll have to guide them by shade-rays. I'll send you and the girls on the least dangerous path to the Hobby as possible. You'll have to leave in an hour."

Catherine sent Nasra to get two units of guards and shade-rays prepared for the Hobby and instructed the girls to wait for Nasra at the House of Shades.

CHAPTER ELEVEN
THE GOSSIPER'S SCUTTLEBUTT

The girls left the courtroom and returned to the House of Shades. The light of Ghasly, Amalgam's moon, illuminated the castle. Lauren wasn't thrilled about venturing through a forest of illusions especially with the animals on the prowl. Renee was indifferent and Amy really wanted to go home. As they approached the house, the girls saw several shades about the entrance, many burned considerably from head to toe. They approached a female ghost helping another ghost into the house and Renee asked what happened to him.

"He was in the purgation fields, frostbitten from his work. He's been given a healing potion from Husk Mold so he'll be fine in the morning, just in time for a return trip to the fields," said the shade sadly.

"Frostbite? The baron cities showed burning fields at the Procession," said Renee.

"It's still winter season. The fields change depending on the season."

"The purgation fields seem awfully cruel and inhumane! Pain and suffering aren't the only ways to redemption," said Renee appalled.

"The Court knows this. After your purging work is complete, your sin is paired with an opposing virtue charm, chastity for lust or generosity for greed and so on, which will be branded into your mark to keep track of how well you practice your virtue. The more virtuous a ghost becomes, the less time they spend in the fields. The purgation fields are just one of the ways we erase our sins but, to be honest, many of the ghosts here have earned their pain."

"His face is so badly burned," said Amy dolefully. "I'm never going to step foot in those fields."

"Keep away from sin and obey the Court rules and it's possible."

The girls entered their apartment in the House of Shades and sat down in the lounges they had created for themselves earlier. For a while, the girls were quiet and waited patiently. Amy was unusually silent in her chair, yet she looked at Lauren with piercing eyes and her mouth twitched as if she was devising a nefarious plan. She sighed deeply, expressing her boredom before she abruptly spoke.

"I can't believe Catherine is going to send me

into that forest."

"Here we go again," said Lauren.

"I know you're enjoying this, being the center of attention in the courtroom, having Catherine cook up these missions so I can spend all day in this ghost world instead of at home with Jason. You want me to die out there don't you? You want some giant animal to eat me up like that snake in the forest so that when you return home you make a move on my boyfriend."

"No Amy, that's your twisted paranoia getting the better of you," said Lauren coolly.

"It sounds like paranoia," said Renee.

"What?" barked Amy at Renee.

"Oh, *come on*, Amy! Why do you think Lauren's after Jason? You've got him already! I've seen how you snuggle with him in school and kiss him in front of Lauren. You pretty much flaunt your relationship before our entire history class."

"I'm not paranoid and I'm not showing off. He loves me and likes it when I draw attention to us. It makes him feel better knowing he's with the finest girl in school," Amy rubbed it in to great effect because Lauren was visibly seething and bit her lip to restrain herself.

"What I'm sick of is risking my life over something I didn't have to be involved with. Ever since my birthday my life has been one hell of a nightmare because of Lauren," said Amy, her eyes quivered with anger. "Now I'm headed towards a forest where that tree creature is waiting for us.

Catherine just volunteers us for this assignment without asking how we feel and you, Renee," she turned to her. "How can you act like this is some sort of adventure? We could die out there!"

"Because I'm not afraid! Catherine wouldn't send us out there unless she thought we were capable of coming back safe."

"You don't know that! She could be sending us out there to hide her own cowardice by *delegating* her work to her stooges. She's chickenhearted and lazy!"

"She's a busy woman Amy, she has other duties around this castle," said Lauren remembering Catherine's rant about her numerous task in the cathedral.

"So you claim! I'm starting to think like the ghosts who leave the baron cities. I don't trust the baron's judgment. We're only sixteen!"

"I'm fifteen," said Renee just to annoy Amy.

"*Even more my point!*" said Amy irked. "This is something those soldier ghosts should handle and you see what Jasmine did to them. We're not old enough to be running through the forests and I still have a curfew for Christ's sake!"

"And I'm sure you've probably broken it before to run out with some guy. Now you can do it for Catherine," said Renee.

"Argh! You two are unreasonable!" said Amy standing.

"Where are you going?" asked Lauren sitting up in her hammock.

"FOR A WALK!" she said and stormed out. Renee and Lauren watched Amy leave before looking at each other.

"Hopefully, for a *long* walk!" said Lauren nastily, the jealousy Amy provoked in her had her yelling at the door.

"Nasra told us to wait," said Renee.

"Oh let her go, maybe she'll get in trouble for making Nasra wait when she arrives. She's been complaining ever since she's got here. Perhaps a stroll through the city is just what she needs to stop whining. Little miss perfect Amy Thompson, I'm the prettiest girl in school, Jason loves me, blah, blah, blah."

A knock at the door twenty minutes later had Lauren wishing it were Nasra, who would find Amy absent and give her a much-deserved punishment. So Lauren wished, but instead of Nasra it was a near pencil thin man, whose body was so small it looked like a skeleton was standing in the hall. He was wearing an overcoat that probably belonged to a normal-sized person but on his body, it appeared tailored for a giant. He coughed hard as if he was straining to expel phlegm but none soiled their hardwood floor. He stood upright and introduced himself.

"Hello, I'm looking for a gossiper mark named Amy Thompson. My name is Harold, I'm the courier of Baronsguard and chief editor of the Amalgam Times," he said in a low voice.

"Amy just stepped out. Are you alright?" asked

Renee as Lauren came close.

"I'm healing fairly well considering how powerful the jinx that cold soul cursed me with was. It gave me ghost pneumonia, one of the worst sicknesses a ghost can get. I guess they never heard the old saying don't shoot the messenger."

"What do you want with Amy?" asked Lauren curiously.

"Gossiper mark Amy has broken a couple of confidentiality rules pertaining to the Procession Raid. I'm looking for her to let her know about her punishment," said Harold. Lauren poorly hid her enthusiasm, in truth she was beaming.

"She's been publishing rumors and classified information about a certain court official and I was sent to stop her libelous statements against one…oh…what's the name…Lauren Walston."

"WHAT!" said Lauren. Her glow dimmed, she remembered the horrible rumors that Amy spread at school and now she was the subject of some. Harold lifted his eyes at Lauren's outburst. He scanned the door to find her name upon it.

"Is that you?" he asked Lauren.

"WHAT HAS SHE BEEN SAYING ABOUT ME?"

"Well I have here some clippings…"

Harold looked in the overcoats' inside pocket and retrieved a few folded sheets of paper. Lauren took them before Harold could fully pull them from his coat. She read the headlines of the articles; all were authored by Sigpos Blarney and investigating the cause of the Procession raid. The headlines read **Abduction at the Procession Raid**, **Shade Girl Miraculously Survives Phoenix Column**, **Phoenix plan foiled by shade girl**, and finally, **Jealousy led Lauren to Amalgam**. Lauren quickly scanned this article.

"According to my source close to the shade girl, finally identified as Lauren Walston, the old green-eyed monster was behind her arrival to Amalgam. Clearly, envy is Lauren's deadly sin and her unrestrained jealousy seems to be catching up with her. Aside from causing the near mortal death of one of our gossipers, she's rumored to be of ill-repute at Royce High for craving attention from every guy in a relationship and many high school girls fault her for their breakup. 'She just kept fawning all over my boyfriend even after he told her I was dating him. *She had to have him!* When she couldn't she'd make up lies about us and said that we said it about each other. We ended up breaking up, thanks a lot Lauren,' said my source quoting a Royce High student *verbatim*."

"HOW COULD SHE!" Lauren screamed. Renee took the article and read it quickly.

"She described herself! *The nerve!*" said Renee incredulously and, secretly, impressed at Amy's audacity.

"I hoped this wouldn't be true, it's quite

unfortunate I got hit by that jinx. I would have put a stop to this earlier," said Harold.

"I hope she suffers for this! That's her reputation not mine!"

"Is this paper widely read?" asked Renee.

"The Amalgam Times is the only paper that reaches every baron city and these particular columns have been wildly popular as everyone was looking for an explanation about the Procession raid. The Court's been unusually tip-lipped about it. It wouldn't surprise me if a most ghosts have read these articles."

"WHERE IS SHE? I'M GOING TO PULVARIZE THAT GIRL!" said Lauren.

"I was hoping she'd be here but more than likely she's at the Gossiper's Scuttlebutt."

"Take me there NOW!" said Lauren.

Lauren, Renee, and Harold left the House of Shades and entered the city district. Renee was still concerned about Nasra returning yet Lauren was livid and no longer cared to wait for her. They passed the demolished Banshee Banquet and took a right down a congested street where they arrived at the bar on Quidnunc Street. Lauren burst through the door and found Amy sitting on the bar counter surrounded by a host of ghosts, laughing and talking gaily.

Lauren walked right up to them and burst through the pack.

"You tramp! How dare you put this garbage in the paper about me?" asked Lauren.

Amy smiled at her and leaned back on her left arm propping herself up on the counter. Harold dismissed the other ghosts around them so that only one remained from the pack.

"I warned you what would happen if you called me out my name. Do it again and I'll dish some more dirt," said Amy smugly.

"Or do it yourself and claim it Lauren's," said Renee disgusted.

"It is Lauren's dirt…now," Amy finished silently so that only Lauren and Renee could hear. Lauren reached her hand back to summon all the strength in her hand to punch Amy but it held firm when she tried to extend it. Rule five was written before her clinched fist. Amy held her breath as Lauren was about to strike but chuckled when she saw the golden letters.

"I guess you have a hearing problem as well. Catherine said once the barrier is up, violence is forbidden!"

"Funny how you get to break all the rules you want while I have to sit and obey."

"Like a dog, Lauren, yes. Like I have to sit and obey Catherine. It's unfortunate for us all. Now it's time that I have some fun."

"This isn't fun for me! Ever since I've got here, they've given me more responsibility."

"So we hear!" said the listening ghost rising and smiling. "Pardon my interruption, but I just wanted to introduce myself to the New Baron. My name is Sigpos Blarney, gossiper extraordinaire and…"

"The one responsible for publishing this trash!" said Lauren angrily waving the clippings. "I mean, don't you even check to see if this stuff is true?"

"I had every reason to believe it was. Amy's been right before, no one had any clue as to what was going on at the Procession. But once I started publishing Amy's articles, Court officials kept pestering me about how I was getting classified information and said she was your friend."

"*EX-FRIEND!* No friend would claim all their dirt is mine."

"I am your friend, Lauren," said Amy. "The last thing I want to see is you get hurt. And maybe if you were able to convince Catherine against us going to this Hobby, we wouldn't be put in harms way."

"You know I can't do that!"

"*FIND A WAY!*"

"This is so embarrassing!" said Lauren close to tears looking over all the articles.

"Gossip like that certainly can be, but it's also, so scintillating. Sizzzz!" said Sigpos licking his finger and touching his hip.

"Oh, I get it! You two are happy now, huh? Amy gets her revenge and you got a good story. You don't care about making me out to be some jealous hussy."

"That depends on how much of this article is true. After all, gossip can have some truth to it," said Sigpos.

"The *truth* is Amy described *herself* in this

article," Lauren threw the jealousy article at Sigpos. "You didn't even get my side of the story!"

"Would you like me to print your story?" Sigpos raised and opened his hand; a pen and notepad materialized onto his palm.

"*No!* I want these stories and anything else Amy's said about me destroyed."

"Too late, Amy's most recent article has just gone to press, part of a special edition on the recent attack at Baronsward Citadel and this castle."

"And what did she say in that?" asked Renee.

"Oh, just that little tidbit about you being the *New Baron!* This is good news Harold; ghosts will be lining up to read about her, we haven't had a new baron since the Drastic Change. It'll surely be the most successful issue of the Amalgam Times ever!"

"That was meant to stay in the courtroom!" said Renee.

"Siggy you know that's against the rules," said Harold.

"I can talk about or publish anything I overhear if the speakers are aware I'm in the vicinity. I made my presence known in the courtroom for those unfamiliar with me as required and Catherine acknowledged Amy during the proceedings. But the guards placed confidentiality on me and forgot Amy therefore it's perfectly legal."

"So this is your fault," Lauren said to Amy.

"I've heard that before," said Amy singing. "Now we're even Steven. I asked you to help me get away from these ghosts, but instead I'm being sent on a mission to find Devon and some stupid book."

Sigpos began writing before Lauren slapped the notepad out of his hand.

"Don't publish that you scumbag!" said Lauren before turning back to Amy. "I hope they toss you in the purgation fields for this so you can get burned like that ghost we saw earlier," Lauren said wishfully.

"Well, first time offenders usually get a light punishment, after that they have to do time in the purgation fields," said Sigpos.

"Not this time, Siggy," said Harold. "Amy Thompson, Baron Catherine herself said that she has read your letters and for your light punishment, you are to accompany Lauren to the Hobby. Catherine stated that your rumormongering is why she *volunteered* you for the assignment. She also says that if anymore gossip was to spread from you, which it seems already has, you'll eat hot coals with the gluttons to slow your loquacious tongue."

Amy trembled at Harold's condemnation while Lauren and Renee smiled. She looked sharply at Lauren and said, "I'm not going to burn my fine ass spirit because of your jealousy so you can forget it." Amy leapt off the bar and brushed past Lauren.

Amy stopped at the bar entrance. *"I'll find some way to fix you, Lauren, and Catherine. Thanks for the gift Sigpos!"* said Amy and she left the bar.

"Man I love her! She might be one of the better gossipers one day," said Sigpos to Harold.

"You just see to it that she doesn't spread anymore gossip. She's already in enough trouble as it is and I don't want my paper to be turned into some sleazy tabloid. Either you find a new venue for your loose talk or you can kiss your job at the Times goodbye," said Harold so angrily he coughed up a little blood. He cleaned himself up with a handkerchief from his coat before he turned to Lauren and said, "I've got to get back to office and salvage my paper's credibility. I promise I'll do what I can to salvage your reputation and I apologize once again." Harold patted Lauren on the shoulder and left the girls and Sigpos for the exit.

"He certainly is mad at me," said Sigpos despairingly.

"You deserve it," said Renee. Sigpos shrugged his shoulders.

"I can't help it, it's in my nature. But I must apologize, I'm sorry, Lauren."

Lauren looked into Sigpos' eyes and saw genuine remorse so she accepted.

"I just wish I could beat her at her own game," said Lauren grudgingly.

"Well, there is one way," said Sigpos, he reached into his cloak and retrieved a large ruby stone. "It's called the Blarney stone, forged out of my own magical skill. This little device improves eloquence, oratorical abilities, and enhances your persuasive skill. It can easily shift any argument in your favor. It might come in handy seeing as how Amy wasn't too thrilled with her punishment.

Maybe you could persuade her to see past your differences or at least to refute the salacious claims she's made."

"Is that the gift you gave her?" asked Lauren.

"Yes, part of a care package I give to all my gossipers in case a rumor we spread gets back to the person it's about. It's saved me several trips to Husk Mold and my life numerous times. Just hold the stone to your throat and it'll meld with your vocal chords. It'll extract itself after you no longer need it."

"I don't think I want anything to do with your kind. I see why they say never trust a gossiper mark, you all should be in the purgation fields twenty-four seven," said Lauren bitterly.

"Oh, come on, gossipers aren't all bad. Good things have come from loose talk, its saved lives; take Paul Avers, the best gossiper ever and my mentor. He broke the Mortalland Rule creating the gossiper communes to keep in touch with his living friends. The way he saw it, he had to create access to two worlds of gossip!"

"Paul broke so many rules gossiping it's ridiculous. He even managed to get word of his summoning, which is impossible! Only God knows that yet he did it! He worked feverishly for that spiritual tabula rasa and finished just before his summoning. His only saving grace from the pyre was the commune's usefulness."

"Where's the justice in that? He gets to break rules and get away with it?"

"Some ghosts appear to get over only to have their problems mount, yet sometimes these same people can save lives with their troublemaking and Paul has saved scores with his inventions."

"So what are gossipers doing in this realm besides causing trouble and getting pardons?"

"We're mandated to keep secrets for our inability to do so in the mortal realm. Trust me; this is very hard for nosy parkers like me, but sometimes I feel obligated to break my confidentiality rules."

"You do huh?" asked Lauren sardonically.

"I can't keep a secret that'll strengthen ghost's faith in our government and news of a new baron will do just that. I know you've just arrived so you probably don't know much about the Dark Phoenix, but he is truly majestic. His powers come from the Judge's mark and the things he can do astounds people to the point that many ghosts actually believe he is God. Distrust in the Court runs high, especially when the barons make mistakes. And with the Phoenix seemingly immortal, continually rising and warring, some lose faith in God."

"News of more help lets ghosts know that God is still working for us, that He hasn't stranded us in limbo which is especially good seeing as how that ancient prophecy never panned out."

"Prophecy?" asked Renee.

"Yeah, supposedly Messina foretold a prophecy of one coming to save Amalgam at a Procession centuries ago, but not many can remember it because most of the ghosts who heard it have long since been summoned. It was one of many false hopes we were given until your arrival and as you'll soon see, news of your coming will fill the Morrigan nation with renewed optimism. I told the ghost world about the new baron in order to prevent souls from turning cold and I'll gladly take my punishment in the purgation fields for my actions. So, in a sense, I see myself not as a gossiper, but a spiritual whistleblower, if you will."

"Whistleblowers alert people to corruption in organizations to save people from harm. They don't spread vicious lies," said Renee.

"I'm a whistleblower in that the Court is an organization, and the great offense they committed is being so secretive about a person who gives us hope. News of Lauren's position will restore many ghosts trust in the Court and keep them loyal to the Judge."

Lauren thought about Sigpos' passion and realized that maybe he wasn't totally without merit. She never realized how uplifting her position would be to the ghosts of Amalgam.

"A whistleblower, Siggy? How honorable of you!" Nasra said approaching with Amy pouting behind her by the door, "A scandalous knight circulating sin under the guise of chivalry. You know our laws and what we discuss in the courtroom should stay there. Your lust for gossip is going to send you to Hell faster than you can say hand-basket! You, Sir Blarney will eat coals tonight instead of Amy on Catherine's order."

"Aye! Such is the fate for the Knights of Chinwag," said Sigpos mournfully.

"I'm sorry about this, Lauren, but now everyone who's responsible for your embarrassment will soon be punished. I have to prepare you three for your training. Catherine will be ready for us in a moment; she's in a meeting with Messina. Let's head to The Guard's Shield to get you suited up."

Sigpos stood and came over to Lauren and placed the blarney stone in her hands, "To make amends for my part in your disgrace."

"Thank you Siggy, confidentiality high!" said Lauren; she gave him a slight smile.

"Smart girl," said Sigpos as Nasra escorted the girls out onto Quidnanc Street.

CHAPTER TWELVE
GUARD SCHOOL

Nasra and the girls left the Scuttlebutt for the castle district. They arrived inside The Guard's Shield, a shop cluttered with weaponry from different areas of the world and ages past like knobkerries, Chinese swords, flails, and grenades. In the immediate front were eight tables where laid small orbs, compasses, pocket watches, medallions and more trinkets. In the middle, racks of weapons all sorts of staffs, swords and axes as well as some odd belongings like fishing poles, nets, ice picks, scythes, and shovels. At the back of the store was the clerk counter standing before a huge circular steel vault door and two staircases leading up to a second landing where more weapons were available for use.

"Pick any weapon you want girls. You'll be a long-staff class so you'll have to pick something with length."

"Long-staff?" asked Renee.

"Yes, the beginner magic rank. After that is short-staff, orb, medium-less, and mark master classes. Ghosts must first learn how to control their mark's abilities and channeling their power through a medium can help. Ghosts prefer something they were fond of in their mortal life, which is why we have a great variety. Most novice ghosts who forgo using staffs for smaller objects end up injuring themselves and others or casting something they can't control."

Amy and Renee couldn't think of any long object favored in Mortalland so Amy chose a trident and Renee a white staff. However, Lauren had a deep affinity for the crusader sword and chose one with a silver guard, black grip, and octagonal pommel.

"I'm going to teach you how to summon them and dispel them for easy carrying. Name your weapons," said Nasra. The girls did as instructed, Lauren named her sword Diane, Amy named her trident after her beau Jason, and Renee picked the name Vanessa for her staff.

"Grasp the weapon firmly, speak its name, and say the charm, *dematerm*."

Lauren went first. She tried and failed but grasped it tighter and said "Diane dematerm," and the sword shrunk infinitesimally small to nothingness.

Renee and Amy got it right on the first try with their weapons.

"Good, now say the name and *materm*," said Nasra.

They tried the materialization spell. All of them had their weapons reappear. Lauren looked at Nasra's orb hanging from her waist.

"Is that ball you've been using a weapon?" asked Lauren.

"Yes, I'm an orb-class. As we get more experienced we no longer need objects and become medium-less and master ranks."

"So how are we to pay for all this?" asked Renee.

"Currency is forbidden in Amalgam. With all the sin caused by the acquisition of wealth, the Judge did away with it. Now any items we need are made through work mandates for ghosts to purge sins."

"What about the coins you gave to the reaper?" asked Lauren.

"That's not money; they're for Messina to track the reapers progress."

Nasra approached the store clerk, "I'll need a gossiper's commune for the Mortalland Shades here."

He went to the back, unlocked a massive magically sealed vault with a password and rummaged around inside before emerging with a white candle that was wrapped with the aura of slightly larger blue candle. Cold mist radiated from it as if it the clerk retrieved it from a freezer. The clerk handed it to Nasra who in turn handed it to Lauren.

"This is the gossiper's commune. It's one of the

best devices that can clearly send messages through Amalgam without the use of an oracle and it protects against eavesdropping and evil spirits in the area. We find them most useful in the New City as our ghosts and mortal friends can communicate between two communes by speaking into them. Be careful with it around pools of water or in the rain, water will destroy it. Catherine has one already and she wants you to keep her informed in your search for the linking tome."

Nasra watched as Lauren tucked it into her waist.

"Now we have to get you and Renee properly fitted for Guard School. Come over here," said Nasra. She led them towards four animated mannequins modeling the male and female guard uniforms.

There were two choices, dress blue or dress white for both genders. Dress blues for women consisted of knee length dresses, stockings, turtle-necked sweaters, high boots, and a cloak that fastened at the neck and fell to the knees. Amy already had on the dress blues working at the House of Shades. The dress whites were like Nasra's uniform, the same attire she wore on gathering night, but said they were for Court officials only. She said, for now, all of them would wear dress blue.

Nasra told them to touch the garments on the mannequin. Once they did their clothes changed from jeans and t-shirts to the guard uniforms.

Lauren felt the warmth they provided and as they left the store, she could feel the uniform generating heat on her body. They left, heading back to the castle gate.

"How did ghosts learn of channeling magic through weapons?" asked Lauren.

"We followed the Phoenix's example. In the early battles, the Loyalists were equipped with odd objects that helped them channel their magic better than us. We interrogated our prisoners and learned the Phoenix taught them to do it. Apparently, when he took the mark off the Vessel the Dark Phoenix was overwhelmed with power. To keep himself from going mad he expelled it all about Amalgam's landscape and waters creating monsters in the process. The Dark Phoenix's pain subsided as he cast the magic through objects and soon he was able to control his power. Since then we've been forging items to help us channel our magic."

They approached a mountain pass near the House of Natives. Lauren could make out an emblem of a shield and a sword atop the cavern pass. Two guards were by the entrance, though they were sitting down, relaxing. As Nasra approached, they stood and straightened up at attention.

"No sleeping on the job boys!" said Nasra as they entered the cave.

Torches lit the pass, the walls were dripping water and Lauren could hear a nearby waterfall rushing along. As they came to an opening in the rock, they saw a ghost fly by, shooting spell from his fly swapper until a charm knocked him down. They stood on the edge of a high ledge. The school was a cavern carved smoothly in a long cylindrical pit with large raised platforms and connecting stone bridges. There were nine levels each had six arched doors along the walls and stairwells leading to different floors.

The energetic animated designs on each floor showed a ghost, fire, water, dew, spectroplasm, lightning, wind, and two other elements. Their symbols were of black mist and white mist. Below Lauren could see ghosts fighting each other with spells represented on the platform where they stood.

"Lead them to my training room, Nasra," said Catherine coming behind them.

Nasra nodded and took them along the chamber through a large arched door directly ahead from where they entered. Catherine moved ahead of the group and placed her hand on a second door to unlock it. Inside was an expansive flat room with a stone floor and a design of three concentric circles with a cross inside the smallest circle. In the far right corner was a dead pool with spectroplasm so that they could refresh themselves. Catherine stood in the middle of this circle, the girls stood in a row before Catherine, and Nasra behind the girls.

Along the left wall was a giant, elaborate clock. It held several smaller clocks inside of it, the smallest protruded out furthest, the rest lay underneath, descending to the largest. A ring circled the clock with a teal fluid running through it.

"This is the baron's training room," began Catherine, "it's where I and the other barons sharpen our skills. This clock along the wall here includes a time-space manipulator. While we train, time will flow normally outside, but in here, we will move much faster. For every minute we have, this room will feel like four hours, therefore, you'll have seven and a half days of lessons. I'm going to instruct you three to use the most of your powers in the short time that we have."

"Can't you set the clock so we can complete our training?" asked Renee.

"The clock uses a special magic element to manipulate time-space and cannot drain completely otherwise it will be useless. Believe me I've maxed out magic in the clock. This room uses illusions that I will use to enhance your education. The magician Vincent helped in improving the illusions to make them more realistic and even though the objects aren't real, they will seem true to life. Are you ready to begin?"

Catherine looked at each but Lauren especially, the girl's nodded hesitantly.

"Good, Nasra, if you will."

Nasra strode over to the clock, adjusted its time, and pressed in a large dial with both her hands. Grass grew atop the stone, and the rock ceiling melted into a blue sky, the empty chamber transformed into a forest, where the sun shone brightly. The trees were lush green; the grass was soft and smelled strongly. Butterflies fluttered, the wind blew gently, and the girls found themselves in a large field of white flowers. Catherine looked around with approval at the illusions as she approached slowly.

"Beautiful isn't?" asked the baroness.

The girls smiled at the realism of the illusions and felt quite at peace.

"First we'll begin with transformation. Ghosting is what we call the transformation of the spirit into its three forms: orb, ghost, and vortexes. Vortexes are a special transformation used in various magic arts such as indwelling and possession but they are of no use to us now. Orbing is a ghost's main mode of mobility and in order to successfully transform you'll have to imagine yourself as weightless and compact. Close your eyes."

The girls did as instructed.

"Imagine yourself in the sky amongst these full, white clouds, soaring freely like an eagle, the wind gently brushing your face. Imagine your body stretched wide, arms extended far, legs spread apart. Now, slowly curly yourself up, arms first, then legs, still soaring… still soaring… still soaring… now… Open!"

Lauren opened her eyes to see herself floating in a glowing ball. Below she could see the grass and flowers, but she couldn't see her body. A golden orb encased her spiritual form but Lauren felt quite normal. She could see the outline of her bubble but she could see Catherine and her surroundings clearly.

"Moving in ghost form is an instinctive as

walking, try it." Lauren tried moving about; just as Catherine said, moving came naturally. The girls took their new forms for a spin; they zipped along the field, performed loops, zigzagged and circled around trees. Lauren and Renee bumped into each other, and said "Ouch!" as it hurt them both. Even Amy had fun swishing through the air, as she always wanted to fly. Catherine called them back before her and they floated above, bouncing in file.

"To return to your ghost form, imagine you're in a fetal position and just extend your legs," said Catherine. As easily as moving, the girls returned to their ghost form. Catherine had them transform several times to make sure they could do it.

"Good. Next are the evanesce and coalesce charms that shades use to separate and rejoin their spirits to their bodies. If you were to say the charm now you'd return to your bodies, however, I've set this chamber so that'll you stay in Amalgam. You'll disappear for a moment if you perform it correctly. First, you'll have to pick a name that describes you but that you don't use often like a middle or nickname."

Lauren and Renee decided to use their middle names, Andrea and Danielle, and Amy chose her extended first name Amerie, which she shortens to Amy.

"Got it? Then say 'evanesce' charm when you've decided."

Renee went first shouting, "*Danielle evanesce!*" She felt an electric tingling about her body and became near entirely transparent for a few seconds before becoming visible again. Amy tried with similar results but Lauren was able to disappear altogether and remain that way for some time before trying the anti-charm coalesce and reappearing.

"It appears you have more control over the charm, Lauren," said Catherine. "Keep practicing and when you get back to Mortalland try it again on your bodies! Some of the best shades I've seen have been able to not only disconnect their spirits but dematerialize their bodies entirely as well as objects in their grasp. I want each of you to become that accomplished."

The girls rested in a nearby cabin and used the spectroplasm in the dead pool next to their lodging to nourish themselves. The baroness decided to give the girls two full days to the subject of magic. Nasra drew nine icons representative of each element in the air with her orb and then extended several lines between them. Nasra called it an element web, showing how each element interacts with each other.

These icons were interconnected by white, red, grey, and black webbing that Nasra described as being the neutral, besting, supporting, and canceling. Spectroplasm was the only element that had a dark counterpart that the baroness said she'd explain later. Catherine began her instruction with the girls sitting before them on three tree stumps in the edge of the meadow.

"First I want you all to understand how magic

relates to the body. When ghosts cast magic, they drain spectroplasm from their husks. Usually this is a small amount but the more complicated spells can drain the spectroplasm entirely. These powerful spells can kill a ghost if they aren't careful or if they don't replenish their energy soon afterward. Shades are similar, you will require more spectroplasm but also food to replenish your bodies, though the latter can wait a bit longer."

"The danger for shades is that a complex spell might kill a shade's mortal body and destroy their husk. You are further at risk if you're malnourished, if there isn't a spirit indwelling your body, and if your spirit has been gone from the body too long. So be careful when casting magic, eat before coming to Amalgam, make sure your indweller is inside your body, and mind your time while in the realm."

"Now, there are two magic orders ascribing to the ghost's loyalty: the Order of the Dark Phoenix and the Order of Messina. Both of these orders are similar but the Dark Phoenix captured control of the brilzen and anemos elements. We have found ways to counter attacks from these elements but we are still at a disadvantage in every magic battle we encounter with a Phoenix Loyalist."

Having explained the orders, she now delved deeper into the study of each element. Catherine then turned their attention to the web. She named each element: cinzeré as fire, aquis as water, anemos for wind, brilzen as lightning, hagio for holy, dwella for dew, necrosidium and biosidium as the death and life elements, and spectroplasm that had no alternative name. Resting in the center of the web is the hagio element that Catherine said was the most powerful element in Amalgam. She explained that spells like aramous and reterium where low-level hagio charms, but its stronger incantations were restricted to all ghosts but the barons, angels, elite reapers, and the Dark Phoenix.

Catherine described the brilzen element as being the second most powerful element owning to its ability to destroy dew barriers, penetrate most wind, water, and fire spells, and manipulate biosidium and necrosidium. She said brilzen magic can propel ghosts across the realm, cause devastating attacks, and noted that it's the element found in the city's chandeliers. She said only spectroplasm spells would be best in countering lightning attacks, because they are neutral to each other.

The dew element, Catherine explained, augments the water and fire elements, while augmenting or limiting the abilities of spectroplasm. The anemos element could best dew, water, and fire, but was neutral to spectroplasm. Catherine said that the Phoenix has effectively used the wind element to create distancing and throwing attacks, impassible wind barriers, and redirecting spells and aerial combat units.

Spectroplasm augmented fire and water charms but many of its spells were most effective on its own. Catherine explained that dark spectroplasm is pure poison, created when spectroplasm becomes stale and stagnant. She explained that it looks like oil yet motionless even if something is thrown into it. Catherine cautioned the girls that it would take their lives instantly and to be careful if they come across some. She said that dark spectroplasm was neutral to every element except dew, which could purify the spoiled element until it returned to spectroplasm.

"The last two, biosidium and necrosidium are elements that naturally occur in the New City," said Catherine. "We find the elements on scenes of high spiritual turbulence such as recent births, deaths, or celebrations focusing on these events like Halloween and the Day of the Dead. In the right amount, these two elements allow ghosts and shades to shift between the ethereal and material planes and can even give or take mortal life."

"They're the least understood elements because they occur so randomly. A maternity ward or morgue has failed to create a single drop yet a single birth or murder can create plenty of it. Necrosidium and Biosidium link to and appear in the gathering plans from their source in the New City, which is why we established Baronsward Citadel to prevent the Dark Phoenix from accessing it. With the citadel destroyed, we'll have to be extra vigilant guarding the plains. Messina gave us a few portals that create these elements so we can access the New City at will. The Dark Phoenix however, relies on his Spirit and his servants to enter the New City."

"How so?" asked Lauren.

"Because the Vessel's Spirit fled Amalgam and therefore, the New City, the Phoenix can indwell susceptible people to induce labor or persuade them to kill others. In the past, his vessels have caused accidents and killed people in order for his servants to enter and exit the living realm. Now, let's begin with the basic defensive spells. Stand up!"

The girls stood and stretched before standing attentively awaiting instruction.

"First, summon your weapons!" said Catherine as a test to see how well they had learned this skill from Nasra; each did it perfectly.

"Excellent! This one is the general shield charm, and because they are quick protection spells, you don't have to summon the holy magic first. Grasp your weapon tightly and repeat after me! Speak loud and clearly! ARAMOUS!"

"ARAMOUS!" said the girls. Their weapons trembled in the girl's hands. Lauren's sword shone gold and turned slightly hot, as did Amy's trident and Renee's staff. Lauren almost let her sword fall and Amy and Renee struggled likewise. Nasra put her arms around Renee to steady her as Catherine approached.

"If your weapon is trembling and warm to the touch you've cast the spell correctly and protecting you at this very moment is an invisible barrier that most attacks cannot penetrate. Observe! *Purgen cinzeré!*"

A fireball shot out of Catherine's sword and

raced towards Renee but dissolved before touching her. Catherine tested Amy and Lauren before moving on.

"Next is the repel spell that will redirect the attack keeping it live to strike elsewhere. This charm can also repel objects so remember this if you're in trouble."

"With this spell, your weapons should be relaxed as the magic isn't as strong, so loosen your grips and repeat after me, RETERIUM!"

"RETERIUM," said the girls.

As Lauren held her sword gently, she could see it shining a dim gold and remained cool and easier to control. Catherine shot the same spell as before that leapt from her sword and approached Amy before swiftly turning away, striking a tree. The tree fell, Lauren and Renee screamed and backed away as the tree collapsed toward them but Amy cast the reterium spell and it swung far behind Catherine.

"Well done, Amy," said Catherine. Lauren was breathing rapidly; scared for her life. Amy however raised her head triumphantly at Catherine's praise. She remembered the guard in the forest using the spell and made sure to memorize it in case any tree limbs tried to pin her down again.

"As you can see, this live spell can remain dangerous. In order to repel and dissolve it totally, repeat after me. RETERIUM INVODIMI!"

The girls repeated Catherine and the baroness shot a spell at Lauren this time. It swerved away and dissipated to nothingness in the air. Catherine spent the rest of their "day" teaching them more defensive spells such as *flectis*, the reflection spell, *invodimi*, the dispel charm with its numerous variants, and the attraction and levitation spells *exeralure* and *ascentate*. She taught the girls how to give extra incantations to the previous charms to add elements with the "erinomi" spell and power "magnus" to the reflected attacks. Catherine said that since Phoenix had captured control of the brilzen and anemos elements, she'd have to teach them how to guard against them.

"Now, to cast a charm from any element you must first summon the element through your weapon. I want to begin with an ice charm, so say *aquis!*"

The girls did as instructed, each got it right the second time; their weapons shone a light blue. Their hands felt like they were dipped in water and a cool chill glided over their hands.

"To cast this charm, say *discus aramous!*" said the baroness.

The girls repeated Catherine's spell; about their forearms formed cool ice rings that created a round ice shield with a pool of water suspended inside the shield face. Catherine created one and then said a spell that changed the training room's sky where dark clouds gathered directly above them. She held up her shield to the sky when a strong bolt crawled from the sky and struck the liquid water in the baroness' shield. The lightning spread about the water and broke the ice ring surrounding it. The electrified ice particles exploded outward, zinging through the air and burying into the ground far from Catherine. The shield repaired itself instantly.

"This shield will protect you from any electrified charms the Phoenix or his witches will send for you. Because the shield is so strong and forged from a powerful ice spell, it takes considerable time to fabricate. Phoenix's brilzen strikes are often very fast which is why we use a fire charm to redirect quick incoming spells in conjunction with our ice shields. We discovered Amalgam fire is partly ionized which we've magically enhanced to allow the fire to conduct electricity. This cinzeré spell will send the lightning snaking through the flames allowing us to contain it safely for a few seconds and in this time, we send it into walls, the ground, or somewhere other than our bodies. Let's try it."

Catherine told them to imbue their weapons with the cinzeré element, which they did with little difficulty. Shining orange-red, their weapons felt as if they were wearing warm gloves. Catherine then demonstrated the spell as before. Another lightning bolt snaked from the sky, and the baroness raised her hand at the incoming blast saying, "*cinzeré voltus!*" Fire exploded from her hand and met the bolt and she swished her hand at the ground; the flame fell to the grass carrying the lightning in it. She tested the girls thoroughly until they mastered both commands.

Catherine then taught the girls more attacks

using each element such as the cinzeré spells purgen cinzeré, pilari cinzeré, and cinzeré en volpus. Amy excelled at aquis charms as they learned geysen aquis, purgen aquis, and vorten aquis. Dew charms were Renee's favorite, because she loved the protection they provided but her particular interest was destruct charms like olien begas and gilren syven that opened access to restricted areas. Lauren liked the spectroplasm element and favored the charms spectro klasto, spectrogeal, and spectrograven. They finished the day going over their spells and retired to their cabin.

The fourth and fifth days were for weapons training. The fourth day, the girls were taught how to fight with their weapons, teaching them how to strike, parry, the vital spots, everything. Catherine described the focus of their fifth lesson as mastering combat during Amalgam's seasons. She had the girls materialize their weapons to battle her and Nasra. Amy and Renee followed Lauren's lead as Lauren easily acquired the massive instruction as if she already knew it.

Catherine also noticed that Lauren advanced faster than Amy and Renee in physical combat and attacked her more aggressively. Lauren fought as if she was an experienced swordswoman and soon she and the baroness were fighting alone while Nasra fought Renee and Amy. Catherine swung her sword at Lauren's head that Lauren easily blocked. The baroness followed with a couple more attacks. Lauren countered, parried, and attacked well. The baroness fought Lauren so intensely that Nasra easily beat Amy and Renee because Catherine and Lauren's battle diverted their attention.

The petals burst off the flowers as Catherine and Lauren moved about. Lauren swung her sword for Catherine's head. The baroness ducked, swirled, and took a swipe at Lauren's back. Lauren swung her arms around from her previous attack and blocked Catherine's strike. Lauren brought her left elbow down and hit Catherine's wrists, making the baroness lower her sword and temporarily knocking her off balance. Lauren then used her sword hand to attempt a downward strike at Catherine's neck. The baroness hurriedly regained her footing to kick her to the ground before Lauren cut her.

Lauren fell; her sword landed away from her as she collapsed. Catherine came for a downward strike as Lauren cast *exeralure* on her sword. It arrived in her hands in time for Lauren to protect herself. Catherine observed Lauren's eyes, they were turning blue and a cool vapor emanated from them. She pressed the sword harder and Lauren struggled against Catherine's sword. Lauren's eyes grew colder and her arms grew stronger enabling her to push the baroness back.

Lauren stood and attacked Catherine faster and stronger, and in her flurry of attacks, she nicked the baroness. Catherine swiftly disarmed Lauren once again and tripped her up. Lauren lay sprawled on the ground defenseless. Catherine asked her to yield; Lauren did, but the baroness didn't remove her sword even as Lauren tried to stand.

"I want you to realize, Lauren, that the Phoenix Cage mark is special. It allows its bearer to siphon off the powers of cold souls, particularly the Dark Phoenix. I've fought the Phoenix several times with it and was able to defeat him, but without his secret I couldn't finish him. Yet, the Phoenix Cage mark retained the magic I siphoned long ago and as its current bearer, you now have access to it. But be careful Lauren, if your anger isn't kept in check you could end up causing more harm than you intend."

Catherine revealed a cut on her left forearm. She removed her sword from Lauren's chin and sheathed it. The baroness grasped her cut and healed it with a charm.

"That's good news then, it should help me against my father's killer."

"Remember what I said about revenge, Lauren. It doesn't seem like you'll need the mark if it comes down to a physical fight. Your sword skills have been enhanced by the Phoenix, but your magical skills are still lacking, so develop them in your free time."

Before resuming their battle, Catherine reached out at the sun as if she was trying to grasp it, and brought her hand down. The sun was drug closer and the cool, spring-like field was set ablaze. The rest season changed to the burn season. The flames danced on the flowers leaves and the trees reacted similarly. The sweltering heat of the field briefly incapacitated the girls. The girls were crouched over gasping. As they struggled for breath, their uniforms changed from sweaters and heavy cloaks to thinner flame-resistant stockings and cloak, knee-length dress, and a shirt.

"What just happened?" asked Amy panting.

"The seasons in Amalgam change just that quickly," said Catherine. "You need to be prepared. If you were fighting the Phoenix Loyalists, they would have killed you while you caught your breath. Let's go on."

Nasra and the baroness fought the girls for a brief moment then gave the girls a break. Nasra pushed the sun farther than it originally was. Dark clouds formed in the sky and a heavy downpour ensued as the girls, sitting on a large rock in the meadow, tried in vain to avoid getting wet. Catherine instructed the girls to observe the trees. Their roots burst from the ground to suck in the water and dew.

"This is what Jasmine is hoping her tree will do to Castle Everlasting's barrier. The holes on the roots will suck in the dew and destroy the barrier for the animals to attack. We can't let that happen."

"Are you planning to destroy the tree?" asked Lauren.

"The animals have it in their grips now, that's not an option. Hopefully you'll be able to stop Jasmine from reclaiming her mark. Let's continue."

The ground was soaked in water, and they battled in a huge deluge. A large surge of rainwater and dew pushed the girls, Nasra, and the baroness from the meadow through the woods and downhill into a river.

Enraged that she was soaked and cold, Amy grabbed hold of a tree and when she found her balance, she ran for Nasra. A tidal wave rushed towards Nasra and she redirected it about her with a spell. Amy tried to stab Nasra in the back, but Nasra grabbed one of the trident's prongs and held Amy off. Nasra tossed Amy into the water and further downstream.

Renee managed to hold onto a large rock in the water and as Amy floated by screaming, she extended her staff to her. Amy grasped it and Renee pulled her onto the rock. Nasra released the wave and allowed it to carry her to the girls. The wave took, Nasra and the girls off the rock and over a ten-foot waterfall.

"I CAN'T SWIM!" said Renee.

On the riverbank, Catherine and Lauren fought as Nasra and her friends tumbled over the falls. Catherine pushed Lauren against a thin tree and with a powerful stroke, cut the tree down as Lauren moved back before the baroness severed her in half. The tree fell and extended out across the falls to the other shore. Catherine jumped over the log and fought to push Lauren over, but Lauren was able to move around the baroness and stepped onto the trunk. She hoped to get to the other side, but Catherine, having witnessed Nasra and the others go over, felt Lauren needed to join her friends. Catherine was able to get Lauren off balance and then kicked her over, the baroness jumped in after her.

The waterfall poured into a lake where a whirlpool formed and drug them all into it. The women fell into a cavern crashing into a pool at the bottom. Inside there was one ramp spiraling up along the wall to the surface but the entrance closed far above. Lauren and Amy were treading in the water recovering from their long fall.

"This is *not* how I intended on spending the start of my sophomore year, Lauren," said Amy strongly. "I swear I'm going to make you pay for this. You'll wish you'd never become a baron."

Lauren didn't let Amy's threat bothered her but realized several of them was missing.

"Where's Renee?" asked Lauren.

"She probably drowned. You know she can't swim," said Amy.

"I—I'm here!" said Renee gasping. She was laying face-up on the rock ramp of the cavern.

"Great, where's Catherine and Nasra?" asked Lauren.

"Up–up there," said Renee pointing above. Lauren and Amy looked up to see Catherine and Nasra running up the ramp as if dogs were chasing them.

"Where are they going?" asked Lauren.

"I told you Catherine was a coward!" said Amy.

The pool began trembling between the girls and they backed away. It bubbled increasingly until a large monster shot up from the water. Lauren and

Amy screamed; it was an enormous worm with rows upon rows of teeth in a treacherous mouth with beady eyes directly above it and nearly a hundred legs on its body. It reached down to swallow up Amy when a fire spell struck the creature and buried its head in the left wall above Renee. Lauren looked above to see Catherine who said, "What are you waiting for? Get out of the pool, pick up Renee, and kill the shenga!"

Lauren and Amy swam for the ramp. Renee was already standing and the girls orbed and flew up the chamber. The shenga was unconscious for a long time and the girls had made it halfway up the ramp before it awoke and charged after them. Exhausted after fighting Catherine and Nasra the girls reverted to ghost form to run up the stairs. Their pace was slow and the shenga had countless legs.

It caught up with them and grabbed Renee who was the most fatigued. It lunged to the level below and carried Renee back down. Renee dropped her staff; Lauren bent down quickly to get it and ran after her. Amy hesitated before deciding to continue up the ramp when Catherine sent a spell blocking the way forward.

"Not being a coward are you, Amy?" asked Catherine.

Amy ran back down to prove she wasn't afraid. Amy and Lauren raced after the creature. The shenga was carrying Renee down to where it emerged which was no longer a pool but a lava pit.

"Help me!" cried Renee. Lauren realized they

would never catch up.

"Wait, Amy," said Lauren. Lauren pointed Renee's staff at the ramp and said "*Purgen cinzeré!*" The ground beneath them collapsed. As they fell, Lauren continued to cast the spell, breaking each floor until they landed one floor underneath the shenga and Renee. As the beast rounded, Lauren and Amy stood at the ready.

"How do we stop it?" asked Amy.

"It's headed toward a lava pit. It might be sensitive to ice. We could make an ice wall," said Lauren.

"But Renee could get crushed," said Amy. Lauren contemplated this quickly as the shenga approached. It was ten feet in front of them when Lauren shouted, "*Purgen aquis!*"

A blast of rushing water issued from her sword as Renee and the beast plowed through. It struck the shenga causing it great pain from the sound of its grating wail. Amy backed up and lost her balance on the ramp edge, her arms swinging in the air. Lauren flattened herself against the wall. The shenga let loose of Renee, tossing her away before rolling over into the lava pit. As it turned over, the shenga pushed Amy off the ledge and Renee fell soon after. The shenga descended at an arch a short distance from the falling girls. Lauren moved swiftly to the edge, pointed her sword at the lake and shouted "*Geysen aquis!*"

A portion of the lava cooled swiftly to rock and then cracked as a geyser of water rushed up, lifting the girls high into the air. The shenga fell into the lava and re-emerged, lunging upward for the girls.

"Renee!" shouted Lauren as she threw her staff up in the air, her arm strengthened as she swung it. The staff flew up swiftly and passed the shenga. Renee caught it and aimed to cast a water spell but the shenga's skin changed to grayish blue. Lauren saw the shenga's transformation and looking to the lava pit, she discovered it had turned to ice. The shenga opened its mouth and swallowed Renee and Amy while the shenga's head slammed into the top of the cavern breaking rock from the ceiling.

The shenga's skin became transparent; Lauren saw its white skeleton, fluids, and Renee and Amy inside. Renee's silhouette pointed her staff to its skin and cast a muddled spell. The worm's stomach erupted in flames and the shenga flailed about in excruciating pain. It regurgitated Renee and Amy and screeched louder than ever. The fluid inside extinguished the flames and covered Amy and Renee in sticky stinking slime.

Its skin turned yellow, Lauren assumed it was dew but she knew only lightning could best dew. Renee and Amy seemed dazed as they hit the ground floor and as the shenga lunged toward them. Lauren pointed her sword and shouted "G*eysen aquis!*" while dragging her sword from the left chamber wall to the right. The geyser issued horizontally instead of vertically, pushing the two out of the way as the shenga bit into the ground fracturing its teeth.

The creature lay still, blocking the water from battering Amy and Renee against the right wall. Its skin turned silver, Lauren thought this was spectroplasm so she pointed her sword and said, "*Spectrogeal!*" The blast from her sword struck the worm and solidified it and the pit. Renee stood after she rested and crossed over too it, then knocked against its hard shell.

"It's petrified!" said Renee. Applause came from above, Nasra and Catherine shouted down to them, "Well done!"

"Good job girls," said Catherine as they left cavern and swam for the shore. Renee rode on Nasra's back and as they surfaced, the girls all sat on the grass under the hot sun to dry. "Relax for the rest of the day; our last day is reserved for something special."

"That was an impressive battle with the shenga. Not many beginning guards has used such quick wit," said Nasra. "They certainly are strong and smart, especially Lauren."

"Yes, her powers eclipse that of normal shades. Watching her throw Renee's staff passed the shenga is a testament to that. Has anything else been happening to you, Lauren?"

"Renee told me I have the power of pyschometry but when I touched a ring my entire bedroom changed to my mother's showing…"

Lauren hesitated; she didn't want to embarrass Anita in her absence.

"A vision of her earlier days, but it was so real,"

said Lauren.

"That is odd," said Catherine. "For you to have lifelike visions I would guess that your powers have been enhanced by the Phoenix mark."

"Also, I've heard my mother's voice in the Baker's Creek graveyard screaming that she can't leave her body," said Renee.

"That's where my father was killed," said Lauren.

"The graveyard?" asked Nasra as she looked at Catherine. "The possessed reaper from the Procession's last stop was near the graveyard."

"Curious," said Catherine. "I'll have Mina look into it. Until then, stay away from there. We'll handle it."

Catherine and Nasra led the girls to the cabin where they rested for their final day of training.

CHAPTER THIRTEEN
THE AMALGAM THEORY

In the morning of the seventh day, Catherine woke Lauren earlier than the rest. Lauren was fatigued and the baroness cut short her well-deserved sleep. Catherine was cautious not to wake the others. However, Amy could be a very light sleeper when she wanted to and she'd been waiting to see why the baroness favored Lauren.

Catherine took Lauren into a small grove of bushes and sat her down on a stump. Amy followed carefully, remaining out of sight and outside the thicket. She retrieved a capsule from Sigpos' care package. The capsule transformed into a mantis that nearly elicited a loud scream from Amy who managed to stifle it and used her mark's magic to turn the ugly mantis into a pretty ladybug. It crawled into the bushes to eavesdrop on their conversation while Amy listened in through her gossiper mark. Catherine sat across from Lauren and looked into her eyes.

"Sorry for waking you so early, but what I have to say is for you alone."

"What is it?" asked Lauren sleepily.

"It's a revelation of great importance but I don't know how you'll respond to what I'm going to tell you. I hope you can handle it."

"Catherine, you're scaring me," said Lauren. "Unless you're going to tell me my mother is dead, I don't think that what you have to say can be any more disturbing than that."

"It might, but here goes. Did you ever wonder why you were chosen to receive this task of baroness?"

"No. You and Messina made it very clear. I ran into the Phoenix's column and received his powers. I am a shade and the Phoenix is partly responsible for killing my father. I want to make sure no other family experiences what I have and I had to become a baron to do this."

Lauren hadn't believed this before, but as she's witnessed the war brewing in Amalgam she realized she didn't want to see anything similar happen in Mortalland.

"That's not all to it. The Phoenix's column is for the most part impregnable. It has electrocuted or burned to death every ghost that came close to it. However, you are the only one who hasn't perished."

Lauren sat slightly surprised but she was still very tired. She was happy to be alive whereas everyone else had died, but wasn't particularly curious as to why. She waited for the baroness to continue, but Catherine was awaiting a response from Lauren.

"Don't you want to know why?" asked Catherine incredulously.

"If this is the big surprise, I guess," Lauren shrugged her shoulders.

"I should have waiting until you were more alert," said Catherine running her hand through her hair and then down her face. She held her hand under her chin and scrutinized Lauren's drowsy face, considering the best way to deliver her message.

"You didn't die because of your mark."

"The Phoenix Cage mark? I didn't have it until Messina gave it to me and that was after I'd entered the column."

"No, your other mark!"

"This mark can't do anything!" Lauren looked skeptically at her left hand mark of the blood cup.

"It's kept you healthy from your painful disease and saved your life in the Phoenix column."

"How so?"

"The mark's magic protected you from the column's fire while simultaneously assuming the Dark Phoenix's traits. I'm sure he was dumbfounded as to why you didn't die and the answer was so close and yet so cleverly disguised.

Luckily all marks appear on the right hand, and the Phoenix probably didn't think you'd have two marks. Even if he did check your left hand he wouldn't have been able to see your mark of the Holy Grail."

Lauren sat impassively, she'd heard of the Holy Grail before, but thought it was something reserved for Christian mythology and never believed it existed. She tried to grasp the gravity of this *revelation,* yet cynicism substituted for surprised. However, since Catherine seemed quite serious, she'd had to ask questions that didn't sound sarcastic. She thought of the Grail's presumed function and offered, "So…does that mean I have…eternal life?"

"No!" Catherine chuckled nervously. "It means you're apart of an important page in history. The Grail caught the Son's blood at the crucifixion and one of its suspected functions was to give eternal life. Yet it serves a different purpose in Amalgam." Catherine scratched her head again and wrestled with her words, choosing them carefully before continuing. "The Judge is the architect of justice, and his plans are set in motion long before we realize it. When the cup caught the Son's blood, it was anointed with a specific mandate in Amalgam."

"To strip the Phoenix of his immortality?" Lauren preempted.

"No. No…not that, his secret will do that remember?"

"Oh yeah. Then what's it for?"

"That requires a bit more explanation that goes into the creation of Amalgam itself. What I'm about to tell you is just a theory, what Messina told me *she* believes is the Judge's purpose for creating this realm. Have you ever questioned what function Amalgam could serve?"

Lauren thought hard and agreed that the conversation should have waited until morning.

"Give me a minute," said Lauren.

"Take your time," Catherine smiled.

Lauren's first guess was obviously purging sin, but according to her Sunday school lessons, the Son died for man's sins. The Judge created Amalgam centuries after the Son's resurrection so what function could Amalgam serve. Lauren thought hard, she wish she'd paid more attention in church and maybe then she could more easily answer Catherine's brain-teasers. Lauren thought about the virtuous un-baptized; good people who died without being baptized or were too young to make that decision themselves. She offered this to Catherine, and though she congratulated Lauren on a good guess, the baroness said she was wrong again.

"Think more along the line about what the Dark Phoenix told you in the meadow."

Lauren remembered the Dark Phoenix's desire for ultimate reconciliation.

"Was Amalgam created to reconcile all souls to God?" asked Lauren.

Catherine smiled, "Not quite, but that's what I wanted you to say. What if Amalgam was created not to reconcile all souls to God, but rather, to test that theory particularly as to how it relates to one person?"

"The Dark Phoenix?"

"Yes."

"Why? Why does God want to test him?"

"God tests us all, but some more than others, to see where our loyalties truly lie. He's done it before remember?" Catherine arched an eyebrow.

"Job," said Lauren.

"Correct."

"That's my favorite book of the Bible, but it doesn't seem to make sense. Doesn't an all-knowing being like the Judge know what's in our hearts?"

"Yes, but there are those who don't know what's in their own hearts and they need an example to follow. Job suffered so that we could see his faith overcome his pain. Yet, every generation or so, one needs a new lesson."

"What lesson?"

"A lesson on character. There are those who wander the earth, going back and forth in it seeking to get any soul they can to join them in their *crusade*. In the end, their crusade is self-serving and whatever excuse they give for their actions, *no matter how logical it may sound*, is actually just a ruse to attain their goal. Those that follow them are to be consumed with them and many of those that stand against these people make a great sacrifice."

"What sacrifice?"

"Death, delayed summoning, loneliness, confusion, anger, and some even turn into cold souls," said Catherine.

"Who are you talking about this time?"

"I'm talking about Nasra, Devon, Jasmine, Etienne, you, me, and all the ghosts of Amalgam. We're all apart of this test. Take for instance this Jasmine. She's a servant of the Dark Phoenix and single-handedly has shed more blood in the past centuries than you could imagine. Her rage is fueled by a false hope, and in her confusion, she's aligned herself with those who stand against the Judge. I met her when she arrived here about three hundred years ago and all she wanted was to avenge her murdered husband."

"I know; I saw it in my dreams. She was cursing you for telling her to move on."

"I advised her to let her past go and she refused. She went on to wreak havoc in Amalgam, the Procession raid is but a taste, and because she has refused to move on, others remain stagnant."

"Nasra?" asked Lauren remembering Jasmine alluded to her in the vision. Catherine nodded.

"And not just her, look at Etienne, immortal with nearly a hundred followers, all with longer than natural lives. If they're following him through and through, their fate is a most undesirable one."

"Why?"

"Etienne has killed a lot of people and so have his followers most likely. His excessive ambition and sheer will to defy the Judge's commandments have brought upon him a most severe punishment when he finally enters Amalgam."

"How do you know what he's done if you can't see his action's in Mortalland? Densen said the mirror dedicated to him was clouded."

"His victims have come to Amalgam. We captured the angel Raziel in Paris five hundred years ago and we believe he possessed the djemsheed. He didn't have it in his possession but about twenty-three years later word spread across the city about a man who owned a cup that gave everlasting life. Gossip travels fast about such things, but not as swiftly as those that knew about the cup ended up dead and most of them were killed by his hand!" Lauren was flabbergasted at the number Catherine hinted.

"From his death toll, we've be able to track his movement. When he arrived in Baker's Creek, in one night over twenty colonial-era guards were killed at Governor Watlington's estate, several more at a nearby dock, and of course, one particularly disgruntled bride."

"Jasmine!" said Lauren intrigued.

"Yes. And from my conversations with Devon before he left to roam the Wilds it seems that Etienne had in mind a plan to break the Mortalland Rule."

"What kind of a plan?"

"One that would prove the existence of ghosts and the afterlife to the living world. I don't know how Etienne was planning on achieving this nor did

Devon but this task lead him to pursue the Mortalland Seal."

"Hmm...why did Devon leave the castle for the Wilds?" asked Lauren. "I can't imagine anyone wanting to live among those animals."

"He has his reasons. Maybe you'll be able to find out but don't worry about his safety just yet. Devon's a powerful ghost; he can take care of himself. He and Vincent make an awesome combination; after all, Vincent's magic enhanced the illusions in this room. Imagine a place where Vincent powers his illusions with an endless source of spectroplasm. It would be quite amazing wouldn't it?"

"Yes," said Lauren honestly.

"It would also offer a great deal of protection, wouldn't you say?"

"I imagine it would."

"Of course it would!" smiled Catherine. "They'll be safe for a while, but the Dark Phoenix and Jasmine *will* penetrate the forest and Devon's life will be in peril."

"He'd better have a great reason for leaving the castle if he's going to be at their mercy," said Lauren introspectively.

"I guess he does, but I've gone off base, who do Etienne, Devon and Nasra all have in common?"

"Jasmine," said Lauren, remembering that she needed Devon for the linking tome.

"And who does Jasmine serve?"

"The Dark Phoenix."

"And what has happened to all the people related to Jasmine?"

"They're still here in Amalgam or living forever in Mortalland."

"But what haven't they done?"

"They…they haven't…left…these worlds."

"And in this world and the mortal, who are we trying to return to?"

"The Judge."

"And who stands in their way?"

* * * *

"Phoenix!" said Jasmine riding a snowy white eagle named Trinity and surrounded by a swarm of fowls of all kinds. The Dark Phoenix atop an exact replica of Jasmine's eagle swooped down from the sky and united his eagle into hers. They surveyed the forest raid from the sky in a basket command post about Trinity's neck that looked like a crown from a distance that could sit three.

"What is Jasmine?" asked the Child Phoenix. He wore a mask similar to Jasmine's only it had two heads not three; the one missing from Jasmine's mask was his face. He was stern and patient, his mood was calm as he talked with her.

"This forest is impenetrable. You could get us through so what are you waiting for?"

"I'm looking for another way around."

"WHY?" shouted Jasmine.

"I don't like the plan."

"THIS IS YOUR PLAN! WHAT DON'T YOU LIKE ABOUT IT AND I'LL MAKE IT SO THAT YOU DO?"

"The problem is Devon, Jasmine," said the Phoenix sharply. "If what you've told me about his powers is true then *when* we capture him he may never tell us the location of the linking tome even with prolonged torture!"

"What are you saying?"

"We can run in there and capture him, but perhaps we should wait until the Court moves."

"Let the Court take him?" Jasmine was confused.

"Obviously they know we're here for him, you've killed the guards they sent to arrest you. But don't you think they'll try again?"

Jasmine nodded slowly, contemplating his words.

"They must know we need the book for the tree to work; they know Devon knows where it is. Baron Catherine must know! They know we won't leave until we capture Devon so they'll have to send someone here to get him. They can't use the portals so they're going to send more guards."

"They'll die, not even the whole of the Morrigan Army can stand against the animals without the Horn of Olives. That instrument is crafted into the rock at Castle Everlasting and it's too dangerous for them to bring it here."

"Right! So what are they going to do?"

"Send small numbers…and…circumvent

us…how?" Jasmine asked thoughtfully. Her mind was racing to catch up with the Phoenix's preemptive plan.

"More importantly is who? Their mission is to find the linking tome, to destroy it. The Court has been trying for years. Devon has known where it is all this time and he's refused to tell the Court. Who would they send to get Devon to divulge the location of that book? Their trying to thwart our plans, Jasmine, you must realize it."

"I don't Phoenix. If Devon will refuse to tell the Court, and if they know as we do that he may not submit to torture, then they must know our plan will fail."

"The Court knows he's too great a risk if we were to capture him. Events have been set in motion so that Devon will reveal the location of that linking tome. It's inevitable at this point; time has finally caught up with him. They'll send someone and if we can get close to *this person* we may not have to torture Devon, but the recipient of his message. But I wonder who they'll send?"

* * * *

"So how does this concern my mark?" Lauren asked.

"Consider this, what does a Phoenix symbolize?"

"Well…it dies, then comes back to life in a new body."

"Who does that sound like?" asked Catherine.

"Jesus," said Lauren.

"Sin offends the Judge correct?"

"Yes."

"And as you know, we call the Dark Phoenix the Great Sinner who purports to be the Savior of ghosts and men right? Therefore, by his logic, he believes he is Christ."

"Right."

"Now I'm going to tell you an interesting fact. The Grail is a powerful relic, too powerful to exist in the material world in its physical state. I was told by Messina herself that she was sent to suffuse the Grail within a bloodline, one whose genealogy tracks back to Jesus' family."

Lauren began to tremble as she buckled under the weight of Catherine's words. Catherine leaned forward and held her hands tightly so that she wouldn't run away. Catherine could see her chest rising rapidly and her hands shaking.

"The Son of Man didn't have any direct descendants, but he did have half-brothers and half-sisters. Messina suffused the Grail within one of them and for generations it has passed through their blood descendants. The Judge instilled an instinct within each of these individuals to baptize their children at birth. This tradition continued without fail until it expired the day you were born."

Lauren tried to run but Catherine held her tight. Her head hurt, and she longed to rid herself of Amalgam. She thought she'd wanted to wake from a dream on the gathering night, but here is where the fairytale should have ended. Catherine barely managed to hold Lauren as she screamed, *"I can't believe this! I can't believe my dad would put this on me, that God would do this to me! I hate you Catherine!"*

Even Amy was in awe at Catherine's revelation and she sat close to the bushes and listened as Lauren screamed. For a moment, she forgot their feud and realized Lauren was not lying when she said the Court had given her more responsibility since she arrived. Then Amy remembered the rumors she spread and with Lauren's familial relation to the Judge, she feared Lauren could have unrestrained retribution. Yet Amy remained cool and plotted how she'd get herself out of this mess. She listened as Catherine began again.

"Your test is to discover why this tradition was broken, why you've never been or decided to be baptized. You, like the Phoenix, also struggle with the Judge. You'll have to struggle to remain pure!"

Catherine struggled to hold Lauren still. Lauren had stood in her attempted flight but Catherine stood and pulled her close, holding her tight to her chest. In their scuffle, Lauren came close to the bushes and the ladybug leapt onto her guard clothes and buried itself in the fabric.

"If you don't decide to do these things, Lauren, you'll never materialize the Grail from within your blood *and that's the key!* It's apart of the final test for the Dark Phoenix to truly reconcile to the Judge."

The baroness let Lauren loose to run, and run

she did, far away. Catherine watched her flee into the wilderness where Lauren ran until she dropped from exhaustion and passed out.

* * * *

A warm sensation filled Lauren's body and soon she regained consciousness from a nightmare in which she struggled to free herself from a birdcage. As she lifted her head and focused her eyes, Lauren could see between trees and brush a brilliant pink-white light she knew was Messina. The radiance dimmed suddenly and the Metatron stood before her. Messina knelt down and extended her hand; Lauren took it and stood slowly with the angel. Messina's purple eyes gazed deep into Lauren's brown pupils.

"The shock isn't too great for you is it? Surely you've always had a burning desire to understand His reasons, its part of your nature as the Grail mark."

She offered her to sit down on a materialized swing extending from a tree branch; Lauren did and they swung gently and slowly.

"It's your frustration and anger at Him that frightens you, isn't it?"

"I don't understand why He punishes the people who love Him the most. He gives everything to people who don't even believe He *exists*! Look at Amy. She has the guy I like, she's popular even though she's mean, and her parents are still alive and together while Renee and I have lost one of ours. The list goes on, I've read how Christians were martyred, but maybe slaughtered is a better word. Didn't Nero feed Christians to wolves?"

"Yes, but it was lions not wolves," said Messina. Lauren sighed despairingly.

"Why won't God come down and help his servants every once in while?"

"He did, but He too was killed. Yet He came into this world knowing He had to die in order to save us, it was this love for humankind that He sacrificed Himself. God has given us the will to choose to obey and love Him or refuse to."

"And those that don't are sent to Hell right?" asked Lauren. "Kind of selfish isn't? Love me or suffer forever in Hell?"

"That's the one directive God asks of every man and woman. You can live a life of wickedness, but if you honestly believe in Him, you might have a chance at salvation. The Judge is everlasting love and He doesn't desire to see anyone of his children punished. He is not some boogey man many people make Him out to be, but the Judge is a God of Justice too, and sometimes his children deserve punishment. You've never met Lucifer, but I can tell you, it's hopeless to reconcile him back to the Lord because he doesn't want to be reconciled."

"Even after centuries in his fallen state, he still seeks to corrupt God's children, using free will as his excuse to lead men and women from God into his ranks. '*Be your own God!*' he said to the angels before he began his futile war for the Throne. In this world, the Dark Phoenix offers a similar excuse, *'I'll reconcile you to God!'* in effect, saying he is God. Small wonder the two couldn't cooperate when the Dark Phoenix entered Hell; there cannot be two gods, yet, their pride is blinding them from realizing this."

"But if God is all powerful, why doesn't he just do away with Phoenix and Lucifer, why do we have to face all this temptation and frustration, why can't He just put the good people back in Heaven?" Lauren asked.

"That day is coming, but until then we must obey the Judge's commandments because of your distant ancestor's choices. We must choose who we will serve, ourselves, God, the Devil, and in this world, The Dark Phoenix. We live according to our beliefs, but only *one* is the Way. Despite your angst and your jaded faith, you know where you stand, Lauren, you're upset because you want to experience that which is deemed sinful because you don't see anything wrong with it."

"*I DON'T ALRIGHT!*" said Lauren strongly as she stood to walk around. "I don't see what's wrong with my dreams, what I want to do with my life. I don't want to be tied down to fighting some God wanna-be. I want to live my life without this hex over my head."

"If that is what you think this mandate is then I'm sorry we pressed it upon you. *I* think the Judge wanted you to stop chasing the answers you seek in your spare time, and live your life discovering the solutions through your work in Amalgam. A unique opportunity to be sure, a chance you seem to want to pass on. But remember what you said in Catherine's chamber and how you felt upon seeing your father in the graveyard before you dismiss this task because you don't want this hex."

"That hurts, Messina," said Lauren honestly ceasing her pacing.

"It should, and it can happen again and again if the Phoenix wins. Even though it seems you've been destined to this task I can tell you honestly that that is not the case. You have to do one more thing before you truly become a baroness. You must show your mark of the Grail to someone other than Catherine and me, as we are the only two who know of it thus far. No one can see the mark unless you have accepted the Judge's mandate to become a baroness in your heart. When you have shown it, you'll have chosen your path."

"Have you forgotten Amy told the nation I'm the new baron?" asked Lauren as she resumed her slow stroll.

"The Judge has granted me intricate powers over this realm. I can easily erase that information from the minds of every ghost in Amalgam, even yours, but I won't on His orders."

"And why not?" asked Lauren sternly.

"I believe you'll see that your barony is not a hex as you think, as many people see that following the Judge is not as hard as the unbelievers pretend it to be."

"The same way you believe I'll meet my father's killer?"

"Exactly," Messina smiled.

"The pressure is too much, now I'm Jesus' distant niece! Am I going to die like Him?"

"Who can say but the Judge?" asked Messina truthfully.

"And am I going to be held to some high standard because I *know* I'm not going to live up to it."

"We all fall short, and trust me; those blood ties are more for the Dark Phoenix than to pressure you. Like every servant of God, particularly those in leadership positions, there is a higher standard upon you because of your purpose. Your mandate is to summon the Grail from your blood and in order to do so, to prevent tainting the cup itself, you must remain as pure as possible."

"Pure? You might as well say that I should join a convent."

"Try your best and remember, Catherine, Nasra, and me are here for you, not to mention your Advocate above," said Messina. "Swing some more, consider your options, and return to the cabin when you're ready."

Messina stood and began to walk away and Lauren sat on the swing when she remembered what Sigpos said to her in the scuttlebutt and decided to ask about it.

"Messina, Siggy said that you spoke a prophecy

long ago. I was wondering if that prophecy was about me."

"Judge for yourself," said Messina and she recited the prophecy to her and was gone as soon as she finished. Lauren opened her eyes on the ground where she had passed out. She saw the sun rising and as it bathed her face with warm rays Lauren thought over Messina's words and the prophecy. She could not help feeling incredibly stressed and sick. Her stomach was as tense as wood and her head hurt as if she'd fallen hard onto some concrete. She vomited were she sat before falling back asleep.

* * * *

The women waited around the cabin for Lauren for most of the seventh day. Baron Catherine stood at the door awaiting Lauren's return, watching unflinchingly for her figure. Renee paced inside the room, occasionally standing next to Catherine to get a glimpse of her.

"She's been gone for so long," said Renee. "What did you say to her, Catherine?"

"That's none of your business, Renee," said Nasra lying on her bed. "Be patient and sit down."

"Poor little Lauren, so much drama," began Amy mockingly. "First she loses her crush, then dies, then her father dies, then she gets some bad news and runs away. Can't she just handle her problems with some dignity? She'll never grow up!"

"Maybe her problems are more serious than

your's Amy. Don't be so judgmental," said Nasra.

"I wonder what she's doing. You think the shenga's got her?" asked Renee.

"Not likely," said Nasra, "Didn't you check to see if it was frozen solid?"

"She just needs some time," said Catherine wearily. "She's been given a great task and it's a bit overwhelming."

"Wait! Aren't we still in the training room? Just shut off the illusions and she'll probably be crying in the corner," Amy said nastily.

"QUIET AMY!" The baroness swirled around and shouted at Amy so loudly that made it Nasra flinch in her bed, Renee fell to the floor next to the baroness, and Amy hit the back of the cabin as if Catherine's voice shoved her into it. The baroness turned back around to look outside. Amy slid over into the corner and started to sob. For the rest of the day, the girls waited for Lauren and an hour before the time Catherine allotted for training ended, Lauren reappeared. She looked exhausted.

Catherine, Nasra, and Renee ran towards and surrounded her. Amy stood at the cabin entrance, seething with jealousy and rage. Just like her birthday party, Lauren threw a fit and got all the attention. Her ladybug, now a butterfly, flittered from Lauren's garments and returned to Amy's capsule. Now Amy had crucial information she could use to blackmail Lauren to get what she wanted or to make good on her threat in the shenga's pool, but she decided to wait and use it when it would suit her best.

"I'm sorry," said Catherine as she hugged Lauren.

"It's just too much Catherine," said Lauren. "It's a lot to ask, and it seems like I never had a choice."

"You do," said Catherine kneeling before her. "You can choose to do nothing; it's within your free will." Catherine distanced herself and Lauren from Renee and Nasra. "Many in the Grail's bloodline have come here and done just that and the war continued. You can make the same choice they did and let the decision go to your children."

"I can't let that happen. That's the problem; there's little room to say no. I pretty much have to," said Lauren.

"You've said yes to a difficult task, but over my years I have seen people say no to a mandate that takes hardly any sacrifice. And like I said before in my chamber; thank you!"

* * * *

Soon after Lauren's return, the baroness, Nasra, and the girls left Guard School for the House of Shades where Densen was waiting in the lobby for Catherine. The girls felt extremely odd having come from the baron's training room after a week of lessons and only forty-five minutes had gone by. Lauren felt like her old simple life (her parent's divorce and losing her crush indeed was simplistic now) had ended and been renewed into something more complex like a phoenix.

"Densen, any good news?" asked Catherine.

"Yes and bad news. The good news is that the Phoenix and Jasmine seem unable to penetrate the forest. The guards Lion Face sent to the Hobby contacted me right before they attempted to arrest Jasmine. They said the animals are stuck at the forest edge because the illusions lead them back to Elysian Fields. The guards never returned however and we fear they're dead. The animals in the Elysian Fields are too numerous to send any more guards. The Phoenix is using the animals to search the forest for the Hobby. The eagles would spot anyone coming close and alert the Phoenix."

Catherine thought for a moment and said to Nasra, "You'll have to go through the mountain and enter the forest from the north. Take the pass of the Oman pike. It's the most direct route."

"Any alternatives?" asked Nasra.

"Barack's Hole is the only other choice," said Catherine. "Both of these ancient stations have enough tunnels that should take you close to the forest unseen. Avoid flying too high to prevent the birds from spying your position. Hurry to the Pike or else you'll have to travel further to Barack's Hole. The seasons are about to change and if you're not through the pike by morning it may be impassable. Densen, lower the castle," said Catherine. He left promptly.

"You'll be able to fly right out, Nasra.

Godspeed ladies, and hopefully I'll see you soon," said Catherine.

The baroness left for Baronsguard. Nasra took the girls to the furthest elevator and went up. They walked up the stairs to the highest floor and went down the hall and up another staircase. Nasra opened the attic door and stood on the roof as the girls filed out.

The roof contained an entirely flat launch pad where the guards, ten in all, sat atop the beasts called the shade-rays awaiting Nasra and the girls. Their bodies were most similar to manta rays, but feathered with larger heads and had peacock-like feathers covering the stinger. Their legs were like ostriches, thin and bent at the joint. The rays stood as their white beady eyes stared down their riders as if they were against flying and even wearing saddles tonight. Four were set aside for the girls and Nasra.

"What are these shade-rays, Nasra?" asked Renee.

"They're Amalgam natives and predators of Mortalland shades. Rays, sirens, unicorns, and centaurs are among the few natives that are entirely tactile to shades. The rest of them only have anatomical parts used solely to destroy shades. Sirens went extinct during the Animal War and nearly all centaurs are loyal to the Dark Phoenix. Natives serve several functions and one is to rid Amalgam of any life forms that aren't supposed to be in the realm. The only beings shades can trust in this realm are ghosts and sadly not all ghosts."

Nasra and the girls boarded the rays. Lauren stepped on the stirrup fastened to its legs that made the ray bend its leg and give out a babyish cry. She seated herself on the saddle, stretched her legs out on its large fins, and held onto the reigns extending from the leather wound around the fins. Nasra instructed them that the trailing rays would follow the lead so they didn't have to worry about guiding them. They slowly rose up, guards following them and flew in a curve rounding about to fly over the House of Shades to the southeast.

CHAPTER FOURTEEN
BARACK'S HOLE

Nasra led the girls and guards from the floating island and swooped down to a lower elevation. Lauren gazed back at the castle; it shined like a Christmas tree with white lights and the golden dew barrier radiated creating a yellow brilliance like a second sun brightening the dark sky for miles. Through the passing clouds, Lauren could see the crater in her dreams below. A sprawling hole, it is as if the Judge snatched the missing earth from the ground. A lake was present in the crater and Lauren could see a small development where a large geyser issued as the castle returned to its original height. Lauren asked Nasra what it was.

"Geyser Worx, it's our spectroplasm processing facility. When Catherine raised the castle, we discovered spectroplasm seeping from the crater's center creating the lake. We built Geyser Worx to acquire, purify, and send it to our man-made aquifer under the castle's foundation via a geyser. The lake is almost tapped; we're becoming more dependent on spectroplasm from the Gorge of Genesis."

* * * *

They flew out of range of the fields and cruised gently into the starlit night sky of Amalgam. An eagle scout was flying a mile from their position. It turned away and flew east, screeching aloud alerting another bird yards away then another in succession until it reached a gestalt lord fowl that flew swiftly to the Phoenix in the Elysian Fields before the Illusionist Forest.

"They're coming," said Phoenix atop Trinity.

"Who?" asked Jasmine riding with the Phoenix.

"Nasra, Lauren, two other girls, and a host of guards from Castle Everlasting," said Child Phoenix.

"The girl who entered your column? Impossible, I locked her up in my tree."

"Inez said they freed her. Catherine must know why the girl survived my column. She must know what's special about Lauren. Since she's alive she could've retained some of my memories and powers."

"What were you thinking of when you regenerated?" asked Jasmine.

"Everything you told me about the linking tome,

my plan to level the castle, and Devon among other things. She's the one that's going to get Devon to talk!"

"They must have a death wish coming this way with so few."

"They're going for a discrete approach. Now it comes to how they are going to circumvent us?" Phoenix mulled their options. "The Oman Pike."

"The seasons are about to change," said Jasmine. "The cavern is filled with wraith-cotton. If the burn season arrives it will ignite the pass before they make it inside."

"Then their only option is Barack's Hole," said Phoenix. "Head for the Pike, if the burn season comes you know where they'll be heading."

"I'll be there to squash them, especially Nasra. Her departure from Amalgam is long overdue."

"This is not the time for revenge. Eliminate the guards with them, but see to it that Lauren survives and drive them towards the Hobby. I'll watch and aid you through your mask. After she gets to Devon hopefully she'll get the information we need out of him, then you can capture them both and I'll find out what's so special about Ms. Walston."

"Yes sir. I'll be back within the hour," said Jasmine as Trinity replicated to an individual eagle and she flew to the mountains where her tree hid among the rock never far from her. She boarded it and raced along the Oman Range for the Oman Pike.

* * * *

As Nasra, Lauren, and company glided in the skies, Lauren thought silently as to what they might encounter on the way. She wondered if the shenga would really be "practice" and honestly questioned whether Renee and Amy would be of more help. She looked to her left. Amy was asleep on her shade-ray while Renee drove her ray closer to Lauren.

"Hey, Lauren, you were great back there. Even though Catherine congratulated all of us, we would have died if it wasn't for you."

"Catherine and Nasra wouldn't have allowed that and besides you got yourself and Amy out of the shenga's stomach."

Lauren didn't turn her head to acknowledge Renee as she answered. She concentrated on following Nasra's lead. She relaxed the reigns, but couldn't rest her mind. Her thoughts lingered on her conversation with Catherine and Messina and Phoenix's dream of ultimate reconciliation that made Lauren ponder the meaning of forgiveness. She thought about how it would apply to Willem and Anita, herself and Amy.

"Something on your mind?" asked Renee.

"Catherine said some things to me that got me thinking, that's all. Amazing isn't it, this world?" asked Lauren trying to change the subject.

"Yes, I would have never thought purgatory and the afterlife could be so interesting: cities and government, animal spirits, mythical beasts not to mention an ethereal war between good and evil," said Renee enthusiastically. Lauren smiled but reminded Renee of the seriousness of the realm and its purpose in salvation.

"What did Catherine say to you by the way?" asked Renee.

"She told me why I was chosen to become a baron."

"And why is that?"

"I can't say right now."

"She wants you to keep it secret?"

"No, but it might be best that I do."

Renee saw that Lauren wasn't going to tell and flew silently alongside her. Lauren focused on the task hand, Devon. She wondered if Devon would look the same as he did in the dreams.

"Names said he was only twenty-six, he should," thought Lauren remembering the rule Nasra described regarding appearance. Then Lauren recalled something she had been meaning to ask Nasra. She jerked her pelvis forward, hoping the ray would comply and pick up speed; it did. She hovered next to Nasra, who focused on flight.

"Nasra, was there some relationship between you and Jasmine?"

"Long ago. How'd you know?"

"The dreams," said Lauren pointing to her head.

"I should have known," said Nasra. Lauren waited for her to elaborate but she didn't. "Well…" she said.

Nasra turned to her and Lauren said, "Tell me about it." Nasra sighed before beginning.

"My family grew up enslaved; property of Governor Watlington. The governor's son, Jonathan, was my first and only love. We were born the same year and we grew up together. He never liked the institution of slavery although he would put on a good show when his hateful mother was around. During my teen years, the governor allowed me to work in the house because of my beauty and he wanted to use my body for his pleasure. It would hurt so much and Jonathan was there to comfort me. We'd talk until the pain subsided and slowly we fell in love."

"But, it wasn't meant to be; two worlds, two different lives. Jonathan made such promises to me. He would take possession of my family and free us. He would marry me in his heart if no priest would in town and we'd live together even if that meant leaving the colonies," said Nasra tearing up.

"Of course that's not how it happened. Around his twenty-first birthday Jonathan met Heather Beaufort—Jasmine—at the governor's ball. Jasmine was the daughter of the Justice of the Peace and from what Jonathan told me, her father was pressuring her to "marry up" in Baker's Creek society to the point that it was driving her crazy. This madness subsided once she met Jonathan. He was a man she could love and met her father's desires. Mrs. Watlington desperately wanted Jonathan to marry Jasmine once she discovered his feelings for me and the governor's infidelity."

"Jonathan said he never loved her, but Jasmine obsessed over him. She was willing to do anything to win his heart from me. So Jasmine and Mrs. Watlington conveniently decided to sell me to the disgusting Mr. Grady. He had a reputation for raping his slave women, brutality towards our race, and was a famed hunter of escaped slaves. As soon as I got to his plantation, he took me into his bedroom and had his way. I was tired of being raped, abused, and overworked, so were the other slaves. We planned a revolt. My soul grew cold!"

"One night when Grady came into the slave house for me I carefully hid a shiv and when he laid me down, I killed him. I repented of my sin as we fled from the South but of course, Grady's friends hunted us with dogs and armed men. They shot each of us execution style but not before the hunters took another turn at us women. They burned our bodies down, though I was still alive; the shot meant to kill me narrowly missed my heart. I…I remember burning at the bottom of a pile of my brothers and sisters, crushed under their weight as my flesh seared," Nasra trembled visibly, tears fell fast, and her voice cracked. "Such was the end of my mortal life." She paused for a while, wiped the fluid away from her eyes, and swallowed hard before beginning again, "I wound up here in Amalgam and worked my purgation mandates trying to move on. I never again saw Jonathan, but guess who shows a few years later?"

"Jasmine!" said Lauren, Nasra nodded yes.

"I was a purveyor in the purgation fields when I saw her cursing Catherine for not allowing her passage to Mortalland. I ordered her to silence or work longer, but I wanted her punished in the worst way, in the Pyre. Jasmine gave me a spiteful look as if she wanted me dead on the spot. She raged how a slave could not order her master and bragged that she became Jonathan's wife; I was devastated. Jonathan's love went to the one person I hated more than Gov. Watlington and Mr. Grady."

"I wanted so badly to end her life and, luckily, I restrained myself. As you can see, she's gone from bad to worse as a Phoenix Loyalist. Jasmine's placed herself against God and there's no coming back unless she miraculously changes, which I doubt. I've always wondered why Jonathan decided to marry Jasmine, but the thought made me cold."

"In my dreams I saw her talking to the Phoenix. When did she join him?"

"Not long after arriving in Amalgam. She disappeared for nearly a month into Mortalland. When Jasmine returned she had been fingered as the one responsible for the Evelyn's tragedy and the deaths of all those sailors."

"How was she responsible? The dream appeared to show a random pirate attack."

"We interrogated some of the pirates after they arrived in Amalgam. Apparently, the pirates owed Jasmine a blood debt for saving their lives. Since she was the governor's daughter-in-law, she learned of Watlington's plan to destroy the Bane at it's hideout on Makon Island. The pirates ambushed and destroyed the Navy's ships and in return, she ordered them to sink the Evelyn. For that Jasmine gained a host of eternal companions in the captain and his crew."

"Eternal? They're still with her?"

"They never leave her side, they need her for protection. Amalgam is a dangerous place."

"I didn't see any pirates in the gathering plains."

"The wolves, Lauren; the pirates were given the order of beasts upon their arrival because of their cruelty to animals. We imprisoned most of them but I think a hundred of them escaped."

"How'd so many get away?" asked Lauren incredulously.

"The captain had nearly four hundred pirates under his command. I never knew what they did to animals though it must've been wolves because the order turns the condemned into the creature the ghost victimized. Did you notice the red circles on the wolf heads?"

"I did actually," said Lauren.

"That's the mark of the order. It binds them to wolf form until the mark's magic wears off. They can't change into ghost form or even speak like their Amalgam counterparts. The animals hate ghosts with the order of beasts and would be sure to devour them if they were to roam the Wilds unprotected."

"Wow," said Lauren dolefully.

"And this is only Jasmine's story; all the Ghosts of the Snow have similar tales. Their lives are increasingly destructive and if they aren't stopped Amalgam could be ruined by their madness."

Lauren pondered their conversation before she moved her ray back and flew with Renee in silence. She glanced at Amy, still asleep. She thought about their feud and decided to forget Jason, but her heart wasn't as rational as her brain. They approached the Oman Pike and Nasra took them lower, landing on a mile-long trail leading to the opening. Moss-like foliage covered the trail, wraith-cotton that had ethereal feelers extending from it.

Their rays ran fast like ostriches, blistering through the mile-long stretch to the pike. The bouncing rays awoke Amy who stretched her arms, yawning wide. Suddenly the ever-precipitous snowfall of Amalgam stopped and the freezing air abruptly grew humid and warm. Night was leaving for another day when Nasra turned to the girls.

"The burn season's coming. Giddy your rays! Ride faster!"

Lauren gazed up to the sky. The gray sky changed to an orange dawn and a visible sight of Lumi, Amalgam's sun on the horizon. The heat was stifling and the girls wheezed as they struggled to breathe. A blanket of steaming haze formed before their eyes. The Amalgam snow was melting and the heat ignited the cotton-filled pass. The trail exploded in flame and Nasra took to the air, "We're too late," she said. The girls and guard's rays followed behind hers. Lauren moved her ray alongside Nasra's.

"So, we're off to Barack's Hole?" asked Lauren.

"Yes."

"What can we expect to find there?"

"It's an abandoned cavern town, formerly the last city before entering the Wild."

"Is that the only alternative?"

"We could go far to the south then east and approach the Hobby from the rear, but that would take at least another day."

Nasra and company flew farther north and below Lauren could see the flames covering the treetops. As far as Lauren could see Amalgam was a grand conflagration. Smoke billowed through the realm filling the sky with dense black clouds. Without the flame's light darkness would cover the realm. Nasra chose to fly a bit lower to keep the smoke from clouding the ray's eyes and just high enough not to burn their transports. Along the Oman range, they soon came to another pass, but this one looked more treacherous than before.

A huge dragon skull was covering the entrance; they'd have to fly through its mouth, and sharp fangs, to enter. The actual opening looked like a large hole in the rock. Nasra swooped inside first; her companions dove in afterward.

"It's going to be tight in here. Hold on to your rays and don't move the reigns," said Nasra to the girls.

Lauren grasped the reigns tight and held on for

dear life as Nasra picked up speed. The ride was a roller coaster, dodging stalactites and dead ends, diving through narrow cracks, and abrupt direction changes that made Lauren's hair stand on its end. Lauren could hear Amy and Renee screaming, their echoes filled the mountain labyrinth.

Nasra slowed as they entered a dark entrance hall from the ceiling, their bioluminescence giving them a little light. There were fifteen massive square pillars supporting the chamber and in between each were statues of dragons, dinosaurs, monsters and gargoyle carved from the rock. Ash, dust, and cobwebs littered the floor and pieces of broken furniture were still lying about in ruin. The air was bitter and stifling. Nasra's ray swooped to the floor and lowered its legs like landing gear. Lauren, Amy, Renee, and the guards' rays landed gently and trotted along with Nasra's to the entrance hall's broken door.

"Wh—what—*ah choo!*—was this place?" asked Renee squeezing.

"This is the entrance hall of Barack's Hole. It was vacated at the start of the Animal War in the year seven hundred and nine Amalgam reckoning, or fifteen hundred and nine Mortalland reckoning."

Lauren saw Renee subtracting the number of Mortalland reckoning from Amalgam.

"So Amalgam's calendar is eight hundred years behind ours?" asked Renee.

"Yes, Amalgam was created at the beginning of the ninth century. After the Great Sin introduced

Mortalland shades into our world, we adjusted our calendars to keep track of shades' stay in Amalgam. We can anticipate when the seasons will change as burn season lasts for approximately ten weeks, dew for fourteen, rest fifteen, and winter for thirteen but the seasons aren't cyclic. Only rest season appears in sequence after each season has come. Our months and dates are the same as well."

A guardsman rode up to Nasra and began a conversation. Lauren recognized the solider as the one she was conversing with in the gathering plains.

"What is it, Alexander?" asked Nasra.

"Three of our guards are missing," said Alexander. "They were behind us when we entered the hole then they vanished. Wait here until I find them."

"Don't bother! They're dead!" said a phantom. It was Jasmine floating above them. Nasra quickly grasped her orb, Alexander his trident. Both uttered a spell and sent it for her. The spells passed through her body, the phantom was unfazed. It gazed piercingly at Lauren.

"I knew you'd be trouble when you entered Phoenix's column. And you Francis," the phantom said to Nasra, "I thought you'd learn your lesson when I sent you to Grady, never come between me and my men."

"My name is Nasra Rallens. Francis Watlington is the mortal name I no longer recognize, Heather! I'm not the governor's property and it was you who came between me and my man."

Lauren watched as Jasmine and Nasra verbally sparred and wondered if she and Amy could meet this end.

"Then how do you explain Jonathan marrying me instead of you?" asked Jasmine's phantom.

"After you sent me away, he probably tried to find comfort anywhere, even in your cold heart. You could never handle fair competition or wait patiently for your blessings. Instead, you went to the Phoenix for power and quick rewards, and in return, you've been in Amalgam longer than mandated and falling further from God. Now show yourself so that we can avenge the guards you've slain and end this feud," said Nasra.

"As you wish," said the phantom as it dissipated and immediately the guards behind them screamed.

Behind Nasra and the girls, Jasmine's tree swooped down from the cavern entrance snatched up the remaining guards and flung them wildly in the air. The sharper roots stabbed their rays and three guards to death. Nasra, Alexander, and the girls dismounted their rays. They ran wildly about the cavern hall; two left the chamber through the entrance door, the tree killed most of the others.

"Take cover in the corner girls!" said Nasra.

"We can help!" said Lauren.

"No! You're all too important to get hurt now!"

A blast destroyed the entrance hall's main door and out came another phantom trailing mirages in its path. The phantom raised its staff with electricity for a swipe at Nasra's head. Jasmine's spirit teleported through the mirages and melding with the phantom as Nasra moved to block. As they clashed, Nasra's reterium spell blocked Jasmine's lighting strike in a brilliant white light forcefully sending Jasmine to the floor.

Alexander cast *purgen icila* and sent an icicle spike aimed at Jasmine's chest. A phantom of Jasmine stretched swiftly in a half-circle behind them, mirages trailing it as she escaped Alexander's attack. Lauren saw Jasmine behind Nasra and screamed for Nasra to duck. Jasmine charged another brilzen strike and swung the staff at Nasra's head who ducked on Lauren's order. Alexander cast *cinzeré arm*, his trident turned orange-white as if it was newly forged, and swung it for Jasmine's head. Jasmine was looking to finish off Nasra when the left face on her mask alerted her to Alexander's attack. A thick layer of ice covered Jasmine's staff and their weapons clashed in steam.

"We've got to help them," said Renee.

"Are you blind, Renee, or do you have a death wish?" asked Amy. *"She's fighting them both and winning!"*

Lauren said nothing as she watched the battle. She realized Jasmine could see everything. Her triple-face mask was telling her who was behind her and what they were about to do. Jasmine turned and swatted Alexander to the ground as Nasra stood. She raised her orb to Jasmine's chest and cast *spectrogeal*. Jasmine cast *reterium magnus*, Nasra's spell struck Jasmine's defense and rocketed back to her. Nasra fell to the ground frozen like a fallen statue. Jasmine cast *spectrogeal* on Alexander who was trying to recover from her last strike. He lay frozen when it hit. Jasmine electrified her staff. She stood above Nasra raising her staff as she said, "Finally, you meet your end!"

Lauren left her companions, raised her sword at Jasmine and spoke, *"Purgen cinzeré!"* The blast leapt from the sword towards Jasmine's chest. The fire blast struck the wall behind Jasmine as mirages left Nasra, showing her body twisting around for a swipe at Lauren. Jasmine struck her down and then swung her staff around for a gut punch at Amy who crashed into the wall.

Renee took her staff and jumped on Jasmine's back. She tightened her body around Jasmine and awkwardly tried to cast a spell on her. Jasmine cast a phantom next to her and entered it, letting Renee drop to the ground. She kicked Renee, sending her skidding along the ground stopping next to Nasra and Alexander.

Jasmine turned back to Lauren, "If you make it to Paradise, leave the gates open for Phoenix and me!" Jasmine smiled as she sent a spell for Lauren's head. Amy stood and cast on the ground underneath Lauren, *geysen aquis*, sending her into the air before the spell could land. Amy ran when Jasmine, infuriated, sent a bolt for her. Jasmine's tree caught her and Amy tried desperately to wriggle herself free. Lauren clung to a second-level tier while airborne and ran along the second level ledge as

Jasmine sent spells up after her, destroying the ledge behind her. Renee stood and immediately a guardsman crashed into her, sending her back down. Renee quickly recovered and helped up the guardsman. She had him cast *spectromel* on Alexander while she restored Nasra.

They stood as the guardsman exhaustedly spoke to them, "We're never going to beat that tree." Nasra saw Jasmine sending spell after spell up after Lauren who ran screaming for her life. Nasra threw her orb at the ground before Jasmine, speaking a spell that turned her orb into a blinding light. Jasmine was stunned and Lauren used this time to orb and return to the ground level. The tree was stunned along with Jasmine, dropping Amy and one other guard still alive in its grasp. Amy and the guard rejoined the group and when they were all together, they entered through the hall door.

"ALEX, SEAL THE HALL!" said Nasra. Alexander turned and cast a powerful cinzeré spell on the rock cavern as Nasra retracted her brilliant orb with *exeralure*. Jasmine stood in the hall alone, eyes still dazed and unable to follow her targets. When she came to, she found that her enemies had escaped and the path to them was sealed.

"DAMN YOU NASRA!" Jasmine screamed.

CHAPTER FIFTEEN
DEEPER INSIDE THE HOLE

The group moved further into the cavern, Alexander cast more spells to keep Jasmine locked away. Lauren heard Nasra breathe onto her orb, a white light shown in the orb's purple clouds and then brightened illuminating the tunnel.

"Ascentate!" said Nasra and her orb floated out in front, guiding them along.

They tread this passage for an hour, the path filling with a stench as it ended into a clearing. They were in a dilapidated hall with decorative wall tiles still hanging, but most of them now marred by black ash.

"What's that smell?" asked Amy covering her nose from the pungent odor.

"It smells rotten," said Renee. "Where's it coming from?"

"Shh! Down there," said Nasra pointing below. Lauren came close, Nasra's orb floated down into the cavern providing light and looking below, she saw the source of the stench. The massive hall was a giant den with numerous high piles of bones scattered about the ground from monstrous creatures and demons. They were high up on an outcropping, the remainder of a bridge that has since collapsed onto the hall floor.

"Oh my God!" said Lauren.

"What is it?" asked Renee. They looked below where they saw amongst the bones, a dragon and Tyrannosaurus rex lay asleep.

"A dragon and a dinosaur!" said Lauren.

"And look! Two of our rays!" said Amy. Moving about the chamber and avoiding the dinosaur and dragon were two of their rays that escaped the battle with Jasmine.

"Are dragon's natives?" asked Renee.

"Yes, dragons are the stronger natives reserved for killing large demons and monsters or safeguarding important places like the Amalgam Towers," said Nasra.

"Are dinosaurs natives as well or where they considered animals?" asked Amy.

"Animals of course! Dinosaurs walked the earth like modern animals and man. I guess the Judge thought they would be excellent predators of monsters and placed them here," said Nasra.

"Usually dragons and dinosaurs roam the Wild with their own kind, but many animals and natives have formed cross-species friendship. After this hall was vacated it looks as if they made it their lair."

"I'd have never thought a dragon could relate to a dinosaur," said Renee. "Then again, I never believed a dragon ever existed."

"Beasts have personalities, too," said Nasra. "They probably compliment each other somehow, as hunters and as friends. Try not to awaken them. Jasmine already has dealt us a crushing blow; we can't have them trying to kill us as well."

"*Exeralure*," Nasra quietly retracted her orb and dimmed its light to not disturb the sleeping creatures. She let it float out again, her eyes focused on it as she guided it about the chamber. Its dim light moved through the bone piles casting demonic shadows along the walls.

"What are you doing?" asked Amy.

"I'm looking for the exit and the map supposedly drawn on one of the walls. If the old stories are correct, this is Barack's Hole central station. It had eight entrances and exits connecting to the Oman pike and other areas. There were two tunnels connected by this bridge and two on the right of us. Its bridge has collapsed. As you can see, the exits across from us have collapsed and these two lead back the way we've come. The last were on the ground level, against the walls, but I don't know where. These stacks of bones might be blocking the way."

"If we're trapped, how do they get out?" asked Amy of the dinosaur and dragon.

Nasra listened to Amy and wondered as well. She saw the many piles of rubble on the floor, barely a clear space on the ground to walk, but when looking up, she found the answer to Amy's question.

"The ceiling," said Nasra. They all looked up; the ceiling had a massive hole.

"Great! We can get out!" said Amy joyfully.

"No! We haven't traveled far enough under the mountain yet. We might emerge and be spotted by Phoenix's fowls not to mention Jasmine is looking for another way to come after us. We'll remain underground and find a tunnel that'll carry us along the range as far as possible."

They waited patiently as the orb moved about the perimeter of the room. Amy had withdrawn into the tunnel so that she could sit as far away from the disgusting odor of the den. Lauren, Renee, Alex, and the last two guards were crowded on the small ledge with Nasra watching her orb weave about the bones. All of them were straining their eyes looking for the door. Nasra quietly whispered a spell, illuminating her orb slightly to better her search.

The tyrannosaur heaved loudly, frightening their rays and breaking Nasra's concentration on her orb. The orb brushed a horn as it wove through another pile of bones, knocking over the top. Skulls rolled from the top and shattered noisily on the floor like a broken vase. A nerve-shaking roar of a yawn from the dragon shook rocks loose from the ceiling. Behind Amy, rocks fell inside the tunnel. It was collapsing. Amy screamed.

"Run, Amy!" said Lauren aloud.

Amy ran out, bumping into Renee, knocking them off the perch and onto the den floor. The tunnel completely collapsed, sealing their only way back with an impenetrable wall. A larger rock dislodged from the ceiling intended to take out the remainder of the bridge and whatever was left on top: Lauren and her companions. They leapt from the shelf as the boulder destroyed the bridge. Renee and Amy scrambled up and backed against the wall before the boulder fell. It smashed onto the floor; the rubble trapped the girls in the corner.

Lauren and Nasra landed in front of the dragon, Alexander and the guards, underneath the tyrannosaur's toothy snout. Lauren could hear the beast sniffing; the swirling air tugged her face as it packed the dragons nostrils.

"Doris," said a deep masculine voice of the dragon, yet its eyes remained close.

"Yes, Mathias," said the motherly voice of the tyrannosaur eyes closed as well. The dragon sniffed the air as he spoke.

"I smell… food… rays… and something… else… can't place it, been a while since I've smelled it."

Doris sniffed the air, her nostrils wrinkling as great huffs of air whipped up the stench.

"I smell it too…smells…smells like…ghosts."

"Ugh! They taste horrible and are hard to digest. What are they doing here?"

"Why don't you ask them?" asked Doris sleepily, her great leathery head turned from left to right.

"I thought my statues would have warned them to stay out. And Baron Catherine dare say she respects our land."

"You know the ghosts. They think they're the greatest creation of the Judge, its no wonder they actually think they're gods. Well see that they leave, or eat them!" said Doris.

"I am hungry…" Mathias stomach growled. "At least they brought sweet-tasting rays with them."

Two wide white eyes pierced the darkness as a ball of flame barreled forward, lighting the cavern with orange light. It burnt to a crisp the last two shade-rays as the dragon stretched its scaly head and neck past Lauren and Nasra and gobbled them up. Lauren could see its throat engorged as their feathered ferries slid down into the beast's belly.

"Throw them up, over the pile!" They heard Amy's voice from the corner. A basketball-sized rock went up above a stack of rocks before falling back inside.

"Don't yell at me. It's already hard enough to move under this all this rubble," said Renee.

"I told you going to this forest was dangerous."

"Not now, Amy, please! Let's try and get out of here!"

"We should dig straight out," said Amy frustrated.

"Yeah and crush ourselves doing it," Renee retorted.

The dragon turned its head towards the pile and blew two fireballs from its nose. The rocks blasted inward as the fire plowed through. Renee and Amy screamed as the fire burned their face and body. The stones cut their skin and broke their bones as they smashed into their husks. The flames engulfed their bodies and Lauren watched horrified as her friends burned. Nasra jumped up, lured her orb into her grasp, and shot a water spell into the pile extinguishing the flames on their skin. She turned as a shadow overtook her; the dragon shut his mouth around her, intending to swallow Nasra whole.

Nasra forced the dragon's mouth open. Mathias blew a plume of fire from its mouth, but Nasra used her aramous spell to redirect the flame around her. Alexander shot bolts of fire to get Mathias to drop Nasra. It singed his flesh, and Mathias rolled on the ground trying to put out the fire.

"ARGH! DORIS HELP ME!" said Mathias. He could barely utter his plea with his mouth open.

Doris had fallen asleep however. Lauren stood to help Nasra but Mathias' tail caught her legs and tripped her and Alexander. One of the guards shot an icicle at the dragon's eye. Mathias blocked it with his wing then swiped off his head with it. The dragon turned its body to face Lauren and ignited his spiked flaming tail. Though he could not crush Nasra with his mouth, he was determined to smash Lauren to bits.

A guard ran towards Lauren to pull her out of the way when Mathias stabbed his chest, turning him to embers. Lauren stood and summoned her sword and took a swipe at the tail as it came for her again. She cut a deep gash into Mathias. The dragon roared in pain causing more rock to fall from the ceiling.

Lauren ran underneath the dragon for cover as a large rock smashed onto Mathias head, making him relinquish Nasra. Lauren helped her up and they fled from Mathias as he fell. Mathias was out cold, his head crashed into the floor before his sleeping mate Doris. As he fell unconscious, he blew a small plume from his nostrils that burned Doris' snout, awakening her as she raised her head up.

"Ow! MATHIAS! You burned me!"

Doris dug her snout into the ground to put out the fire.

"Lauren, Alex, get Renee and Amy," said Nasra. She threw her orb into the piles of skulls and breathed forcefully. The orb blew the rocks away from the girls into the cavern. Lauren and Alexander found Amy and Renee covered in blackened scars. Their legs were fine, but from the waist up, they were severely burned.

"Oh God! Can you move, Renee? Amy?" asked Lauren.

Lauren grabbed Amy gently by the arms. She choked in pain; her throat filled with necroplasm resulting in a bubbly groan.

"Stop, please stop...it hurts," said Amy gagging. Alexander picked up Renee.

Nasra retracted her orb and used it to blast away several piles of bones uncovering the exit, a thin tunnel. Doris soothed her burns and turned her attention to Nasra. Doris ran to the archway and swung her entire body into the wall, blocking the exit. Her tail crushed the wall above the tunnel, collapsing rubble atop her destroying their hopes of escaping. Doris wailed with pain, she was hurt, but stopped the ghosts from escaping. Nasra saw what Doris had done and ran to attend to her companion's health before continuing to search for an exit. Nasra saw Amy and Renee's charred bodies and pitied them.

"They'll need spectroplasm to heal these wounds," said Alex.

"We have to get them to a dead pool. We'll have to carry them on our shoulders," said Nasra.

Mathias regained consciousness as Lauren slowly picked up Renee, her arms growing thick and powerful to lift her friend who weighed more than she did. Lauren was able to quite easily sling Renee on her shoulder and carry her without difficulty. Nasra similarly slung Amy on her shoulders and turned to Doris, who was struggling to stand after her wall charge. Alexander stood ready to protect them from the awakened dragon.

"Where to, Nasra?" asked Alexander. Nasra searched the chamber, the ceiling exit looking particularly tempting but she took her orb and had it blast away the soot from the wall covering the Barack's Hole map. She found a tunnel that ran underneath the chamber to an underground lake. The map depicted a stairwell leading to it. Nasra blasted the rubble on the ground and found a hole in the floor where Mathias' head broke the ground. There was a pass underneath. Mathias stood, his wings outstretched and he rubbed his head with his three-fingered claw. He sat on his haunches and stroked a large knot that was swelling more.

"Damn ghosts!" said Mathias when he caught Doris in a glance pained against a wall; he ran to her.

"Doris! My love, are you okay?"

"Yes! I sealed them in, they can't escape! Finish them Mathias. They'll be a well-deserved meal after this!"

"You'll get the thickest, juiciest one, Doris," said Mathias as he turned to devour the ghosts and discovered they were once again alone in their den. Mathias heard screams coming from the ground and found their escape route. He found them sliding down the tunnel shrinking into the darkness. The dragon blew a flame after them as he clawed through the ground enraged that they escaped.

Nasra, Alexander, and the girls tumbled from the tunnel in free-fall for a few seconds before crashing onto hard rock. Nasra's leg broke on impact, Lauren landed on her feet but her legs and hips were only sore, not broken. Alexander fell luckily on his bottom, his armor protecting his body. Renee and Amy hit the ground wholly in pain because the fall agitated their burns. A heat surge and light preceded Mathias' lethal plume, giving Nasra, Alexander, and Lauren enough forewarning to move Amy and Renee before the fire scorched their landing site.

* * * *

Alexander and Nasra stood and Nasra limped around surveying their new surroundings. They were in another hall like above but its tiles were all but broken and merged with the rock cavern riddled with stalagmites. It was unfinished. Lauren looked back to Renee and Amy. They were squirming as sharp pains surged through their bodies.

"Is a dead pool nearby?" asked Lauren.

Nasra searched the cavern and found one a few feet ahead. Four dense stalagmites with concentric patterns on them surrounded a pit filled with spectroplasm. Beyond it was their path between sharp rocky stalactites dripping water and spectroplasm was a twisting cavern.

"Over there! Pick Renee up and don't worry about hurting them. Their pains will only be a memory once we get them to the pool."

Lauren gently picked up Renee, took her to the pool, and laid her beside as Nasra did for Amy.

"Stand back, Lauren," said Nasra as she whipped out her orb and held it at arms' length above the dead pool.

"Iseo Quegdren," said Nasra and the spectroplasm in the dead pool swirled and white light cracked through the fluid like lighting.

It rose up in a large surge like a tidal wave and with a swoop of Nasra's arm, bathed the two in spectroplasm. The fluid seeped into their burns and melded them away into smooth brown skin with a hint of pink to identify them as Mortalland shades. Lauren watched as they gradually healed and silently mouthed the spell Nasra used in case she needed it again. In minutes, Renee and Amy were fully healed and able to move on their own once again. They stood up uninhibited by pain as Nasra moved the excess spectroplasm back into the dead pool.

"Thank you, Nasra. I thought I was done for," said Renee breathing deeply.

"Don't mention it," said Nasra as she entered in the pool and, with another spell, healed her broken leg. From above, the station hall was collapsing further as Mathias shouted of his hatred for ghosts.

"You wanted to enter Barack's Hole, now stay here forever!" said Mathias. Rocks fell from the tunnel entrance, he was sealing up the hole.

"Well it looks like we're trapped save for that pass," said Alexander. He pointed forward, the only way to go into a rock cavern so dark it looked like a portal to outer space.

Nasra stepped out the pool, and with Alexander and the girls ready to proceed, she led them on. Nasra lit her orb as before while they tread a narrow ledge along the right. They entered into another hollow, this one different as Lauren noticed rock stalactites whose razor sharp tips filled with what appeared to be rushing water. They stood before a wall of tall stalagmites that stood as a barrier at the edge of sheer blackness.

Only the light from Nasra's orb and their bellies

offered illumination. Renee moved forward and climbed a stalagmite to look out. Before them was a massive underground lake. Lauren and Amy followed, their luminance shown through the spikes and lit the water like moonlight. She didn't even see a ripple in the water, it was absolutely still.

"It's a lake," said Renee.

"It's so black and it's everywhere!" said Amy.

"Is this dark spectroplasm?" asked Lauren.

Alexander and Nasra climbed a stalagmite and looked at the liquid. Nasra let her orb hover above it; the fluid did look like oil but it was motionless. She ignited her hand, saying *cinzeré illumine*, to take a better look. A white-light flame wrapped about her hand from the tip of her fingers to the wrist.

"Yes, and it will kill you instantly," said Nasra.

"Can we cross it?" asked Lauren as Nasra retracted her orb.

"We'll see. *Purgen cinzeré!*" said Nasra and a fireball shot from her orb across the lake. The red light illuminated the darkness until it faded out like dying flame. As far as they could tell, the lake never ended.

"It just goes on and on," said Renee despairingly.

"We should go back! This is suicide!" said Amy.

"There is no way back!" said Alexander hopelessly.

"We'll have to try and fly across. Everyone orb and hopefully we'll make it across," said Nasra. They all transformed into their ghost orbs and rose up.

"Fly fast and straight. Don't move unless I tell you," said Nasra. Her orb was glowing at different intensities as she spoke. They flew across the lake; the girl's orbs wavered in the air, a clear indication of their fear. They flew in silence for nearly an half an hour when Renee spoke.

"I'm getting tired, Nasra."

"Me too," said Amy.

"Same here," said Lauren.

"Wait, then," said Nasra as she and Alexander transformed to ghost form. Nasra shot another fireball from her orb with the same result as before. The fireball streaked past a small island where a battered winged creature slouched in a chair. The creature rose in surprise as the flame flashed by and looked fiercely in the direction from which it came.

"It's too far," said Amy ghosting. "We're going to die!"

"Don't despair," said Nasra.

"She's right! We can't make it!" said Lauren.

"You'll never make it! You'll never escape!" rang a maniacal voice in the darkness.

"Who is that?" asked Renee frightened. The girls ghosted and all five floated in place.

"I'm the siren of the still lake and you're trespassing," the voice said again. Undeniably female, it scared them all for it seemed to come from everywhere in the darkness and was high in pitch.

"A siren! I thought they were extinct!" said Renee.

"So did I," said Nasra.

"You must be the ghosts that attacked Mathias and Doris. I'll see that they're avenged. You'll be submerged in this dark spectroplasm and sent to the Judge, who I hope will see the inherent evilness in his Amalgam ghosts and throw you in Hell," said the voice.

"If there's no going back and the girls are tired, then let's carry them Alexander and fly fast," said Nasra.

Nasra pulled Lauren along and Alexander took Amy and Renee by their arms and flew straight. They pushed themselves moving as fast as they could when they saw her. The siren's face was slim and heart-shaped with a sharp chin, small red lips, thin nose, and her eyes held pink pupils. A long scar blemished the right side of her face from her forehead down to the chin. Her figure was humanoid, but her ragged wings draped from her featherless arms. Feathers covered her massively muscular human-like legs, but her feet were gigantic talons. She began to sing as they neared:

A siren of peace, I am Selene
Sprung from songs of the Judge
Once beautiful and serene
Now troubled and cold I carry a painful a grudge
I am the first and last of my kind
Because of the ghosts of Amalgam

The dark spectroplasm depicted a vision of the siren begging the ghosts not to attack the animals seeking refuge in her sanctuary. It was the cavern they were in except the dark lake was not present. Instead, there was a massive and beautiful hall carved from the brown rock with bright white and yellow lights emanating from the stalactites that streamed thin lines of colored water into the hall's numerous small pools. The sanctuary was populated with pink sirens conversing in a heated debate with the ghosts. Leading the ghosts was the Child Phoenix and his witch Gretchen.

I tried to help the spirits of men
Yet they betrayed me
So I broke my vow to serve them
But that is a sin

The hall, embroiled with anger, erupted in violence. The girls could hear the screams and voices in the image as the ghosts attacked the sirens and slain all of them. Selene screamed and stalactites fell from the ceiling killing some of the ghosts. The Phoenix and Gretchen fled with their Loyalists and Selene sat holding the bodies of her sirens. She cursed them and refused to serve ghosts again when Metatron appeared. The siren pointed to her slaughtered kin as she passionately expressed herself to Messina.

I cursed the ghosts to Messina but she said:
You know your purpose
To serve ghosts and animals alike
You've killed those you were to protect
And will be punished with solitary

Messina's voice resonated throughout the chamber from the vision. It was stern and angry. The siren screamed in the vision and the stalactites burst filling the chamber with spectroplasm and water when Messina collapsed the entrance to the hall as she left. Lauren was afraid as they neared the siren, cluttering the ceiling were those same stalactites. The vision ended with Selene alone with the bodies of her sirens.

I received this quiet place
Wide open and peaceful
Free from the cold face
Yet here they are the arrogant and deceitful
And like my sirens you'll share the same fate

She sang a high musical note that pierced Lauren and her company's senses, irritating their ears and giving them massive headaches making it hard for them to stay airborne. The siren song burst the water-swollen stalactites pouring out water in powerful jets that filled the cavern creating a deafening sound and a blinding mist. They dodged through the streams trying to continue forward, but it was becoming increasingly difficult because of their number.

The chamber became terribly cold and the girls struggled to fly in the blistering chill reminiscent of Amalgam's winter season. They moved cautiously through weaving, dodging, and stopping when a jet came close and moving round quickly as Lauren looked above to see another raining down. The siren set her trap. A wall of jets barred the way, completely encircling them. They could not run through because the force would shove them into the lake to their death.

"She means to kill us!" said Renee. The girls and Nasra ghosted before the wall of water.

"Can anyone see a way around?" asked Nasra. Lauren looked down the hall of water, more jets to the left and right. Though Lauren and her friends could not tell, they were in a maze of water columns with no exit, only a path to the siren.

"No," said Lauren. Amy and Alexander similarly shook their heads no.

"Besides, the vision showed Messina collapsing the exit. We're stuck in the mountain!" said Renee.

A sea serpent lunged from the jets, the water washing off its spectroplasm. It attempted to bite Lauren, but her reflexes were too quick and she spun away from the snake's bite. The serpent whipped its tail for a successful strike at Renee, who fell below, before it disappeared into the wall of water behind them.

"Renee!" said Lauren as she orbed and flew in a

dive and saved Renee before she hit the dark spectroplasm. Lauren returned to her companions with Renee unconscious in her arms.

"If she means to keep us here to feed her disgusting snakes then she'll wish more than ever that we'd never come at all. *Follow me!*" said Nasra.

Lauren materialized her sword, feeling she needed protection from any more snakes that might suddenly fling out the water. They flew in ghost form through the spiral hall of jets while serpents jumped in and out of the water walls. Some lunged down the hall wriggling like sidewinders before they struck only to miss and claim water as their spoil. They arrived in the center with the siren and floating above her Nasra spoke to the songstress.

"Stay your wrath and let us through for the sake of your health native!" said Nasra.

"No cold soul shall ever order me so boldly while trespassing. Have at you wretch!"

A larger serpent reared from the black spectroplasm. It flung itself for Nasra who asked for Lauren's weapon. She threw her sword to Nasra who sidestepped the instant the serpent attacked and severed the head from its thick neck in one strike. She then took the head and swung it at the siren so fast she couldn't move before it clobbered her, sending her flying into the lake.

As the siren gurgled in the spectroplasm, the jets calmed and solidified. The mist subsided and the turbulent lake settled. Nasra and the girls floated down to stand on her island as the siren tried desperately to escape her murky lake, but like oil it stuck to her wings.

"Still wishing the cold face would learn their place?" asked Nasra. The siren cried in a childish high-pitched wail.

"How is she still alive?" asked Lauren.

"Spectroplasm doesn't harm natives," said Nasra.

"I hate you. Why did you do this to me…WHY? All I ever wanted—"

"Was a quiet place, we heard. It was you who broke the silence!" said Nasra flying out to the siren, picking her up from the waters, careful not to touch the spectroplasm. She placed the siren back on the island and Selene sat on the ground a drenched, sulking mess. Nasra used her orb and a water charm to wash her wings.

"You said your name was Selene, *the Selene* from the Animal War?" asked Nasra. The siren nodded affirmatively.

"We thought you were dead," said Nasra.

"I was sealed up in here!" Selene spat through her teeth.

"You mean we're still stuck here? NOOOO!" said Amy. Her voice echoed through the cavern so loud it made Lauren and Alexander anxious the stalactites might reopen. Amy's outburst terrified her companions. No one wished to be stuck in the mountain surrounded by deadly spectroplasm. Renee moved in Lauren's arms, regaining

consciousness. Lauren wasn't sure if she wanted to awaken to more bad news.

"The ghosts who sealed you inside, the Phoenix and his loyalists, why did they want to kill those animals?" asked Nasra.

"They were pursuing them, trying to discover if animals could be killed. The ghosts were torturing those poor animals until they managed to escape. They came to me for sanctuary. I tried to make peace with the ghosts but they would not hear of it. They had to see if animals could die, to discover any weaknesses they might have in case the animals turned on them. They started killing my sirens so I attacked the ghosts. They murdered all my sirens before I could drive them out."

"Messina's punishment was too harsh. She closed my womb and told me to stay here for the remainder of the Animal War. Selene, the progenitor of Amalgam's sirens, rendered barren because of ghosts. Instead of rejoining the world, I stayed behind. I can't stand the sight of your kind. Amalgam is for purging sin and many of you missed Hell by a nick of the bottom, yet your immoral behavior endures and you desire more power. Ghosts deserve nothing more than any other creation of God, yet you believe your worth is higher!"

"So the few ghosts who killed your sirens are representative of us all, is that it?" asked Nasra.

"I know your history and hear of current events from Mathias and Doris," said Selene. The lake turned to a vision of the Procession raid and the ghosts entering the skyscraping forest behind the siren for the girls and Nasra to see. "As a whole, you're the worst creation of all realms, pure evil in every way."

"First of all, no creation of God's is inherently evil only by our choices do we become evil. Secondly, the Procession incident was not an attack. The ghosts ran into the animal forest through fear. They were fleeing a dangerous ghost named Jasmine, who imprisoned this girl here," Nasra pointed to Lauren, "and rallied the entire animal kingdom against the Court with the disappearance of their leader Estoc. If you wish for peaceful relations between animals and ghosts then you should help us."

"What's happened to Estoc?" asked Selene angrily.

"He's missing and the Phoenix is blaming the Court for his disappearance leading the animals to war with us."

"The Phoenix?" Selene grunted, "Another ghost responsible for animal suffering!"

"Isn't he the one depicted in your visions destroying your hall?" asked Lauren.

"Yes," said Selene.

"Why didn't he kill you?" asked Alexander.

"He wanted me to join him, if my peace stance changed to violence Phoenix figured he'd justify his war with the ghosts. I never figured out why he wanted to use animals to war against other ghosts. I figured it was just in your savage nature."

"He needs the animals to achieve his goals. He'd kill your animals and any ghosts that stand in his way," said Nasra.

"Typical of ghosts," said Selene. "That's why I refuse to leave my hall!"

"But wouldn't you like to do something to prevent ghosts and animals from fighting again?" asked Lauren incredulously.

"I would but…"

"But nothing," said Nasra. "Like it or not Selene, we're on the verge of a second Animal War. If you do not want to see animals hurt again, then get out of this rut and protect them, help us stop the Phoenix! We need you to help us across this lake to reach the Hobby. There you can see for yourself the damage Phoenix is causing."

"And what business do you have at the Hobby?"

Nasra informed her of their quest to find Devon.

"Baron Catherine is doing what she can to find Estoc and bring peace between us. An old peacemaker alongside Catherine will help her in that regard." Selene thought hard for a long while, returning to her chair to ponder her options and struggling to come to grips with living among the ghosts again.

"Fine…if Phoenix is the true cause of another war then I must stop him, but let me rest a moment." Amy faked a cough.

"Excuse me; we still have a little problem of getting out of here!" said Amy.

"Amy's right," said Nasra surveying the cavern. "And with our rays dead it's going to take days to travel on foot to the Hobby. Devon will be captured by then."

"How far is the nearest shore?" asked Lauren.

"Don't worry about escaping, I'll get us out of here," said Selene. She found the severed snake's head by her chair, dipped it in the spectroplasm and had Nasra *spectrogeal* it. Selene then threw it at the ceiling with incredible speed and strength. It burst through the rock allowing fresh air and a ray of light in from the Amalgam sky that brightened the island. The siren was of immense strength as she picked up Lauren, still carrying Renee, and Amy with her talons and flew up with Nasra and Alexander in her arms, out of the black lake to the surface of the Oman Range.

CHAPTER SIXTEEN
THE ILLUSIONIST'S HOBBY

"You could have left that cave at anytime?" asked Amy.

"After my punishment was over, yes," said Selene. She flew them in the shadow of the Oman Range faster than any winged creature in Amalgam could manage.

"And how long ago was that?"

"Four hundred and ninety years."

"DEAR GOD! Why didn't you leave?" asked Amy.

"Self-imposed isolation, Amy."

"At this rate we'll be at the Illusionist Forest in less than an hour," said Nasra.

Lauren held Renee tight, which was doubly hard when she awoke to see the mountains flying beneath her legs. Renee looked above to see the siren carrying them.

"I guess we lost," said Renee. "She's carrying

us to her nest to eat us."

"No, she's taking us to the forest," said Lauren with a smile.

Selene flew closer to the Oman fields where Nasra turned her attention to the mass of animals gathered by the forest edge. Selene flew lower, careful to avoid drawing the attention of the birds in the fields. Lauren and her company finally stopped on a mountaintop near the northern edge of the Illusionist Forest. Its treetops and most of the foliage were aflame due to burn season. Screams reached them from the Oman fields, the animals wailed as fire scorched their skin as they attempted to enter the forest.

The larger animals gathered far to the west, the rear guard. The smaller animals like rabbits, squirrels, and rats were being used to ascertain the location of the Hobby. The eagles, ravens, and other fowls were scouring the forest from the side as thick plumes of smoke rose from the treetop fires. Lauren could see the forest trees were shifting. She could feel the heat from below and even the rocks they stood on were warm. Lauren wished that Gloria was here, thinking that she could keep the animals off them while they looked for the Hobby.

"It looks like the war has begun," said Selene. "I'm going to talk to them."

"It's too risky now. Wait until we get to Castle Everlasting," said Nasra.

"We could use more guards," said Lauren dismayed at the ferocity of the animal horde.

"Without the Horn of Olives, we don't stand a chance against the animals," said Alexander.

"What does this horn do?" asked Renee.

"Animals only weakness is a deep, penetrating sound," said Nasra.

"We can slow them with our magic but the Horn of Olives is the only true defense we have against them. The animals were unstoppable until Catherine told us to make the horn. The sound tortured the animals, paralyzing them with pain, and they surrendered to silence it. After that, Catherine struck a peace treaty with Estoc and redistricted Amalgam. Animals would live in the Wild's District while we would condense our territory to give the animals more freedom."

"So that's how the war ended," said Selene pensively.

"Hopefully we won't have to use it this time," said Nasra.

"How will we enter the forest?" asked Renee, functioning again.

Nasra stood on a larger rock and looked below to see animals in all directions by the forest. They would be exposed as they approached from the north as the high rocks gave way to level ground.

"We'll have to orb and fly fast," said Nasra.

"And what do we do when we get in the forest? It looks like the trees are moving. How will we stay together or know where we're going?" asked Amy.

"Lauren, did your dreams show a path inside?" asked Nasra.

"No," said Lauren. "Could Gloria get us through? She is an animal mark!"

"Doubtful, some of these animals are so cold, they'd probably kill her too and under the command from the Phoenix, they'd have to attack us," said Alexander.

"I can fly you to the forest edge, but once inside..." began Selene.

"You could crash into one of those trees and we'll be at the mercy of the animals," finished Alexander.

"Hello," said a small gnome, startling Lauren's group. He was dressed in a blue pointed hat with white star designs and was standing only a few feet away from them. Lauren thought he looked like the garden gnome statues she would ride past occasionally on her way to school. His beard was white by the chin but darkened towards the bottom due to dust and grime. He was wearing a gray cloak that would explode to red or blue. His face was reminiscent of Santa Claus. The gnome stood looking at them indifferently with his hands cupped at his waist. He was accompanied by two others gnomes that looked quite similar to him although wearing different clothes.

"A cave gnome! Who are you?" asked Nasra.

"I'm Inkadreh, leader of the city Bignome and my companions are Bladin and Horace. Is there something in the forest that interests you?" asked the gnome curiously; his voice was husky and strong.

"Yeah, the Hobby!" said Amy.

"AMY!" said Nasra, rebuking her divulgence of their destination.

"Ah! If it's entry to the Hobby you seek then I can't help you there, but I can get you into the forest."

"I can get them into the forest," said Selene.

"You can die trying," said Inkadreh strongly. "My gnomes and I had to create a new passage to the forest and to the delicious forest fruit because of predators in the area. We can use that passage."

"What do you want in return?" said Nasra. "Nothing comes free, right?"

"Protection through the forest, I'm here to meet the Hobby's magician. We gnomes have a particular interest in how he creates the illusions. Seeing as how the animals can't penetrate the forest, I hoping he'll teach me a charm that will protect our cave dwellings against them and our natural predators, the wizenlocks. That way, we won't have to relocate whenever they come around again. What do you say? Do we have a deal?"

Nasra consulted her company with a glance at each of them. All of them nodded yes. Nasra picked up the gnome and lifted him to her eye level, Horace and Bladin looked up to Inkadreh with wide eyes.

"Take us to this passage," she said.

"Head half a mile straight and you'll find a cave hole," said Inkadreh.

Nasra followed the gnome's direction as they

traveled exactly half a mile before coming to a hole that was only five feet wide.

"Jump in," said Inkadreh. Bladin and Horace went in first, Nasra and Alexander dove in next, Renee followed, then Amy.

"Can you fit, Selene?" asked Lauren.

"We'll see," she said bashfully.

Selene wrapped her arms and wings about her body tightly and tucked her talons down after she leaped above the hole. She slid down nicely and Lauren entered last. They slid down and came to the gnome city of Bignome. Lauren and her company had to crouch and walk as they moved through the city that looked like a rock beehive. There were several half-cylindrical carvings in the rock with rectangular holes and smooth ledges connecting each level of gnome houses. It looked recently abandoned however.

"Where is everyone?" Renee asked the gnome.

"They left for our shelter. They feared the animals would find this city and destroy it. Bladin, Horace, see if you can find any food in our stores, I'll go with Nasra to the Hobby," said Inkadreh. His gnomes left their company and began ascending a staircase towards a small cave a few levels above.

"Around to your left is a small tunnel that will take you underneath the forest. You'll have to crawl to get through but it's going to take some time."

"How long is this tunnel?" asked Nasra.

"About eight miles to the exit, but I must warn you, the Hobby will create illusions even in this tunnel. We had trouble creating this passage; it took us years to finish because of them. Remember, whatever you see, is not real," said Inkadreh. They came to the tunnel; it was big enough for an adult human to crawl through comfortably. It was long and dark, and though nothing appeared odd now, Nasra expected that to change the closer they got to the forest.

"Eight miles, huh? Well we won't have to crawl," said Nasra as she orbed and floated inside.

The other ghosts orbed as well, the gnome could fly, and Selene packed her wings tight. She followed last, crawling almost as fast as she could fly. As Inkadreh promised, the illusions transformed the empty hollow into a massive bug hole where centipedes, maggots, spiders, and all manner of creepy crawlies wriggled on their bodies. The girls ended up ghosting and crawling, as avoiding the falling bugs in their orb form made them crash into the cavern walls. This made it worse, however, with bugs slinking up their arms and legs so the girls reverted back for the remainder of the arduous journey.

They flew for several minutes, close together until the tunnel curved upward. They ghosted and Nasra blew in her orb and the giant boulder covering the tunnel exit rocketed off. They surfaced into a clearing. The girls anxiously escaped, rubbing their arms off and shaking their hair to get rid of the buggy sensation. Selene, being the last out, placed the boulder back and there Amy, Lauren, and Renee sat propped up against it for while to rest. Nasra walked the perimeter of the forest hoping to catch sight of the Hobby or a path.

"Rest comfortably," said Alexander. "I don't believe the animals have come this far."

Lauren looked at the trees as she caught her breath. She saw the leaves were red and creating the burning fire. It was searing, humid, and becoming hotter by the moment. All around them in this clearing the trees moved about, their roots crawling along like searching fingers. Lauren looked around to see something familiar. In her dream, the forest was green and wet, not flaming red.

"Would you happen to know where the Hobby lies?" Nasra asked the gnome, but he shook his head no.

"Lauren, did your dreams show you a path here?" asked Nasra.

"Only a crossroad with eight paths but I think it was created to send people back to the fields."

"Then I suggest the best course would be to head further east. I would expect that the reason the forest shifts even this deep is because the Hobby is further inside. With any luck, we'll come across the true path."

The girls stood and followed Nasra as she made her way to the eastern side of the clearing. As they approached the trees, however, they moved faster, dropping flaming leaves to the ground.

"We'll have to orb again. Stay close everyone!" said Nasra as orbed and entered the forest.

The girls followed and Selene flew after them, Alexander following behind. Much like the black lake, Lauren and her company dodged the trees. The heat from the trees was unbearably hot, even the sizzling air pained them. They flew east uneventfully for half an hour when the forest ahead disappeared like a mirage.

Floating in midair, they came to a gorge with a river running beneath yet the further Lauren and her companions flew, the distance to the opposite edge increased. Looking back, Lauren realized they hadn't advanced at all. They ghosted and returned to the closest shelf.

"Looks like we can't get across; you think it's just an illusion?" asked Renee. Nasra looked inquisitively at the gorge.

"I can't tell and I don't want to try and cross," said Nasra.

"Why not?"

"As we fly, the illusions may make it seem like the edge is receding and we could easily be stalled at a dew barrier. If we were to attempt to land after flying we could fall into the gorge. I'm not too familiar with the Wild's geography but I think this could be the Ilana River. Its current is very swift and supposedly inhabited by a terrible sea monster."

"It is," said Selene. "A giant sea serpent called Leviathan often spawns up here, and its offspring would sometimes swim upriver and find their way into my cavern. I believe he's here now, given the number of serpents in my cavern."

"So there's no use trying to swim across," said Nasra.

"Should we go back?"

"We could, but we could also wind up at the forest edge."

"So we're stuck!" said Amy frustrated and she plopped onto the ground.

Lauren sat next to her, while Nasra, Alexander, and Renee considered their options. Lauren picked up a couple of small rocks and started to juggle them to pass the time. She started to grow impatient after a while and started thinking over her dreams. Lauren realized how Vincent designed the forest to keep them out. Even a powerful witch like Jasmine couldn't penetrate the illusions and Lauren wondered why they even tried.

Lauren filled with despair; they had come so far only to be stuck wandering in a magical forest and leaving meant certain death by the animals. She'd hoped to find Devon, to find the answers she sought, but now felt like Amy was right, maybe they shouldn't have come at all.

"Maybe we should try and find this crossroad," said Alexander. "Nasra, you and I could try two of the paths and if we don't come back, they'll know not to go in those directions."

"They'd still have six paths to choose from, and only five would remain in their company. They may not make it to the Hobby even if they were to split up. If Jasmine hadn't killed our guards we could've tried it."

Lauren had stopped juggling to listen to them talk. Not once did they even consider the certain death they'd face if they were wrong which made her question whether they were totally altruistic or completely foolish. After several more minutes, when Alexander and Nasra were finally deciding on returning to find the crossroads and sacrifice themselves Lauren stood to dissuade the idea.

"Look, you two aren't going to kill yourselves! We'll just go back to that rock, crawl back to the mountains and fly around until we find some other way around *this stupid gorge!*" said Lauren as turned and flung the rocks into the distant right. Two of the rocks fell below but one bounced in midair and rolled off some invisible obstruction before tumbling into the depths. Everyone saw it and moved swiftly in that direction. When they arrived, Nasra blew a white powder from her orb that turned golden when it struck the invisible object. The particles formed the shape of a collapsed tree.

"It's an invisible bridge!" said Nasra happily.

Lauren stepped to the edge and raised her foot where the powder previously lingered. Amy did not want Lauren to get the glory this time and moved quickly onto the invisible log while Lauren was still gathering her courage. She closed her eyes as she walked along and it appeared as if Amy floated on air when she should have fallen.

"Wow! That Amy sure is brave!" said Alexander smiling.

Lauren watched her as she went across jealous that Amy could best her whenever she desired. Amy crossed the chasm in its entirety and did not stop until Nasra called out after her.

"Amy, you've cleared it. You can stop now."

Amy opened her eyes to a flaming staff in her face. She screamed as six ghosts leapt from hiding behind the tree trunks and the seventh held her hostage.

"So much for Vincent's theory that the illusions would keep us safe," said the ghost holding Amy.

"Don't hurt her!" said Nasra. "We're guards from Castle Everlasting!"

They all began to cross the log until the leader warned them not to proceed. Renee and Selene remained behind on Nasra's instruction as she and Alexander slowly approached the bandits stopping midway on the trunk next to Lauren.

"Access to the Hobby is strictly limited in times of war. A true guard would know this!" said the ghost.

"I do. My name is Nasra Rallens, district purveyor of the New City. We're looking for a ghost named Devon Knight and we believe he's here."

"They know Master Knight, Reinhardt," said a ghost to the leader holding Amy. Reinhardt chose his next words carefully as he held Amy tighter.

"It could be a trap," Reinhardt whispered to his companion. "And what's with the gnome?"

"He showed us a path inside the forest," said Amy.

"Did he? It's a wonder how he found a way inside and every other creature is stumped at the forest edge!"

"Are you going to stand there and threaten a young girl or are you going to use your common sense and let us through. If we were Loyalists wouldn't we be fighting now?" asked Nasra.

"What's the problem here?" asked another ghost riding a brown horse.

When he emerged from under the shadow of the trees, Lauren knew it was Devon. He had dark brown skin, brown eyes, black hair, a strong build, and a melancholy countenance. He wore a thin blue tattered vest, a white shirt that looked stained with blood, and loose black pants they blew in the wind. His sapphire necklace blinked white light and as he approached the tree appeared. The bridge was a long, large, and smooth tree trunk, broken at the flare and buried firmly in the ground where the ghosts held Amy. Reinhardt and his cohorts respected him, clearing a path and standing straight as he dismounted and fronted the pack.

"Master Knight…"

"Devon, please, Reinhardt," said Devon, his voice strong but with a tinge of boredom.

"Right. These ghosts have broken through the illusions," Reinhardt shook Amy in his arms and then pointed at Lauren and her friends. Devon looked sharply at Nasra's company and spoke gently to Reinhardt.

"Did they say why they've come?"

"They're looking for you. I know how you and Vincent feel about the barons and Morrigan guards and since they've somehow managed to get this far into the forest, I was going to take them prisoner."

"That won't be necessary. So why are you searching for me?" Devon addressed his question to Nasra who moved closer and pulled Lauren along. They came within a few feet of Devon before he raised his hand to have them stop with a foreboding expression.

"We have an emergency with the animals as you know," Nasra began. "What you may not know is why. We have reason to believe the Phoenix and his witch are after you." Reinhart and his companions laughed gaily, yet Devon appeared flattered.

"They've been after me for some time. That's why I came here, so I wouldn't have to fight or run any longer."

"They're not going to leave until they know where the linking tome to the Book of Marks is," said Nasra. Devon was unfazed and actually appeared quite frustrated.

"I *told* Catherine a man had it on the ship, I *never* knew what became of it!" said Devon patronizingly.

"His name was Duncan and I *know* you died hiding it!" said Lauren, coming from behind Nasra angered by his blatant denial.

"We've risked too much coming here for you to pretend to not know where it is. I know about the Evelyn's sinking. I know Duncan told you to find

Etienne and that you drowned weighed down to chests. Now, I need to know where you buried that book!"

Devon's tense face relaxed, he was humbled and intrigued by Lauren's assertions but didn't entirely believe her and said warily, "Why should I trust you?"

"Because I've been given a mandate by Messina herself to stop the Phoenix and my business has brought me to you. That's proof enough I'm the one to trust!"

Lauren's sudden boldness surprised every ghost at the gorge except for Reinhart who appeared starstruck.

"Oh my God! It's Lauren Walston! The new baron everyone in the cities has been talking about! They say she's indestructible! She survived the Phoenix column and everything!" said Reinhart ecstatically. Lauren knew Amy's article had reached every city in Amalgam and the story of a new baron was no longer secret but popular and embellished. Lauren looked at Amy loathsomely but Amy shrugged and grinned smugly in Reinhart's custody.

"Everyone?" asked Nasra disbelievingly.

"Never trust a gossiper mark," said Reinhardt.

"Isn't that the truth!" said Lauren spitefully at Amy.

"Enough! Come with me," said Devon.

* * * *

Lauren walked close behind Devon, now walking alongside his horse, as he led them through the magic forest. The illusions gave way in his presence revealing the forest secret. Most of the trees were motionless, the mobile trees were illusions and would steer intruders into the stationary trees. Devon took them on a dirt road to the Hobby; the road Nasra was hoping to come across a good distance back. This road was fairly straight and after Devon spoke "Vanishing Shelter" to a wall of foliage that trimmed itself to ankle height they entered the Hobby.

It was a truly a hamlet with many small bricked houses flanking the sole road leading from the entrance and dead-ending at the manor. Sunlight filtered down mostly on this lane, leaving much of the town in cool shade but rays of warmth seeped through the branches and spotted every house. The trees in the town were multicolored like autumn and every house looked comfortably snug in their shadows. Lauren wondered if the leaf piles collecting before their houses would suddenly rise like the maze at Castle Everlasting and camouflage the entire town.

Here it was not as hot as the rest of the forest, whether this was because of Vincent's magic or the cover of taller trees Lauren couldn't say. A white vapor wisped through the town, the last remnants of ice melted by the burn season that hadn't yet escaped the forest ceiling. Lauren had seen many beautiful sights in Amalgam, and the Hobby was but another. The realm truly deserved its name and she savored the occasionally picturesque sights because she knew it would not be long before she'd witness another brutal event.

Ghosts were sitting outside playing card games or using magic to entertain the town's children, which Lauren thought was an odd contrast to the horror unfolding at the forest edge. The citizen's were preoccupied with their daily tasks and they didn't hear a single conversation discussing the animals but they were talking about the castle raid and of course the new baron.

"You all must be pretty confident that the animals can't reach this town," said Renee.

"In the near three hundred years since Vincent and I founded this town there has yet to be a penetration of the forest. Many consider it as safe as Castle Everlasting, that used to be a compliment before a few hours ago," Devon chuckled.

"Look, we have to get you back to Castle Everlasting. Baron Catherine has some questions for you that need answering," said Nasra.

"I'll never again see the inside of the castle so long as I'm in Amalgam," said Devon.

He led them to the manor and swung open the doors to the small foyer. The inside of this splendid looking house was everything but impressive. The interior was entirely wooden and appeared eaten through by termites with many holes in the floor and the lumber was weather worn. There were a few paintings but all the glasses were broken and lying on the floor in shards. Steps were missing in large gaps in the staircase and railings were nonexistent. There was no light except the dim daylight coming from the curtain-less windows. Lauren thought that only the cathedral in Messina was more disappointingly deceptive.

"Nice," said Amy who dodged a large spider sliding down from the ceiling.

"Vincent!" Devon called out. From the second landing came the magician Vincent Vengrass wearing an immensely shredded, nearly transparent cloak dotted with small stars and blew gently in the air. He is a tall Hispanic man with short curly black hair, brown eyes, with a stubby nose and was a very strong as his muscles bulged through his torn robes.

"Yes?"

"Guards from New Elysian are here, Vincent," said Devon. "And they've found a way through your illusions. Are you doing anything productive with the time you spend *alone* in your chamber?"

"It's our first penetration ever and now I'm a fraud!" said Vincent, his baritone voice projecting like an announcer, rolling along with melodic tone inspiring excitement and enthusiasm in all listeners. "What do they want?"

"To speak with me," said Devon.

"I'm going outside to take a look around," said Amy repulsed by the manor's interior evading the spider on her way out. Vincent descended the stairs, approached and greeted Lauren's companions.

"So how did you manage to sneak into my

forest?" Vincent asked Nasra.

"The help of this gnome here," said Nasra. She pointed to the little gnome standing by her side who waived gingerly at Vincent.

"We're going to have a long talk," said Vincent kneeling to the gnome.

"And I'm interested in seeing how the illusions are created," said Renee when introducing herself.

"I'll show you and some other magic," said Vincent.

He stood, raised his empty hands, materialized a red cloth and transformed it to a rose with a wave of his hand. Renee took it and the rose formed a flowery patterned dress on her guard clothes. He then clapped his hands and the manor's interior changed. The walls became golden, the broken wooden floor changed to a magnificent marble surface that reflected the golden light of a massive chandelier. The wooden stairs changed to exquisitely carved arched steps and the railing was white with large diamonds for posts. About the mansion were several elaborate statues of mythical characters and creatures.

"Entertain her companions while we talk," said Devon as he escorted Lauren out of the manor for a private conversation.

CHAPTER SEVENTEEN
DEVON'S TALE

Devon took Lauren around the back of the manor by the windmill where they sat on a wide tree stump. A stream ran behind them, creating a soothing trickle that relaxed the two of them. The windmill added to the serenity with a cool breeze. Devon shuffled his weight, trying to get more comfortable before he spoke.

"So you're the new baron?" Devon began. He claimed to have read about her in the Amalgam Times and said it was a miracle that she survived the Phoenix column. Lauren admitted surviving the column, but denied the trashy stuff as rumors created by the vengeful gossiper mark in her company and Devon believed her. She divulged minor details that led to their arrival at the Hobby and about her new abilities but didn't tell him about her second mark.

"Why are you looking for the book?"

"The Phoenix is hoping to bring the castle down with a mark inside. They attacked Castle Everlasting a week...I mean, a few hours ago, but couldn't get it from the Book of Marks."

"So they're coming for me," said Devon knowingly. "And how do you know so much about me?"

"The Phoenix column. I can see his memories. He must've been thinking about capturing you and, as you know, he's right outside this forest," said Lauren.

"And Catherine and Messina forced you to become a baron over a chance run-in with the Phoenix?" asked Devon hostilely.

"I'm doing this because of what happened to my father," said Lauren, remaining cool to his gruff remarks.

"What happened to him?"

"He was killed by a ghost. I live in the New City, and the ghost was able to kill my father because of the Dark Phoenix."

"I see. It's a damn shame what the Phoenix has done to our worlds," said Devon gravely.

"I decided to help Catherine and Messina fix this place."

"Humph! You've got your work cut out for you," Devon said glumly.

"Tell me about it! Just getting here was hell in itself. Why do you live so far away from the baron cities?"

"Not everyone trusts the barons or agree with the purgation process. Many ghosts think the Judge stranded us in limbo as punishment for the Great Sin. They believe the Court is nothing more than an oppressive mock government in a land of undesirables. They think the barons subject spirits to torture and mandates to satisfy their own sick fantasies. Catherine once said to me how the Dark Phoenix is standing in ghosts way from leaving Amalgam, yet many easily see the Court as the one standing in *his* way."

"After all, if Phoenix was to win we'd all live in Heaven saint and sinner alike which why he has so many followers. Many Phoenix loyalists are ghosts like me who have been in Amalgam for centuries whereas others are summoned in a few hours. Ask as to why and Catherine will only say you haven't been called. The Court says ghosts should let go of their past yet how are we to progress when we're stuck here?"

Devon bit his lip and kicked a couple of flowers in reach of his extended leg as he sat on the stump. He was obviously as frustrated as Catherine suggested he'd be and Lauren considered his words about how ghosts viewed the Court, realizing she'd be seen similarly if she was to continue on as baron. Devon sighed before beginning again.

"After the summoning of my fellow Evelyn sailors, I began roaming Amalgam's Wild lands to find some purpose until my time. I met Vincent in the gathering plains and we became friends. He also disagreed with Court policies and desired a separate home far from their cities so we established the Hobby. Then the tree rider began stalking me, why I never knew until today. Vincent helped create a haven for me and in return I used my power to ensure our people would never have to leave."

"How so?" asked Lauren. Devon showed Lauren his mark, on the back of his hand was a dead pool. He cast his hand over the ground where a small pit formed and inside was liquid spectroplasm.

"You can create dead pools?" asked Lauren amazed, Devon said yes.

"It's a rare ability. I don't know of anyone else who can do it."

"Catherine said you were powerful! All I can do is see visions when I touch things. *You* can heal your own wounds and cast as many spectroplasm spells as you want right?" asked Lauren; she thought a little flattery might help him open up to her.

"Yeah, among other things," Devon gloated dejectedly. "The town relies greatly on my ability to spawn these pools. I'm tied to supplying food for the town. Never in my life have I've been so constrained and even now I'm not used to it."

"What? Being responsible?" Lauren joked.

"No, caged in Amalgam without a reason as to why or an end in sight. In the old days, after governing this place, I had to leave the forests for a few months so that witch and the wolves wouldn't assume this was my permanent sanctuary. I actually let them find me when I was away from the Hobby but only after I'd made sure I'd escape before they gave chase. It worked a long time, but a few years back they realized I resided here."

Lauren heard Devon talk of Jasmine but was more concerned about how some ghosts are summoned immediately and questioned why her father departed so suddenly.

"Are there many here like you? People that haven't been judged?" asked Lauren.

"There are but few as long as I and most have become cold souls," said Devon disparagingly. "I can see why they go cold though, being idle and lonely can only make a spirit evil. As hope fades and prophecies go unfulfilled, it seems like I'll never leave. Oh God, I long to enter the Paradise Realm, it's the only place where the soul is finally at rest and content with endless love from the Maker."

"How do you know what's in Paradise?"

"I've spoken with numerous fallen spirits."

"The reapers?"

"No, reapers rarely talk to anyone other than to their purveyors. I meant the ghosts that have fallen from Heaven. Were you in the gathering plains during the Procession?"

"Yes."

"The fallen were the spirits that hailed from the sky. Since the Paradise tower collapse, Messina forcefully removes spirits and angels from Heaven.

They look like shooting stars when descending."

"I remember them," said Lauren eyes wide as she recalled the horrific experience of the Procession. "Why are they cast down from Heaven?"

"The angels are cast out because they became too prideful or envied the positions of fellow angels. Instead of sending the angels to Hell, the Judge occasionally sends them to Messina where they are without the Judge's Touch. I hear its excruciating for angels to be out of God's presence for any significant time. Other angels are in Amalgam to satiate their curiosity about human race. They tend to keep low profiles however; many disguise themselves as ghosts and wander between the towns remaining neutral to Amalgam events. The ghosts however, are sent for a number of reasons, some good, but mostly bad. But anyway, I don't want to delay you any longer, what do you want to know?"

"Everything about the Evelyn's sinking, especially where you buried the book," said Lauren firmly.

"Since you have the gift of psychometry, you can see for yourself. Touch my fatal scar; they're my lungs. Lauren stood and moved around and placed her hands on his back and closed her eyes. Devon took a deep breath before he began his tale.

* * * *

The fiery red-orange sky turned star-studded

black, the forest morphed into a sandy beach, and the manor transformed into an old port. Lauren stood next to Devon on the Evelyn, which is about to depart the dock. The smell of the salt water filled her nostrils; the moonlight flickered excitedly over the dark blue harbor water imprinting white rippling waves on Laurens brown pupils. Chaos ran rampant about the port as sailors gasped at the inexplicable destruction of a large ship and the death of all the sailors onboard. Lauren observed Devon in the vision and realized that he was still wearing his death rags to this day. Like a deity whose voice stretched from the heavens, Devon's voice accompanied Lauren through the vision.

"I first met Duncan the night the Masterson sank but we died on the Evelyn a month later…"

"Interesting night," said Duncan as he boarded the vessel after parting with two men he was talking to moments ago.

"Unbelievable! A ship of that size sinks as if it sails underwater. I'd say sabotage was behind it. What say you?" Duncan smiled at Devon. Devon was lazily mopping the deck of the Evelyn watching the water claim the grand vessel.

"I can only imagine," said Devon mutedly not looking up at him.

"Ah come on!" said Duncan taking away Devon's mop and placing it against the rail. "Don't work yourself to death. Take a break. You want to anyway."

Devon surveyed the deck and realized none of

the other sailors were working.

"I'd guess poor craftsmanship," Devon ventured as he sat on the ship's rail and Duncan leaned against it, elbows propping him up. Lauren moved close to them and listened in.

"The Masterson? It's the governor's personal carrier," said Duncan excitedly.

"Maybe they scuttled it," Devon took another guess loosing up to Duncan.

"And left all those sailors onboard to die? It had to be sabotage! Maybe a small explosion created a large hole to sink it."

"I didn't hear any gunpowder ignite," said Devon thoughtfully.

They watched the guards bustling about with a curious gaze as the Evelyn slowly sailed from the dock.

"What's your name and where are you from?" asked Duncan.

"Devondre Knight, my friends call me Devon. I'm originally from Jamaica, you?"

"Duncan, from France, but well-traveled like yourself I assume." Devon nodded in agreement. "Knight, that name isn't Jamaican is it?"

"It's not my family name, but I don't want to talk about why I took it."

"Ah! Well, do you have any family?" Duncan continued.

"My parents died a while back, since then the Evelyn has been my home and the crew my family."

"Ah…" said Duncan with satisfaction. "Are you

a loner? Or let me rephrase, would it be hard to let go of your shipmates were you to take up another profession?"

"I'd miss them, but I'm willing to try new things."

Duncan smiled as they gazed out to sea. The Evelyn was approaching the outer islands.

"What do you do?" continued Devon.

"I'm an assistant for Dr. Robert, a psychologist who is researching the supernatural. We study the behavior of ghosts and travel to areas where unexplainable phenomena occur to investigate the underlying source."

Devon laughed for a moment. "Did you say ghosts?" he asked giggling. Duncan replied yes quite seriously which made Devon stop laughing and ask more serious questions.

"So what kind of phenomena have you linked to ghosts?"

"Mist bellowing without fire or precipitation, books flying off shelves, psychic disturbances, and objects moving without any perceptible force; things of that nature."

"And you try to find a spook behind it all? I'm ignorant to all this because I don't believe in ghosts."

"Are you a religious man?"

"Yes."

"So you believe that we all have spirits?"

"Yes," said Devon with a drawl knowing what Duncan was getting at.

"Then why don't you believe in a ghost which is basically a spirit?"

"When a person dies their spirit goes to God not wander the earth. A spirit leaving Heaven to come back to knock books of shelves and slam doors sounds a bit ridiculous to me. Heaven can't be that boring."

"I've spent my life trying to get people like you to believe that ghosts do exist. You say you find it hard to believe a ghost would come back to slam doors to startle people. Well think of it this way, what if a person murdered a co-worker in a cellar. The victim's ghost can't directly talk to a mortal or touch one and this murderer is about to kill again. So the ghost tries to smash objects to bring attention to the situation and save the person."

Devon's skeptical expression gave way to a thoughtful stare. Duncan saw that he was persuading Devon.

"Interesting, I never thought what a dead person would do to get someone to listen to them," said Devon.

"That's what we do. We communicate with the dead," said Duncan trying to arouse more interest in Devon.

"You talk to the dead?" Devon asked cynically, once again withdrawing from the conversation.

"We know there is an afterlife and soon we'll prove to the world that ghosts haunt our world trying to complete unfinished business. We'll explain the paranormal behavior as the superior functioning of our very spirits as we ascend upon death into higher beings. It will be one of the most important works ever untaken by man."

"I wish you luck," said Devon jumping off the rail, ready leave Duncan's company. Duncan pulled him back and revealed the linking tome. Devon's eyes widened as the book gave off a cool air that chilled his face and its transparent cover gripped his attention.

"What is that?"

"We don't know but whatever it is it has some correlation to the jewel we were tracking tonight, the jewel placed aboard the Masterson before it sunk," Duncan let this slip.

"So you do know what happened to the Masterson!" said Devon backing away.

"I know that what we were tracking was placed aboard the Masterson. I doubt it caused the ship to sink. Besides, I didn't do it! I was standing here the whole time! We pursued it because it was believed to reveal ghosts to the naked eye."

"I'm sorry, Duncan," said Devon bending for his mop. "But I've heard enough and as for that book I suggest you chuck it overboard before it does something to the Evelyn."

"Okay, Devon. One day, when we've recovered the jewel you'll see as Dr. Robert and I have and know the truth."

"I thought Duncan was insane even after seeing his magic book but now I know it was I who was blind. The Royal Navy stopped our voyage and

returned us to port to investigate the sinking and the deaths of the guards slain after we left the dock. The ship, cargo, everything was inspected and the crew questioned. I didn't tell the officers of Duncan's possible involvement with the Masterson or of his book. After all, neither he nor his friends ever went close to that ship."

"I don't know how Duncan managed to hide it, but he had the book with him the night the Evelyn sank. I didn't talk to him until we set sail again."

Lauren stood on the ship again next to Devon, the ship swayed gently with the sea; the air was cool and breezed swiftly. The night was unusually dark, tumultuous clouds shrouded the stars and moon, and the sea was a mirror image of the depths of space. In the midst of the gloom sailed the Evelyn, its watchful crew on edge in this unnatural darkness.

"We didn't speak at first nor did we get far on our voyage. There was a storm that night and we had hardly passed Crow Island when we heard a call from the crow's nest..."

"Sail ho!" said the watchman. *"Pirates! It's the Baker's Bane!"* Lauren could see a large ship emerge from the blackness of the night sea and ran to the ship's edge along with Devon to see the Bane approaching.

"Duncan and I were on deck that night. It's like the Bane materialized out of thin air. The most feared pirate group, the Spiral Rapier and their infamous leader Captain Corven were after us. They reputedly decimated three of the Royal Navy's

battleships on Makon Island and were feared for notifying future targets by sending severed wolf heads. We were totally unprepared; who would have thought Corven was brazen enough to attack us so close to the shore."

"Devon, stay close to me," said Duncan. "I need your help."

"Don't start, Duncan," said Devon as he unsheathed his sword.

The Bane shot its cannons directly into the Evelyn's rudder, stern and hull, blowing up its cargo that included explosive materials. A loud explosion knocked everyone to the deck. Fire spewed in every direction and eyes glowed with amber flames. The menacing pirate ship mysteriously remained enshrouded in shadow though the fire burned the Evelyn's hull.

The explosion deafened the sailors, sending them to the deck, and they were too shocked to stand. Devon's vision was blurry when he opened them again. His head hurt and as he glanced around, he saw Duncan lying on the deck, rubbing his temple. The two had bumped heads. Devon slowly stood up when Duncan grabbed his arm.

"I'm immortal and I can keep you alive if you do as I say?"

"If you do as I say maybe in the morning we won't be swimming with the fishes," said Devon coolly. Duncan stood and took Devon's sword from his hands, bared his chest and ran himself through.

"What are you craz—you're not dead!" Devon

was perplexed.

"And you won't be either if you stay close to me, I can't lose this book."

The pirates swung from their ship to the Evelyn. Two of them landed behind Devon and another two behind Duncan.

"Behind you!" they said in unison. Devon withdrew his sword from Duncan's chest and kicked him toward the pirates. Duncan collapsed on them and Devon swung around to fight the pirates behind him. Lauren watched fearfully, wanting to take her hands off Devon to end the vision afraid the pirates would cut her to pieces. Nevertheless, she held on, grasping his back tight because in the vision she hid behind a rail and peered over to see.

"Can you imagine what was going through my mind? We were being attacked by pirates and Duncan was talking quite calmly with a sword through his chest!"

Devon fought the two pirates with skill. He elbowed one off the ship as he punched the second in the nose knocking him down. Devon picked up a sword from the downed pirate and tossed it to Duncan. Duncan grabbed the sword to defend against the charging pirate running towards him. He blocked the pirate's strike and eventually managed to kill his assailant when yet another appeared before him. Devon was using two swords to fend off more pirates that arrived to kill them.

Slashing, blocking, and ducking, Devon moved between two battered pirates. He hit one to his right on the temple with the sword's handle and pushed the dazed pirate into the other sending them both to the deck. Duncan wasn't fairing so well. The pirate he was dueling had disarmed and cornered him trying desperately to kill him if Duncan would stop swerving. The pirate fainted and Duncan fell for it. His sword entered under Duncan's collarbone, the pirate left the blade in, rendering his left shoulder useless for now. Duncan screamed in pain as blood soaked his shirt.

Devon heard his cry. It broke his concentration and the pirate he was fighting disarmed him and gave chase. Devon raced to Duncan's aid and away from his attacker. He jumped over a dead sailor's body and managed to push Duncan's assailant off the ship. Duncan looked around anxiously for a weapon and a lantern in a window caught his eye. He smashed it with his right elbow and grabbed it.

"Duck, Devon!" Devon complied and Duncan hit the pursuing pirate across the head breaking the lantern and igniting his scarf. The pirate screamed as he tried to put out the flame and Devon tossed him overboard to help him in that regard. Devon looked around and made sure no pirates were coming before inspecting Duncan's wound.

"Pull out the blade damn it!" said Duncan in tears. Devon snatched the blade from the wound swiftly. Duncan's pain subsided and Devon watched the wound closed quickly.

"What are you?" asked Devon.

"Immortal, I told you," said Duncan panting.

Devon looked around the ship as he saw his comrades falling but many were still holding strong. The pirate force outnumbered them threefold and the ship was sinking fast from the hull breech. "We're going to have to get out of here," said Devon.

"Where? We're miles from port."

Devon looked to the starboard side and saw some of his fellow sailors taking their chances in the sea. All of them were moving in the same direction and looking further in the darkness, he glimpsed the shadowy Crow Island in a flash of lighting.

"Come on, Duncan, we have to swim."

"Wait!" Duncan pulled him back. "I can't die, but I don't want them to get this book. Should I be captured and if you escape, find a man in Baker's Creek known as Etienne Robert and give it to him. Tell him what happened to me—augh!—tell him you're *alone* and he'll reward you with everlasting life!" Duncan struggled to speak, his wound, though healed, was sore. Devon nodded that he understood.

"We hit the water and swam for our lives. It was slow at first, there were so many bodies floating and the water was red. I know because my sleeves were white that night. I heard the pirate captain calling out after Duncan."

"Duncan, do you think you can get away? That island is too far from shore. You'll be stranded even if you manage to hide from us," said Captain Corven from the Bane.

"They know your name, Duncan! What do they want?" asked Devon struggling to talk above the water.

"They must know about the book! But how?" asked Duncan.

"I made it to shore first. It was obvious that whatever Duncan had in his possession was the cause of the Evelyn's tragedy but nothing could prepare me for what I witnessed next. The water in the sea turned white, as if it froze suddenly then thawed instantly. Everyone in the water, sailors, pirates, tons of fish, even Duncan died instantly like the sailors on the Masterson."

"Duncan!" Devon called after him. Duncan bobbed in the water.

"So much for immortality," said Devon. The book in Duncan's coat floated out. He looked out to the water and saw all the dead bodies in ocean.

"After seeing what happened to my sailors I couldn't let the pirates get their hands on that book. The pirates shed too much blood on its account and I'd see to it that it was all in vain. I took it far onto the island. I stopped running by a brook where I hid by a grove of trees and bushes. I sat for a while, resting before opening the book to see what was inside. The book was filled with animated pictures, marks."

"I got lost in the pages until I heard someone approaching so I hurriedly wrapped the book with fabric from my shirt and buried it as deep as I could underneath the wet soil where I sat. I buried it in

front of three massive trees, and to remember where I buried them I carved three letters at their base, an E, V and L for Evelyn."

"He's around here somewhere," said a pirate. Devon crouched close to the tree's flare and hurriedly carved the L. When he finished Devon emerged from the bushes and tried to run away but ended up with a pistol in his face.

"Hello chap," said a gun-wielding pirate. "Search him," he said to his companion. The pirate patted Devon down but found nothing. He peaked inside the tiny grove and searched a bit but in the darkness, he couldn't see the freshly turned dirt or even see well into the bushes.

"Where'd ya hide it?" asked the gun-wielder.

"Hide what?"

"Don't play dumb with us. The book! We saw you take it from Duncan at the shore."

"I must have dropped it."

"Then you're no good to us," the pirate cocked the gun.

"Yes he is. We can torture him till he tells the truth!" said his partner. The gun-wielder rolled his eyes when his partner blew his bluff.

"I know that idiot!" the gun-wielder shouted. "Take 'em to the captain. He'll see that we find the book for our client."

"At that moment, I realized the pirates were under orders from someone else, but I never figured out who sent them."

Lauren followed the pirates as they took Devon

to the shore and tied him to two chests they pillaged from the Evelyn to sail to the Bane. Captain Corven was sailing on a rowboat along with a few of his pirates when the Evelyn's fire spread to their ship. One of the pirates in Devon's boat fell into the water at the sound of the Bane's armory exploding. He couldn't swim and ended up capsizing the boat trying to get back in.

"I fell into the water and sunk fast, I drowned before the pirates could rescue me," Devon shuddered slightly when he mentioned the drowning.

"I watched as a spirit from the shore. The water killed most of the remaining pirates; it froze over again as it did when it killed Duncan. The Royal Navy finished off the captain and the rest of the Spiral Rapier after the explosions brought them from port. We wound up on the island in spirit, pirates and sailors, looking at our bodies until a sailor resumed the fight."

"What was it all for? The sailor asked and that question remained with me since then. Only when the reapers arrived did the fighting stop," said Devon, he sighed again. Lauren removed her hands and the vision dissolve back to the Hobby and the forest.

"Now you know, it's on Crow Island but that's about as descriptive as I can get besides what I've told you already. God! It feels good to have that off my chest."

"Thank you, Devon," said Lauren coming

around to sit on the stump. "Crow Island, at least I'll be able to start there. But I'm worried, by now those trees could have been blown over by a storm or dug up to build houses," said Lauren disappointedly.

"Then take this," said Devon as he took off his torn white, bloodstained shirt, his chest was bare underneath his vest. "Using your psychometry this shirt should guide you to the linking tome."

"How?" Lauren asked as she took it.

"It will give you a sensation when you get close to someone or something belonging to a dead person. In my case, it should zero in on the remaining fragments of my shirt."

"Shouldn't your whole shirt be in Mortalland?"

"I returned to Mortalland a few months after the sinking and de-materialized it."

"Why do you still wear your death rags?" asked Lauren.

"It's reminder of the Evelyn and its crew so that I will never forget that night or the location of the book. I know Catherine wishes ghosts would remove their death rags but I have no intentions of going cold rest assured."

"Did you ever find out why the water froze over?" asked Lauren.

"Catherine said the Mortalland Seal was trying to re-stabilize the mortal and ethereal realms. The seal separated these two worlds and when the water froze it was casting an ethereal seal charm that took the life of any living thing caught in it."

"Why would Catherine tell you this?"

"She wanted me to become the New City's district representative. She saw my mark and realized my potential and said that since I'd fallen victim to the seal's effect, I should govern the city to see that it never happens again."

"Why'd you turn her down?" asked Lauren.

"I didn't want the responsibility."

"I didn't either when Catherine asked me to become a baron but I understand her reasoning. I have to help them and I want answers," said Lauren mournfully.

"Your father," said Devon. Lauren nodded.

"And Messina believes you'll discover who killed him while fighting the Phoenix? Humph! Catherine said the same thing to me before I refused," said Devon.

"I believe them and maybe you should too. Already I know who was responsible for the Evelyn's sinking." Devon looked at her with great surprise.

"Who?"

"Jasmine...the tree rider. She ordered the pirates to raid the Evelyn and the pirates were turned to wolves by the order of beasts."

"Wow! They've been chasing me for centuries. My God! My God!" Devon said this many times more.

"Imagine Devon, had you taken the position, you could have discovered Jasmine was responsible earlier and possibly prevented my father's death."

"And how could I have done that?"

"While waiting to be summoned, you could have found the Mortalland Seal and destroyed the New City or at least arrested the ghost before they murdered my father."

"It's possible," Devon said thoughtfully.

"By becoming a baroness, I'll do what I can to fix Amalgam and maybe you should consider returning to the castle to do some good. After all, you're already serving the people here, you might as well work for the Court and get the justice you deserve," said Lauren enticing him with her secret motive.

"The Judge and the Court forbids revenge if that's what you're suggesting. And I don't want revenge; I want to leave this place! I want to move on!"

Lauren realized she was provoking his anger towards the Court and decided to stop pressuring him. They sat in silence for a moment before Lauren broke it.

"Did you ever try to find Etienne?" asked Lauren.

"No, I didn't see the point. I was already dead, no need for eternal physical life and I hear he's very hard to find."

"Hmm, I better go meet up with Nasra and the others. So what's the plan if the animals break through the illusions?"

"They won't. I'm fully confident in Vincent's illusions. The Hobby's manor is the safest place to be right now. It can even take several appearances, confusing any intruder if they try to enter. The animals will never penetrate the forest or the manor as long as the Eye remains intact."

* * * *

"So this is where the Illusionist Forest gets its name," said Inkadreh. He was staring into a large collection of enchanted mirrors in the manor's attic. Renee was gaily riding a carousel Vincent had magically created for her. She watched and listened as Vincent presented the Illusionist Eye to Nasra and Inkadreh. Inkadreh rejoined Vincent and Nasra as their host explained a giant orb on a pedestal that pulsated with various micro images of shifting trees, the forest chasm, a rock monster and other obstacles that protect the town. The mirrors projected the illusions into the forest.

"And this single orb is creating the illusions?" asked Nasra.

"In addition to these mirrors, yes," said Vincent. "The Eye is what I call my illusion creator. It's my finest, most powerful and complex spell I've ever cast."

"You should be proud. You're undoubtedly the greatest magician in Amalgam. I feel entirely safe within the Hobby," said Nasra.

"He is not the greatest magician nor are you safe within this town, Nasra," said Inkadreh, his voice changing to a sinister childish tone. "Your illusions,

Vincent, are not as strong as mine or my witch Miranda because of one simple flaw. *They're not designed to kill!* That's the true power of an illusion." Inkadreh's small body grew wider and taller stopping around four feet. His wrinkled face and grayish white beard shriveled to a clean-shaven boyish face.

"Had you devised lethal traps in your magic, Jasmine and I would not be moments from destroying this *Hobby* of yours." His ears extended slightly beyond that of the regular gnome's size to that of a human child. His cloak changed to a mantle and his pointed hat morphed to his dirty black hair.

"Phoenix!" said Nasra. She withdrew her orb to defend herself. Vincent withdrew his wand, turned to Renee, who was now standing cautiously in the corner, and told her to run.

Phoenix turned to the Eye and breathed fire onto the orb engulfing it in flames. He stomped the floor breaking shards of wood that he elongated and sent them into the mirrors shattering them all. The forest trees ceased moving and the animal host rushed forward. Coming from the mountains, far apart from the animal mass, was Jasmine atop her tree. She breezed through the trees like wind more smoothly than she had in the Skyscraping Forest and would be at the Hobby in a matter of minutes. Devon and Lauren headed back to the manor when he stopped Lauren suddenly and looked deep into the woods.

"What is it?" asked Lauren.

"The trees have stopped moving. THE EYE!" said Devon sprinting towards the manor.

In the attic, the flames from the Eye reached the ceiling filling it with dark smoke as the Child Phoenix battled Nasra and Vincent. The broken glass on the floor made the battle more perilous for Nasra and Vincent to defend themselves.

"Bladin and Horace were illusions; I fed the gnomes of Bignome to the wizenlocks after subverting them to dig the tunnel. Do you know how long that took?" said Phoenix. He posed this question to Nasra as he stood guarded against an impending attack.

"*Fractis Spectrohusk!*" said Nasra. From her orb, husk-eating organisms clouded in green acid spray barreled toward the Phoenix. He conjured a wind gust that sent the spell against the wall then another to push Nasra to the floor.

"Over a year, the illusions kept giving the gnomes terrors of tunnel collapses, water breeches, and giant gnome-eating moles. They were difficult to control and a less determined foe would have given up, but I stayed the course because I knew one day I would have the satisfaction of blinding this Eye."

Vincent raised his wand, it glowed green, and shouted "Sallo Azeck!" The spell rushed for the Phoenix's head yet missed the Great Sinner as he transformed into a phoenix bird. The spell whizzed out the window and the Phoenix swooped for

Vincent. His claws dug into Vincent's chest and his sharp wings scratched his face. He fell to the floor and his wand rolled along the ground. Nasra stood and saw the Phoenix assailing Vincent. She attracted his wand and shouted *"Vincent, catch!"*

Phoenix flew off the magician and caught the wand in his beak. He transformed to ghost form, releasing the wand from his mouth and catching it in his right hand. He shot a powerful brilzen lighting bolt attack from his left hand, frying Nasra who couldn't cast her fire charm swiftly enough. Vincent moved quickly, he grabbed Phoenix's wand hand and pointed it at the Phoenix's head.

"Fatalis Morteli!" shouted Vincent. The spell raced from his wand into the Phoenix's mind and for a brief moment, the Great Sinner felt the immense anger, despair, and sadness preceding his death. He remembered the crowd gathered before him and the blank stares on their faces as he stood in protest with fire in his hand and oil drenching his body. He touched the torch to his body and flames encapsulated his mortal shell. The Phoenix screamed in pain. Back in the Hobby, his body exploded in red flames and in his horror, Phoenix flung Nasra out the attic window with his lightning. He created a wind gust to push Vincent against the wall away from him as he desperately tried to shake the fear of his mortal death from his mind. When Lauren and Devon arrived outside the front of the manor Nasra was falling out the window and she slammed into the ground. Lauren and Devon rushed to help her.

"Nasra what happened?" asked Lauren.

"Inkadreh, he's the Phoenix. He destroyed the Eye and is fighting Vincent inside," said Nasra. Her legs and arms quivered rigidly because of the severe burns. Devon formed a pool beneath her and bathed her wounds in spectroplasm. She healed quickly as Devon charged into the manor after Vincent.

"No, Devon!" said Nasra leaning up from the pool with spectroplasm dripping heavily from her foreboding arm. Devon stopped before the door.

"He's the only family I have left."

"He wants you! There's nothing you can do against the Phoenix."

The door swung open and out came Renee who ran into Devon.

"Lauren! The Phoenix is the gnome!" said Renee breaking the news too late.

"Are you alright?" asked Devon.

"Yes," said Renee.

"Move aside. I've got to help Vincent." He tried to enter but Renee held on to him.

"The house is taking different forms. I got lost trying to find my way out."

"I know how to get through," said Devon, clutching his necklace, but as he was going to enter he heard another girl call out.

"Run! Run!" said Amy. Behind Lauren and her company flew Selene, carrying Amy and Alexander, who were escaping the chaos of the town.

"Jasmine's coming. She's tearing up the forest. She'll be here any second."

Nasra, fully healed, stood as Selene dropped Amy and Alexander, landing behind them.

"Two enemies and two important people. We'll split you two up and go in separate directions. Renee and Amy go with Devon and Alexander. Selene and I will get Lauren back to Castle Everlasting so she can recover the book," said Nasra.

Another blast destroyed the attic and set the whole manor on fire. Through the black smoke came another orb, dark grey with stars. It landed and Vincent ghosted. His garments were shredded and exposed deep scars on his chest and right leg. Necroplasm seeped from these wounds; he was bleeding but appeared strong.

"Phoenix will have a tough time getting out of that death terror."

"Vincent!" Devon gave him a strong hug.

"Can we go now!" said Amy panicking.

"Vincent, can you make me look like Lauren and make Lauren appear like me?" asked Nasra.

"Yes, but why?"

"To confuse them; you know where to look for the book right, Lauren?"

"Yes," she said.

"Devon, I trust you'll see her to safety but after that…please take care," said Nasra.

"Hurry! Stand side-by-side," said Vincent. Lauren and Nasra stood shoulder-to-shoulder and

Vincent placed his hands on their faces and crossed their images onto each other.

"Amazing," said Selene at the transformation. In their disguises the two women modeled each other perfectly; height, weight, and all, but their voices remained unchanged. Jasmine cast a spell and a tree behind Vincent fell swiftly, intersecting the group. Amy tried to cast it away but Vincent pushed her aside. Jasmine's tree moved in, expelling wolves as it had done during the Procession.

"Fetch Lauren and bring her to me," said Jasmine.

Devon, the real Lauren, Selene, and Renee where on the right side of the tree, while Nasra, Vincent, Alexander, and Amy lay on the left. Immediately the wolves ran for Nasra as Vincent pulled her up, Alexander grabbed Amy, and they all ran between the burning manor and a row of houses to the left for the woods. Vincent was creating illusions to confuse the wolves as they made their escape. Devon, Selene, Lauren, and Renee made for a pass near the windmill that would take them further into the forest.

In the manor's attic, Child Phoenix couldn't free his mind from Vincent's death terror and had to regenerate. His column stretched to the sky from the manor roof followed by a bird's screech that blended to a boy screaming. A flaming phoenix bird emerged from the column and landed on the fallen tree. It transformed to human form as Jasmine approached him.

"*Where are they?*" Phoenix screamed.

"Lauren and Vincent went into the forest to my left, Devon and the others to the right," Jasmine said quickly.

"I'll take Lauren and Vincent! Get Devon! Force the location of the book out of him then take the pirates with you to Mortalland and find it! I'm going to kill Vincent for that death terror of his."

The Phoenix turned back into a bird and pursued his targets as Jasmine propelled her tree into the forest after Devon. Devon whistled for his horse that appeared behind them running at top speed. Devon quickly climbed her. Renee tried to leap on but she fell through it and hit the ground.

"Sorry, Loretta can only carry the dead, not shades," said Devon. Jasmine came charging through the forest after them. Selene swooped down and picked up Renee and Lauren and flew straight out as Devon followed. Selene tried desperately to fly up and out of the forest, but Jasmine shot spells at the trees, breaking off branches that kept Selene within the forest.

"I can't get them out of here with her blasting every tree in sight!" said Selene.

"*Spectro Klasto!*" Devon shot magic behind him. The spell leapt from his hand. It struck the roots on Jasmine's tree breaking many on the right side. Her trunk sunk and lost some speed. In that small window, Selene was able to rise from the trees, braving the smoke of burn season that provided excellent cover from the eagles and flew north to the Oman Range, hiding behind the huge mountains all the way back to Castle Everlasting.

"Devon, this has gone on long enough!" said Jasmine as she shot a bolt of electricity underneath the horse's hooves. It fried the beast and it tumbled violently before falling unconscious. Devon flew off and rolled on the ground hurt but his wounds healed instantly. Jasmine lifted and bound him by the tree's roots on a nearby trunk.

"I'm tired of this! You've delayed my plans to seek revenge on Etienne and look where it's gotten you, stuck in Amalgam leading a rabble of cheap conjurers. Now, tell me," she said, the roots tightened and Devon screamed. "Where did you hide the linking tome? *Tell me right now or you'll spend the rest of your time in Amalgam in greater pain.*" Jasmine's white staff crackled lightning and inched closed to Devon's face. The menacing face of the Child Phoenix on her mask melding into electric bolts emitting from the staff.

* * * *

Selene landed on the summit of the mountain due east of the Lanise crater. Above them floated Castle Everlasting but it was so high no creature in Amalgam could ever hope to reach the city foundation.

"There's no way I can reach that height," said Selene gasping for breath. She didn't stop for a moment's rest on their return flight. Immediately the ground sank beneath them and soon they were in the courtroom standing on the stone pit. Densen was standing next to Catherine, who was deep in thought. He looked surprised at Lauren and the supposedly extinct siren.

"Nasra? Why did you leave Lauren?" asked Densen.

"No it's me!" said Lauren in her voice. Densen was confused for a second until he waved his hand and Vincent illusion melted from Lauren's spirit.

"Clever, Vincent!"

"Catherine, Phoenix is after Amy and Nasra. We have to save them," Lauren said anxiously.

"Shh! She's guiding the portal through the Hobby searching for them and as many residents of the Hobby as possible." Densen approached and took them outside the courtroom, shutting the door leaving Catherine in silence.

"Selene is it?" asked Densen, the siren concurred. "Welcome," he said bewilderedly, for lack of a better term. "Please wait here, I hope you'll be of service to Catherine during our negotiations with the animals."

They walked down the hall towards the stairs.

"I'll take you to the embassy tower. When you get back to Mortalland find the book posthaste and destroy it. You have the location from Devon right?"

"Yes, but Amy and Nasra…"

"Are our concern now. Catherine will contact you once she has something to report."

Densen led Renee and Lauren to the Everlasting's embassy tower as the fate of their friends remained unclear. Passing through the realms Lauren found herself flying towards to her body, which was in school during biology, her last period of the day. In her hand materialized the gossiper's commune and Devon's shirt, Lauren quickly stuffed them in her backpack. The spirit that indwelt her body leapt out as Lauren returned. She hovered invisibly over a sleeping student sitting next to Lauren, giving her such a chill it woke her. After righting herself, Lauren saw her body's host wave goodbye, a teenage girl about her age dressed like a grunge pop star, before orbing to Amalgam House. Lauren sat in class trying to copy notes and readjust to mortal life but it was hard as her thoughts lingered on the safety of Amy and her Amalgam companions.

CHAPTER EIGHTEEN
ANITA'S SECRET

"Do you think they'll be alright?" asked Renee.

"I hope so," said Lauren as they met in the hallway leaving school. "Maybe we can catch Amy's body before she leaves."

"It may not be Amy but her indweller!" said Renee hurriedly as Lauren took off down the halls to Amy's class. "How can we tell if it's really Amy?"

"We'll ask her."

Lauren and Renee poked through the crowd but didn't have to search long as Amy was exiting French class and she appeared to act like the Amy Thompson she always knew.

"There she is!" said Renee.

"Hello, Lauren, Renee," said Amy.

"Amy! Is it really you?" asked Lauren. Amy approached closely to whisper in Lauren's ear.

"She hasn't come back."

"Then how did you recognize Renee and me?"

"When indwellers enter another's body we can access memories in the person's mind. We're trained to acknowledge relatives, friends, family, and some Court servants. The rest is forbidden for the true host's privacy."

"Oh, then who are you?" asked Lauren.

"Traci and I know all about you, Lauren, the new baron, and you're only sixteen!"

"Yes," said Lauren distractedly thinking of her friends.

"I'll hope to see you at Amalgam House. Ask for me so we can get to know each other."

"Where are you off to?"

"Amy's mother doesn't like it when she's late so I have to hurry to the car. And I can't be seen talking to you much longer. I know you two have been having problems so I have to keep the image up but nice meeting you. *No Lauren, I don't want to talk about what happened at my party!*" said Traci as she stormed off.

"What do we do now?" asked Renee.

"I guess we go home and wait for Catherine to contact us," said Lauren, clutching the gossiper's commune in her pocket. "I'll give you a call so we can start searching for the book."

When Lauren arrived home, she immediately went to her room and waited for her mother to return from work. It was a Thursday, she'd been gone in Amalgam for a day and she hadn't spoken with her mother since the police visited. Lauren wanted an update in their investigation though she knew it probably wouldn't yield much new information. Anita arrived shortly after Lauren and went straight to her bedroom with several bags of clothes, the mail, and her work portfolio. Lauren followed her inside and found her sitting at her dresser reading the mail, bags on the bed and her hair down.

"Hey, Mom!"

"Hi! Not doing the Moonwalk anymore?" Anita looked up at her daughter.

"Moonwalk? I can't...," Lauren began but then realized that the pop girl spirit from Amalgam house possessed her body and was probably dancing in her skin.

"Oh, um...I've mastered it now so I'll try salsa next."

Anita put down the mail and scratched her head tiredly before standing up and going through her bags.

"I bought you a dress to wear to the funeral."

"The funeral?" asked Lauren coming in to look at the black gown Anita was removing from one of the bags. "When is it?"

"You forgot that it's tomorrow? Jesus you've been acting strange lately," said Anita inspecting Lauren with her eyes.

"I meant what time?"

"Three. Willem's family made the arrangements; we'll be sitting in the second row at Grace's Angels Church. I want you to be ready at two thirty. The pink bag is yours," said Anita whose melancholy behavior was unlike anything Lauren had ever seen.

"Is something wrong, Mom?" asked Lauren pulling the bag towards her.

"I miss him, Lauren. I just wish we could have worked out our problems before he died."

"What problems?"

"He didn't tell you at the graveyard?"

"We got there too late…" Lauren paused.

"I see," Anita said sadly.

"We had different desires for this family. Willem wanted to create a media empire after his paper took off a few years back. He was always at the office. I just wanted my husband for a while. You're off at school, my career is dead after being out for so many years, and we're not in need of money. I was just sitting around the house. For the better part of last year we hardly saw each other."

Lauren remembered Willem's absence but thought it was because of Willem's business not their marital problems. Lauren didn't fully trust Anita's explanation. She wondered if she could press the truth from her mother with what she learned from the psychometric vision.

"W—was anyone…cheating?" asked Lauren shyly.

Anita quickly turned her back to Lauren and

collapsed on her bed sitting facing a wall with her hands covering her face. Tears rolled down her wrists and she wept uncontrollably before she screamed, *"It was a mistake!* I never...I never should have went to that bar with my friends. I just wanted to go out like Willem and I used to."

"I didn't mean it, Mom...I'm sorry, I'm going to my room," said Lauren as she made for the door. Lauren felt horrible; this time she made her mother cry.

"No, no...I've been meaning to tell you. I just didn't want you to hate me." Lauren stopped and came over to her mother and knelt by her side.

"I was so stressed, Lauren. I wanted to leave and go somewhere, for some...some release. I met up with some of my old college girlfriends and they took me to the city. We went to dinner, the movies, shopping, and dancing all in one day. It was the most fun I had in years. We were at the bar and the wine was good, it washed all the problems away, momentarily at least." Anita wiped her eyes.

"Then I met *him*...I was so caught up in the moment I had forgot I was married. I can't even remember his name. We danced the rest of the night and he offered to take me home. We went to bed and Willem must have walked in because I heard them arguing after I asked him to leave. I was devastated and ashamed. I caused Willem to run into Natalie's arms and ruined this family. It's been me all along and I couldn't bear to tell you the truth so I blamed our problems on him. I couldn't take my only daughter turning against me now that Willem was leaving." Anita's tears were subsiding but she was still upset.

"I would never turn against you, Mom. I just wanted to know the truth."

"There's more...," said Anita turning her head away.

"What? Tell me, Mom, please," said Lauren pleading sitting next to her and holding her hand.

"I got pregnant by that man!"

Lauren's heart leapt and tears fell without her knowing. Her trembling hand reached her mouth before she could retract it.

"Never get drunk, Lauren. It'll ruin your life, but you know that don't you," Anita said through a sad smile. Anita continued solemnly.

"I told Willem three weeks after that night. He was so angry it was a good thing I told him over the phone. You thought you've seen the worst the night of the pool party, you didn't. I tried calling him for weeks but he wouldn't respond. I hardly saw him until the last time he came here with Natalie and after you got hurt. I've been trying to keep it a secret as I thought of giving it up, aborting it, all possible options and when Willem died, I was very worried because his family has been upset with me since they learned of the affair."

"Jesus, Mom, you should have told me," said Lauren.

"What can you do about it? It's my mess, I have to take responsibility for it and as you can imagine it's been hard. I've been so selfish to put our family in this situation. I even considered sending you to live Willem to keep it a secret from you."

"Willem told his family and they've pretty much ignored me ever since. I was told I couldn't ride with the family convoy to the church. They said I dishonored him, although, you can if you wish." Anita paused slightly as new tears streamed down her face. "I really messed up, Lauren." Anita cried out as Lauren comforted her.

"I'm here for you, Mom, despite what the Walstons do. I don't want to ride with them if my mother can't. Just promise me, no more secrets!"

"I promise! Give me a hug, baby," said Anita.

Lauren squeezed her mother tightly before handing her a tissue. Lauren thought about having a sibling. It was bittersweet, exciting because she'll have a little brother or sister but depressing because of the circumstances. She wondered whether it would be a boy or girl, what his or her name would be. She thought maybe the baby was why Willem was reluctant to reconcile and the driving force behind the divorce. Lauren returned to her room with the bag containing her dress where the telephone had been ringing in her absence. It was Renee, who asked if Amy had called and for the time of her father's funeral because she wanted to attend.

"No, I haven't heard from her."

"Do you think she'll call if she made it out of Amalgam? Maybe she hasn't yet because she's still mad at you?"

"She'll call, just pray for her safe return."

"When do you want to look for the book?"

"My father's funeral is tomorrow so the day after."

"Where did Devon say he buried it?"

"Underneath three trees somewhere on Crow Island."

"Amy's from that island!"

"Yes and we could really use her help. Devon only gave me his shirt and the physical surroundings which are three hundred years old."

"His shirt? Oh, psychometry, right?"

"Yeah."

"Well, I'm sure that'll work. When she calls count me in, okay?"

"Sure."

Lauren hung up the phone and spent the rest of the day watching television, trying to rest her mind but she questions filled her head. Having finally heard the truth from her mother Lauren questioned her personal need to continue the search for the linking tome. Only the contents of Willem's final anamnesis and his murderer's identity remained a mystery. Lauren wondered what Willem had to say in this final anamnesis. Goodbye was obvious and possibly more information about their divorce, but what else? Would he still be upset? Would he ask her to continue as baron? The only way to know was to unlock the message.

As to Willem's assailant, Messina's assurance

she'd encounter the ghost was comforting and with her training, Lauren was confident that she could avenge Willem. She still planned on taking her revenge and to suffer the consequences in the purgation fields, though the ghost outside the House of Shades made her fear the pain she'd endure. Lauren quickly dismissed these thoughts as selfish. She had a responsibility to her friends, who put their lives in jeopardy to save hers and whose fates remain uncertain. She recalled Willem's anamnesis and realized she had the privilege of *knowing* her father is still alive in spirit whereas everyone else has to have faith.

She wondered if her father had done anything that would keep him out of Heaven. She wasn't sure if he'd ever committed any serious wrong seeing as how he and her mother held secrets from her. "There is one way to find out," thought Lauren. She got the idea to touch her father's body in hopes of receiving a psychometric vision but Lauren wondered if she wanted to know more truth. She thought of what she would feel at the funeral when looking at her father's body. She realized it wouldn't be goodbye but possibly see you later. Lauren thought the remainder of the night about her responsibility to Amalgam. The stress began to make her sick though and nothing soothed Lauren's stress like sleep.

* * * *

She awoke energized though the depressing prospect of attending her father's funeral quickly sapped the enthusiasm out of her day. She showered and dressed, she wore a knee-length black dress with veiled sleeves and a hat with a veil bow. Anita wore a similar black dress but without the veil and no hat, she styled her hair so that it was curly and shimmering.

They rode to Grace's Angel Church, which wasn't too far from Amalgam House. There was a long line to enter the church. Willem had many friends from work and around the town, not to mention reporters covering burial of their late employer. Lauren saw Renee standing outside by a large oak tree along with an unexpected guest, Jason. She got out of the car and walked causally towards them. Her heart leapt as she approached her friends. She was braver, however, as the occasion didn't lend itself to excited feelings.

"Hey, Renee," said Lauren before turning to Jason. "Hi Jason, didn't expect you to be here."

"I thought I'd come for support. I really admired him, he was so successful because he worked hard and believed in himself. His passing was such a tragedy, I felt compelled to come."

Lauren smiled listening to Jason's thoughtful words before she said, "Have you seen Amy?"

"She's good, same old Amy Thompson," said Jason and Lauren realized Traci was good at indwelling Amy. A caravan of black vehicles diverted her attention as Willem's hearse and the

Walstons arrived into Grace's Angel Church lot. Lauren saw they were fully dressed in black. Many attendees cried before the services even began and Lauren listened as they spoke of the strange circumstance in which Willem passed.

"They still don't have any suspects. Who could have committed such a terrible crime and escape without a trace?" Lauren's ears filled with similar talk until the funeral began.

"Lauren, over here!" said Anita waving her over from the middle of a line that had formed by the church's ramp.

"I'll see you all after the service," said Lauren as she left them to join her mother.

An elderly woman stopped Lauren as she moved past the line. It was her grandmother, Rebecca yet Lauren called her a Grandma Betty. She stood at four-eleven, very thin, but her face was still energetic at age eighty-four. Her husband, Lauren's grandfather, passed earlier and she never remarried. When Lauren asked why Betty replied, "There's no one in the world like your Grandpa." Lauren believed that that was true love and not Amy's passion for Jason.

Betty was dressed in a very old-fashioned brown waitress dress. Anita said Betty wore that uniform when giving birth to Willem. The one that itched all day long with the cake stain she never washed off when she dropped a patron's dessert as she went into labor. It covered nearly ever inch of the body besides the arms and the knees.

"Well I's say, it's my son's lovely daughter, Lauren. All growed up and you'ful," said Grandma Betty.

"Thank you," said Lauren. "You're looking spectacular as well."

"Oh hush chile. I'm ol', no sense flatterin' an ol' lady as to her 'pearance. I'm ready Lauren, ready tuh see my son again. Tis a shame he was taken from you and me," said Betty, her eyes filled with tears and she hugged Lauren as tight as her strength allowed. She felt a soft pillow of flesh press against her skin. "I's wish he could've watched you grow as I's saw him. Tuh not have dat strong fatherly presence wit you is something no youn' girl should bear."

She sighed before speaking again. "He nevah harmed no one, nevah wanted to. If only I could speak tuh de person dat did this and ask 'em why they took him I'd be content. If de Lawd is willin, my body will remain strong 'til I'se know."

"Hopefully we'll all find out soon, Grandma," said Lauren. She reminded herself to tell her grandmother why if she ever found out from Willem's killer, but Lauren doubted Betty would believe a ghost was responsible.

"I know Willem and Nita were havin' problems but I love her! We love her 'spite what my chilen' might say. They're angry 'cause they loved their brother and he always confided in his siblings. The marriage failin' hurt 'em as well. They've angry wit everyone, the police, g'aveyard caretakers, frensic doctors. It's not an attempt tuh spite you or Nita. I won't rest 'til my chillen' are back on good terms wit yo' mother."

"Thanks, Grandma," said Lauren comforted by her grandmother's explanation as she kissed her on the cheek before moving to stand in front of her mother. The line began to move inside slowly and the weeping became more audible. Anita clutched Lauren's shoulders tightly. Lauren could feel her hands trembling and looking back saw her mother staring fearfully at the open casket where Willem lay. After talking to her grandmother, Lauren finally realized that she would never see Willem in his physical state again with his body's burial. Unknowingly Lauren hoped to the anamnesis would also bring him back to life as her reward for finding the linking tome. This realization provoked a stream of tears to run down her cheek.

Lauren could feel Anita's grip tightening as they grew closer to the body and was relieved that they weren't sitting in the front row. She wasn't sure Anita or her shoulders would be able to take it. Many were viewing the body before they sat. Grandma Betty was rather subdued as she paid her respects to her last-born child. Anita arrived at the second row and sat quickly. She turned her head down as shaken nerves overwhelmed her and broke down crying aloud.

Lauren was curious as to the state of her father's remains, so she moved closer to the casket. She found Willem, eyes closed, face serene with a smile and cosmetics applied liberally. His arms cupped about his abdomen and on it was his wedding ring. Lauren wondered…she reached in with her trembling index finger. She closed her eyes before her finger touched the ring and when she felt the cold gold, she hesitated before opening her eyes.

The pulpit and her father's casket vanished replaced by Willem sitting at his office desk, pouring alcohol into a short glass, weeping intensely and drinking fast. On his desk was a gun, a small pistol and a single bullet. He slammed the glass to the table, shaking the wine in the bottle as he cried out, "WHY GOD?" He was wearing the same clothes as he did in the vision from Anita's ring so Lauren knew it was the same night. Lauren saw the full effect Anita's unfaithfulness had on Willem. He was going to commit suicide!

"I've sacrificed so much for this woman. I tried so hard to win her heart in college. I prayed I'd be the man she'd marry," Willem wailed, head on the desk.

He laid his head on the table for moments, silent before moving swiftly for the gun, loading it hastily and putting it in his open mouth when Natalie entered his office.

"Mr. Walston, I have here for you the photographs for the accident on Bishop Street," said Natalie, flipping through an envelope with pictures. Willem removed the gun and hid it below his thigh. He placed the glass and the open bottle in a drawer for it to ruin a few documents inside, fixed his clothing, and wiped away his tears.

"Here they are," she said handing a few pictures to him and smiling.

"Thanks," said Willem, looking into her eyes and forming a slight smile.

"Something wrong? You seem a little…sad." She gave a concerned smile, one that picked up Willem's spirits.

"I'm tired, deadlines you know." Willem straightened up and tried to appear professional.

"You shouldn't work so hard and *late*. Go home, get some rest!" she strode over behind his desk.

"Home is no place to find rest tonight," Willem said gravely.

"Not even at that nice house on Evelyn Lane?" Natalie sniffed the air. "Was someone drinking in here?"

"Ah, no…I mean yes. Trying to stay awake…no rest from the news."

"Certainly not," said Natalie as she moved a chair from the corner of the room and placed it by his seat. She plopped her folder on the desk and leaned over to explain her report on the accident. Willem awkwardly tried to reposition himself and get comfortable as Natalie sat closely. Lauren could smell her perfume through the vision. It was strong and Willem loved it.

As she sat talking, Willem moved closer to her until they were face-to-face. Slowly they began a seductive conversation. Willem divulged about

Anita's affair and his secret crush on her. Natalie confessed her love and they kissed. The dream faded when Willem's brother, Ronald touched her shoulder to usher her back to her seat as the funeral was about to begin.

"Don't worry, Lauren. He's in a better place now," said Ronald to console her, most people thought she had become frozen with grief.

As she returned to her seat, she saw Natalie in the congregation. Lauren felt that she owed Natalie thanks for her seductive charm that prevented Willem's suicide. She wondered if the Judge would forgive Willem for any unfaithfulness he might have experienced with her as she sat listening to the preacher. The eulogy and service was short and sweet with the preacher having very positive comments on Willem's life and a multitude of the mourners agreed vocally. The proceedings continued outside underneath the tent covering Willem's plot. As they laid his casket in the ground, Anita fainted and Uncle Ronald carried her into the fellowship hall of the church by Lauren and her brother-in-law. When the service was over and Anita was feeling better, Lauren rejoined Renee and Jason.

"Is your mother okay?" asked Renee.

"Yeah, she just had a fainting spell."

"Good, I hope her spirits lift soon. I'm going home, take care okay?" asked Renee.

"Wait," said Lauren, she approached Renee and took her aside. "I know you've been to the graveyard. Have you heard your mother's voice lately?" Renee smiled abashedly.

"Yes. She says there people talking to her, other spirits. They're trying to help her but its going to take time. There's something going on, I can *feel* it, and that graveyard is the source of it."

"Remember what Catherine said and promise me that you won't go back there."

"Why?"

"Because something *is* happening there and something *has* happened already. I don't want you to get hurt."

"Lauren, I…"

"Renee," Lauren grabbed her arm. "Remember my father and promise to me you won't go back there."

"I promise."

"Good…take care." Renee got inside her father's car and left but Jason waited around for Lauren.

"Your mother must have really loved him," Jason began and Lauren turned to him.

"She did; I wonder if Amy feels the same way about you. Why are you with her by the way?" asked Lauren.

"Obviously she's cute, funny, and I think she'll help me grow socially so I can meet new people."

"You can't do that on your own?"

"No way! I'm far too shy to walk up to girls and start conversations. I was lucky that Amy found me attractive and I hope that we never break up because

I don't want to go back to being alone. She's introduced me to so many new people and experiences. Every day that I'm with her is exciting. I'm no longer the geek that sits alone playing video games and watching television. I'm popular and more interesting now!"

"But you were interesting then. They didn't see it!"

"This is what I want to be, Lauren. The guy people actually call and see if they want to hang out. The guy the girls actually notice when he walks down the hall."

"A lot of girls notice the shy, silent guys. I did and I thought you knew."

"Knew what?"

After braving the shenga, Jasmine, a dragon, dinosaur, and siren Lauren found her courage. "Did you ever like me, Jason?"

"Sure I did," said Jason and Lauren's heart leapt again. "You're a great friend." Lauren felt almost as hollow as the day Willem died.

"That's not what I meant! Did you ever want to be more than my friend?"

"At times. You're very funny, artistic, and we have good conversations but…"

"But what?"

"You're just like me, introverted and quiet. Amy's just so different. She's a very positive person; she doesn't let anything or anyone bother her. And I just get that feeling…it's hard to explain," Jason shrugged as he finished.

"I see...I better go check on my mom. Thanks for coming," said Lauren as she walked away. *'Positive person! Perhaps, he's mistaking Traci for the true Amy!'* thought Lauren; she felt sick as well as empty. To lift her spirits, Lauren thought of what Messina said about human's vain pursuits and felt Jason's desire to be popular was blinding him from true happiness with her, yet somehow this didn't help her much.

Lauren returned to the fellowship hall where Anita was eating a little food. She was talking with the Walstons once again; they threw aside their petty feud after witnessing Anita faint. She was conversing lightly even with Natalie who had arrived inside to check on her. Lauren sat next to her mother and waited patiently as a majority of the attendees expressed their condolences. As the evening drew to a close Lauren and Anita arrived back to Evelyn Lane followed by Uncle Ronald to ensure their safe return. He passed them, headed home, as they pulled into the drive. Lauren and Anita didn't talk as they entered the house.

Lauren joined her mother in her bedroom and sat on the edge of the bed while Anita stretched out. They talked about the beautiful funeral service and the kind words of Willem's mourners. Anita asked what Lauren was thinking about when she stood at the casket but Lauren, though she promised her mother they'd no longer keep secrets, had to obey the Mortalland Rule and said, "I was reflecting." The phone rang and Lauren answered. It was for

Anita. She confirmed dinner for two tomorrow at a restaurant called Gisele on the Outer Banks. Lauren heard of Gisele before and if she wasn't mistaken it was the most expensive and elegant restaurant in Baker's Creek.

"Who was that?" asked Lauren.

"A business prospect, his name's Mr. Lasitier. He runs a tourism firm in Baker's Creek. He told me that one of Willem's old associates had referred him to me. He asked if I had any experience in advertising which I have and he offered me a job."

"But dinner?" asked Lauren worriedly. With the affair still lingering in her mind she wondered if she was meeting this man socially.

"An interview over dinner. We're meeting at two o'clock, tomorrow. That reminds me, I have to prepare my portfolio, my resume," said Anita planning aloud. Lauren got up and eased to the door so Anita could get to work.

"You looked nice today, Lauren," said Anita before Lauren could sneak out. "I bet Jason was impressed."

"Not really, Mom," said Lauren.

She left her mother for her room to lie on her bed. She tried to force out thoughts of her and Jason's conversation re-entering her mind. Her telephone aided in this as it rang, startling her. She picked up the phone and said hello.

"I'm so glad you made it out safe, Lauren," Amy's acid voice flowed from the phone.

"Amy, is it really you?" asked Lauren, ignoring

her sarcasm for now.

"*I can't believe you left me to die, running for dear life while Selene flies you and Renee out of that forest!*"

"Amy, I'm sorry but it sounds like you made it out safely, 'cause you're back to your normal self."

"You being sarcastic?" asked Amy.

"*No, you are!* I'm just letting you know how you sound. *Be happy you're alive!*"

"Maybe I would be calm and happy now if it wasn't for Nasra's *stupid* idea to wear your body as a disguise. Phoenix never stopped chasing us because he thought Nasra was you! But stupidity does have its faults because now she, Alexander, and Vincent have been captured."

"WHAT?" asked Lauren.

"Yeah, Phoenix caught up with us and nearly killed the three of them once he discovered Nasra wasn't you. Vincent told me to hide under some bushes and made it look thicker than it was. I watched the Phoenix torture them and that could've been me! I told you two it was dangerous going out there, I told you to tell Catherine not to send us but *noooo!* You had to be *Ms. New Baron*, you had to put our lives in jeopardy and now, three of your friends are missing."

"What do you mean, missing?"

"Phoenix and Jasmine took them away. When I met up with the guards they said Phoenix might have jailed them in some tree prison Jasmine has somewhere."

"What about Devon?"

"I don't know, weren't you with him?"

"We got separated."

"You left him too, huh? Well I didn't see him."

"Oh God," said Lauren.

"Oh God is right, their going to need Him to save their lives or you."

Lauren had had enough of Amy's crass and selfishness. She wanted to tell her never to come back to Amalgam if she felt so cold towards Nasra and everyone else but she restrained her anger.

"Me?" asked Lauren baffled.

"Yeah, Catherine had me tell you. She said the Phoenix contacted her and said that they'll be kept alive as hostages to trade for the linking tome. He said you'll have to find it soon or they'll kill all three."

The air burst out of Lauren lungs and she felt nervous as if acid left a gaping hole in her stomach at the thought of lives depending on her to find the linking tome.

"We need to get started right away," said Lauren.

"We…you mean *you!* I'm not going along with this anymore. I'm done! Catherine said I had to go to the Hobby for my punishment, that's it."

"AND SHE ALSO SAID YOU'D BE PUNISHED IN THE PURGATION FIELDS FOR THOSE LIES YOU SPREAD ABOUT ME!" Lauren yelled with all unrestrained passion. Anita called from downstairs about her screaming and Lauren said she was

watching a television show and got a little into it. She returned to her conversation, Amy was still snapping at her.

"You've must have lost your damn mind if you think you can talk to me like that. When I see you again, you'll be wishing that car had killed you!"

Lauren realized that this cattiness would be the kind of time waste that would suffer her friends. She had to get to work as soon as possible and would need Amy's help to investigate Crow Island. Lauren quickly thought of a clever way to get her to help.

"Amy, I don't have time for this! If you don't want to eat coals in the purgation fields then I suggest you help me find the book. I don't want any arguing or attitude, just help me and Renee out and I'll ask Catherine if you can get out of punishment."

"THAT'S NOT ENOUGH! I don't want to go back there anymore! I don't want to see a fucking ghost ever again in my life! *If* you can do that, then I'll be happy to cooperate!"

"Done!"

Lauren told Amy about the directions Devon gave her and about his shirt that should provide a clue if they were getting close. "Have your mom pick me up at Gisele's tomorrow so we can start looking."

"Tomorrow?" asked Amy surprised. "I just got back from Amalgam less than ten minutes ago and I caught a cold!"

"The sooner we get done, the sooner you'll

never see a ghost again. Goodnight Amy," said Lauren sweetly and cut the connection to dial Renee's number.

Lauren was happy to finally control Amy for once and she didn't have to use the blarney stone to do it! She told Renee the good and bad news about Amy's return and Nasra, Devon and Vengrass' capture. Renee was saddened at the news and expressed her desire to begin the search immediately. Lauren relayed Anita's dinner appointment at Gisele's tomorrow and Amy's plan to pick her up at the restaurant.

"Why is she going to dinner?"

"She claims to have a job interview," said Lauren disbelievingly.

"You don't trust her?" asked Renee.

"How many job interviews take place at restaurants?" asked Lauren.

"Quite a few. Some businesses looking for long term relationships with employees want to be as accommodating as possible," said Renee professionally. "You're not suspicious of your mom dating so soon after your father's death are you?"

"A little."

"Don't be. I'm certain she has more respect for your father than that. You'll see you're just being paranoid."

"I hope so. Are you coming along tomorrow?"

"I'll see, my Dad is having some friends over and I may have to clean up. I'll let you know."

CHAPTER NINETEEN
THE SEARCH BEGINS

It was the third Saturday of September and the weather was becoming cooler with each day. Lauren awoke excitedly in the morning ready to begin her search. She thought finding the book would be much easier with Devon's shirt and Amy's knowledge of Crow Island. Expecting to get a little dirty, Lauren dressed in her jeans and a long sleeve black shirt, putting on Devon's shirt underneath to conceal and carry it. Lauren tucked her gossiper's commune in her pocket because Nasra instructed her to keep it on her at all times.

At breakfast, Lauren asked her mother if she could join her to the Outer Banks to meet Amy. Anita agreed after Lauren explained that Amy's mother would ensure she'd be back in time and that she and Amy decided to mend their friendship with some time together. Lauren waited for Anita's appointment, reflecting on Devon's vision and writing down clues to refresh her memory. Renee called and said that indeed her father needed her so she wouldn't be able to join her and Amy. At noon, Lauren heard her mother showering and at one she was ready.

Lauren then went downstairs to see Anita dressed semi-professionally in a dark pantsuit and her hair done in a wrap. Anita carried her large portfolio briefcase and gathered her keys as they headed out the door for the car. They rode across Arthur Sound on the same bridge the night of the gathering. It was far more comfortable for Lauren the second time around and soon they were on Crow Island. Turning into the lot of Gisele's Lauren found Amy and her mother waiting patiently. Lauren moved to get out of the car when Anita stopped her.

"Lauren, I'm not going to pick you up from the hospital again am I?"

"No, Mom."

"No fighting this time, promise?"

"I promise."

Lauren hurriedly ran over to them. Amy politely greeted her and Amy's mother was happy that she also made an excellent recovery but they all shied away from talking about the birthday party. Both girls sat in the back seat quietly for most of the ride until they passed a house close to Amy's when Devon's shirt began to feel cool and snug on Lauren's torso as if she'd just emerged from the water. Lauren looked at the house they were passing and asked who lived there.

"That's Peter Townsend house," said Amy.

"The creep at the party?" asked Lauren.

"What do you mean?"

"He's a disgusting pig, whistling at girls and talking about their bodies. Oh, and he felt me up when he pulled me off you."

"What does he have to do with the book?" asked Amy annoyed.

"The shirt got cool as we passed his house, it might be there," said Lauren.

"Good, at least that's a start. He lives two blocks from my house, we can walk once we get home. He's pretty smart in math so I'll call him up and ask if he can help me with some algebra homework. I'm pretty sure I can convince him to let us look around," said Amy lifting her breasts.

Lauren wasn't thrilled about meeting Peter again. She often steered clear of him at school and he mostly kept away from her for fear of another groin kick. She was happy however, that Amy knew him and since her psychometry hadn't failed before, Lauren was sure the book lay inside their house. Amy's mother pulled the car into the Thompson drive and Lauren and Amy walked inside to her room. Amy called Peter and asked if he could help with her homework.

"*Yeah, I always make time for a pretty lady.*" Lauren heard Peter's voice blaring through the phone.

"I'm bringing my friend, Lauren…"

"*When did you two start talking again?*" asked Peter inquisitively. "*I thought the two of you were still at each other's throats over Average Joe Jason Birch.*"

"Careful, Peter, he is my boyfriend and Lauren and I have settled our differences," said Amy annoyed.

"*Well I'm glad you two made up, can't wait to see you both.*"

"We'll see you in a minute," said Amy as she hung up the phone. "Let's go."

Amy grabbed her books and backpack and they walked downstairs. Amy told her mother she was leaving and the girls walked swiftly to Peter's house. Moments later Lauren and Amy were on the Townsend's porch and Amy knocked three times. Peter opened the door wearing a blue shirt and jeans eating a bowl of chocolate cereal with milk dripping down his chin.

"Hello. Come inside, don't be shy," Peter commented to Lauren when she appeared hesitant to enter.

"No!" said Lauren. Amy gave Lauren a puzzled look.

"No what?" asked Peter.

"I want an apology!" said Lauren.

"For what?" Peter asked contemptuously.

"For feeling me up while Amy and I were fighting!"

Peter laughed heartily despite seeing Lauren

become madder.

"I'm sorry, but when I reached around you moved really quickly and my hands slipped."

"Yeah right!"

"Oh let it go! Besides, you should be proud. It felt *real* good!"

"DON'T EVER TOUCH ME AGAIN OR NEXT TIME I'LL KICK YOU SO HARD YOU'LL NEVER HAVE CHILDREN!"

Peter looked disturbed as Lauren walked in. Amy came in with Peter and Lauren heard her trying to make peace between them. As she waited for Amy, Lauren examined the sizeable family oil portrait with Peter and his parents. Peter's father was a large man with graying black hair, black eyes, and an imposing presence. He was dressed in a dark black suit and a blue tie that, by the artist's skill, appeared silk.

His mother was very attractive, eclipsing Natalie. She smiled in the picture; her teeth showed through thick mahogany lip-colored lips. She was of medium build but her arms, neck, and chest were visibly muscular. Peter was just a boy when it was painted but he held the smirk that would later irritate many girls at Royce High. He was standing next to his father dressed exactly like him. It hung on the wall beneath a staircase and to the right of a brightly lit hallway.

To the left was a nice white carpeted room with multiple glass tables and lamps with white furniture. Further down could be see a den more conservative than their extravagant living room where Peter was lounging around before they arrived. A video game was paused on the large television and multiple games spread out before a beanbag chair. He led them to this room when Lauren took a peak down a brightly lit hallway before it. She could see the light was coming from an open door to the backyard. Outside Lauren could see a small excavator and asked Amy to look. She did and asked Peter about it.

"What's going on outside, Peter?" asked Amy.

"Oh, my parents are planning a garden. Luther got fed up with Vera's *whining* so he ordered a group of landscapers to come and fix it up back there. You know remove a few old trees, plant a few new ones, spruce it up."

"How's it coming?" Amy continued.

"Fairly uneventful," Peter plopped into his beanbag chair, "So, Lauren, are you over Jason yet?"

"Can we not talk about that?" asked Amy putting her bags down on the floor.

"Just curious, I wanted to see if she's available. There shouldn't be any hard feelings seeing as how you two have made up," said Peter snickering. The shirt grew cooler on Lauren's body when she stood in the hallway and after listening to Peter talk about the trees she asked if they could go outside.

"I guess," said Peter putting aside his bowl and standing to lead them outside. He moved close to Lauren as they exited the house, Amy followed him and Lauren.

"So Lauren, do you any free time? I'd *love* to get to know you."

Lauren gave him a disgusted look.

"Honestly. So we can be friends," said Peter earnestly.

"I *know* who you are Peter," said Lauren flatly.

"Really? What good news have you heard about me?" asked Peter stopping to turn and face her.

"Good?" asked Lauren disgustedly.

"In math!" said Amy. "She's heard you're one of the smartest students at Royce High."

"Oh," said Peter disappointed. Lauren surveyed the back yard with a keen eye. There was no cluster of large trees present and she could only see the dug up ground and the excavator. They approached two women sitting to the right at a sleek steel table engaged in a light conversation.

"Is that your mother there, Peter?" asked Lauren of one of the two women at the table who looked like the woman in the painting.

"Yes, my mom, Vera, and her loony sister Aunt Carrie. Carrie has been putting into Vera's head that supernatural garbage about our house having bad spiritual energy and other such rubbish. She's always believed those silly rumors about this town being haunted."

"Hey, Pete, brought some friends over?" asked Peter's mother.

"Yes, Vera," said Peter.

"*How many times have I told you to call me*

Mom?" asked Vera, who was quite displeased. "It's very disrespectful."

"Sorry!" said Peter rolling his eyes. "*Damn* my mom can be a *bitch* at times. I don't complain when she calls me Pete."

"It's not nice to speak of your mother like that," said Amy.

"It's true!" said Peter.

"What was this machine digging up, Peter?" asked Lauren.

"A few trees to make room for a gazebo. When it's finished I would like to have you over when we dedicate it," Peter smirked. Lauren had enough and felt like punching him; she balled up her fist until Amy nudged her.

"Calm down. Is this the place?" Amy whispered.

"I think so but without the trees I can't be sure. Let's me see if I can find the brook." Lauren looked between the remaining trees for a small stream.

"Can we get closer to see the equipment, Peter?" asked Amy placing her arms around Peter's waist.

"I don't see why not," Peter's voice deepened. "Just be careful by the excavator, the ground's a little wet over there."

Lauren noticed the fluid sensation decreased the further she went from the house. Since they were outside, Lauren wanted as much visual confirmation as possible to make certain they were in the right place. She moved carefully around the excavator machine holding onto one of the remaining trees on the property. The ground was soft and wet where she stood. The pond next to gazebo had been set in the ground and the water had wet the ground. Lauren looked at the base of the remaining trees but could not find any carved letters.

Lauren thought about Devon, Amy didn't know what happened to him after they left Amalgam so he might have escaped Jasmine. She withdrew her gossiper commune to speak with him. She called his name a few times silently and tried to look as inconspicuous as possible. Peter and Amy were not far behind and Lauren could hear Peter talking seductively to Amy. Their conversation distracted Lauren.

"I've always known that you liked me. What are you doing with that nerd Jason? He's so boring and goofy; he's more suitable for your friend here."

Lauren's anger burned. She turned and shouted, "Don't talk about Jason like that!" She loosened her grip on the tree but slipped on some mud. The commune left her hand and fell into the pond, evaporating into vapors. Peter laughed loudly, while Amy helped her up and Vera and Aunt Carrie came over to help. Lauren was filthy, covered in mud on her right side from her arms to her legs. Peter had collapsed to the ground in his gaiety.

"Shut up, Pete!" said Vera as she approached.

Amy helped Lauren to a chair where she sat panting for losing the gossiper's commune. Lauren realized that saving her friends was now going to be much more difficult without contact with the Court.

"I told you it was slippery over there," said Peter.

"Ha, ha Peter," Amy said mockingly. She glared at him while running her fingers through Lauren's hair to comfort her. "Slow you breathing, Lauren. Don't shake yourself to pieces."

"I've lost it, Amy!" said Lauren panic-stricken.

"I'll say," said Peter. "Throwing a fit over a boy who doesn't even like you and both times it's ended in disaster."

"Lost what?" asked Amy coming closer when Lauren beckoned her by nodding her head.

"The gossiper's commune! It fell into the water and it was my only way to contact the Court."

"Don't worry about that now. Besides we can go to the Amalgam House if we need to speak with Catherine," Amy whispered.

Lauren calmed, she remembered the ghost house has an oracle as its administrator.

"Are you okay, darling?" asked Vera. Lauren nodded yes. "Get her some ointment for her elbow," said Vera to her sister. Lauren realized it was bleeding when Vera mentioned it. "What were you looking for?"

"I just wanted to see the pond," said Lauren.

"Oh, I always wanted one. When I first got here, I told Luther I wanted a gazebo and a pond so we could sit and watch the sunset."

"That was good thinking," said Aunt Carrie returning with the ointment.

"Where is Dad, by the way?" Peter asked his mother.

"He left two hours ago."

"What for?"

"He found something in the dirt."

"Oh, what?" asked Peter indifferently but Lauren and Amy looked up curiously.

"It looked like a pile of caked up dirt but when he washed it off he phoned a couple of appraisal shops and left afterwards. I hope it's worth something, whatever it was. Would you like a glass of water, Lauren?"

"Yes," said Lauren as she rolled up her muddy and bloodstained shirt. Vera asked Peter to get the water while Aunt Carrie liberally applied the ointment to Lauren's elbow. It burned intensely.

"I hope that ointment cures clumsy," said Peter as he left.

"Ignore him, he's spoiled," said Vera glaring at her bratty child.

While Peter was away and Vera and Aunt Carrie talked about how to add value to a house, Lauren and Amy leaned to each other but they didn't have to say a word. They both knew that the linking tome had been uncovered.

"Are you *sure* this is the place?" asked Amy seriously.

"It has to be; the shirt and my psychometry and are telling me it's here and Peter's father found something under the dug up trees. He's out looking for an appraiser, my God!" said Lauren realizing how hard it would be to find the linking tome if it was sold.

"You think he might sell it?" asked Amy.

"Possibly, but my psychometry is telling me the book's still in the house. We have to hurry; he might be bringing someone to the house to appraise it."

"Well let's get inside and get to it. I'll keep Pete with me, you start looking."

Having soiled her clothes, Lauren had the perfect excuse to head to the bathroom. Peter was bringing out the glass of water but changed directions when the girls returned into the house. Peter told Lauren where she could find a bathroom on the ground floor and he and Amy followed her back into the house. Amy mouthed, "Start looking!" as Lauren parted from them and then convinced Peter to step away from his video game to help her with some algebra.

As she left for the bathroom, Lauren neared the staircase and the shirt grew noticeably cooler than before. She went upstairs and as she did, Devon's shirt felt wetter and colder with each rising step. She realized the book must be upstairs and hurried up before Peter or anyone came looking. Lauren then followed the sensation, as she went down a hallway. Lauren saw yet another small bedroom, clean and undisturbed, a guest room she assumed, but the shirt grew dryer and warmer.

Lauren tried the side of the second floor but to do so she'd have to cross the foyer on a balcony exposed to the ground level. She started walking but had to run back when Peter came into the room headed for the kitchen for drinks. Amy stood by the door laughing at Peter's jokes about Irwin, a senior jock and "varsity dumbass" as Peter described him. Lauren crouched down by the walkway yet Amy saw her up above. She mouthed for her to move before intercepting Peter who was returning with the drinks taking him back into the kitchen claiming she wanted a root beer instead of fruit punch.

Lauren moved across when the shirt started to chill her bones and a drowning sensation overtook her. She knew this was what Devon felt when he sank into the abyss and it stung worse than in her vision. Near one door, her body felt colder than ever and the stinging more painful. Lauren used the evanesce charm to drop her body and phase through the door. She cast an unlocking charm on he handle, she learned from Vasteck, before coalescing into her body and entering. Inside, she found a small study and a desk with a telephone book, phone, and mud in the center. She moved around the desk and felt immense despair.

There on the table was the remaining dirty torn cloth from Devon's shirt. Lauren touched it slightly and closed her eyes as hopelessness besieged her. The book had been completely uncovered leaving her without a clue and a deep fear that the linking tome is now in the possession of a museum or private collector and her Amalgam friends were doomed. Lauren composed herself and focused on the cloth when she entered a vision.

She could see the book being unearthed and taken inside by Luther who took it upstairs. He put on a pair of latex gloves, washed off the mud, and entered his study. When he opened the book, it grew in size expanding to the size of a photo album, but filled with numerous pages like a gigantic dictionary. Luther was astounded and sat for a while with his mouth open before carefully flipping a couple of pages. He cleaned up his desk and reached for the phone book. He called a shop in the vision but Lauren couldn't make out the name, Luther's excitement confounded his lips and only a word could be heard "boutique."

The vision ended when Luther agreed to an immediate meeting and picked up the book to leave. From below, Lauren heard Peter wondering if she'd gotten lost or sick. She got up to rejoin them below before Peter discovered she wasn't in the restroom but paused for a moment. She thought about taking the cloth with her to look over the vision more carefully, but decided it would be best to leave the room undisturbed.

Lauren left the study and returned slowly from the upper level hoping to remain invisible and not let anyone know she was up there. She returned to the foyer and looked into the kitchen to see where they were when Peter said, "There you are!" from behind her. Lauren turned to him, he was smiling, and Amy was hanging on his arm.

"Get a little lost or were you somewhere you

shouldn't have been," Peter's eyes lifted to the second floor.

"*I* was in the bathroom then *I* came out looking for you two," said Lauren with sass.

"Uh huh," said Peter sardonically. "Is that why you're still dirty?"

Amy slapped Peter's chest, "Please, Peter! Lauren just needed something stronger than soap to remove these stains," smiled Amy before she sneezed and wiped herself with a tissue. "Why don't you get some detergent from the laundry room so Lauren can get cleaned up?" She flashed a gorgeous smile at him. Peter blushed before curving his mouth into that grating smirk and said, "Sure."

He left promptly while Amy and Lauren conversed. "No book! Was it not up there?" she asked.

"I found the cloth Devon wrapped it in, but Peter's dad took the book with him," Lauren said.

Peter returned with the detergent and he and Amy went back to the game room while Lauren headed for the bathroom. She rejoined them soon and found Amy playing into Peter's advances for a date, flirting heavily, and agreeing to go out with him. Lauren got upset because she was planning to cheat on Jason but she held her tongue. She couldn't stand it when their flirting grew a bit physical but Amy noticed it was bothering Lauren and stopped Peter by asking him to get her a cream soda this time.

When Peter left from the room, Lauren asked,

"What are you doing?"

"What?" Amy asked irritably.

"You're dating Jason!"

"*Hello!* Jason isn't related to the man who has our book. I'm getting friendly with Peter so I can hang around to see if Luther's going to bring the book back. I'm trying to keep my ass out of those purgation fields and I'll do whatever it takes. By the way, if Jason asks, we're over."

"WHAT?"

"Trust me, Lauren; he's only after one thing despite the nice guy façade. I'm going date Peter until we can find the book. Besides, you should be happy, now that he's single again you can have him, if you don't mind my sloppy seconds," Amy giggled, which incensed Lauren. "Peter?" she asked.

"Yes," Peter said returning with the drink.

"Does your father have a cell phone we could call?"

"He doesn't have it on him. I heard it ringing upstairs when I called to have him bring home some breakfast. I had to eat cereal instead."

"Give me a call when your father returns?"

"Why?" Peter asked cynically.

"We're curious as to what he could have found."

"He'd never tell. Luther's very secretive when it comes to his business."

"We're just interested to see if your family has hit the jackpot. If that's the case, maybe you could take me around Baker's Creek in the new car you're parents will buy for you. Please, can you tell me what it is?" asked Amy batting her eyes and rubbing his hand. Peter dreamily imagined riding in a new car with her, but Lauren knew he was indulging in some perverted fantasy and rolled her eyes at the thought.

"Yeah, I'll call you," he said, licking his lips and forming a wet smirk.

Lauren huffed in frustration. Amy's plan did have some reason to it but she felt Amy had just grown tired of Jason. She felt like fighting but remembered her promise to her mother. When Amy's mother arrived at the Townsend's Lauren left furious at Amy, at herself for losing the gossiper's commune, and arriving too late to get the linking tome. They rode in silence to Gisele's where her mother was waiting in the car ready to return to Evelyn Lane. At home, Lauren let her anger out on the phone with Renee who immediately inquired about their success.

"Any luck finding the book?"

"Yes and no," said Lauren frustrated.

"What's wrong?"

"Devon's shirt led us to Peter's house today. It seems Peter's father found it in their yard and is now trying to get it appraised."

"*Are you serious?*" asked Renee.

"Yes, do you know how hard it could to be to track down that book if he's sold it?"

"It could be difficult but for now let's hope he

hasn't sold it. That should be our next move, to find out if he has it."

"Oh Amy's got that covered," said Lauren spitefully.

"How so?"

"She was all over Peter today. She's no longer dating Jason and what's worse she insults him like he's just another one of her disgusting exes."

"Maybe she knows, Lauren. He is a teenage boy after all and what she said is probably true. So is Peter her new beau?"

"No, Amy said she wanted to *date* Peter in case Luther returned with the book."

"That was a smart move, Lauren. She was just flirting with him to help us out."

"I won't buy it. I knew Amy would drop Jason sooner or later I just knew it!"

"Give her a chance. What better way to make up for the pool party than by trusting her on this one?" Lauren's anger subsided, she knew Renee was right. They ended the conversation with Lauren agreeing to be slow to anger when it comes to Amy's behavior.

✦ ✦ ✦ ✦

At school on Monday, Lauren didn't see Amy until history class but she did see Jason who appeared quite brokenhearted. Jason tried to talk to her but she avoided him for now; she wanted to see if Amy would talk to him during history class.

When Lauren walked in Amy was sitting with Renee talking intensely. Lauren hurried over when Amy and Renee excitedly waved her over.

"Bad news, Lauren," said Renee.

"He sold the book?" asked Lauren expecting disaster.

"No, it seems Luther's gone missing," said Amy before sneezing.

"*What?*"

"I called Peter this morning; his dad never came home after he left. Peter didn't come to school today because he and his mother are worried sick," said Amy.

"My God," said Lauren sadly. "Do they know where he was last seen?"

"His car was last seen heading out of town going towards Farmington Wells."

"Why would he go so far away? There are plenty of appraisal shops in Baker's Creek."

"Maybe he was trying to get a second opinion," offered Renee.

"His family said he'd never leave for a long period of time without calling them," said Amy. She blew her nose into a tissue while surveying Lauren who was deep in thought. Lauren was perplexed and though her mission remained the same, it has taken quite a spin to include a missing person.

"Maybe he was going to Farmington Wells like you said Renee and ran into a bit of trouble," said Lauren.

"What do you think we should do?" asked Amy.

"I suggest you continue to remain close to Peter," said Lauren affably though Renee caught the sarcasm in her response. "Hopefully he'll keep you informed with the police effort. Renee and I can…well, what do you suggest we do?"

Renee thought for a second then spoke. "Treat this like a missing person's case and call every place he may have visited. Where does he like to go around town?"

"I could find out," said Amy.

"Do that," said Lauren. "We know he was going to an appraisal shop so we can start by calling all of them in Baker's Creek."

"We could start with those furthest from town," Renee added, Lauren concurred.

"We'll need a picture of Luther so we can show it to the store clerks. Can you find one at the Townsend's, Amy?" asked Lauren.

"Sure," said Amy.

Jason walked in before the teacher who closed the door to start class. Lauren sat and watched him look confused at Amy before sitting at his usual desk. It was too painful for Lauren to bear. When class dismissed, Amy and Renee were waiting on Lauren to pack up her books but she saw Jason trying to get her attention.

"Hey, I'm going to talk with the teacher about the homework. I'll meet you in the cafeteria," said Lauren. Amy looked over at Jason, who looked quite pathetic in his heartbreak, then smirked at Lauren and made for the door.

"I'll see you later," said Renee as she left with Amy discussing more ways to find a missing person. Jason hurried over and Lauren stood upright to prepare for his questions and deliver some sad news.

"Lauren, what's up with her?" asked Jason bewildered. "She told me this morning she wanted to break up."

"I guess she's preoccupied with schoolwork and doesn't have time for a relationship right now. I'm sorry, Jason."

Jason appeared as if he was about to cry but he quickly composed himself.

"A few weeks ago she was fine now she acts like I'm disgusting. She was the prettiest girl I ever met and the best thing that ever happened to me, that *will* ever happen to me." Lauren was hurt by his comments and out of jealousy, anger, and sadness, she snapped at Jason.

"Well that's how girls like Amy will treat you! Carry you around until you've served their purpose then forget you ever existed. And...I—I just wish you could have used better judgment! You would've been happy with me!"

Jason was stunned, as if the world suddenly just became too cruel and cold. Lauren left for the cafeteria, but could hardly stomach her lunch as she sat with Amy and Renee. The rest of the school day passed swiftly because all Lauren could think about was her callous comments to Jason.

CHAPTER TWENTY
DISTURBING COUNSEL

After school, Lauren went home and started on her homework. The images of Jason's heartbroken face continued to distract her. She threw aside her work altogether when she received an excited phone call from Renee.

"*You'll never believe what I found today!*"

"What?" Lauren asked impassively.

"Remember how I've been looking for books on ghosts and spiritual abilities? Well I found my best one at this store today. Get this; it's called *The Amalgam Theory* written by none other than Etienne Robert!"

Lauren's indifference turned to excitement; she couldn't believe what Renee was saying and asked her to repeat the title. She heard correctly and thinking Etienne had learned what Catherine told her, she asked Renee what the book described.

"It described the gathering, Procession, and

other Amalgam ceremonies in detail. Some of the information is wrong like monsters driving the carriages instead of reapers and brutalizing stars falling from the sky for punishment was mistaken for ghosts, but the book was largely accurate. It's as if the person who wrote it had been there. And they wrote it some time ago. This book was published back in fifteen seventy-six."

"Interesting," said Lauren thoughtfully.

"What?"

"Catherine said Etienne was planning to break the Mortalland Rule, but it seems he's already done it."

"That little detail is missing from the book, but at least we got our next clue," said Renee. "They also do some appraising at the shop. I didn't ask about Luther or how they came across the book because Dad didn't have a lot of time in town today."

"Where did you find this book?" Lauren asked seriously.

"A store called Knowles' Divination and Boutique on the corner of Coral and Bridge Street. Wanna make a quick visit tonight?"

Lauren realized this might be the right shop, remembering Luther said "boutique" in the vision.

"Yeah, meet at my house, say around seven o'clock!" said Lauren.

Lauren hung up the phone and immediately called Amy and informed her of their plans. Amy said she'd see if she could join them, but was doubtful because her mother wanted the family to have dinner together tonight. A few minutes from seven, Lauren was sitting on the porch burning Luther's image into her eyes. She procured a picture from Amy, who managed to drop it off while her mother was in town for groceries. She would not able to join them today because her mother couldn't spare the time to pick her up. Soon after, Mr. Dupree pulled his car into the drive with Renee in the passenger side.

Lauren walked in the house and told Anita where they were going and that Renee's father would be taking them. Anita gave her permission and they left with Barry. He took them through town crossing Sailor Lake on Bridge Street. Lauren looked at the graveyard as it passed on their right, silent and dark as usual. She saw Renee turn to it, and Lauren wondered how the investigation was progressing in her mother's case. However, with the loss of the gossiper's commune Lauren would have to wait until they returned to Amalgam House to get any information.

Knowles' Divination and Boutique was a small shop that looked squeezed between two others. Written in black letters on painted white wood was the shop name with no lamp to illuminate it. A pink neon sign in the shop window that read "Gifts and Novelties" was its main advertisement.

"How long will this be?" asked Barry.

"About ten or twenty minutes, right, Lauren?" asked Renee.

"Yes," said Lauren as she got out of the car. Barry sat in the car on the curb, turning off the engine as the girls crossed the street.

"Do you know who owns the shop?" Lauren asked Renee.

"No, but I'll ask when we get inside."

The store was square in shape and everything except for the glass entrance door was completely wooden from the floor to the chairs, even the ceiling fan. The counter was on the left side and the merchandise to the right. Bookshelves stood against every wall and in the center were numerous tables filled with candles of various scents, incense, powders, liquid concoctions, and more books. There were many trinkets related to divination such as tea leaves, runes, bowls and calendars. Renee approached the counter and rang a small bell for service while Lauren checked the bookshelves for any more titles related to Amalgam. A man came out from a side room through a beaded curtain, smelling of incense and looked as if he didn't desire to be disturbed. When he saw Renee, his countenance changed to lively and inviting.

"Hi, Renee, did you find *The Amalgam Theory* enlightening?"

"I did, Dylan. In fact, I brought my friend who has some questions about its authors."

"Is that her?" asked Dylan.

"Yes," said Renee, she turned to Lauren, who placed a few books back on the shelves, approached the counter, and shook his hand courteously.

"Pleased to meet you, but I can't offer you much help seeing as how these men have passed on some time ago and the only documented account I could find of Robert's life claimed that the failure of the book forced him and his associates to move to the New World to escape their creditors."

"Is there any information as to how the authors came up with these theories?" asked Lauren.

"No. In the book they claim to have spoken with various people who've seen ghosts and I assume that those eyewitness accounts were their sources. It wasn't a popular book nor was it particularly scientific. One person every five years would ever check it out and those that read it believed it only to be conjecture and fantasy."

"Someone must be reading it seeing as how it's still in circulation, right?" asked Lauren.

"It's no longer in print and that's one of the only copies left. Would you like to purchase it so we won't have to list it in our inventory?"

"You're trying to get rid of it?" asked Renee.

"Yes. As I said, no one's read it in quite some time."

"I'll take it, how much?" asked Lauren.

"No charge, glad to be rid of it. Anything else I can help you with?"

"Yes, we were wondering if a man named Luther Townsend may have visited this shop in the past few days," said Lauren holding out his picture to Dylan who studied it for a moment before handing it back saying he hadn't seen him.

"Is he someone who may have an interest in your studies?" asked Dylan pointing to the book.

"Yes, he went missing a few days ago and we were wondering if anyone had seen him."

"I'm positive I would have seen him had he come in. We haven't had many customers in the past week."

"Who owns this shop?" asked Renee.

"Dr. Stephen Knowles," said Dylan. Lauren couldn't remember why, but the name sounded familiar to her.

"What's he a doctor of?" asked Lauren.

"Parapsychology," he said.

"What's that?"

"It's the study of paranormal phenomena," said Renee. "He might be someone we could talk to."

"He's always interested in meeting guests from his shop," said Dylan.

"Do you have his address?" asked Lauren.

"Yes, its thirty-seven hundred Psychologist Park, building one off Cherry Street."

Renee whispered to Lauren, "That's out near Baker's Creek city limits like going to Farmington Wells."

"Anything else?" asked Dylan.

"We're finished. Thanks for the help and the free book," said Lauren.

"Please come again. Nice seeing you again, Renee."

"Oh, I'll be back," said Renee assuredly.

"So are you going to talk with this Dr.

Knowles?" asked Renee as the girls exited the shop.

"Yes. I want to know where he found this book. Since his office is on the outskirts of Baker's Creek, maybe he met Luther before he disappeared. I'm going to set up an appointment immediately," said Lauren. She arrived home and set an appointment with Dr. Knowles' secretary tomorrow at six o'clock. Lauren then tried to recall when and where she'd heard his name and remembered the news broadcast the night of Amy's party that a Dr. Knowles was petitioning against the grave excavation.

* * * *

On Tuesday evening, after an explanation to Anita as to why she was going to see a psychologist, a school project Lauren answered, they arrived five minutes early. Having remembered Dr. Knowles' name, Lauren was interested in his reason for opposing the excavation and made it a priority to ask. Anita pulled into the parking lot of a collection of red-bricked buildings overlooking a wide pond with willow trees and a white fence. The wooden sign near the entrance simply read Psychologist's Park. There was only one car in the parking lot since it was after work hours. Lauren got out of the car and Anita asked her to be ready in an hour before driving off. Lauren knocked on the door of building one; a blonde haired girl with a red sweater and blue jeans about Lauren's age opened it.

"Hello, Lauren is it?"

"Yes."

"Welcome, I'm Melissa, I spoke with you yesterday right?" she asked moving aside so Lauren could enter.

"Yes, I was glad you could pencil me in so suddenly."

"Not a problem. Dr. Knowles' in the back, wait here," said Melissa. She entered the first room on the left and Lauren could hear her telling the doctor he had a visitor from his shop before returning to answer a call at the reception desk. Lauren stood in the middle of the lobby surveying the room and waiting patiently. There was a television to her left with a brown couch facing it and three matching wicker chairs. A plastic tree was behind the couch and a brown ceiling fan was operating in the room. To her right was a waist-high counter where the patients checked in and further down the halls were two doors on the left and right.

The doctor entered the reception area and greeted Lauren. He was about six feet tall and muscular, his face was wrinkled and stern, wearing a red sweater like his granddaughter, and brown corduroy pants with brown shoes. His hair was gray and looked a mess in one spot that gave Lauren the impression that he had been scratching his head.

"Hello, Lauren, I'm Dr. Knowles. How are you doing?"

"I'm fine."

Immediately Knowles' eyes were drawn to

Lauren's scar at the top of her head that still hadn't healed, but he didn't ask of it.

"Come on back," he said and led her into the first room on the left. It was a small room with a wooden floor and a well-polished, stylish wood desk with two chairs in front and back. A miniature refrigerator sat on floor to the left of his desk. There was also a recliner and chair to the left, tilted back fully and rumpled as if he or a patient had recently lain there. On his desk was an open book he was reading moments before. He immediately took a seat after offering Lauren to sit down.

"I assume you have an interest in the paranormal? Why else would you be here right?"

"Right."

"Now Dylan told me you had some questions about a book, although he didn't tell me which one."

Lauren placed *The Amalgam Theory* on his desk. He turned the book around, put on his glasses and leaned back with the book, flipping through a few of the pages.

"I was wondering where you came across this book."

"Paris, France, five years ago. This was one of the more interesting works I've read although its theories are incredibly hard to prove because of the nature of the world it describes. A purgatorial world of spirits, secrecy, and magic, an interesting theory on the afterlife, I've read it at least a twenty times."

"No kidding," said Lauren surprised.

"What about this book interests you?"

"How did the authors come up with these theories?"

"Eyewitness accounts for their human interviews and I assume they used mediums or were mediums themselves and talked with the spirits of this realm. They could've been misled by demons though. They tend to play pranks on the living especially if the medium has trouble discerning a demon from friendly spirits. Are you researching this book for a report at school?"

"Personal interest."

"Ah," the doctor smiled. His eyes focused squarely on Lauren's and he hardly blinked which made Lauren a little uncomfortable.

"What happened to your head if you don't mind me asking?" asked Dr. Knowles, his eyes lifting briefly to the lasting remnant of her injury before focusing back on hers. Lauren felt the oddest sensation that he was reading her eyes for honesty.

"I was in a car accident this summer."

"Were your injuries serious?"

"Not really. This scar is all that remains," Lauren smiled nervously. Dr. Knowles hummed quietly.

"Any more questions about the book?" he asked.

"No, but I have a question about one of my friends. His father went missing and the last time we heard from him he was searching for an appraiser. I heard he found something in his yard before he disappeared," said Lauren as she passed him the picture. He looked at the picture stoically. Lauren couldn't get a read on any of his emotions. Nothing seemed to surprise him unless he was a master of concealing expressions.

"His name is Luther Townsend," continued Lauren. The doctor looked at the picture a moment longer then said he'd never seen him.

"Was he a close friend?"

"He's my friend's father," said Lauren. "We're praying for his safe return."

"I'm sure the police will be able to find him."

"Also, were you the one protesting the grave excavation? I think I heard your name on the news a couple weeks ago."

"Yes I was. It's bad business disturbing the dead. Some secrets die with their bearers and its best to leave it that way. If it's important hopefully the knowledge will be rediscovered later, but just to carve a few letters on a blank slab seems awfully trivial don't you think?"

"It must be important to the families," said Lauren.

"What about the families whose loved ones were killed excavating the grave? I wonder if they think it was important," said Dr. Knowles.

Lauren agreed, as she knew the mystery wasn't nearly as important the cost of her father's life. If Dr. Knowles had not said this so conversationally she felt she would have been much more offended. Since he said it in ignorance of her relation to one of the victims, she let it slide. The only clue Dr. Knowles had indicative of her hurt feelings was the silence in which they sat. Lauren began to fan herself. Either by Lauren's change in mood or room temperature, it was becoming warmer in the office.

"Is it getting hot in here?" asked Dr. Knowles.

"Yes."

"Would you like a drink? Say tea?"

Before she could answer, Dr. Knowles belted out, "Melissa, make some of my favorite tea!"

He pulled out from the small refrigerator a chipped chalice and went to the bathroom to wash it and check the thermostat. Lauren busied herself by looking at the numerous items in his room. Minutes later, he returned and Melissa brought in the tea and poured it into his cup.

"I wash this cup all the time so it's clean. It's one of my antiques."

"It's very pretty."

He handed the cup to Lauren and once she touched it, she received several visions. She was back in the cathedral of Messina and witnessed two angels plundering the treasury. One of the angels took hold of the cup in her hands now and gazed at it longingly while the female took an hourglass and similarly studied it. The vision shifted and Lauren saw the same angel giving the cup to a young man in a bar. Her vision changed again to the room in which she sat, Luther and Dr. Knowles were having a heated discussion.

Luther had in his hand a book page that the

doctor unsuccessfully tried to wrest from him. Luther tried to leave the office, but Dr. Knowles pulled a gun from the desk and shot him in the head. The vision rippled like a curtain in the wind to outside the Psychologist Park. It was in the evening and Dr. Knowles had fastened large rocks on Luther's body and submerged him in the water.

Lastly, the vision switched to the lighthouse and led her eyes to the keeper house and through a trap door on the floor. The vision guided her eyes under this door into a pass underneath the cliff that led below the lake to a chamber containing a portal device like the one in Amalgam House. There several men and women praised the doctor for discovering a page from the linking tome and they reveled in the joy of drawing closer to finding the book.

Dr. Knowles advised his followers to be patient. He said that the page did not have the mark he needed to activate the portal but it was possible the complete linking tome might have one. They planned how they would find Luther's house and assigned people to the task before leading his ecstatic band out the cavern through a vault that exited at a plot in Baker's Memorial graveyard. When the vault cover closed, Lauren could see the name on the tombstone was Pierre Channing.

"Lauren? LAUREN?" Dr. Knowles clapped his hands and Lauren woke from her vision.

"Yes?"

"Is the tea too hot?" he asked, looking puzzled.

"No, it's fine." She drank the tea with difficulty because her hands were shaking with fear. She wanted to go immediately but her mother wouldn't be back for another forty minutes.

"Taste's good, but its run right through me. Where's your bathroom?" asked Lauren.

"Down the hall, last door on the right."

She excused herself, leaving the cup on his desk, trembling as she went to bathroom where she thought to place a call to Anita from the lobby. She was frightened that Dr. Knowles might overhear but she wanted to get as far away from him as possible. Questions were running through her mind. *That cup must have been the djemsheed, how did he get it? He must be Etienne! How am I going to tell Peter and Vera what's happened to Luther?*

Lauren peeked out from the bathroom as Melissa was walking by and asked if she could call her mother to pick her up.

"Is something wrong?" asked Melissa.

"Woman troubles you understand."

"Oh, what's the number?"

Lauren gave it to her and she called Anita. Soon after, Lauren left the bathroom and returned to the doctor's room who sat looking into his cup, swishing the tea around. Unknown to Lauren, Dr. Knowles could see muddled visions of her accident, her journey in the reaper carriage, and a segment from the Procession raid.

"Dr. Knowles, I'm feeling a little sick, do you mind if I step outside and get some air?"

"Sure, go ahead."

Lauren walked to the bench at the pond and sat looking into the water. Minutes later Dr. Knowles came outside and sat next to her. Lauren tensed sitting next to a murderer; a cold shiver ran along her spine and her stomach tied and became as taut as steel. She winced and rubbed her belly, the pain emerged from her knotted muscles, and her joints began ache as if she was on the verge of a pain crisis from her disease.

"Sometimes Melissa makes the tea a little strong. It can unsettle my stomach at times and if you're not used to it you may feel nauseated."

Lauren wondered if the doctor was being honest. Her heart trembled as she thought of Luther lying underneath the water and his killer sitting peacefully beside her. Dr. Knowles scooped a handful of rocks from the ground and tossed one into the lake.

"Have I answered most of your questions, Lauren?"

"Yes," Lauren rubbed her belly to keep up the deception, but she really felt like vomiting because of his disgusting presence.

"Good," said Dr. Knowles tossing another in. Surprisingly it landed into the water exactly in the same place as the previous one.

"The nauseating feeling can take some time to go away, but I can calm your stomach now. Look into the water and breathe in and out. Take note of your breathing as you watch the water ripple.

Breathe in when you hear a splash and breathe out when you hear the next one."

He threw one in and Lauren did as she was told because she couldn't help it. The water mesmerized her. He threw in another and another and another. Lauren was breathing at a rhythmic pace and was slowly relaxing.

"Imagine you're lying down on each ripple and floating along with them. Think of a color that would describe the emotions your feeling. What is that color?"

The color that popped into Lauren's mind was red. The image of Luther's blood from the vision remained painted before her eyes. Once again, she felt that she failed to move fast enough to save an innocent man's life.

"Red," she said in a dreary tone. She swayed slightly, feeling as if she was riding the tiny waves of the water.

"Let red become the color of the ripples." The doctor threw another rock in the water.

"Imagine that as you come to the end of the ripple you submerge into the water. It's very warm, and it runs up over your feet, past your knees, warming your stomach, loosing the muscles in your neck. It's covering your eyes and they feel full. It runs through your hair and massages your scalp."

Lauren was doing as he said and she was slowly more willing to let Dr. Knowles in on the information she withheld from him at the beginning. There was something strange about the water that fixed her gaze upon it. Lauren was so focused on the ripples closest to her that she didn't take notice of the entire pond rippling as if a giant ghost child was inside kicking up his bathwater. Visions of Lauren's adventures in Amalgam cast upon the lake and the doctor eagerly studied them.

Lauren fell into a trance where she could barely hear herself speak but knew she was whispering many secrets. The water submersion sensation wholly took over her and comforted her most of the time but only when she wanted to refuse a question did the soothing feeling take on the impression of drowning and the red water the consistency of blood. Deep in her consciousness she knew she was being tortured.

The time passed sooner than Lauren expected. Anita arrived and while they were sitting on the bench and the pond quickly became calm. Anita honked her horn twice but Lauren didn't move. She suddenly heard Dr. Knowles' voice in a clear normal tone. He had to snap his fingers and clap his hands in her face before she came to. When she did, Lauren was aware of her surroundings though a bit disoriented.

"Are you okay, Lauren?"

"Yes, I'm fine."

"You must have got a little sleepy during your story. I've never heard anyone speak at such great lengths before."

"What was I...um...talk–"

"Talking about? School mostly, but also about a

guy named Jason. You seem like the shy, silent type, but underneath there's a social butterfly waiting to burst forth. Your mother is waiting for you. You should hurry."

"Thank you, Dr. Knowles. It's been nice talking to you," Lauren said hurriedly, moving quickly to Anita's car.

"I'm glad I could help," said Dr. Knowles as he stood and waved to Anita.

Lauren got in the car. As Anita drove off, Lauren watched Dr. Knowles returning indoors. His head was down and he seemed worried and a bit fearful as if he had heard some terrible news.

* * * *

On the way home, Lauren's head felt exceedingly heavy as it did when she was receiving visions but this time she was able to stave off unconsciousness until she arrived home. Retreating to her bedroom and laying down, Lauren fell asleep and dreamed a particularly violent vision. She was floating toward a colonial-era house, one with square windows all in a row, with a rectangular door and a decorative crown designed as a patch of flowers. Lauren phased through the door into a living room with elegant eighteen-century furniture where a warm fire was burning in the fireplace and a strong scent of African jasmine filled the home. Lauren saw a handsome young man reading a very large book by the fire in a sturdy chair, awestruck and engrossed in its pages. The book was massive and wide, it's cover and pages almost extending past his arm's length, yet he used the chair's arm rests to support the heavy tome.

She heard sounds from the kitchen, the clanking of cookware and a woman humming an unfamiliar ballad. When this woman entered the room, Lauren knew it was Jasmine who was wearing a satin gown and a pearl necklace and looked radiantly beautiful as opposed to her appearance when she sat talking with Kradleman. She seemed to glow from a feeling of euphoria, as she glided towards the man in the chair and wrapped her arms about his shoulders like a snake trying stealthily to constrict an unsuspecting prey.

She snuggled him tightly, but he didn't want to be bothered while examining his important text. She glanced at the book, the graphic icons and numerous names didn't particularly interest her. She asked him to put it away and play with his new wife, but he said in response that his father had given them the most peculiar wedding present. She kissed him on his neck and whispered in his ear, convincing him to come upstairs in ten minutes.

He watched her ascend the stairs before returning to his reading; she flicked off a gown strap with her finger and bid him to follow. He closed the book with a mournful, brokenhearted countenance. It shrank in his hands until it was the size of a regular book which seemed to strike him as odd still but as if he'd expected it. He placed it inside a loose floorboard under the rug and stood to agitate the fire rekindling the dying flame. A loud burst shook the room, startling Lauren who looked behind her to see a man entering the house who ran through her for the newlywed. This intruder was tall, thin, yet very muscular who took the man by surprise and held him hostage at gunpoint.

Walking in searchingly was a companion burglar, who surveyed the house for any other people. He is a young man of medium build and stood at six-feet tall. He appeared highly intelligent with a determined, inquisitive countenance as if he was analyzing everything he saw. Lauren recognized him from the vision in Dr. Knowles office as the man in the bar who received the djemsheed from Raziel. He focused on his companion and their captive before asking aloud, "Are you the owner of this home? Are you Jonathan Watlington?" he asked with a faint French accent before sneezing.

"Yes!" Jonathan said.

"It's him alright, Etienne. I've seen him before in town," said Jonathan's captor.

Etienne acknowledged his friend's statement with a smile before his face twisted and he sneezed again. Though Etienne spoke with a heavy accent, Lauren realized he and Dr. Knowles must be the same person because their voices were similar.

"We were told by a maid in your father's house that he gave you a book. We need it!"

"I don't know what you're talking about!"

Jonathan struggled to speak under his captor's muscular arm.

Etienne strode forward pondering while removing a weapon from his waist. He pointed it at Jonathan's head as he drew within the limit of his extended arm.

"We don't have much time! I'd advise you not to hold us up much longer, your father did, and he died for it," he said coolly. Jonathan sighed listening to his startling words. Etienne and his companion were distracted from their interrogation by the sound of footsteps pounding on the stairs; Jonathan's wife was returning downstairs. Etienne sent a shot as soon as she entered the living room; it struck the wall close to her but she didn't flinch.

"Jonathan!" she said.

"Your wife?" Etienne asked partly wondering why she didn't draw back at his shot and observing her disheveled clothing exposing sensual parts of her figure.

"Yes!"

Etienne studied her before sneezed yet again and withdrawing a handkerchief to wipe his nose saying, "Je deteste ces fichues fleurs de jasmin!" He focused his eyes again on Jonathan's wife before speaking again.

"You must be Heather Beaufort, I'm sorry, Watlington. I read about your lavish wedding. Beautiful, isn't she Pierre?"

"Gorgeous," he replied gazing over his left shoulder. Lauren realized she was witnessing

Jasmine's wedding night. She looked at Jasmine who appeared more like a strong, beautiful mother than an evil witch. Though attractive, Nasra far eclipsed her and Lauren could see why Jasmine had trouble winning Jonathan's heart.

"Too bad we're on the run; we could have stayed and had some fun. Now where's this book, Jonathan? Tell us or she dies!" Etienne pointed the gun towards her and from the manner in which the woman glared at him Lauren thought their duel could end in a stalemate.

"Un—undah-da fl–floorboard," Jonathan gasped.

Pierre spun Jonathan to his left by the fireplace to lift the rug for a look at the floorboard while Etienne shifted his gun towards Jonathan. Pierre procured the book from the floor and stood to open it. Pierre opened it slowly and it slowly grew in size. Pierre struggled to hold it before studying its pages; he glanced up at Etienne with a smile. Etienne moved forward, keeping his eye on Jonathan at first but then fixing his gaze on the book.

Jonathan looked intently at the gun, he feared it, but anger grew in his heart as he thought of his slain father. He lowered his right hand to the poker by the fire and carefully removed it from its holder. Heather saw what he intended to do and her demeanor changed from rage to absolute fear; she was frightened her husband was going to be hurt. Lauren saw what Jonathan was going to do and clutched her chest in anticipation.

He moved fast; Jonathan swatted the gun from Etienne's hand and it skirted along the floor. Etienne reeled back gripping his bloodied hand that swelled with pain. Jonathan swung it back at Pierre, the sharp end striking his temple. He lunged forward and grappled with Pierre managing to push him to the floor aided with pure fury and Pierre's daze. Etienne reclaimed his weapon pointing it at Jonathan who had bested Pierre and was going to deliver a deathblow. Jonathan heard Heather scream his name when a shot rang out.

Jonathan looked at Heather who was running to stand before him and fell swiftly to the floor dead when the bullet struck her. Pierre used this moment to retrieve a dagger and fatally wound Jonathan. He collapsed to the floor breathing ever more shallowly, crawling towards his bride until he died. Etienne and Pierre picked up their bodies and took them into the night air. They dumped them in the lake before returning inside to reclaim the book then the vision shifted again.

Etienne and Pierre were now at the docks, parting with Duncan who boarded the Evelyn. They hid in the bushes and withdrew their weapons, Lauren knew, to search the harbor floor for the Mortalland Seal. They made quick work of the guards before diving in. They swam for long periods within the hour, but surfaced occasionally because, as Lauren learned by their gripes about the djemsheed's magic, the water still stung their lungs.

Pierre returned to the water while Etienne remained on the rocks when suddenly the water froze just as it had done with Duncan. Pierre's lifeless body floated to the surface and Etienne stood stunned.

"Mon Dieu! Quelle magie peut prendre le sang immortel?" he asked bewilderedly.

Etienne fished Pierre's body from the water and tried to revive him before giving up, leaving his corpse on the rocks to flee from arriving police. Etienne drove his carriage furiously away from the docks. He contemplated aloud how to rendezvous with Duncan unaware that his immortal brotherhood would soon be completely broken. The vision dissipated to the burned out jasmine candle on Lauren's bed stand and she wept into her pillow. The dream was bittersweet; Lauren witnessed Jasmine giving her life to save Jonathan's which was proof that she had some compassion in her. Somehow, Lauren rested a bit easier with this knowledge; maybe Jasmine would show mercy to her captive friends.

CHAPTER TWENTY-ONE
RETURN TO AMALGAM HOUSE

"It sounds like he hypnotized you! But throwing rocks in a pond to do it sounds very strange. What did you tell him?" asked Renee. Lauren called Renee and told her everything about the visions. She regained her memory of her discussion with Dr. Knowles and realized she had divulged too much about her adventures in Amalgam.

"About the linking tome mostly, what it is and why we're after it. Renee the Court is going to punish me for this."

"You weren't in control of yourself, maybe they'll have mercy. Are you positive he killed Mr. Townsend?"

"My visions haven't been wrong so far."

"You're right. Should we call the police, phone in an anonymous tip?"

"I'd say so but he's our only lead to the linking tome. If they lock him up we may never find it."

"We still have the lighthouse lead to go by though. Why do you think Luther only brought a page to his interview with Etienne?"

"Peter said his father was secretive about his business and he probably didn't trust anyone with the entire book. Luther must have hidden it somewhere."

"You think he could have kept the book at home?"

"Possibly, or in his car, I didn't see what Dr. Knowles did to Luther's car in the vision."

"Do you think he knows how to use those marks?"

"He's been alive for some time, I'm sure he's figured out how to use magic marks. Calling the police sounds like a good idea now. He needs to be picked up before he can do some more damage," said Lauren anxiously.

"Maybe we should contact Catherine's first," offered Renee. "We shouldn't put cops in harm's way if they can't handle him."

"Can you get us a ride to Amalgam House?"

"I'll try. Is Amy coming along?"

"I'll give her a ring and see if she can make it."

Lauren called up Amy who sounded groggy over the phone and said she might be coming down with the flu. Lauren told her about Dr. Knowles and their plans to go to Amalgam House tonight. Amy said she was too sick to go though she would like to hear Catherine's advice once they returned. Lauren was able to ride with Barry and Renee to Amalgam House as Anita was on the hunt for jobs. They arrived at Amalgam House as before, Mr. Hitchen approached the gate and let them in. He had Renee tell her father they would provide transportation back home and he drove away.

"What's the nature of this visit?" asked Mr. Hitchen.

"Is there a way to contact Baron Catherine from here?" asked Lauren.

"Yes, but usually you have to schedule an appointment. Catherine's a busy woman and she may be unavailable especially now. Didn't she give you a gossiper's commune?"

"I lost it," said Lauren sorrowfully. "How are things going with animals?"

"The negotiations fell through. The baroness and Selene have been appealing desperately to the animal leadership to turn away from the Phoenix but they won't listen. They've captured the Roland Shipyard and are now amassing in the Lanise Crater to lay siege to Geyser Worx and the castle."

"What about Jasmine and the Phoenix?"

"The Phoenix and Gretchen have been leading the animals in their conquests, but Jasmine has disappeared. We have no clue where she or her giant tree is. I'm aware that Catherine's given you an assignment related to the crisis, I hope you've brought her some good news."

Lauren felt bad; she didn't have any good news at all. They entered Amalgam House. Tension pervaded the mansion where ghosts were bustling about, hastily at work.

"In order to safely contact such a high-level person as Catherine, you'll have to get permission from Mina. Wait here in the lobby until I return."

Lauren and Renee took a seat in the lobby near the piano, listening to the boy ghost practicing again with his teacher. He had become quite good with the one tune and the music soothed Lauren's troubled mind. While they waited, Lauren saw a familiar ghost dancing towards her. She was a young white girl dressed in a red skirt, black shirt, and bangles on her arms with big bushy brown hair; Lauren's indweller was conversing with a companion whom Renee recognized as her indweller.

Renee's indweller was a black girl dressed more modernly with close-fitting blue jeans and a white short-sleeve shirt. Her black hair was in a ponytail, her face was very round, her lower back arched and she walked a bit awkwardly. Lauren thought maybe an injury in a mortal life or birth defect imprinted onto her spectral gait. The female spirits waved once they noticed the girls and approached them to talk.

"Hi, Lauren, what's been up?" asked her indweller, the ghost was be-bopping and listening to a tape player that played what sounded like eighties tunes.

"The Court has me running around town. What's your name by the way?"

"Oh, Mary and this is my friend Joy," said Mary. "Sorry I didn't get to introduce myself. We have to return here as soon as the original host returns."

"Where's Traci?" asked Lauren of Amy's indweller.

"Haven't seen her in a while, she's probably been sent to indwell another body. She's one of the best and they have multiple hosts. By the way, how did I do indwelling you? Did anyone ask about a change in your behavior?"

"Only my mom," said Lauren.

"Cool," Mary said happily.

"See, I told you, you were getting better. If you'd stop *dancing* in your hosts bodies you'd be as good as Traci," said Joy.

"I heard no complaints from my dad, Joy," said Renee.

"Thank you," Joy said appreciatively.

"I've been wondering about your ability to see inside our thoughts. Is there a way I can keep my personal life a secret? I don't want my privacy invaded," said Renee.

"Indwellers aren't allowed to access the secrets of a host unless the situation is deemed critical," said Joy.

"But how can you tell what's a secret and

what's not?" asked Renee.

"Once we enter the mind, we see thoughts as colors," said Mary. "Red represents passionate feelings, blue as peaceful, gray as sad, yellow as joyous, green as desires, and white as neutral."

"The darker shade of these colors means it's a secret," said Joy. "The more intense feelings are harder to access and the indweller risks losing his or her own personality if done wrong. The better indwellers can access strong secrets without risk to themselves. They are able capable of distinguishing the mixed colors like teal and orchid, the more complex feelings beginners are taught to stay away from."

"The better we are at discerning these colors the more likely we can mimic your true behavior," said Mary. "Usually we are required to request of our first host to become their lifelong indweller which is why we were hoping to speak with you two." Mary breathed deeply. "Lauren, Renee, we would like to become your personal indwellers," said Mary in anticipation. Renee nodded yes and Lauren agreed as well.

"Sure, you did well the first time," said Lauren.

"YES!" said Mary and Joy as they jumped in delight.

"I can't believe it! I'm indweller of the new baron!" said Mary. Lauren cringed every time someone referred to her title.

"I'm glad we've found hosts!" said Joy breathing relief. Lauren and Renee felt like celebrities as the two spirits praised the girls and themselves. Lauren instructed Mary to drink from her vial occasionally when she enters the Amalgam Realm and to bring some whenever she indwells her body. Mary said she'd already been instructed by Nasra to do so and that she has access to refills here at the house.

"It's comforting knowing that ghosts can't easily take over a person's character like in those horror movies," said Renee.

"I wouldn't say that," said Joy warily.

"Why not?" asked Renee.

"For certain demons and ghosts like Phoenix loyalists, their specialty is deception and a rite of passage for their beginning indwellers is opening the most intense emotions immediately to see if they can handle them especially those dealing with love or hate. In half the time we're taught the Phoenix's indwellers are trained to access the entire mind and assume multiple identities in full."

"Pardon us," said Mr. Hitchen returning with an elderly Caucasian woman garbed in a black veil dress with tattered brown hair adorned with a pearly necklace and arm bracelets.

"Lauren, Renee, I'd like to introduce you to the oracle Mina," said Mr. Hitchen. The girls shook her hand.

"I've been waiting to meet you Lauren. I was hoping you'd come here as soon as you returned from Amalgam but I understand if you were sidetracked. I see you've brought a friend," Mina released Lauren's hand and shook Renee's.

"You're the one who has a relative in the graveyard, right?" asked Mina.

"Yes," said Renee, she smiled widely, expecting to hear some good news.

"We're on top of it. I've managed to calm her down a bit, but freeing her is going to take some time. But don't worry about her; she's safe for the moment. I was impressed when Catherine told me that you could hear her crying out without much formal training of your oracle abilities. How did you learn the craft?"

"I read about it, although, I was browsing books on mediums. They taught me how to clear my mind to listen to spirits," said Renee.

"Interesting, but you must know that our craft is very dangerous. Medium abilities are similar to oracle skills but we are taught to listen to Messina's voice who guides us to distressed spirits. I would suggest you not try to contact spirits without a gossiper commune or other devices approved by the Court until you've been formally trained and mastered the techniques."

"I won't," said Renee.

"I see you've been making friends in the time it took me to move this old vessel of flesh to the lobby. Mary, Joy, did you get their approval?"

"Yes!" they said.

"Good. Then if you two will excuse us, we have business to discuss. Mr. Hitchen, lead the way to my office," said Mina. Mr. Hitchen led the women up the stairs of Amalgam House to the second floor. On their way up, Lauren explained to Mina why they were here, including her encounter with Dr. Knowles.

They reached her office, easily the largest in Amalgam House and appeared wholly dedicated to contacting spirits, with incense, soft music provided by an enchanted harp, and dim warm light. A strong chill blew in the air Mina said originated from her constant contact with Amalgam. Purple gossamer curtains shrouded a pitted section in the room's center. Unlit candles surrounded the curtains outside except by the entrance pulled by an unseen force. Lauren and Renee would have to throw on blankets to stand comfortably.

"My God! This room feels like Amalgam," said Renee rubbing her arms. "You're not cold at all, Mina?"

"My spirit and body are more Amalgam than Mortalland. This room is comfortable to me. It sounds like this Dr. Knowles obviously has had some scheme planned for some time. If only I knew which faction he was linked to I might be able to tie more of our open cases to him."

"How many people in the New City know of Amalgam besides the Court?" asked Lauren.

"Several hundreds, if not more, and they are not just limited to the New City. Two groups like the Reis Clan and the Saved operate in the New City. The Ghost Watchers and the satanic cult the Tongue of the Dragon are international factions. Dr.

Knowles might be involved with anyone of these groups. I definitely understand your concern about him and since you lost the commune, it was a good idea that you came here. Unfortunately, I'm tied up with the graveyard case. There certainly is a presence there enslaving the spirits."

"I knew it," said Renee.

"You were right but you're not nearly strong enough to deal with it. In truth, I can't handle it. It's extremely powerful and very intelligent; I'm having trouble discerning who it is."

"Is it hiding its identity?" asked Lauren.

"Yes, even toying with me. It seems to be a demon or a powerful spirit. It's been a terrible challenge trying to exorcise it. It won't leave even with my strongest prayers. I'm surprised that you weren't harmed by it, Renee. Maybe the spirit felt you weren't a threat. Stay away from there unless your business takes you there," said Mina, opening a drawer and retrieving a wooden box.

The girls watched as Mina set up her device. The box had a set of headphones attached to it with a small hole in the center, a rubber band, and a sheet of purple silk. She folded the silk into a bag and blew into it before tying it with a rubber band. Mina placed it into the hole and amazingly, it stood on its on and remained inflated as if it was breathing. Inside the bag, a small white light shown through the cloth turning the silk sheet into a soft purple light.

"What are you doing?" asked Lauren.

"This little box is called the oracle telephone and this curtained section is the booth. Place the headphones on your head, clear your mind, and listen carefully to hear Catherine's voice. You'll know when you've reached her. Come Renee, you can tell me more of what you learned in the graveyard while she talks with Catherine," said Mina as she and Renee left the office.

The curtained entrance closed and Lauren cleared her mind. At first, Lauren couldn't hear anything. Then she heard a sound like wind, before a subtle voice came whispering through, faintly saying hello. Immediately the candles outside the curtains lit and labarums, ankhs, borromean rings, and fish symbols appeared on the screen. The booth illuminated greatly from a light that burst from the ceiling and the voice through the headphones became as clear as any telephone in Mortalland.

"Hello," said Catherine.

Lauren opened her eyes believing Catherine was in the room but all she saw was the purple bag pulsating rhythmically to Catherine's voice when she again said hello.

"Catherine, this is Lauren. I'm calling from Amalgam house because I lost the gossiper's commune during my search, I'm sorry."

"It's okay. Tell me why you're calling," said Catherine.

"I wanted to ask you about a person named Dr. Stephen Knowles. Does the name sound familiar?"

"No," said Catherine. "Who is he?"

"He's after the linking tome and has killed one of my leads to the book. I believe he's Etienne!"

"What makes you think that?" asked Catherine curiously.

"He had given me some tea to drink and when I touched the cup I could see the angels taking it from the cathedral. I think the cup was the djemsheed. I also saw a vision of Etienne receiving it from Raziel and of him killing Jasmine when she was alive for the linking tome."

"Tell me how you came in contact with this man?" Catherine's voice was audibly concerned and intrigued. Lauren told her all about their search since returning to Amalgam up until her suggestion of calling the police.

"This is an interesting and dangerous element. One of our portals was stolen from Amalgam House a year ago, but we never discovered who or how, only that they must have been shades to know of the portal. For Dr. Knowles to have it, the djemsheed, and a book authored by the oldest shade about Amalgam can only mean he is Etienne."

"What do you suggest?"

"I agree with Renee. Stay away from the local authorities for now because he may react violently. I suggest following up the lead at the lighthouse but be extremely cautious! Now that Etienne, or Dr. Knowles, has the marks on those pages, it would be wise to assume he knows how to use them. If that's the case he'll be too strong for you, Renee, and Amy to handle alone and you'll be ill-equipped to combat such a man. The djemsheed has made his body impervious to most mortal and ethereal weaponry. You'll have to come to Amalgam immediately to retrieve a mortis blade. Use it to undo his immortality and send his spirit to the Judge."

"Wait...you want me to kill him?" asked Lauren bewildered.

"Unless you can convince him to take his own immortality with the djemsheed, I'm afraid you'll have no other choice," said Catherine.

"I've never killed anyone Catherine and I'm not about to start now," said Lauren appalled.

"Lauren, his existence is an abomination of God's decree. Man should not live forever in sin, and you'll see to it that he does not. I'll have Mina support you with guards as you investigate the lighthouse. Have Mr. Hitchen open the third floor portal and tell Mina what I said about the guards. Do you understand?"

"Yes, Catherine," said Lauren disappointed.

"I'll see you soon," said Catherine. The light from the bag ebbed to darkness as the bag deflated. The candles outside the curtains went out and the curtain pulled itself back to allow Lauren an unobstructed exit. A blaring siren sounded throughout the house. Lauren covered her ears and walked towards the office door as Mina and Renee came back inside.

"What's that noise?" asked Renee plugging her ears.

A few guards rushed into the room and grabbed Mina by the arms to escort her out.

"Mina, multiple suspects have surrounded the perimeter. We'll have to get you out through the tunnels," said the lead guard.

"Have Mr. Hitchen bring Lauren and Renee…" Mina commanded as the guards took her away.

Screams filled the mansion. Lauren and Renee walked out onto the second floor where they saw guards heading outside. Raised at a forty-five degree angle, the lobby's willow tree is where most of the ghosts and shades exited the mansion. Underneath its foundation was a tunnel leading to sanctuary. Mr. Hitchen ran up the stairs taking several steps in a single bound. He pushed his way through frightened ghosts telling them, "Secure all sensitive documents, take your weapons, and get to the tunnels!" He stopped moving once he found the girls.

"What's going on?" asked Lauren.

"Intruders, possible assassination attempt," said Hitchen. "Looks like a witch and she's brought animals that are moving up the grounds for the mansion. I have to get you out of here. Hurry, follow me," he said taking Renee by the arm.

"Jasmine," said Lauren. "Where's Mina?"

"We're taking her to a car waiting to carry her to the Ghost Shack," said Mr. Hitchen. The girls followed Mr. Hitchen closely as he led them downstairs.

"Catherine said she was opening a portal on the

third floor for me to reach Castle Everlasting. Can't we just go there?"

"When this house is under duress all portals are shut down."

"Where's the tunnel entrance?" asked Renee.

"Under the willow on the ground floor; the other exits have been compromised."

They reached the ground floor and ran past the piano for the tree. As Lauren, Renee, and Mr. Hitchen neared it, a guard screamed, "Take cover!" A large explosion blew a gap in the front of the house sending rumble flying all through the lobby. The ghosts were unharmed but the rubble crushed several shades to death transitioning them to full ghosts. Lauren and Renee were able to save themselves by lying flat on the ground. Lauren looked up to see wolves attacking the few living people inside. Their eyes were red with the most ferocious scowl, their mouths drenched in blood, and the order of beasts shone brightly on their heads. Several drove Mr. Hitchen away when he tried to help Lauren and Renee.

Following the wolves was the intruder. It didn't look like Jasmine, but a barely recognizable, horribly scarred female. Her face was mangled and hardly identifiable. Lauren and Renee were terrified and made quickly for the tunnel entrance. The woman raised her hand, the trees drooping branches stretched to the ceiling and pushed against it setting the tree down to cover the entrance sealing the girls inside the house.

"Hello, Lauren," said the woman.

"Jasmine?" asked Lauren. The woman nodded affirmatively.

"Do you know how terrifying it is riding a motorcycle on a dark night when a spook suddenly appears out of thin air ready to swipe you with a staff?"

"You killed this woman?" asked Lauren.

"I needed a vessel to speak with you. You and Nasra played a nasty little trick on the Phoenix and me. I was sorely disappointed when we missed capturing you *again*. But at least we managed to snare a few useful captives and now I've found my best one."

"I won't cooperate with you. I'm not joining or helping the Phoenix in anyway."

"Me neither…if…you were talking about me," said Renee swinging slowly next to Lauren.

"I'm talking about him," Jasmine looked behind her as a wolf dragged in a body by the ankle. As the body drew closer, Lauren realized who it was and shouted, "Jason!"

"I've been watching you ever since you arrived back in Mortalland. When I discovered your love for this boy, I knew he'd be an excellent tool to hasten your search. I'll give you three days to find the linking tome and bring it to the office at the Baker's Creek Lighthouse for an exchange or else you can count on Jason becoming a lost soul forever."

"He's got nothing to do with Amalgam or your

war. Don't bring him into this," Lauren pleaded.

"Wrong! He's going to be your motivation. Three days, Lauren, and if you fail, I'll make you an orphan when I kill Anita. Consider her safety mercy for now." The woman's body suddenly convulsed and fell. A vortex of cold air left it and entered Jason's nose. His body started to move and then he stood. Jason raised his hands and the girls turned upright. Jasmine in Jason's body moved forward and kissed Lauren deeply on the lips. Lauren's was startled. She'd dreamed of this moment since she met Jason, but this wasn't a cool night in front of the lighthouse.

"You better hurry," said Jasmine in Jason's voice. "I don't have much time. *Now get moving!*" The vines flung her and Renee out the gap in the mansion. Renee broke her ankle and Lauren her wrist as they landed in the middle of the Amalgam House lawn. Renee reached down, repaired her ankle, and did the same for Lauren's injury. Flames erupted from the ground level of the house and leapt to the second level, brightening the darkened property. The girls watched the fire spread for a moment until Jasmine's wolves gave chase from the house. They stood quickly and ran for the gate.

Lauren held it open for Renee to exit as a wolf jumped for her. Lauren slammed it closed in its face knocking it to the ground. The wolves no longer gave chase once Lauren and Renee left the premises. The girls had to walk nearly two miles to the nearest phone to call Barry to come pick them up. After an unsatisfactory explanation about why they had to walk to a phone and weren't dropped off, Barry grounded Renee until she could tell the truth about their business at the mansion. He also promised Lauren that Anita would be receiving a call from him once they got home.

CHAPTER TWENTY-TWO
THE SÉANCE AND PURGATION FIELDS

Barry dropped Lauren off at Evelyn Lane and sped away. Lauren thought to explain to Anita what happened herself but decided to let Barry be a concerned parent and she will play her role as an unruly child. Besides Lauren needed to think about how she would get back to Castle Everlasting. She entered her room and stretched out on her bed leaving the bedroom door open. Once the phone rings, it would offer no protection from Anita's fury. The phone rang fifteen minutes later and soon Anita was storming up the stairs. Anita entered her room and said heatedly, "Don't even pretend to be asleep Lauren. No one goes to sleep in this house when they're in trouble."

"I'm sorry, Mom…"

"You're not sorry, Lauren. If you were sorry, you wouldn't be going behind my back getting rides to some strange mansion. Now what happened at that house?" asked Anita intensely.

"I can't tell you. It's forbidden."

"Don't tell me you've gotten yourself involved in some cult down there," said Anita concerned as she came into the room and sat on her bed.

"It's not a cult, Mom."

"Are you telling me the truth?"

"Yes, I promise."

"They didn't brainwash you did they? How could I tell?" Anita wondered aloud while lifting up the lids of Lauren's eyes.

"Mom stop!" said Lauren swatting her hand away.

"*Then what were you doing there?*" Anger swelled again in Anita's voice.

"I can't tell you."

"What did we say about keeping secrets? I've told you what happened with your father and me," said Anita. Lauren breathed deeply. She could not fabricate a credible lie but she did manage a clever diversion.

"You told me, it's better to discuss these things when the time was right like after I finished my exams? Right now it's not a good time to tell you what goes on at that house, but it's the exact opposite of a cult."

"Okay, but until that time no phone, no going out except for school, and definitely no friends."

"*But, Mom!*"

"No buts, you're grounded. It's one thing to keep a secret because it might hurt your feelings, but when your life's in danger I have to take responsibility," said Anita taking Lauren's room phone out the jack and her cell phone.

"I'm going to call the police to find out what goes on at that house and you're staying in until you feel like talking," said Anita as she left Lauren in the room.

Lauren did not press the matter. She learned how to evanesce in Amalgam so leaving was not the problem, lying to her mother was. Lauren wanted to tell the truth but she also wanted to keep the laws of Amalgam. Anita would not believe her anyway. Punishment did have its benefits, Lauren thought, now she could plan her next move in peace. Her thoughts lingered on Jason. *How did Jasmine know where to find him? She did say she had been watching me, but how? I wish I hadn't been so mean to him. She gave me three days, starting tonight or tomorrow?* Lauren wasn't certain so she gave herself two.

Lauren paced in her room. The cavern was her next step but Catherine warned her about going without guards and the mortis blade. She had to get to Amalgam but the only portal outside of the now destroyed Amalgam House is in Etienne's possession. Lauren concluded she would have to await contact from Mina to go to the Ghost Shack. Whether Mina made it safely to the Ghost Shack was uncertain. Lauren worked on the premise that they didn't make it and needed to come up with an independent plan. After an hour or so, no other ideas came to her except to go to the cavern unaided.

Lauren considered flying to Renee's house but realized she had never been to Renee's house because she always came over. She could go to Amy's house but the trip would be extremely far. In that time her mother could return and if Lauren was to leave her body without its spirit Anita would call for an ambulance again when she'd be unable to wake her. Trapped, Lauren realized that being grounded sucks and spent the rest of her evening practicing her evanescing and materializing. She soon mastered the charm and was able to dematerialize entirely as long as she wished with objects in her possession. Yet this newfound ability didn't avail her situation as leaving her bedroom empty would have Anita phoning the police thinking the cult had abducted her. Instead, Lauren dressed for bed to rest for school tomorrow.

* * * *

At school Wednesday, Lauren walked into history class to hear Renee and Amy discussing auras. Renee noticed Amy's aura was a bit faint and was explaining to her how they are believed to signal malfunctions in the body and a weakened aura could be suggestive of illness. Amy appeared quite feeble due to her cold and had numerous bruises and cuts.

"How'd you get all bruised up, Amy?" asked Lauren.

"Being sick. I fell down the stairs, twice actually, going to the bathroom. My parents won't let me walk by a flight now," smiled Amy as she rubbed her head. Renee offered to heal her wounds once they had some privacy. "How did things go at Amalgam House?"

They told Amy about what happened at Amalgam House and Jason's peril. Amy cried when they told her Jasmine threatened to kill him in three days.

"How did she know to take him?" asked Amy.

"I was trying to figure that out. I can't imagine how she or anyone else could be watching us," said Lauren.

"And three days? The book is more lost now than it was before," said Amy desperately. "Any idea where it could be?"

"Our only clue is the lighthouse," said Renee.

"Then let's go after school..." Amy said hopefully.

"We can't," said Lauren coldly. "Mina didn't tell me where the Ghost Shack is and we need a mortis blade from Amalgam. Unless we can magically get to Castle Everlasting, we're out of luck and I'm grounded," said Lauren.

"Me too. Dad put his foot down hard; he grounded me for the whole month!" said Renee.

"How did Jasmine get into Mortalland?" asked Amy.

"We don't know," said Renee.

"And there's no way to call Catherine and ask her where this Ghost Shack is?" asked Amy.

"We lost our communes," said Lauren. "How about you, Renee, think you can reach Catherine with your oracle abilities?"

"No, she's too far away and I've only been able to reach ghosts in the New City. But…"

"But what?" asked Lauren.

"Last night I had this dream where I'm walking across Bridge Street's bridge singing this odd verse, but it's not my voice coming out of my mouth."

Lauren asked Renee to describe the voice and when she did, Lauren knew it was Messina. She then asked Renee to repeat the verse.

"I lie in ruin abandoned and alone. My family has forsaken me; my heart is empty. My garden grows untamed, bitter fruit rests on stone and marble. From my window, I read only inscriptions and in the shadow of death, I am a refuge. Step through my door and you will find your path."

"She's trying to tell us where to go!" said Lauren.

"I hate riddles. This Messina is playing a joke on us!" said Amy exasperatedly. "What do you think it means, Renee?"

"Refuge… family forsaken me… door…

window…," Lauren thought aloud. "It's a house! An old one near a garden of stone and marble…near Bridge Street?" asked Lauren confused.

"That's where I was walking in the dream," said Renee.

"What can you see from Bridge Street?" asked Lauren.

"Coral street, the Baker's Light, Sailor Lake, the Memorial graveyard... a graveyard! A garden of stone and marble! But there aren't any abandoned houses near that graveyard!" said Renee.

"I've never seen one," said Amy.

"How many graveyards are in Baker's Creek?" asked Lauren.

"There's one at Grace Angel's Church," began Renee.

"I didn't see an abandoned house nearby," said Lauren.

"There's one by that big church near the museum. Another by the hospital," said Renee thinking of more.

"And on, and on, and on…and Jason will be dead by the time we find them all. It'd be different if we had a car and no nagging parents takin' us everywhere. How are we going to drive around and find all these graveyards?" asked Amy.

"Mom is busy with her new job," said Lauren.

"Yeah, I asked Dad to take me around too much as it is!" said Renee.

"And my mom doesn't want me going out since I'm sick," said Amy. "What about a séance?"

The Ghosts of Amalgam: The Linking Tome

Lauren and Renee looked at each other, pondering Amy's suggestion. Both their faces expressed the fear of engaging in such an activity.

"I don't think we should try that and I don't know of any mediums we could use anyway," said Lauren.

"I do," said Renee. "I came across one while looking for these books; her name is Rosa Lunde, a medium who owns a shop on Norde Street."

Amy looked at Lauren, who was pondering the thought.

"We could try! We could have her contact Catherine and find out where the Ghost Shack is. It could save us a lot of time!" said Amy.

Lauren considered this a moment longer; though no one had ever said anything against séances, she knew engaging in this activity might bring a severe punishment upon them but they were pressed for time.

"It seems like we're out of options. Since the lighthouse is just a clue, the sooner we get there the better because we might have to look elsewhere. I say we do it," said Lauren.

"For Jason!" said Amy. Lauren nodded yes, Amy smiled slightly before her face cramped for a sneeze.

"How far is Norde Street from here?" asked Lauren.

"A couple of blocks, we could walk there if we can somehow find an excuse to tell our parents!"

"We could stay after school, say it's for study

hall or detention. Your parents will believe that," said Amy chuckling despairingly.

"Yes, they would!" said Lauren.

Lauren called Anita and told her she had study hall opting for that lie in favor of detention with the hopes of avoiding any more punishment. Anita agreed to let Renee's father drop her off home. Amy ended up in the bathroom vomiting, her fever worsened, but she remained at school to accompany Lauren and Renee to see the medium. Once the bell rang, the girls met in front of the school and began a swift trek to Norde Street. Fifteen minutes later, they arrived at a small house where in the window of what looked like an average residence was a board advertising psychic readings and spiritual consultations.

"I won't be able to stay long. Mom's got a party planned and I'm still sick," said Amy sniffling.

The girls knocked on the door, a Caucasian woman opened it. She was in her thirties and wore tattered blue jeans stained with paint, a yellow sweater, and sandals with socks. She placed her right arm on the frame while holding the door open with her left and shifted her weight on her left leg while waiting a response from the girls.

"Rosa Lunde? The medium?" asked Lauren.

"Yes?"

"My name's Lauren Walston and these are my friends Amy and Renee. We were wondering if you could help us contact a spirit, a Catherine Salindras."

"The fee is thirty-five dollars cash and no refunds if the spirit can't be contacted," said Rosa.

"Why no refund?" asked Amy.

"Because I can perform a séance perfectly and the spirit may not show up. People expect to see a spirit every time, but sometimes the dead person is simply unavailable. The dead do have things to do; the afterlife is a busy place after all."

"We know," said Lauren.

Rosa's face tightened, confused by Lauren's assertion, but she cracked a small smile as she watched them pull their funds together. They handed her the money and she invited them inside. She directed them into the living room to sit while she changed clothes. The girls moved through her messy kitchen, where a bowl of cereal sat mostly finished, a few flakes still in a pool of milk, the pantry was open with food bursting forth, and rice spilled across the floor.

In the den, which was cleaner, the girls sat on a tacky plastic-covered teal couch and listened to the trickle of an algae-filled green water fish tank. They read from a huge collection of magazines pilled in the den until Rosa emerged minutes later. She had put on a white t-shirt and a sheer black veil blouse with a scarf tied around her head. Something about her attire made Renee think she had just changed into her costume and she remained suspicious of Rosa as she led them into the basement.

On the lower level, they found immediately in front of the stairwell a large round table, and further against the wall, a collection of amulets and talismans. To their left was an old television with knob turners for station selection and a single couch atop a dirty brown carpet. To their right was a bar with a couple of barstools and a host of snacks spread atop of it.

They sat around the table dressed with a white tablecloth and two five-arm candelabrums with five white candles each. Rosa put some instrumental music into a CD player and lit several incense sticks in the room. She invited the girls to partake in the snacks she had in the basement, saying they needed full bodies to energize themselves in order for the séance to work properly. The girls were not going to do this but Renee said she read the same thing in her books and all the snacks were wrapped individually and untouched.

"I don't trust Rosa's no refund policy," said Amy quietly to her friends while finishing off some beef jerky. "She might just do some hokey act and tell us Catherine's busy. How will we know if it's working?"

"We should sense a temperature drop or some other feeling. Occasionally when people contact spirits, parts of their body feel the pain the spirit felt when they died," said Renee, snacking on a couple of crackers.

"And how will they answer us? Can they talk?" asked Lauren.

"Depends, if she's genuine she could channel the spirit to talk through her or at least use the old rap once for yes, twice for no. Don't worry about our money, I'll know of she's pulling our legs. I actually tried this once before, but I couldn't get it to work.

"When was this?" asked Lauren.

"When I first started to hear ghost voices, right before I met you. I had tried to perform one out of a book but all I ended up doing was burning a lot of incense. Thank goodness you were at school the next day or Peter would have definitely made me cry in front of our class! But so far so good, she's trying to relax us with this music and the food," said Renee.

When the girls became full from the snacks, Rosa turned off the music, asked them to sit at the table, and led them in a breathing exercise.

"What are those scents, Rosa?" asked Renee as they returned the table.

"Cinnamon, frankincense, and sandalwood," she said burning the last of the incense with a lighter. "It aids in meditation and opening the consciousness." Renee gave Lauren and Amy a nod to confirm that Rosa was genuine so far. Rosa then proceeded to light the white candles, all but four, which she placed on the white table. They were ready to begin.

"Pick up a candle and we'll charge it," said Rosa lighting hers and then the others.

"Now, close your eyes and imagine white smoke rising from the candles," she said with a slow breathy tone. They did as instructed all of them focusing deeply. "Pass them to the person on your right using your right hand and take the candle on your left. Breathe in through your nose, out your mouth. Keep your minds absolutely blank." They followed her instructions flawlessly.

"Now we'll begin. Most sought Catherine Salindras, we ask that you move among us, speak with us, grace us with your presence."

Rosa repeated this instruction ten times, finally she called again, this time they felt heat about their bodies as if their skin was on fire.

"I feel warm," said Amy with her eyes closed.

"Me too. My skin feels hot and tight," said Lauren. "Is this normal?"

"Yeah," said Renee confidently, "Catherine probably died in a fire since I feel heat all over my body. Let's try and make contact. You ready, Rosa? Rosa?"

Renee opened her eyes to see Rosa breathing fast and swallowing hard as if someone had shoved a lump of coal down her throat and she struggled to disgust them. The girls fixed their eyes upon the hired medium.

"What's wrong?" asked Amy.

"I…I didn't think it would work," said Rosa struggling to maintain her poise.

"What? What do mean you didn't think it'd work?" Renee asked heatedly.

"Because it's never worked before! I've always said that the dead were busy when customers wouldn't see a ghost," said Rosa trembling and

breathing rapidly.

"You're a con artist!" said Renee.

"I knew she was a fake!" said Amy.

"I—I th—think I should um…go," said Rosa rising to stand but Renee and Amy held her down.

"You're not going anywhere until we got our thirty-five dollars worth!" said Amy.

"And the information we need," said Renee. Seeing as how Rosa reached Catherine, Lauren felt she had done her job and immediately took charge to get the information they sought. She silenced everyone and told Amy and Renee to cover Rosa's ears. They each placed a hand on Rosa's ears and carefully held the candles over Rosa's back and focused once again before Lauren proceeded to ask her questions.

"If you are here with us, rap once if for yes," said Lauren.

A forceful blow struck a closet door to the right near Rosa's bar full of goodies. Rosa jumped and looked to see where the knock was coming from but Amy and Renee held her tight and in their grips. She started to cry saying, "This is insane!" Lauren switched to her shade eyes to see if Catherine was in the room, but she wasn't, somehow the baroness was making the sound without being present. Lauren renewed her questioning.

"Catherine, this is Lauren. I'm sorry about this approach but as you probably know Jasmine destroyed Amalgam House and I can't get to Castle Everlasting because I don't know where the Ghost

Shack is. Do you understand me, rap once for…"

They heard a rap and Rosa shook again.

"Jasmine has taken a friend of mine prisoner, Jason Birch. She's holding him until we get the linking tome. I can't continue my search without the mortis blade or the guards. I need to know where the Ghost Shack is so I can get the blade before Friday or Jasmine will kill Jason. Will you tell me where it is?"

They heard another rap.

"How do we get her to answer this with a yes or no question?" asked Amy.

"Does anyone have a map and a penny?" asked Renee. They all shook their heads no.

"Should I look upstairs?" asked Amy.

"You might break the connection," said Renee. Rosa looked at her bewilderedly. Renee answered her awed gaze with, "Yeah, I read about this stuff, I know how it's done!"

"You girls are spooks! I thought that the rumors in this town was a bunch of nonsense, I didn't people actually practiced this stuff!"

"Oh, but you saw it fit to exploit them didn't you?" asked Renee.

"You better stop this; the ghost we've brought up could be the one that killed those reporters!" said Rosa frightened.

"Oh shut up!" said Amy with a curved smile.

"Renee, you're an oracle, can you let her speak through you," said Lauren.

"No way!" said Renee strongly but hushed. "My

skills aren't developed yet!"

"Catherine, will it hurt if you speak through Renee?"

They heard two raps.

"Come on, Renee, we'll help you through it."

"Just try to relax," said Amy. "Breathe in your nose, out your mouth, and calm yourself."

Renee however was panting and breathing very fast clutching her chest. Rosa became even more terrified now that Renee was becoming frightened.

"I don't feel right," said Renee. Lauren grew frustrated, first at the swindling medium and now at Renee. She grabbed Renee's clutched hand on her chest and placed it on the table rubbing it slowly.

"Follow me. Breathe in," said Lauren drawing a deep breath, "and out," said Lauren exhaling. Renee mimicked this and soon her head was down and her chest was rising comfortably. Her head wavered back and forth and then she lifted her eyes. Catherine's voice emanated from Renee's dark lips.

"I'm very disappointed in you, Lauren," said Catherine. "Names is recording a list of your offenses in his book. I'm going to have to defend you in court."

"But..."

"BUT NOTHING!" said Catherine through Renee and Rosa squirmed like a child watching a horror movie. "Though your intentions were noble, you performed a séance with this medium who has no ties to the Court. Your motives are the only thing that might save you and your friends from being put to death! Now you must definitely come to Amalgam. The Ghost Shack is off Bilmore Street. Look for a dry-rotted wooden house near Vernon Cemetery. Come immediately and tell this medium to never speak of what she's seen!" said Catherine and Renee returned from her trance.

"I don't want to do it," said Renee.

"Renee, it's okay. You've already done it," said Amy gravely.

"Seriously?" asked Renee looking to the girls. Amy arched her brow and smiled at Renee.

"Oh...," said Renee sighing relief. They all turned their attention to the fearful Lauren.

"What's wrong?" asked Renee regaining her composure.

"We're in trouble with Catherine for performing this séance," said Amy. "And we're going to be in trouble if we don't get back to the school soon. Sorry I can't go with you two, but Mom is going to freak if I'm not home in time for that party."

"I guess it's just me and you," said Renee to Lauren who nodded sadly. The girls left Rosa in her home for school, but not before strongly advising against speaking of what has transpired or anything she may have heard to anyone and Rosa, looking deathly afraid of the girls, appeared inclined to keep silent. In fact, as soon as they left, Rosa used their money and some savings to stay a hotel where she immediately called a realtor to sell her house.

* * * *

"Bilmore Street, is it?" asked Barry taking the girls to Vernon Cemetery. They had returned to school quickly where Barry picked them up. She fabricated a story to explain her immediate need to visit the graveyard. Both rode in the backseat while Barry drove and spoke to them. "What kind of religion requires three annual trips to visit their deceased ancestors, if you don't mind me asking, Lauren?"

"It's not a religion…more like an orthodox annual celebration of…death," said Lauren.

"How do we plan on getting back with this one?" asked Renee. Lauren shook her head with uncertainty. She was running on fumes for ideas to get around town and felt horrible that she is in trouble for trying to save a life. Arriving on Bilmore Street, they passed the dry rotten house Catherine described. In the cemetery was Mr. Hitchen moving about the graves with their indwellers Mary and Joy.

Lauren and Renee separated their spirits from their bodies as Mary and Joy indwelt them. Mary and Joy, in their bodies, got out of the car and paid respects at a random grave before leaving with Barry. Lauren and Renee approached Mr. Hitchen, who led them to the Ghost Shack.

"Glad you two made it out of Amalgam House. Sorry I wasn't much help," said Mr. Hitchen.

"Is Mina safe?" asked Lauren frustrated.

"She got wounded heading to the car. Regrettably, a couple of the wolves managed to maul her."

"Is she alright?" asked Renee.

"She's hospitalized for the moment but she's old and may not pull through."

"I hope she makes it," said Renee sadly.

"In her condition she was unable to contact you with our location," said Mr. Hitchen.

"No one else could get the location of this house to us?" asked Lauren.

"We were trying to bring you two along but there were a hundred wolves on the grounds. We've been trying to set up base here and find those lost at Amalgam House. The earliest we could have reached you would have been Friday."

"*FRIDAY!*" said Lauren stopping. Mr. Hitchen was stunned and speechless at her outburst. Lauren continued walking for the shack while Mr. Hitchen and Renee hung back.

"Is there something wrong?" Mr. Hitchen asked Renee.

"We're being punished in Amalgam," said Renee.

Mr. Hitchen and Renee rejoined Lauren inside the scraggly old wooden house. It was a one-room building with a sink in the corner and a broken mirror next to a toilet for a bathroom and clear indentations where a stove and a bed once stood. On the floor was a large trapdoor that Mr. Hitchen opened after casting a complex spell on the woodwork. He then led them down a lengthy ladder into a tunnel. They walked through the underground halls and into huge chamber supported by numerous concrete pillars and wood beams where tightly packed desks filled the room.

Ghosts and mortals were organizing tables, desks, and documents and Lauren realized why Mr. Hitchen said the earliest they could contact her would be Friday. However, seeing this room she knew that would have been a stretch. Battery powered lamps provided the main source of illumination although generators by the walls gave power to some other equipment.

"This is the Ghost Shack. Doesn't look like much but it's made for necessity."

Mr. Hitchen took them through the large room and down a nearly pitch black corridor. They came to a door. The frame had been made of strong, thick oak wood and the door itself was a solid five inches thick. A shining dew barrier sealed the door radiating a dark shade of blue.

"These are dew barriers, right, Mr. Hitchen?" asked Renee.

"Correct!" he said. "Do you know how to dispel barriers?"

"Catherine taught us *diktat invodimi* and a few others; I was wondering which charm you were using?"

"It's called a*sue terin*. This particular one is very strong and can destroy many weaker barriers."

Renee and Lauren made note of it while Mr. Hitchen dispelled the barrier and entered the portal room. It was already open, the portal guard said

Catherine notified him in advance and the girls wasted no time entering Amalgam.

* * * *

On the other side, Lauren and Renee stepped foot in Catherine's quarters at Baronsguard. The baroness was waiting and as Lauren was about to speak Catherine said, "It seems you two have already been saved from a terrible fate but you'll still have to be reprimanded. Follow me."

Lauren was relieved somewhat when Catherine said this. The baroness continued talking, leading them through the curtained archway in her chamber and down a flight of stairs. "Messina came to me in a dream moments before your arrival with your judgment. She considered Mina's injury, the destruction of Amalgam House, your importance to Amalgam, and the time it would have taken the three of you to find Vernon Cemetery if you acted on the oracle she sent before deciding on your punishment. She said it was possible you would have needlessly suffered this Jason Birch. Who is he?" asked Catherine stopping to turn to her.

"A friend," said Lauren. "He goes to my school."

"Ah! Messina said that you are guilty of breaking Amalgam's anti-séance rule and the sin of Sloth. Messina had given you an oracle to decipher to locate the Ghost Shack but you sought a medium because you were unwilling to work hard and find the cemetery. The two of you were not trained to handle the situation if you'd reached a demon or an evil spirit. Since you two were slow about doing your spiritual work, the two of you are going to have to learn a little haste. Renee, you'll be sentenced to work alongside Lauren in the purgation fields for participating and Amy will receive the same fate when she comes back. Go to the House of Shades and await your summons to the purgation fields after this meeting."

"This isn't right. I had to do it Catherine," said Lauren.

"Lauren this is a merciful judgment! You're lucky to have covered Rosa's ears during the séance or we could have tried you for violating the Mortalland Rule. We've done it before and the condemned received the pyre penalty. Those sentenced to the pyre will burn now until the end of Amalgam. *Be very thankful.*"

Lauren was indeed thankful after hearing Catherine's words but felt extraordinarily guilty about having contacted Rosa and hung her head as they moved on.

"Have you heard from Nasra, Vincent, or Devon?" asked Lauren remembering of her friends.

"I couldn't rescue them from the Phoenix; he bewitched my portal and made it wander off course. I believe he's imprisoned them in the spectral tree. I was thrilled Amy was able to escape, but I was heartbroken to hear of Vincent's and Nasra's capture. I don't know what became of Devon."

They emerged behind Catherine's bench in the courtroom. Densen, Names and Graves, Lion Face, and Selene were waiting patiently. The mood was causal as Catherine instructed Renee, Selene, and Lauren to the jury box and the district representatives took their place at the podiums.

"I've called this closed session for an update on our readiness for war. Names, have you found a ghost with the mark of the tree?"

"Yes, other than Jasmine there were two in all of Amalgam at Barons Donovan and Samina's cities and there I interviewed each one. They were very compliant as it seems Jasmine has greatly offended them by created her tree prison out of the guardian tree spirit known as Kradleman. They agreed the mark of the tree has the following powers. For all trees, with the tree's permission if sentient, the mark can grow, shrink, and control their trunks and roots, force the absorption of dew, hear the voices of Amalgam trees, and possibly awaken the sentience of Mortalland trees. They also can command the use of a favorite tree more strongly than others if the bearer preferred a particular type."

"How is Jasmine controlling these trees without her mark?" asked Lauren.

"Some ghosts retain minor functions, especially if they've had the mark for some time. I believe, however, that Phoenix has granted her a patch mark, one to enhance the power Jasmine retained after her mark was removed," said Catherine.

"That's a fair assumption, Catherine," said Names. "She's probably using the residual functions of her tree mark to control the roots of the one she rides. The willow at Amalgam House obeyed her commands probably because it's Jasmine's favorite type of tree."

"And the spectral tree? That's not a giant willow yet it upped and moved," said Lion Face.

"The Phoenix could have moved it. He does have animal muscle; with their numbers, it would have been easy. I doubt Jasmine can use her residual powers on such a large tree however and if she remains without her mark the tree is useless. With Jasmine's threat it seems she still can't find it," said Catherine.

"What threat?" Lion Face asked. Catherine told the representatives of Jasmine's demand.

"Why three days?" asked Densen.

"She didn't say but I'm for it as well to bring this war to its knees before it gets running. Lauren will find it and see that Nasra and the others are freed and we'll have to find some way to stop Jasmine from lowering the castle. Are the guards prepared for war, Lion Face?"

"Yes, I've personally enhanced many divisions courage with my braver charm and we were able to secure Geyser Worx for now, but we can't hold for long. Jasmine and Phoenix will need spectroplasm to feed their tree and we've inconvenienced them by draining the lake to only a few thousand gallons. For a tree that size it won't be enough."

"Good thinking, Lion Face," said Catherine. "The Horn of Olives, Densen?"

"Cleaned and tested," said Densen.

"Let's think worst-case scenario. If Jasmine gets her mark, lowers the castle, and the animals infiltrate the city, what do we do? Guards can only hold the animals back but for so long. Is there a plan to find Estoc or kill the Phoenix and Jasmine?" asked Lion Face.

"Estoc is for all purposes missing. There's been several investigative units sent out but none could find him. Don't worry about Jasmine, she can't get past me, but the Phoenix is the main problem. If he gets past our defenses there's nothing I can do but stall him. Lauren, have you made any progress discovering the secret of the Phoenix?"

Lauren had been so busy trying to find the linking tome that she had forgotten about that mandate.

"No, Catherine," said Lauren. The baroness sighed.

"We may not be able to stop him if the castle is leveled. Our only hope is that the barrier can keep him outside the castle. Lion Face put every effort into tapping that lake dry so Jasmine's tree won't be able to break it. I'll put the other baron cities on alert to protect their reserves. Other than that, let's pray for another miracle from God to save us. Selene, take Lauren and Renee to the House of Shades. I'll be with you two after you've finished in the purgation fields," said Catherine.

"We could send a regiment of our best guards to try and destroy the tree before it levels the castle," said Lion Face.

"That would be a suicide mission, but it's certainly an option we'll have to consider," said Catherine. Sigpos appeared in the hall and whispered into Densen's ear before vanishing again.

"Bad news from Baron Jonah, a few ships of Phoenix Loyalist slipped by his defenses and are sailing for New Elysian. They should dock at Roland Shipyard within the next twenty four-hours," Densen said disparagingly.

Selene stood and took Lauren and Renee out of the courtroom as the baroness, Lion Face and Densen continued discussing war strategy. Selene led them down the stairs of Baronsguard when Lauren decided to ask why the negotiations failed.

"Although the animals were happy to see me they said Catherine herself claimed responsibility for Estoc's capture. The lionesses of Estoc's pride believe it was Catherine using a tree that lifted him from their pride."

"But that was Jasmine!" said Lauren.

"I know but we couldn't get through to them. The only thing that can stop the animals would be to find Estoc and I don't believe that would help. They want ghosts to pay for all their sins past and present in this coming battle. They've changed so much since I've gone. All they feel is rage. I should have never left," said Selene sorrowfully. "Thankfully Catherine gave me a second chance. I'm now Head of the House of Natives and I oversee all native activity at Castle Everlasting. I'll do everything in my power to ensure we win this battle."

Selene led them to the House of Shades and dropped them off at the door. Lauren and Renee made their way to their room. It remained just as they left it. Lauren needed to relax as her job in New City was stressing her out. Minutes later, a knock on the door shocked both Renee and Lauren. They hadn't expected Catherine to arrive so suddenly. Renee opened the door, it was a ghost carrying a stuffed black pouch slung over his shoulder wearing a cap pointed at the top and surrounded by many smaller tips. A small scarf was tied around his neck, his shorts fit loosely, and his shirt fully buttoned.

"Delivery from the Amalgam Times! Special run! All baron cities papers reacting to the current crisis!" said the man holding retrieving a newspaper from his pouch.

"Oh, thanks!" said Renee.

"Has Harold made those changes he was talking about?" asked Lauren, coming to the door looking loathsomely at the paper.

"Yes, he has. We no longer have a gossip column and now only ghosts bearing journalistic and scribe marks can work at the paper. We're making sure all of our information is accurate from a variety of sources like Court officials on and off the record and public announcements."

"Good, now Siggy and Amy won't have a way

of embarrassing you in future papers," said Renee.

"Not necessarily. Sigpos has joined with a couple other gossipers like Sarah Finke, Joshua Medlers, and Polly Muror to create his own magazine. It's going to give every paper in Amalgam some stiff competition."

"Yeah, right! They won't sell a single issue. No one trust gossiper marks," said Renee.

"Ghosts say never trust a gossiper mark, but what they mean is never trust them to keep a secret! Sigpos was partly responsible for the Amalgam Times success and recently published our most successful issue ever about the new baron."

"Ugh!" said Lauren as she left the door for her hammock. Renee pointed to Lauren's name on the door and then to her. The deliveryman knew he'd upset her and made a quick exit.

"Well, I've got more deliveries. Good luck, Lauren," he said.

Lauren waved at him as he left their door and went down the hall, knocking on the next door. Renee watched as residents in the next apartment rushed him with outstretched hands for the paper and he produced several more than his bag appeared to hold. Renee looked down at Amalgam Times headline that read: **ANIMAL ATTACK IMMINENT.**

"Let me have one," said Lauren.

Renee gave her the Amalgam Times and the Everlasting Papers while she read the remainder. Lauren read the articles below the top story that had other headlines related to the looming battle. *Phoenix asserts this is beginning of the end, Catherine orders civilian evacuation, Guards on edge about animal numbers, Lake tap spurs famine fears, Amalgam House Destroyed.* These all came from Lauren's papers. The Genesis Gazette, Ruin Scraps, and the Ages Past described their cities respond to the coming battle.

"Listen here, Lauren," said Renee reading from the Genesis Gazette. "Baron Donovan has pledged his undying support for Baron Catherine and the citizens of Castle Everlasting. He has petitioned the baroness to leave the Amalgam portal open for the Genesis Guard to reinforce the Everlasting Guard. Baron Catherine refused, however, saying that doing so would weaken his city's defenses and has kept his offer as a last resort. How bad is this, Lauren?"

"It seems to be a nationwide concern; every paper is talking about it."

"Listen," said Renee, another article caught her attention. "Rumors abound that Phoenix has recruited the service of Gretchen Reis, his lady general known for her remorseless brutality and brilliant strategy during the previous Phoenix Wars to ensure victory. Having nullified the Judge's ability to use the Brilliant Flash during the Amalgam Seals War, there may be nothing that stands between the Phoenix and Castle Everlasting's Chamber of Three Doors."

Lauren became increasingly worried. She

wondered how Catherine was handling it as she and Renee could barely keep pace with events in the New City. They read each paper and by the time they finished there was another knock at the door. This time, it was a small fairy.

"Greetings, Lauren and Renee," said the ball of winged light in a high-pitched girl voice. "You two are to catch the Morrigan Train in the city district west of the Ages Tower. You will depart at three o'clock and arrive in the purgation fields at three thirty. Here are your tickets." The little fairy produced two long tickets much larger than her body and Lauren took them. "You two are to follow Sloth to that section of the field."

The fairy flittered down the hall where other fairies were busy delivering tickets, weaving through a multitude of ghosts headed to the train. As Lauren and Renee headed out the house, they saw they were not alone as many more were departing for work. They followed them out of the castle district. Passing through the city wall there was an expansive arched staircase with a large platform that had a walkway extending to the right alongside the mountain that the ghosts treaded.

Following this procession, Lauren and Renee came to a large glass building, a modern train station created in a U-shape that swallowed the tracks and sheltered the trains. There were two steam-engine locomotives, gold and blue regally decorated with ornate golden bands that stretched to the caboose. The furthest train, the gold one, was for unloading, the blue train for loading. Lauren and Renee handed their tickets to an usher and boarded the blue train.

The train cars were more like subway cars with gold bars and triangles to hold and comfortable leather-like seats. At first, Lauren questioned this but seeing the burnt ghosts holding onto the bars and others squirming painfully in their seats from the unloading train, she realized not many ghosts would prefer to sit. Gold carpet covered the aisles and every other car had a small booth for lifestones, which a passing ghost explained where used to store spectroplasm, but all were unmanned now. The train departed immediately, taking them into a tunnel. Upon emerging, they looked out the window to a massive lake to the right and another structure a passing ghost described to them as the sunken aquarium. Once again, the mountain overtook their sight for ten minutes before the windows turned blazing red. They had arrived.

* * * *

Lauren and Renee left the train from a similar station and filed out the front on direction of their fairy guides. The area behind Baronsguard was like a lake of lava and black smoke. Right away, Lauren spotted the outcropping Catherine mentioned but all she could see was the rock, no cages. They approached a wide gate, funneling all those who arrived towards seven Minotaurs. They were standing on a gargantuan slab of granite, the last part of the station floor before the field. The archway leading into the field read SALIGIARIUM. Each Minotaur had its tail wrapped around it a different number of times, the one on the far right had his once, the next twice, and onward until seven.

Lauren and Renee managed to be near the front and could see that their Minotaur with "Sloth" carved into his head. The fairies organized the gathering and the Minotaurs lead them to different parts of the field. It was so expansive Lauren thought it had to be the largest portion of land dedicated to any function at Castle Everlasting. Lauren witnessed firsthand how the ghosts purge their sins. Those following Greed were carrying hot coals barefooted across the heated field that charred their arms and chest as they stacked them in large piles. Gluttony followed Greed where his ghosts had to gorge themselves on the stacked coals.

Lauren saw ghosts tied to thorn-covered trees where native goblins shot flaming arrows at them. These were the wrathful, defenseless against their aggressors. Renee caught Lust shackling ghosts to chairs by a lava river where up sprang flaming shape-shifters that took the image of their lovers and embraced them for affection. Envy led his throng to a portion of the lake where the lava met the water and burned it to a super hot steam. His ghosts were chained to the lake edge where their eyes were bathed in the evaporation but weren't allowed to lift their heads. They watched the prideful make their way up a natural trail on the mountain where Pride shackled them to the cliff wall. Heated steam blew across their bodies as hot spikes tore into their husks repeatedly.

Sloth led them to an ash-covered field section and instructed them to remove all footwear and run barefooted to the only water source in the fields. It was a great distance, and they would take buckets to douse a row of everlasting flames behind them. As they ran along the ashes, their feet would burn slightly but if they stopped, they caught fire up to their waists. Emerging from the ash to chase after them were green snakes that would bite anyone too slow to escape their bite. Their hot poison slowed them down and many more snakes beset any straggler caught by one these swift serpents as their lower body burned from the flames. After several laps, Lauren and Renee succumbed to them like several in their group tonight though Lauren couldn't hear anyone scream because her wails drowned out her companions.

After two hours with no rest, the fairies cut short their purging. The little fairies, as tiny as they were, could touch ghosts and shades and carried the girls back to the train. Arriving at the station, Catherine met Lauren and Renee. The fairies dropped them off in front of her but they couldn't stand and fell to their knees. Catherine raised her hand and cast a powerful healing charm that healed both of them immediately.

"We're running out of time so I had the fairies bring you back. You'll do your virtue work in the New City. Hurry back and go immediately to the lighthouse. Take these with you."

Catherine retrieved a mortis blade and gossiper's commune from her cloak. Lauren took the gossiper's commune and stuck it in her clothes, but Catherine held off on giving the blade to her. She held it out the dagger in her hands and told Lauren to look at it. Lauren unsheathed the dagger, its curved ornate glass handle radiated ice blue light, but thousands of miniature brown and black organisms wrapped around the blade. She sheathed it quickly.

"The bacterium on the blade can eat a person to death quickly and entirely but in order for it to work you must make contact with the person's bare skin. We created them when the djemsheed was lost. The djemsheed's magic is regenerative, healing old organs and wounds, ensuring longevity. We also use these blades to eat the false skins of the Phoenix Loyalist and regenerative creatures before they can heal but they work doubly strong on humans so be careful when using it around mortals. It'll take care of Etienne without a doubt."

"Why would the angels give Etienne the djemsheed?" asked Renee.

"Before we sealed Cedric in the Burrow, he said they stole the items from the treasury in hopes that the Phoenix would one day reacquire them to aid his entry into Paradise. The angels passed these items including the djemsheed to mortal associates. Etienne is one but he's obviously not trying to help the Phoenix or Jasmine. Maybe the angels didn't trust the Phoenix. They were smart to hide these relics in Mortalland and the Phoenix himself has done the same with prized possessions. They know it's the one place we can't monitor well."

"They don't seem to have problems monitoring me. Jasmine said since she arrived in the New City she's been watching me. That's how she was able to kidnap Jason," said Lauren.

"What method did she use to speak with you, flesh-crafted skin, or through an agent?"

"She used one of her random victim's bodies," said Lauren disgustedly. "Why?"

"Phoenix loyalists are known to use special skin, flesh created from spectroplasm that's regenerative and tough to destroy with mortal weapons. I was wondering if she was using this to follow you. It's quite deceptive but can be distinguished because it lacks the natural feel and texture of human flesh yet it works well enough for them. Be on guard for anyone who might look a bit odd while on your search. I had a few guards to change your parent's memories to let you off punishment. Consider that a courtesy."

"What about the guards that was supposed to join us?" Lauren asked.

"I'm sorry, Lauren. We can't spare anymore after the Amalgam House incident. Many of the guards from that facility are lost. You're on your own now."

Lauren took Catherine's message with a heavy heart as they left Baronsguard for the embassy towers and were teleported from Castle Everlasting back to the New City.

CHAPTER TWENTY-THREE
THE LINKING TOME

Lauren and Renee returned to their bodies, awaking with all suddenness in their bedrooms as their indwellers departed. Lauren held the mortis blade in hand and the gossiper's commune materialized in her pocket. It was Thursday morning and Lauren felt the mounting pressure to save Jason. She got out of bed to dress for school when Anita knocked on her door. Lauren opened it and her mother, looking sad, told her to answer the phone. Anita replaced the phone in her room; she couldn't remember why it was in her bedroom.

"Telephone dear, it's Mrs. Birch. I'm afraid its bad news concerning Jason," said Anita.

"What is it, Mom?" asked Lauren, trying to be believably ignorant but knew Mrs. Birch was calling about her missing son.

"Jason's missing."

"What! What happened?"

"He disappeared Monday evening. The Birch's are worried about him. Jason's mother wants to know when you last saw him."

Lauren took the phone and adjusted to speak with an upset Mrs. Birch.

"Hello, Mrs. Birch," said Lauren politely. "Are you okay?"

"I'm managing," said Mrs. Birch tearfully. "I got your number from Amy. When did you last see Jason and did he seem in trouble at all?"

"Not that I'm aware of. I last saw him in history class. He was happy like he usually is," Lauren lied, knowing Amy recently broke up with him.

"Did he say anything like he was planning to run away?" asked Mrs. Birch.

"No, do you think he ran away?" asked Lauren.

"I just want to keep all options open. I'm worried; there have been a lot of mysterious things happening in Baker's Creek. I don't understand how the police cannot have a single suspect your father's investigation. Now my boy has gone missing and I'm scared for my baby," said Mrs. Birch weeping audibly now.

"I'll pray for his safe return and I'll keep my eyes and ears open for him," said Lauren.

"Thank you. I'm going to call the police in a few minutes and inform them of the situation. I wouldn't be this worried if he was with his friends, but they haven't seen him either."

"I can't imagine how you feel, Mrs. Birch. I'll let you know if I hear something okay?"

"Thank you, Lauren. Tell you mother I said thank you," said Mrs. Birch sobbing as she hung up. Lauren slowly put her phone back in the cradle. She was sad as well; withholding information from a heartbroken mother upset her.

"What did she say?" asked Renee, whom Lauren called after talking with Mrs. Birch.

"She just found out that Jason is missing. She wanted to know if I had seen her, of course…" Lauren closed the door to her room before speaking again, "I told her I hadn't."

"Poor Mrs. Birch," said Renee.

"We must find this book before Jasmine hurts Jason. See if you can come to my house after school, okay?"

"Will do," said Renee.

Renee was ready to set out when Lauren called. Barry was happy to drive Renee to Lauren's as Anita was once again working the night with her new boss Mr. Lasitier. Amy said she couldn't join them because of something big unfolding at the Townsend's house and wanted to go back home to find out what was happening. Barry dropped off Renee at Evelyn Lane.

"Aren't we supposed to be going to the lighthouse?" asked Renee.

"There's a passage from a grave at Baker's Memorial that will take us to the cavern," said Lauren.

They walked to Baker's Memorial. Lauren saw the police tape still hanging around the grave of the unknown and walked past solemnly. Renee could only hear her mother silently weeping with other spirits in the graveyard as they approached the grave of Pierre Channing. There they stood over it like mourners before Renee spoke.

"How do we get in? Do we say a password or something?"

"We'll use the evanesce spell," said Lauren. "Hide your body behind a tombstone; make it look like your sleeping." Renee did as instructed and they evanesced. Renee's body drooped silently by the tree and Lauren de-materializing entirely.

They moved below the ground where they fell down a long, deep vertical tunnel. Inside the plot was a rope ladder leading back up. Lauren thought Renee could have brought her body if only she knew a way to remove the massive stone slab covering the plot. The pass was very dark, so Lauren used the *cinzeré illumine* spell to light their path. Her hand ignited in flame and they moved deeper into passage. They came to a door similar to the one at Amalgam House. This one glowed green. Renee recalled an incantation Catherine taught them to break the dew barrier and unlocked the door allowing them to proceed.

After climbing over waist-high rock obstruction, they entered a wide chamber lit by two standing torches. Numerous rock pillars carved during digging supported the ceiling. Etienne's desk from his office was in the cavern, a chair, and several crates of folders. The desk was facing a deactivated portal in the middle of the chamber. At the opposite end of the room was a ramp carved-out of the rock that went up two levels, reaching another dew-sealed door. Renee observed the portal while Lauren checked the desk.

Lauren went to the desk and pulled open two of the drawers finding nothing of use until coming across an address book. The first section of contacts labeled the Saved. There were phone numbers and addresses of people living in Baker's Creek, nearly a hundred. The remaining contacts were town dignitaries in high positions of Baker's Creek society such as the mayor, police chief, several judges, city council members, and the head of public works.

Lauren materialized and found one particular letter from the judge denying Dr. Knowles' request to stop the excavation. For a moment, she wished the court had sided with him. Maybe her father would still be alive. Lauren continued to search through his belongings and found an intriguing letter:

Dear Dr. Knowles,

You were correct in assuming that a rival sect is watching us. Several of the Saved have done a little counter-reconnaissance on these spies and learned the following. They appear to be residents of

Mexico yet some are descendent from Spain, fluent in English and Spanish, and incredibly wealthy on par with you. There seems to be a strong sense of kinship among the group and we conclude that they must be all closely related, perhaps family. We do not know if they are in possession of the Telas-Dod or the Spear, but we believe they are responsible for the destruction of the Dragon Tongue sect.

Furthermore, we have seen them on several occasions in the graveyard, on the lighthouse grounds, near your shop on Coral Street, and drawing close to your office at Psychologist Park. I believe a confrontation is inevitable, although, if they are not immortals, I do not believe they will be a match for the Saved.

Interestingly enough, Douglas claims to have spotted a young man following our spies! He is the only person who has seen him, and says this boy has managed to spy on our nemeses without drawing their attention. If we can locate him, perhaps he can yield valuable information that will help us destroy our enemies!

As to the girl who visited your office this week, Lauren Waltson, she's the daughter of Willem Walston, owner of the Daily Watch who died during the excavation. We've had her house under surveillance for almost week now. The only irregular activity about her is her random visits across town. Lauren happens to be friends with Renee Dupree, the girl usually hovering around Teresa Dupree's grave. We could kill Renee and put an end to her snooping or kidnap her for information about Lauren and the linking tome. These options, of course, are yours to consider.

Happily Saved,
Dylan

This letter from the seemingly genteel Dylan frightened Lauren. Dylan's warning of another sect competing for Amalgam's relics had Lauren wishing she had her own group to help her. It also made her fear for the safety of Renee's body in the graveyard. Lauren hastened her search, but the last drawer was locked. She de-materialized her arm and reached through materializing her hand to grab whatever she could find. She felt only a piece of paper which she de-materialized and pulled from the drawer. It was a single page from the linking tome.

When Lauren touched it, she entered a psychometric vision of Etienne killing Luther. The scene wasn't too different from before with exception to Etienne saying he'd spare Luther's life if he told him where the book was hidden before shooting him. Lauren focused harder and the vision changed like a ripple of water to earlier that day, with Luther observing the newly recovered book from the dirt. The vision was similar to the one at the Townsends except it continued with Luther standing to exit his study after using the phone. He stopped suddenly, book in hand and deep in thought. The vision changed to Luther walking by his large picture to open a door on the side of it where he took a flight of stairs to a cellar. Inside Luther ripped the page out of the book and the vision ended dissolving back to the desk and Lauren in the cavern.

Though it wasn't an "x" on a treasure map, it was close enough and Lauren was satisfied with another clue in their search. Renee had moved from the portal, up the cavern ramp, through the barrier door, and into the keeper house. She returned running into the chamber soon after.

"Someone's coming, Lauren, hide!" said Renee.

"Hide? We're invisible!" said Lauren.

"No! They can *see* us. One of them looked right at me! We have to go! *Now!*" said Renee as shadows stretched across the wall. Lauren stood up and evanesced, the page in her hand also dematerialized and they searched for a place to hide. They chose to hide behind the rocks that obstructed the cavern entrance. The two men entered the cavern searching wildly about the chamber, their flashlight beams swishing along the walls. Lauren and Renee recognized one of them as Dylan.

"Are you seeing things, Brandon?" asked Dylan searching for intruders.

"No! I swear I saw a ghost girl coming up the keeper house floor."

"Positive? Was she cute?"

"No, I mean yes. Seriously, I thought Master Knowles was going to seal the grave entrance?"

"He started to with those rocks but since the excavation didn't go on as planned he didn't see the need. But you said you saw someone so let's see if we can find her…I don't see anything," said Dylan after a few moments. "Besides the cavern door is sealed with a dew barrier and the tomb with a pass phrase. Only the Saved know the password to break the magic on the vault and few shades know a spell powerful enough to dispel the barrier."

"I also thought I saw that annoying girl from the store with a friend in the graveyard moments ago too."

"Renee? Now *she's* cute!" said Dylan.

"I heard you suggested kidnapping her if she kept coming around."

"Yes, Master Knowles thought Renee might be a medium and was communicating with the spirits lingering in the graveyard. He didn't want the spirits talking to her about us. Good thing he didn't as she led us right to Lauren," said Dylan.

Lauren and Renee listened with intrigue; they were astounded that these people were watching them.

"Oh my God!" said Renee. "Are these the people keeping Mom in the graveyard?"

"I don't know," said Lauren. "Sounds like it, but Mina said it was a spirit holding them hostage not shades or whatever these people are."

Renee remembered what Mina had told her but she believed that these people had something to do with her mother's imprisonment. She listened closely to their conversation.

"Didn't he assign her to you after Matt died?" asked Brandon.

"Yeah, she's been our best lead since Luther popped up with a page from the book."

"That was quite a momentous day. I thought we'd never reach Amalgam until Luther showed up with a linking tome page, no less!" said Brandon.

"Lot of good it's done us. This thing still doesn't wanna work." Lauren and Renee heard a loud thump. Dylan kicked the portal.

"Let's hope that Lauren can lead us to the whole book and then I'm sure Master Knowles will find a portal guard mark to activate it. Otherwise we'll have to go the more dangerous route."

"What's that?" asked Brandon.

"Kidnap the girls. Force them to talk about Amalgam and take it from there."

"We should have done that a long time ago!" said Brandon exhaustively. "We know that they're shades. We know where they live and we know they're connected to that ghost mansion. We should have flexed our muscle long ago."

"You know that ghost mansion is guarded and you know the Master doesn't want to go back after losing his wife stealing this portal."

"It was her fault! She chose to live a mortal's life; her memory would be completely erased had not Etienne given his children her surname. I know the Master took her loss hard but that mansion must have portal guard ghosts and the only reason he won't go back is because of her!"

"Well now that's not the only reason. Master Knowles told me that someone else is out there watching the girls, protecting them even. You never heard how Matt and the others died did you?"

"Are you going to tell me now? I've been curious since they went missing," said Brandon.

"Apparently someone or something must have driven their spirits from their bodies and then kept them from returning."

"They lost their spirits?" asked Brandon bewildered. "Ah! So that's how you kill one of us. No wonder Dr. Knowles took his immortality after they found the body. I thought he had executed them but I was afraid to ask since no one questions the Master."

"He didn't know what to think at first. When he realized their spirits were gone he had Paula channel them but they wouldn't return. Matt's body was still alive but a body without a spirit is as good as dead and it took every bit of the good doctor's heart to remove his immortality."

"He doesn't like to lose one of us. He treats us like his blood family," said Brandon appreciatively.

"We are his family so you can understand his reluctance to act on the girls. The witch that attacked him a few days ago really spooked him. That's why he's moving his office here, he doesn't want to put his granddaughter in danger and our contacts at the station claim detectives are looking for him for questioning."

"For what?"

"Luther's death."

"How'd the cops find him?"

"It seems the Master and the witch put on quite a spectacle having at each other. Some passer-bys called the police to investigate the strange lights in the area. When they arrived they found Luther's body in the pond, a tree had collapsed and surfaced his body. They found his office wrecked with a few traces of blood so they've been looking for him both as a missing person and in connection with Luther's death."

"This must have been the big event at the Townsend's Amy was talking about," Lauren said to Renee.

"Does he know who the witch is?" asked Brandon.

"He said he'd never seen her before. He really wants us to step up the search now that she's involved. Master Knowles thinks the book is in Luther's house. We already have it under surveillance."

"The witch their talking about has to be Jasmine," said Renee.

"Sounds like her," said Lauren. Lauren realized that Jasmine was ensuring they would get to the linking tome before Etienne and his Saved and relayed this to Renee.

"Then what's stopping us?" asked Brandon excitedly.

"The witch! Whoever she is, she's got the

Master spooked into being a little more cautious, after all he barely escaped with his life. He believes that this witch is the same one that killed our Saved, the people at the excavation, and he thinks she's after the book too!"

Lauren gasped; she felt a heavy pain in her chest. She trembled and struggled for breath. She turned around and slumped down from the rocks. Lauren drew her knees to her chest and dug her head into them as she sat crying. Dylan's words mixed with sadness and Catherine's encouragement in her chamber.

"We mustn't be careless now. We'll remain invisible for now and at the right moment we'll strike!" said Dylan. His words merged into Catherine saying "Messina has the utmost confidence you'll encounter you father's killer."

Messina's prediction had finally come true and sooner than expected. Not only had she discovered who killed her father but she'd already come face to face with the person who had done it. Jasmine had slain her father and in only a few short weeks of serving the Court, she'd discovered it was her. Renee was listening so assiduously to Brandon and Dylan for news of her mother that she had not noticed Lauren crying.

"Well, I don't see anything. I'm heading back to the lighthouse," said Dylan.

"Right behind you," said Brandon. "How do you think the Master came by the djemsheed?"

"He's never told anyone, not even his son."

Their voices faded as the headed up the ramp.

"Unbelievable isn't it, Lauren?" asked Renee until she saw Lauren crying. "Lauren what's wrong?"

Lauren drew a deep breathe as she lifted her head, tears rolling down her cheek and said slowly, "You heard them didn't you? What they said about Jasmine and the people in the graveyard."

Renee thought briefly then said somberly, "Jasmine killed your father, oh Lauren, I'm so sorry."

"The Phoenix must have helped her into Mortalland somehow and that's when she did it," said Lauren gravely. "And now, because of the Phoenix, Peter's father is dead just like mine. Catherine was right. Phoenix isn't virtuous nor his ghosts. They're all selfish, killing innocent people like Dad and Mr. Townsend in their pointless war. If they'd just done their time in the fields they could've been in Paradise by now. When I see Jasmine again, I'll make sure both her and Etienne are sent to the Judge. I'll kill them both!"

"Careful, Lauren. Remember Catherine's advice. Vengeance is God's not yours."

"God has given me the mortis blade and I'll do my part and send them from the New City to the pyre at Castle Everlasting. That'll be my vengeance!"

Satisfied that they had enough information, Lauren and Renee moved up through grave. Renee re-entered her body while Lauren materialized and they hurried back to Evelyn Lane. The journey was quick for both of them, the girls thought about their respective loved ones the entire time and neither spoke as they returned to Lauren's house.

* * * *

Searching Lauren's house they found Willem's binoculars. From Lauren's bedroom, Renee peered into the houses across the street that might be used to scope out their house. She gave every passing and parked car, every window, and every person strolling the streets a close examination.

"I can't see anything," said Renee.

"Use your shade eyes. The people watching us are shades themselves and probably invisible to mortal eyes," said Lauren absentmindedly, her thoughts dwelled on her father as she lay on her bed.

Lauren could think clearly about what she would do to her father's murderer. She contemplated what she'd need to kill Jasmine once she saw her again. The mortis blade was her most obvious weapon, to destroy the flesh-crafted skin she's been parading around in to eavesdrop on them. However, having witnessed Jasmine's destruction, she feared her limited skills would not be enough to take down Phoenix's great witch. Renee changed her eyes but still could not see anyone and gave up a few minutes later.

"If the Saved are watching us then we shouldn't

go and get the book until we can find some way to get his spies off of us. Otherwise they could take it from us once we've found it," Renee said thinking aloud.

"There isn't time, Renee," said Lauren solemnly. "Tomorrow's Friday, and if we don't get the book Jason dies."

"Didn't Jasmine say bring the book to the lighthouse?"

"Yes."

"This is bad, Lauren. Those men came from the lighthouse. Does Jasmine intend to kill them too?"

"Seems like it."

The phone rang; Lauren picked up, it was Amy.

"Big news, Lauren, sad but big. It seems the police have found Luther's body in a lake at Dr. Knowles' office."

"I know," said Lauren flatly.

"How?" asked Amy awestruck. Lauren told her what happened in the cavern.

"I'm sorry, Lauren, truly, but that's not all I learned. It seems that right before Luther's body surfaced the Townsend's noticed some people poking about their property on several occasions. With the news of Luther's death, they've requested police protection until these people are caught and Luther's murder investigation has been solved."

Lauren relayed Amy's message to Renee as they talked.

"We might be in luck," said Renee.

"Why?" asked Lauren.

"Seeing as how no one should be able to get into the Townsend's house unless the family approves of it, Etienne and his Saved can't get to the linking tome."

"Dylan said they had contacts at the police station. The cops watching the house could be the Saved," said Lauren.

"Yeah, but they're being kept in check by Jasmine right? It seems the path is clear. We should go for it," said Renee.

"It's too dangerous. Do we just walk in and take the linking tome from the house with Jasmine and the Saved watching us? And if we get the book, we can't just give it to Jasmine so she can get her mark back and give Phoenix have access to the Book of Marks. Maybe its best if we wait."

"But what other options do we have?" asked Renee.

Lauren thought hard, thinking of her resources, the gossiper's commune, Renee's medium skills, the mortis blade, everything. She even thought of their indwellers when Lauren formed a plan.

"A diversion!" she said sitting up.

Renee's brows tightened as they tried to figure out what Lauren had in mind.

"We make all eyes watching us follow our indwelt bodies away from the house and then you, me, and Amy can enter the house as spirits, find the book, and have Amy take it out."

"That's a good idea," said Renee. "We could make it look like a night on the town!"

"If we could get Peter to go with our bodies that would be even better to keep up the deception," said Lauren.

"I don't know, Lauren, Peter's pretty depressed," said Amy over the phone. "It would take something great to lift his spirits, something like..."

"A date with Renee," said Lauren smiling at her.

"No way am I going out with that disgusting boy!" said Renee.

"You know he has a crush on you and he was whistling at you at Amy's party. Besides, it wouldn't really be you, it'd be Joy. I'm sure she can keep his hands off your body."

"Oh, alright, I just hope he doesn't think I like him after tonight. What do we need to do now?"

"First, we're going to call our indwellers then we'll call up Peter to send our condolences and offer him a ride out on the town with us. We need something time consuming but can also be cut short like..."

"Dinner and a movie! I like it already, but let's get this plan straightened out so we'll know where we're supposed to be at all times," said Renee.

The girls sat and plotted their entry to the Townsend's house. An hour later, Amy called up Peter and asked if he would like to join Lauren and Renee for a night out and that Renee was interested in him. Though he was very depressed, Amy talked him into it. Amy also said she needed to use his computer to finish her math homework and asked if she could stay inside while he went out. He agreed. Using her commune, Lauren reached Mary and Joy at the Ghost Shack and soon after their orbs were flying across the New City for Evelyn Lane. Anita was meeting Mr. Lasitier at his office on Crow Island and was happy to take the girls to Amy's house once she promised her they'd be home in time for school the next day.

As they passed the Townsend's for the Thompson residence, Lauren surveyed the street to find the Saved's stakeout. She didn't see any dark cars or people hiding in the bushes but she did see the police. Lauren thought they were the Saved hiding in plain sight. At Amy's house, Mary and Joy indwelt Lauren and Renee's bodies. Amy lent Joy her cell phone and exchanged numbers so they could reach each other. Amy brought her backpack along to put the linking tome in should they find it.

Amy, Mary, and Joy then went to the Townsend's by way of Barry's car. Renee and Lauren traveled along in the woods in orbs. Joy and Amy got out of the car to talk with Peter, who instructed the police to let them on the property. Lauren and Renee watched from a distance.

"Do you see anyone scoping the house?" asked Lauren looking around.

"No, maybe Jasmine gave them a frightful scare," said Renee.

"They're going inside," said Lauren as Joy and Amy walked into the house. Moments later, Peter and Joy were returning from the house. Amy stayed inside to use the computer. As Barry drove off, Lauren and Renee saw a black car pull out from under the trees, following them to town, the police lit their lights and sirens and sped after them.

"That must have been them. The cops after going after them," said Lauren.

"Looks like your distraction worked," said Renee.

"Let's get inside then," said Lauren.

Lauren and Renee moved through the walls of the house entering into the Townsend's large kitchen. Lauren saw Amy's backpack on the floor in the den against the couch. Amy came downstairs from Peter's room with a book in hand and spoke to them.

"Vera's upstairs in her bedroom crying her eyes out so she won't be bothering us," said Amy whispering. "Where do we go now?"

"The cellar," said Lauren.

"Wait, let me evanesce!" said Amy as she sat on the couch. She situated herself with her head down over the book in her lap as if she was reading intently before evanescing. In spirit form, Amy joined her friends, Lauren led them down the hall on the right of the staircase where she found the cellar door, and they passed through it.

In the dark cellar, they cast *cinzeré illumine* to aid their search as they moved through the wine racks. Artwork, boxes, wine racks, and family busts filled the room. Cloth draped over an old couch that Renee stumbled over and searched before moving on to an already opened box, while Lauren looked behind the paintings.

"I can't find anything," said Renee.

"Me neither, any luck, Amy?" asked Lauren.

"Not yet!" she replied.

"Wait," said Lauren, "I feel something."

She continued to move about feeling a cool sensation coming from the second row of wine. About the middle, she felt the chill becoming stronger. She laid flat on her stomach and there she discovered the linking tome strapped under the lowest rack.

"Found it!"

"You did?" asked Renee. Lauren moved her hand to take it but phased through. She needed Amy's help.

"Amy, go upstairs and get your body." Amy left promptly; she coalesced into her body and returned to the cellar door. She jiggled the handle but the door wouldn't budge; it was locked by an old-fashioned bar lock. Renee saw the bar fastening the door and went to open it. Amy jerked harder on the door, so hard that when Renee cast her levitation spell on the lock, Amy would set it back down. Renee stuck her immaterial head through the door and told her to let go of the handle. She then cast *ascentate* on the bar and Amy entered. She went to where Lauren was kneeling in wait.

"It's taped underneath the lowest shelf," said Lauren standing in the second row next to the middle rack. Amy hurried over, knelt down, and unstrapped the linking tome.

"Yes! I'm free and my boyfriend's safe! I hope Jason forgives me; I'm going to make it up to him. Whoo-hoo! No more ghosts! You better keep your end of our bargain, Lauren!" said Amy. She extended the linking tome to give to Lauren.

"Keep it, I can't hold it. Call up Joy and have her return to the house so we can get out of here. And don't worry about our bargain; I'll make sure you never come back to Amalgam."

Amy felt a bit silly when Lauren didn't respond to her pestering. Amy placed the book in her backpack and called Joy. She returned upstairs to do her homework while Lauren and Renee waited invisibly in the den. Vera came downstairs in a white gown looking extremely fatigued and moved slowly to the kitchen. Lauren got up and followed her watching curiously, as Vera opened the fridge. She poured a glass of water but in her sorrow, missed the cup. The water spilled onto the floor before it wet Vera's bare foot who returned from her grief long enough to pour the glass, clean the mess, and replace the pitcher.

Vera's heartbroken countenance recalled to Lauren's mind Anita's face when she learned of Willem's death. She passed through Lauren rubbing her shoulders as she returned upstairs. Lauren could feel the sadness within her and continued to watch her slow trek up the stairs back to her bedroom. Lauren heard Amy talking to Joy on the phone who then came back downstairs to relay the message.

Amy told Lauren that Joy said they'd arrive in about fifteen minutes.

"Ask if she saw the black car pull out behind them," said Lauren; Amy asked Joy.

"She said yes but it turned onto Bridge Street…she says it's not following them but the police were still pursing the car," said Amy.

"Good," said Lauren. "Let's head outside into the bushes, we can't let anyone see us leaving the house. Amy, you can come out when they get back."

Lauren and Renee crept out the house and took cover in the nearby brush. The girls waited anxiously until Barry's car pulled alongside the road. Peter and Joy exited the car with Mary in the back seat. Screeching tires and a revving engine roared from the street curve. Its headlights were bright and blinding as it approached the Townsend house with all speed.

"What the hell? *It's them, Lauren!*" Renee screamed.

The same black car seen earlier sped from the opposite direction stopping alongside Barry's car. The passenger pulled a gun and shot a tranquilizer into Barry's neck. Garbed in black and wearing balaclavas, the assailants got out of the car and tranquilized Peter as the police cruiser pulled up behind Barry's car.

"Take the girls, all of them," said a man emerging from the police car.

The four men shot Renee and Lauren's indwelt

bodies and placed them all inside the first car. One of them picked up Peter and rushed him inside the house, opening the door with his key and returning swiftly outside. The leader approached Amy and shot her as well. He picked up her body and approached Lauren and Renee in the brush and said, "Follow behind our car; we're heading for the graveyard." Lauren knew the voice; it was Dylan.

"Take him home and return to the graveyard and don't harm him on Master Knowles orders," said Dylan about Barry to the man who was going to drive him and his car home. Two men joined Dylan. Another man drove the police car to tail Barry's chauffeur and gather him once his task was complete. Dylan returned to their car and sped off for the graveyard.

"I thought Joy said they lost them? Now what are we going to do?" asked Renee.

"We'll think of something but first we have to keep up," said Lauren as she and Renee orbed and flew as fast as they could after the car.

CHAPTER TWENTY-FOUR
THE DJEMSHEED AND FIRST SECRET OF THE PHOENIX

The car pulled into the graveyard's parking lot. Dylan and the Saved revived the girls and had them get out. Lauren and Renee arrived and transformed to ghost form. They couldn't fabricate a plan to free their friends so they had to play by the Saved rules for now. Dylan told Lauren and Renee to enter their bodies, saying the Master loathes indwellers, before they crossed to the cavern's grave entrance. He spoke a pass phrase, "Immortality is the path to Amalgam." The vault raised and opened like a casket lid; they entered the cavern.

Dr. Knowles and all of his Saved awaited their arrival all casually dressed, male and female, young to very old. In the center by the portal Dr. Knowles stood strong, his arms tense, fist clutched loosely, and legs shoulder length apart. His eyes focused on the girls as they filed in, but when he saw Amy, Lauren noticed the same murderous gaze in the vision of Luther's death.

"C'est cette petite sorcière mauvaise!" said the doctor angrily. He raised his hand and out shot a blast of freezing water that condensed into an icicle that pierced Amy's abdomen, nailing her to the wall.

"NO!" Lauren screamed as Amy's eyes closed and her body became limp, drooping on the icicle. Blood ran down her stomach onto the floor. Lauren and Renee ran to get her off but the icicle fastened her to the wall.

"AMY!" said Lauren tearing as her finger ran over the wound. Lauren was deeply saddened; she had not apologized for her jealousy and repaired their friendship. Now that Amy was dead, it was too late and she grieved again for losing a close friend. She clinched her fists, her anger burned towards Dr. Knowles.

"WHY DID YOU HAVE TO KILL HER?" asked Lauren approaching the doctor to attack him but Dylan held her back.

"She tried to kill me after you left my clinic!" said Dr. Knowles.

"Amy was at home sick!" said Lauren.

"She was sick after our fight. Why was she after me? Acting on orders from the Court or you?"

asked Dr. Knowles.

"Maybe you got the wrong person, *Etienne!*" said Lauren.

Dr. Knowles paused, "How do you know my *real* name?"

"I know a lot about you. The oldest shade, the djemsheed, all your murders, and that you're Raziel's little stooge."

"How? How do you know about my past?" asked Etienne curiously.

"The same way I knew you killed Luther when I visited your clinic, but I'm not going to tell you."

"Hmm...psychometry I'd guess!" said Etienne ponderously as he moved forward. "I could have used someone with that talent. Too few shades amongst my immortals; rarely did I manage to save a person who had a near-death experience and was blessed with powers from the afterlife like myself."

Etienne removed the spike from Amy's abdomen allowing her body to hit the cavern floor without pause. He took her backpack and opened it, finding the linking tome inside. He looked at it with much fondness as if he was reliving a great memory.

"I haven't seen this little item since Pierre and I took it from the Watlington's house centuries ago," said Etienne.

"Why do you want to open a portal to Amalgam?" asked Lauren.

"Pyschometry told you a lot about my plans, huh?" asked Etienne. "Well I also learned a great deal about you, Lauren. The new baron the ghosts have been babbling about, your secret love Jason and you told me just what I needed to reclaim the linking tome."

"You didn't answer my question," said Lauren strongly.

"I've been searching for the linking tome for two reasons. One, to fulfill my mother's dying wish and finish an age-old quest to prove the existence of life after death and two, to free the angel Raziel who has given me immortality and a dream to pursue. I made a promise some time ago that Pierre, Duncan, and I would be the only three to share in immortality."

"But after the Mortalland Seal and the Evelyn's tragedy caused their deaths I realized no one knew who they were or what they contributed to humanity's greatest discovery. It made me think, what is true immortality? I realized that living forever unnoticed is only half of it, filled with the eternal stress of living, loneliness, and hard work to remain anonymous."

"Here! Here!" said members of his group.

"True immortality is reflected in men such as Napoleon Bonaparte or Jesus Christ, even infamous people such as Hitler or Judas Iscariot. They left their mark on history and the world. The simple mention of their name kindles ambition, love, hate, betrayal, or respect. I must be one of them but only fond, loving memories will follow the name of Etienne Robert. I'll be remembered as the one who dispelled the fear of death with physical proof of the spiritual realm. My Saved will join me in this true version of immortality along with Pierre and Duncan in spirit."

"After their deaths went ignored I decided to create a larger network of disassociated citizens to expedite the search for the Mortalland Seal and this linking tome. It was fortunate that we learned of the Amalgam portals so that we could forego the search for the seal and look solely for the linking tome. Now here we are," Etienne knocked on the wooden desk, "moments from becoming the first men and women to prove death is an insignificant threshold to a better world."

"So you killed Mr. Townsend and countless others so you can be read about in history books?" asked Lauren.

"They still live in the afterlife," said Etienne causally flipping through the pages of the linking tome.

"You sound like the Phoenix! Now I see why the Court has kept such secrecy about Amalgam. Look at how you, Phoenix, and Jasmine regard human life. You've placed no value on it."

"Jasmine? Dylan's mentioned that name before. The witch whose been causing all the trouble lately. Is she your little friend down there?" asked Etienne of Amy.

"*NO!*" said Lauren angrily.

"Who is she?"

"Someone you killed in your quest to prove

there's an afterlife. You shot her in the house where you found the linking tome."

"Ah yes, and she's become a powerful witch seeking vengeance…how dramatic! Next time we meet I'll be sure to finish her."

"What do you plan to do once you reach Amalgam?" asked Lauren.

"Bask in the Amalgam sun, make snow angels, run wild in the plains I could only glimpse in the old Parisian pub, and then return with my fellow compatriots and spread the good news of the afterlife. With this portal operational, everyone can enter the world themselves should they think we're lying."

"Don't you know that you'll break the Mortalland rule? You could be sent to the Pyre!"

"I don't care much for rules. They're made to control the weak while the powerful bend them to their will. Besides, I broke that rule when I wrote The Amalgam Theory. I was a bit frightened when you told me about that law, but once this portal is open, I'll acquire thousands more followers, maybe even millions, and I'll make the Court to overturn their sentence!"

"And how do you intend to do this with both Phoenix and Jasmine trying to kill you?"

"The Phoenix I can handle. Raziel told me the Phoenix's secret and I learned the missing clue to undo his immortality after I hypnotized you. I'll use the marks from this linking tome to crush him and his witch. My Saved here will aid me if I can't handle them both."

Lauren was surprised, elated, and relieved, to hear Etienne knew the secret of the Phoenix. However, she remained calm. Lauren didn't want to show her ignorance as Etienne has already shown his. She had to discover what he meant by learning the missing clue from her and with Etienne unaware of the Phoenix's massive army that far outnumbered his Saved, Lauren realized she might have some solid information to use as a fair trade.

"And what is this secret?" asked Lauren bitingly.

"Can you keep a secret?" asked Etienne.

"Yes."

"So can I!" said Etienne. His attention was fixated on the book that made Lauren mull Etienne's desires and she discovered how to tempt him into telling the secret.

"What if I told you that there's a whole treasury of items like the cup Raziel took from the cathedral of Messina?"

Etienne's was perplexed at the mention of the church. He had never broken his vow to Raziel and he wished he could have hypnotized Lauren longer to get every ounce of information from her. He stalled to feel Lauren out, hoping she would slip up as he unknowingly already has.

"Who say's the djemsheed came from a cathedral?"

"I know it came from the cathedral because I've been there and a baron told me what was inside the treasury," said Lauren. "I'll offer you a deal. Tell me the secret of the Phoenix and I'll take you to the cathedral after you enter Amalgam. After all, wouldn't you be even more successful in your quest by bringing home treasures like…the Holy Grail? You'll prove the existence of *God* with that!" Lauren was making a tempting offer for Etienne. His tongue slid along his teeth and licked his mouth while considering her proposal.

"I would," said Etienne. "But I don't have to make any deals with you. You're my prisoner! You and your friends only have the option of sparing yourself much pain and suffering by doing whatever I ask including taking me to the cathedral. If the Phoenix shows, I'll speak the secret," said Etienne approaching. "And if you don't make good on your promise, you and your friends will die!"

Lauren didn't have much of a choice in the matter and consented. She knew Etienne was a ruthless man and he would surely cause her friends great harm if she refused. Lauren's only hope was that Catherine would be able to rescue them once they entered the ghost world.

Etienne turned his attention to the linking tome and found a portal guard mark. He used the sequester wand inside the book to place it upon his right hand and activated the portal. His Saved cheered loudly as the biosidium sprayed from the rungs and they gazed in awe at the white snow-covered fields of the gathering plains, the rolling hills, and the high trees and mountains in the distance.

"Do you see my Saved, the wonder of the afterlife?" Etienne said with maniacal gaiety. His Saved clapped and surrounded him in delight before a brilliant light blinded them. Electricity flowed over the portal entranceway, wholly engulfing the portal's rungs. From the bolts emerged a solitary threateningly evil eye, the lightning was impenetrable and Etienne and his Saved backed away.

"What is it, Master?" asked his servants.

"I don't know!" he said raising his arms to protect himself from the lightning.

The bolts scooped up the biosidium and bathed it over Amy's body; the lightning gave her heart a strong shock, restarting it. Suddenly Amy's body convulsed and she screamed as she rose up swiftly, pushing Renee aside. She put her hands on her head and shook it violently. Everyone in the cavern was astounded, they all thought Amy was dead but now she was more alive than when she entered the cavern. A misty vortex issued from her nose, ears, eyes and mouth and then Amy's body dropped back to the cavern floor, breathing once again but very shallow. Renee backed away as the mist passed her to exit the cavern.

"She's possessed!" said Etienne.

Etienne shot a few spells at the mist but missed. Etienne moved towards Lauren and grabbed her tightly. *"What possessed her? Was it the witch?"*

"I didn't know she was possessed," said Lauren.

"Don't lie to me!"

"I'M NOT! I SWEAR!" said Lauren grimacing from his grip.

"Dylan, Brandon, Douglas, find that spirit and destroy it!"

The men he called ran out of the cavern pass and went up out into the graveyard. They did not search long as the mist formed into a brilliant bluish white orb floating above the unknown grave before diving below the dirt. Under the surface the orb spread over a full skeleton with old worn clothes in a wooden casket and with a powerful spell reanimated it. The skeleton swiftly clawed its way from the ground breaking through in the presence of the Saved. Jasmine stood, her spirit fitted over the skeleton like a body, moving in tandem as if they were one. Using the wind element she broke a branch from a nearby tree and used it to channel magic spells.

The branch glowed red-hot and pointed at Brandon who received the full blast of her *pilari cinzeré* spell that turned him into a walking torch from a column of fire. He ran for the water screaming. Dylan and Douglas ran back for the cavern but Douglas caught another spell enveloping him in flame. Dylan ran quickly for the grave entrance, jumping down the gap and breaking his leg. It healed as he ran back through the cavern door. Dylan shut the door behind and enchanted it with dew magic. He entered the chamber where Etienne, Lauren, and the Saved stood.

"That girl was possessed by the witch, Master!"

said Dylan. *"She materialized from the unknown grave and attacked us…"*

The cavern door flew into the cavern crushing Dylan in its path pinning him into the ground. Jasmine entered the cavern slowly as the electricity flowed from the portal. The cavern was overwhelmed with light as a large ethereal phoenix emerged. The bird stretched its wings, flying through Jasmine, bathing her skeleton with spectroplasm and a flesh-crafting spell on its way to the graveyard. Jasmine's skeleton grew muscles, sinew, flesh; even the tattered cloth grew in abundance and stitched itself forming and an old but elegant evening gown. Jasmine stood, entirely physical wearing a white silk gown, a pearl necklace, and a bracelet, her death rags. A small bullet hole near Jasmine's chest remained on her newly crafted body; her fatal scar dripped blood and the fresh wound made Lauren realize that Jasmine had not moved on for a moment since her death that terrible night centuries ago.

The spectral phoenix spread throughout graveyard plots reanimating the decaying corpses inside their tombs. Spectroplasm pieced their bodies together giving them the strength to breakthrough their coffins and dig through the dirt. They screeched like tortured men and women and were agile, dangerous, and intelligent, moving quickly for the cavern. Their screams terrified the Saved, Lauren, and her friends. The electricity covering the portal continued to bar entry to Amalgam offering no escape for Etienne and his Saved.

Etienne was amazed that the young woman he'd slain years before was standing in his presence just as alive and beautiful before he killed her. Etienne stood guarded as Jasmine approached him in the cavern. Lauren noticed her skin; it was slightly waxy, like the most realistic mannequin ever produced. The flesh-crafted skin preserved her features well; it was extremely deceptive with hair, some wrinkles, and appropriate changes in light.

"Etienne Robert, I've waited so long for this night. Tonight, I'll finally have my revenge," said Jasmine as she threw down the tree branch and materialized her staff. Etienne clapped his hands mockingly, his face austere. His eyes were holding her gaze without fear or the intrigue earlier.

"Interesting! Truly! I remember killing you and your husband, I remember how *easy* it was. I'm glad you've got some training but it's all been in vain. This isn't going to be a tale of revenge against the evil Dr. Robert. As you discovered at my clinic, I haven't been without practice myself!" said Etienne withdrawing the djemsheed. "And this little trinket is going to be your undoing for you should know that with it I cannot die."

"Your longevity is actually quite delicate, Etienne. Tonight truly is cause for celebration, you will reach Amalgam but you won't return. I'll need that blade you carry, Lauren, to strip him of his immortality."

Suddenly fearful, Etienne snapped at Lauren,

"What blade?"

The screeching intensified as the zombies entered the cavern and attacked the Saved. The Saved drew several objects through which to cast magic. The first zombies fell to wall of magic but their wounds healed quickly and were soon walking again. The Saved and the living dead fought throughout the cavern. Etienne and half of his followers moved out of the cavern through the graveyard pass while others exited through the keeper house. Etienne confronted Jasmine head-on to keep her away from Lauren and the zombies steered clear of him, all under the control of the Phoenix, who wanted Jasmine to exact revenge.

"Lauren, help me," said Renee. A zombie had pushed her to the floor and was trying to bite her. Lauren removed the mortis blade from her pocket and stuck it into the zombie's back. The bacterium on the blade devoured the creature entirely leaving no trace of it aside from worn death rags that gently fell on Renee.

"Get up," said Lauren, extending Renee her hand. "We have to get Amy's body out of here!"

Renee stood but then froze, transfixed at a particular zombie coming her way. Lauren followed her gaze and found the decayed body of Renee's mother, Teresa coming towards them.

"Hello, Lauren, Renee," spoke the zombie in a voice not of Renee's mother, but a deeper, more sinister voice she'd never heard before.

"Who are you?" asked Lauren angrily.

"I am the Spirit Phoenix. Jasmine tells me you have a secret concerning my ultimate fate. A secret Amy knew but one we couldn't pry from her mind even with torture! I must know what this secret is and I will not kill you tonight so that I may discover it. As long as you don't return to Amalgam to try and save Castle Everlasting I'll spare Jason, your Amalgam friends, and your mother from a terrible possession, one that might complicate the life forming inside her."

"Don't go near my mother! You've taken my father away from me. Don't you dare come close to Anita or Jason!" Lauren said infuriated.

"*It was you keeping my Mom in her grave! What have you done with her?*" screamed Renee tearfully.

"She's with me, slowly turning to a lost soul with the other dead in the graveyard. *They belong to me!*" said Phoenix gurgling through spectroplam. Unlike the other zombies, the Phoenix shoddily reanimated Teresa's body, Lauren thought, to frighten Renee.

"Mom," said Renee tearfully.

"I promise you'll regret this, Phoenix," said Lauren, her voice quivering with rage, lifting the mortis blade.

"*Don't make claims you can't back up!* Stay in Mortalland if you wish to save your loved ones," said Phoenix as Lauren watched it move out the cavern through the lighthouse exit. Lauren kneeled to check Amy's body; she was breathing again and her heart was beating steadily.

"She's alive! Renee, help me take Amy's body to the surface! I've got to find Amy's spirit," said Lauren destroyed more zombies coming towards them.

"What happened to her and her indweller?" asked Renee sadly, she crouched down by Amy's body to lift it.

"Jasmine must have captured Amy in Amalgam," said Lauren. "I should have known when Amy came back late from the Hobby that something was up," said Lauren. "That's how she knew about Jason. She unlocked Amy's mind."

"What do you think became of Traci?" asked Mary. Joy filled with despair. The girls saw her sadness and assumed the worst for Traci.

"How did she get into Mortalland?" asked Renee. "Etienne's portal didn't work until he got the portal guard mark. Jasmine possessed Amy before that and all the other portals are in the Court's control."

"I don't know. I just hope Nasra and the others are safe," said Lauren.

"I can't believe Jasmine has been watching us all this time," said Renee as she picked up Amy's legs.

"She must be a master of possession," said Mary. "If you couldn't tell a difference in her attitude or aura, she must have disguised herself very well."

"I could tell," said Renee. "Only I thought Amy was sick, but I won't make that mistake again."

"Mary, Joy, go to the Ghost Shack and tell them we need help here if they can spare it," said Lauren as they struggled to carry Amy's body out the cavern. The two indwellers orbed and flew out of the cavern for the Ghost Shack. Jasmine saw the indweller's orbs who screamed to the Phoenix to stop them. He did, his spectral bird engulfed their orbs and grounded them with the spectrograven spell and scarred their psyches. They lay on the ground amidst the conflict delirious and immobile.

The battle spilled into the graveyard and the lighthouse grounds. It was a deadlock as no amount of magic could destroy the zombies and they couldn't overcome the immortal Saved. Etienne and Jasmine fought by the lakeshore. Lauren watched as they dueled realizing that neither had the advantage and the only weapon to turn the duel was her mortis blade.

Etienne was casting spells from marks inside the linking tome. *"Brilzen Batos!"* said Jasmine conjuring lightning through her staff. She turned and swung her staff for Etienne's midsection but he blocked the strike with *aramous*. Etienne raised his hand and blasted Jasmine with a fire spell, but she redirected it. Zombies joined their fight and Etienne backed towards the water to defend himself as his Saved surrounded him. Jasmine looked to Lauren and her friends. A zombie came for Lauren; she struck down it and two more with her mortis blade.

"Where should we take Amy?" asked Renee.

Lauren looked around to find a small wooden

dock with a rowboat at the side, the Baker's Light ferry. Lauren looked to the lighthouse to see some zombies fighting the Saved on the lighthouse grounds but none near the bridge and Coral Street.

"Put her inside the rowboat and row to Coral Street. Call for help and get her to the hospital if you can."

"*Lauren, watch out!*" said Renee.

Lauren turned to see Jasmine in front of her who quickly snatched the mortis blade from her and pushed her to the ground. She cast *purgen explodos* on the rowboat, blasting shards of flaming wood into the lake.

"I need this. Wait here, the zombies won't hurt you," said Jasmine.

She tossed the blade in the air; the spectral bird caught the dagger's handle in its beak and flew to the lighthouse grounds. It dropped the blade to a zombie that destroyed the Saved on the opposite shore. The Spirit Phoenix continued to swish across the grounds immobilizing the slain Saved spirits. The bird returned the blade to Jasmine who strolled to where Etienne and his Saved where fighting. They were lined up against the shore and fought off their zombie attackers but were outnumbered and being pushed into the lake. Etienne dipped his cup into the lake then cast *spectro sintegara* in the second bowl. He then drank the water.

His elderly features peeled off like dried clay to reveal his youthful appearance. Etienne expectorated a wall of gray fire that evaporated the spectroplasm in every zombie coming towards his Saved. The deceased remains fell to the ground lifeless. Etienne continued to sip from the cup slaying the creatures en masse and balancing the battle. Meanwhile, Jasmine was annihilating his Saved, piercing their skin with the mortis blade.

The battle drew close to an end. Etienne, Dylan, and Brandon, were all the Saved that remained to battle Jasmine and six zombies. They surrounded the Saved and Jasmine moved into the circle. With the mortis blade clasped firmly in her hand, she charged for Brandon. Etienne blew a plume at her, but she escaped into a mirage and the flames passed through. She killed both Brandon and Dylan easily before moving on Etienne. Jasmine studied Etienne before speaking.

"After I kill you, the reapers are going to carry you to the gathering plains where I have animals waiting to slay your Saved immediately but for you I have a special surprise. An eagle will bring you to me at the spectral tree so I can torture you before you're thrown into the Demon Recess."

Etienne hurriedly flipped through the book, smiling when he selected a snake-charmer mark. It produced an ethereal hood-spread cobra visible only to shade eyes and the dead that was poised to strike Jasmine's body of unnatural skin. The snake wrapped its body around Etienne guarding him from the Phoenix's zombies. It destroyed one that came close to Etienne with a lightning fast strike while he tried to reposition the hefty book in his arms.

"This snake's venom will eat your skin before you can heal yourself. I'll enter Amalgam and when the Phoenix comes for me, I'll speak his *true name* to undo his immortality! Do you hear me, Lauren?" Etienne raised his voice.

Lauren listened as Etienne divulged the Phoenix's secret. She changed her eyes to see the snake protecting Etienne as it changed its elemental colors like the shenga. The Phoenix sent two more zombies to silence him, but the snake obliterated them both with quick bites to the stomach. It then lunged for Jasmine and narrowly missed her legs as she jumped high into the air casting *purgen cinzeré* at Etienne who blocked it. The snake followed Jasmine who hovered in the air.

"I was told the first secret by Raziel, the second and third secrets were told to two others, associates of the angels Cedric and Marcela." Jasmine listened as Etienne spoke and thought Phoenix was right. The angels had betrayed him. The snake was crafty enough to continue knocking around all the other zombies away with its tail while focusing its fangs on Jasmine.

"The Phoenix was given a new name upon receiving the Phoenix mark, a name identifying him as a false God…"

"*Silence, Etienne!*" said Jasmine. She cast *sonorous imperilious* at him, but Etienne easily deflected it because she was off balance dealing with his snake.

"Speaking that name will strip him of mark and

immortality, returning him to a mortal ghost. To protect that name Phoenix created three false names that simultaneously thwart and facilitate him. Speaking one of these names to the correct Phoenix spirit will splinter his mark, giving that spirit's power to his vanquisher and greatly weaken him, forcing the Dark Phoenix to regenerate slowly for months."

Jasmine charged her staff with the aquis element as the cobra shown red. She formed an ice wall in the split-second the snake charged for her. Its fangs sank into the ice and it reeled back in pain. Jasmine formed several icicles and sent it towards the beast piercing all parts of it. The snake turned blue to sooth the pain.

"If you use all three decoy names, however, he'll wholly regenerate over seven years. His splintered marks will be stripped from those who've claimed its pieces and he'll be given a different false God name," said Etienne, carefully watching Jasmine. Etienne knew he was doomed; he couldn't speak the Phoenix secret because he couldn't identify the Phoenix form flying above him and didn't want to waste the decoy name.

Jasmine cast *cinzeré enferris* on the beast vaporizing it. She then cast a phantom of herself behind Etienne, one that held the mortis blade over his head while Etienne watched his snake withering in flames. Her mirages stretched to the phantom and then Jasmine was there, mortis blade in hand. Etienne spoke quickly, "Discover his *true name!*"

Jasmine sunk the dagger into Etienne's head; he disintegrated to dust as the bacterium consumed him. The djemsheed he carried and the linking tome fell to the ground by his clothes. His spirit stood above his body's ashes and clothes, still powerful. Jasmine cast the silence charm on his mouth so he could not tell anymore of the Phoenix's secret. Jasmine was tense but elated because she had finally killed Etienne.

Three reaper carriages arrived to collect the Saved. Etienne and Jasmine stood ready to resume their battle, but neither wished to anger the reapers. Etienne and his followers boarded the carriages after the Phoenix freed the immobilized Saved for the gathering plains. As the carriages departed, Jasmine picked up the djemsheed and linking tome then approached the girls.

"These belong to the Phoenix," said Jasmine holding the djemsheed. "Pick her up and carry her along."

Lauren and Renee lifted Amy. As they struggled with her body, Lauren saw Mary and Joy twitching listlessly underneath a tree.

"Mary, Joy; what did you do to them?" asked Lauren.

"Phoenix scarred them. They'll be of no further use to you."

Jasmine led the girls and the remaining zombies into the cavern pass through the trap door in the keeper house. They emerged into a storeroom containing a variety of tools and objects from

Etienne's shop. Jasmine ordered a zombie to take a lengthy chain off the wall. She escorted them into the tower to begin the trek up the many stairs.

The Baker's Light was tall, with hundreds of stairs at a height of two hundred and ten feet tall. Encumbered with Amy's spirit-less body and Jasmine's demands for haste the journey wasn't pleasant for Lauren and Renee. She took them to a bedroom where the girls laid Amy's body down. There was a small portable heater and the remaining items from Etienne's office.

Jasmine placed the linking tome down on a desk and searched until she found her tree mark. She rubbed the mark first then used the sequester wand to remove it from the page and place it on the backside of her right hand. Having placed it atop the Phoenix patch, they melded to form the dark tree mark.

"This new mark will allow me to control any tree with or without its permission," said Jasmine happily, closing her eyes, feeling the strength surge through her body. "It's been such a long time since I've been without my full power."

"Bitch," said Lauren.

"What was that?" asked Jasmine threateningly.

"Why did you kill my father?" asked Lauren angrily.

"Your father was at the wrong place at the wrong time. Ages ago, when I returned to Mortalland, the first thing I did was find my body in the lake where Etienne had dumped it. I buried it and left the grave unmarked. As the cemetery grew, I inadvertently created the chiseling widow ghost story when I appeared to scare people away. However, people became more interested until finally they decided to excavate my grave."

"I needed my remains to let Etienne see me in my original state as the helpless woman empowered by the Phoenix to avenge her husband. Phoenix caused the Coral Street accident, filling the scene with necrosidium through which I was able to enter Mortalland just before the excavators were going to unearth me. This time they got the message."

Lauren thought this was the most trifle excuse for the death of her father. She couldn't bear telling her grandmother that Willem was killed by an evil ghost on such frivolous reasoning.

"What happened to Amy?" asked Lauren.

"She's locked up in the spectral tree. You didn't believe that story I told you. A dense thicket wouldn't fool the Phoenix, nor was he fooled by Nasra's disguise. Unfortunately, I was and had Amy not persuaded the Phoenix to spare their lives, I would have killed her on the spot. She made a pretty convincing argument that day."

"What did she say?" asked Lauren.

"She described how useful captives she, Nasra, and Vincent would be. She said I could model Nasra's deception for my entry into Mortalland and that Vincent could make my spirit look like hers to doubly aid in deceiving you. An excellent idea, especially when I had to evanesce to retrieve the linking tome. She said that you and Nasra were particularly fond of each other and that keeping her alive would motivate you to find the linking tome. When it came to herself, Amy said she knew a secret about you and the Phoenix, a secret she was going to tell but a charm confounded her lips. We tortured her for long time but she couldn't speak it. It was only after I indwelt her did I learn a powerful spell sealed off the secret and I was thankful all the more that we spared her."

For a moment, Lauren thought Amy betrayed her, but realized she managed to save many lives. Lauren wondered whether Amy was using the blarney stone to devise such a plan or if she was intentionally trying to sabotage her. Lauren assumed the secret Amy learned must've been about her Holy Grail mark and that she must have been snooping on her conversation with Catherine. Lauren was grateful, however, because it was the sole reason they were all still alive.

"What about Traci and Alexander?" asked Renee.

"They're dead which was particularly pleasing to me since Alexander was a close friend of Nasra's," said Jasmine coldly. Lauren shook her head.

"Life is meaningless to you, huh? It doesn't matter to you what happens to the families whose lives you've affected?" asked Lauren.

"No," said Jasmine. "They leave this realm and enter the next. Phoenix will reconcile them to God and we'll sit happily in Paradise except for those who've stood in our way like Etienne, Catherine, and you."

"So how many Jasmines have you made in your life?" asked Lauren. Jasmine chuckled with a bitter smirk cracked upon her lips.

"If they're like me, I look forward to increasing our ranks."

"She didn't make any Jasmine's or even cold souls that day, Lauren," said Renee whose gaze penetrated Jasmine eyes. "She made more Court servants."

"Cute, Renee. Not that they'll have much of an influence once the battle is won tonight."

"So why are you doing this, Jasmine?" asked Lauren disappointedly.

"If Phoenix will bring us back to God, why not settle grievances with our enemies? Why trouble God with justice and salvation when we can do it ourselves?"

"Because your justice is flawed, Nasra was right about you…"

"Nasra will be dead and so will you. Who cares what she thinks of me now that I'm stronger? That reminds me of your *weak* lover, Jason."

Jasmine nodded her head and the zombies brought Jason to her, unconscious and tied. They placed him on the bed next to Amy's body when Jasmine crooned, "They're so sweet together. Having been in both their bodies I can tell you Lauren that they're very much in love. Jason desperately waits for the day when they can make love and Amy is genuinely considering breaking her vow of chastity. His emotions burned red for her but when I searched Jason's heart for your place, I found you were associated with white. Do you know what that means?"

"Neutral," said Lauren heartbroken. Jasmine chuckled before speaking again.

"Ah, I can see your pouting face at Amy's party right now! Remember that anger you felt? It's the same anger I held for Etienne after he took my husband away. The only difference is I married Jonathan whereas you've only had a kiss from Jason and that was from me!" Jasmine laughed.

"Sadly, we have something in common," said Lauren.

"What do you want to do with them?" Teresa Phoenix asked Jasmine.

"Take them to the lantern room and tie them all up to the beacon stand. Use truss shackles so they can't de-materialize and search them for any devices the Court may have given them. We can't chance Lauren's return to Amalgam!" said Jasmine strongly.

The zombies moved accordingly to Jasmine's instructions. They left the bedroom and moved up the remaining stairs to the lamp room where Jasmine and the zombies stripped of their cell phone and gossiper's commune. A zombie shackled them to a post cropping from the beacon stand that held up the first order Fresnel lens. The zombie carrying the chain lashed it around the post securing it with a heavy lock leaving a decent amount of slack. Teresa Phoenix brought forth the truss shackles and bound the girls' arms together inside the chain.

"You're going leave us here? How will we get unlocked with the lighthouse keepers dead? How are we supposed to get help for Amy and Jason?" asked Renee wrestling against the chains.

"I'd be more concerned with how you're going to save yourself. Your parents will be looking for you sure enough, but who'll think to look here? And as you said, without the keepers manning the lighthouse it could be days until you're freed, maybe even weeks. Without food or water, you'll pass away eventually. Since I can't kill you now, I'll see to it that it happens in due time. We'll come back for your spirits to discover this secret when we return from Amalgam."

"I'll clean up the mess in the graveyard, replace the other bodies. Except this one, I'll scatter it in the wind," said Teresa Phoenix. Renee looked fiercely at Phoenix and Jasmine.

"I'll have my wolves guard the tower outside below to make sure they can't escape," said Jasmine. She went below and cast a spell on the stairs that broke several of the top steps. The metal warped and raised to seal up the lamp floor making it inaccessible from the tower. Spirit Phoenix crept out onto the watchtower deck and belted a painful wail in Teresa's voice as the remains withered to dust and carried off in the wind.

"STOP IT!" Renee screamed as tears filled her eyes, she sat crying and Lauren tried to comfort her.

"Interesting news," said one of the zombies from below, his voice was audible but muffled as they moved down the stairs. "I was searching through Etienne's desk and found his address book. It seems Etienne has a son and granddaughter, a Jacob and Melissa Lasitier. Etienne assigned Jacob to watch Lauren's mother Anita for information about her and his granddaughter works at his clinic. I thought the information might interest you."

"I promised myself I'd kill anyone associated with him," said Jasmine contemplatively. Her footsteps clanking with metal steps ceased, the message enthralled her. "Where are they?" she asked firmly.

"Returning from Crow Island for Evelyn Lane. He heard his father found the linking tome and is coming here after dropping off Anita."

"Will I have the time?" asked Jasmine.

"The battle can't begin without you and the animals are still situating the tree in the crater. You've waited years for this night. We can wait a little longer. I'm returning to Amalgam to check on the animal progress. We'll use the portal in the cavern to transport you to the other side."

"What if Lauren's mother gets in my way?"

"I made a promise not to hurt them as long as Lauren remains in Mortalland. Make sure I'm not made a liar unless Lauren breaks her end of the bargain."

"Certainly, Phoenix. I'm going to Evelyn Lane to finish this."

Lauren's heart raced, Jasmine would be in her house waiting for her mother, Jacob and Melissa to return. Phoenix had made a bargain with her; one Lauren didn't accept but certainly felt compelled to obey. She never entertained the idea of staying in Mortalland because she knew Catherine could not stop the Phoenix without his secret. She had to escape, but doing so would endanger her mother.

CHAPTER TWENTY-FIVE
THE LIGHTHOUSE ESCAPE

"We have to get out of here," said Lauren screaming. "I can't let her get within sight of my mom, or Melissa and Jacob. Ugh!" Lauren gritted her teeth and jerked her body against the chains in frustration. The wolves were howling from below; Jasmine's watchdogs were on guard.

"These stupid chains, *Andrea eva...eva...nex!*" said Lauren as her body couldn't de-materialized to spirit because of the truss shackles.

"I can't say the spell. It's hopeless," sighed Lauren. Jason moaned as he woke up. He looked at his neighboring captive Renee puzzled.

"Renee?"

"Yes, Jason, it's me," she said.

"How'd you...how'd we get here? And why are

we chained up?"

"We don't have time to explain, Jason."

Jason looked next to him and saw Amy's body, her clothes blood soaked.

"Amy? Oh my God, what happened to her? What the hell is going on?"

"Jason, please don't get excited especially since there's nothing we can do for her now," said Renee. Lauren sighed deeply.

"What is it?" asked Renee.

"We have to get Amy's spirit back to her body."

"What?" asked Jason.

"Now that Jasmine's out of her body it'll die and I'm not sure how long she'll have to live with that wound. If her spirit was inside she could heal herself," said Lauren.

"If I could get free I could help her," said Renee.

"Can somebody please explain why we're locked up in the first place?" asked Jason becoming angry.

"*NO!*" said the girls.

"Jason look, no more questions until we're out of here," said Lauren firmly. "Any suggestions?"

"Let's talk out the problem, like we did with the Townsend house," said Renee. "So what are we up against? We're shackled to this platform and can't de-materialize. The lamp room has been sealed shut and no one knows we're here. Even if we somehow freed ourselves Jasmine's wolves are outside waiting to rip us to pieces."

"And don't forget we can't get down from the tower to be eaten without committing suicide at two hundred feet up," said Lauren.

"Since we can't help ourselves who can we call for help?"

"Our indwellers are scarred outside in the graveyard so we can't get out a message to anyone. Even if we could, Mina is hospitalized, and Catherine is probably too busy with the war..." Lauren offered.

"Anyone else, friends, relatives, anyone from Amalgam?" asked Renee.

Names came to Lauren's mind, Nasra, Densen, Selene, Devon, Lion Face, Vasteck and Gloria.

"Mr. Vasteck and Gloria!" said Lauren.

"Oh yeah! Great, how do we contact them?"

"They took our communes and our cell phones. Maybe your oracle skills can at least get a message to them."

"You think it will work?"

"It's worth a shot."

"Slide close to me then," said Renee. Using their legs the girls moved their bodies close together.

"Take my hand, relax, and clear your mind," said Renee to Jason. Renee prayed for this to work and said, "Most sought...what's his first name?"

"Kevin, Kevin Vasteck."

"Okay. Most sought Kevin Vasteck, we ask that you move among us, speak with us, grace us with your presence."

Renee repeated this over and over until the fourth time. They felt a chill in the lamp room and Renee's body became tense as she channeled Vasteck's message through her, "Hello, Lauren."

"Mr. Vasteck my friends and I are in trouble. Jasmine, the tree rider has imprisoned us at the Baker's Light. Could you free us?" asked Lauren.

"What's wrong with her?" asked Jason, bewildered that a male voice flowing through Renee's lips.

"Quiet!" said Lauren.

"Yes, Gloria and I were just strolling Kepchar Street," said Vasteck.

"Be careful, Vasteck, there are wolves on the lighthouse grounds."

"We'll hurry," said Vasteck.

Renee's body went back limp before she spoke, "Did we reach them?"

"Yes and now we wait," said Lauren. "Hold on, Mom, just hold on," Lauren said to herself.

"They won't be too long, I'm positive," said Renee. She was right, within ten minutes the wolves were howling uproariously until they were suddenly subdued and below they could here a spell cast on the lamp room floor. Moments later, Gloria and Vasteck were standing before them.

"Nice to see you again, Lauren. I'm sure Baron Catherine would like to see you as well considering what's about to happen at the castle."

"I'd like to help but my mother needs my help more than anyone. Can you get these chains off?"

"Let's see," said Vasteck. He knelt down beside Lauren and she turned her body to give him a better view of their bonds.

"Materialized truss shackles about the wrists, woven by a chain and lock, the lock sealed shut with dew magic and the key broken off inside. Umm...she really wanted you to stay put."

"How'd you get past the wolves?" asked Renee.

"Gloria got us past the wolves," said Vasteck distractedly, trying to concentrate on the chains.

"It's obvious they were once human given the order of beasts," said Gloria. "My mark told me they were pirates. I made the air smell like the sea to subdue them but they were frightened and ran away. I guess aspects of their former lives spark painful memories," said Gloria.

Mr. Vasteck was fumbling with the lock, casting various dew destruct charms on the chains and lock.

"Damn, these shackles! Every time I cast a dew charm on it, it breaks the magic for a second before becoming stronger. Know any powerful spells that can undo it, Lauren?"

"What's the one Mr. Hitchen taught us? *Asu...Asu...*" Lauren's lips were confounded, she couldn't speak. "I can't say it!"

"Yeah, dumb of me to ask," said Vasteck. "Truss shackles inhibit the restrained from saying spells or performing transformations that would free them." Vasteck looked at the beacon platform and the chains wrapped about the post. "Mortal lock and ethereal charm," said Vasteck. "*Gilren syven*," said

Vasteck on the lock, its dew magic broke then he grasped the lock with his ethereal hand and froze it entirely with aquis magic.

"Break the lock, Lauren. Smash it somehow."

Lauren turned her body around and lifted her foot to kick the lock shattering it entirely. The chain broke free of the beacon and Vasteck unwove it from their bonds but they stood confined by the truss shackles.

"If Vasteck weakens the magic for a second could you finish the spell, Lauren?" asked Gloria. Lauren said yes but questioned how she'd get free. Gloria asked her if she knew how to de-materialize, and Lauren replied affirmatively. Vasteck thought this over for a moment and then said, "We'll see. Get ready to speak it in three, two, one, *olien begas!*"

Lauren's tongue was free to speak the charm; but she de-materialized instead and her shackles fell to the floor. Vasteck then used *asue terin* to weaken her friend's bonds while Lauren grabbed hold and de-materialized them.

"Thanks," said Lauren. "Renee, fly down and heal our indwellers." Renee disconnected her spirit and left the tower. Soon she returned with Mary and Joy following behind her, psyches restored.

"Sorry, Lauren," said Mary.

"Don't worry about it. In fact, I'm glad you're here. I need one of you to indwell Amy."

"Joy, you're the better indweller, you do it," said Mary. Joy transformed into a vortex and filled

Amy's body.

"This injury is deep, Lauren," said Joy as she stood in Amy's body. She pressed the wound on her stomach and appeared quite fatigued.

"Amy!" said Jason. He tried to hug her but Joy changed her voice to reflect her own higher pitched voice. "I'm not her, Jason, name's Joy." Jason was startled and stepped back confused.

"Amy's going to need medical attention soon. I don't know if her spirit returning will completely heal it. In Amalgam the pink gel must be closing on her face by now," said Joy.

"Don't get excited, Joy," said Renee pressing her hand against the wound. "I can patch this to stop the bleeding. I'll need something to sterilize the wound." Renee tore the bottom of her shirt and wrapped it around the wound to slow the bleeding.

"How do we get down?" asked Renee looking around.

"I can get down but you, Jason, and Amy can't follow. Let's take a look outside," said Lauren.

She materialized her sword, her arms swelled with strength enabling her to break the beacon chamber's glass. They stepped onto the observation deck to look below. Halfway down the girls saw a hoist jutting from the tower. Lauren thought the Saved might have been using it to lift Etienne's belongings up the tower.

"The hoist," said Renee. "Think there's enough chain in the keeper house to reach it?"

"I'll see," said Lauren. She evanesced and orbed

to the keeper's house. Inside, she found a rope and another chain both totaled sixty feet in length. Lauren materialized and tried to lift them both. They were far too heavy for her to carry but her *ascentate* charm made them light as a feather. She orbed and returned to the tower, stopping at a window a floor below the observation deck. Lauren phased through it and materialized into an empty room lit only by the moonlight. Dropping the chain and rope, Lauren opened the window, tied the chain to the tower stairs, and threaded and tied the rope through the chain. She then flew back to the deck materializing once she arrived.

"Tie this rope to the posts. I've tied it to a chain in a room below us," said Lauren. "If you can get in there then you'd be able to walk down the tower steps."

"Good idea," said Renee. She was helping Jason as they walked out onto the deck. She propped up Jason alongside the lamp room door as she joined the girls. "Renee, help me," said Lauren. They tied the rope creating a necktie knot. Lauren gave it a couple of firm tugs, making sure the knots were secure on both ends before returning up top.

"That should do it," said Lauren. Her attention turned to the south. From the lighthouse, she could see Evelyn Lane. Renee saw her looking out, concerned for her mother.

"Go to her, Lauren. I'll see that we get down from here!" said Renee.

"And we'll be here to help," said Vasteck.

"Thanks. Mary, come with me. If I can stop

Jasmine I'll need you to indwell me so you can watch over my mom."

"Right behind you," said Mary. Lauren dematerialized and orbed and with Mary, left for Evelyn Lane.

* * * *

"Joy, do you think you can get down by yourself?" asked Renee.

"I—I don't think so," said Joy. "I'll need lover boy here to support me."

Jason was happy to hold her but Renee took his hand away and she supported Amy's body.

"You must be tired, Jason. Try and go alone."

Renee paired up with Joy and the girls began their descent. Jason went first and was strong enough to move on his own entering the room with little trouble. Renee didn't want Joy to exert Amy's body like Jason did and used their shackles to slide down the rope with Joy holding onto her waist. When they were all inside the room, they descended the tower and Renee plotted their next step along the way.

"We need to get to Evelyn Lane and Amy to a hospital. I want to call and check on my dad; he could pick us up if he's okay."

"We have to get to a phone first," said Jason.

"Let's go to the keeper house, there's probably one in there. Joy can lay Amy's body down there as well until we're picked up," said Renee.

"Not to mention I have to call my parents and tell them what happened to me although I don't know what I'm going to say," said Jason. "I don't even know how long I've been gone."

"Almost two days. We'll help you figure out something," said Renee.

In the keeper house, they found a telephone and dialed Barry first. Renee explained their assailants had stolen something from the Townsends and took them to the lighthouse to cover their crime. She said they were also responsible for Amy's injury. Barry said he was coming to pick her up and was going to call the police once she was safe. Renee added that she wanted to stop by Lauren's house to check on her because she managed to escape and was going to call for help. While waiting, Renee found some alcohol to flush the puncture before wrapping a clean cloth around it. Afterwards, Renee along with Vasteck and Gloria, deliberated how to best explain Jason's disappearance.

* * * *

Arriving at Evelyn Lane, Lauren entered the house screaming for her mother. All the lights were on, the house shown bright yellow and white.

"MOM? MOM?" Lauren shouted.

"I'll check upstairs," said Mary.

"Please," said Lauren appreciatively. Mary flew upstairs and searched first in the bathroom then the extra bedroom opposite Lauren's. Lauren searched the living room, then Anita's room. She searched the kitchen and then the den, using both mortal and ethereal eyes. Lauren dreaded the thought that Jasmine had already killed them with the mortis blade. Surely not a single piece of flesh would remain if she did and yet she saw no clothing in a pile that appeared to have fallen with its bodily support. Lauren returned to the stairwell where she called for Mary.

"Is she up there, Mary? Mary?" No answer came. Lauren ran upstairs, instinctively going to her room. Bursting through the door, Lauren saw Jasmine holding Mary hostage with her left hand de-materialized and the other materialized pointing her staff at Mary's neck.

"How in Amalgam did you escape so fast?" asked Jasmine.

"*Where's my mom?*" asked Lauren fiercely.

"I'd hope they'd be here," said Jasmine. "The battle is drawing closer and I still have two more Saved to kill."

"You've taken your revenge on Etienne let it end there!"

"I made a promise, one that I'm going to keep."

"What about the promise that if I stayed in Mortalland you wouldn't harm my mother?"

"Phoenix made that promise. Whether or not I'll uphold it depends on you. You've escaped and though that doesn't break the deal, it's disconcerting. You're going to return to Amalgam aren't you?"

"Yes," said Lauren.

"Insolent child! Can't you see what we're trying to do?"

"Looks like you're trying to kill more people! Phoenix offered me the chance to join him but I refused. For God sake Jasmine, just take the pain in the purgation fields like everyone else."

"I'll never step foot in those fields again."

Lights flashed through the window as a car was heard pulling into the drive. Jasmine moved to the window and looked out, in the driveway was Jacob's car. Jasmine tossed Mary aside and drew out the mortis blade.

"If your mother screams, I kill her," said Jasmine. Her body phased through the window and Lauren ran after her, landing on the ground a few paces behind her. Anita was getting out of the passenger side when Jacob saw the specters coming from the window. By Jasmine's appearance, Jacob could tell she was a cold soul. He placed the car in reverse and floored the accelerator.

"Dad!" said Melissa from the back seat terrified at the speed her father peeled out the drive. The open passenger door narrowly missing Anita's swollen belly who was about to reach in for her portfolio.

"*What the hell!*" said Anita startled.

Jacob braked in the middle of the road to place the car in drive. Anita saw the terror on his face and looked in the direction of his gaze to see a swirling thick cloud of moisture from which Jasmine materialized. Anita didn't scream she fainted.

Jasmine raised her staff and shot a bolt of fire at the hood of Jacob's car. The blast ignited the hood and much of the car's interior.

"Melissa, get out!" said Jacob as he pounded on the door. He burned his hand trying to pull the handle yet he forced himself out. In her panic, Melissa couldn't open the backseat door.

"*STOP IT!*" Lauren said as she materialized and jumped on Jasmine's back. Mary came from the second floor and landed behind them. Jasmine threw Lauren to the ground in front of her. She withdrew the mortis blade and raised it to stab Lauren but Mary drew a wand and cast *exeralure* on the blade. It came to her, de-materializing in her grasp. Jasmine turned to her and shot a death terror charm from her staff. The spell struck Mary in the head and instantly she began running away in fear.

As Jasmine cast the death terror on Mary, Lauren swiftly cast *exeralure* on the mortis blade. It materialized in her hands and she reached up and cut Jasmine's bare forearm. The organisms on the blade ate her flesh turning her to dust in seconds. The djemsheed and linking tome fell to the ground along with Jasmine's death rags. Lauren cast purgen cinzeré on the book and the linking tome burned to oblivion. The djemsheed was still on the ground but Jasmine couldn't touch it without her body.

Jasmine's spirit stood in front of Lauren and she lifted her staff to swing at Lauren but her mark glowed and became warm. Jasmine paused; the Spirit Phoenix was requesting she return to

Amalgam. Jasmine looked to Jacob's car, melting in flames with Melissa still trapped inside and no sign of Jacob. She saw Anita lying on the ground unconscious with her hand over her heart.

"Looks like my job is finished anyway. I'll see you sweetie," Jasmine said to Lauren as she orbed and flew for the graveyard.

Lauren searched for Mary but her spirit was running far down by Norm Street. Lauren materialized her sword, and held it firmly as she cast the strongest water spell she learned in training, "Geysen Aquis!" She pointed the blade up to the sky and stroked downward. A water surge fell like heavy rain on top of the car, extinguishing the fire. Lauren ran forward and opened the backseat. She pulled out Melissa as Jacob opened the other passenger door screaming for his daughter.

"She's fine," said Lauren. Lauren picked up the djemsheed as they moved inside the house. Jacob carried Anita inside laying her down on the couch. Melissa sat in a chair and Jacob crouched beside her, comforting her. Lauren got her a glass of water.

"Who was that ghost?" asked Jacob.

"Her name was Jasmine. She's the ghost that killed your father and the rest of the Saved."

"MY FATHER'S DEAD!" said Jacob.

"Yes! You won't even find their bodies; it was eaten by this blade." Lauren raised it so he could see it and explained its function. Melissa and Jacob wept silently. Lauren didn't provide much sensitivity when giving this heartbreaking news since Etienne was a cold blooded murderer as well as many of his followers and they themselves were most likely not much better.

Another car pulled into the drive. It was Renee and Barry carrying Jason and Amy's body with Vasteck and Gloria floating invisibly alongside. Renee, Vasteck, and Gloria entered the house and found them in the den. She approached cautiously seeing Anita lying on the sofa.

"Is Anita safe?" asked Renee whispering.

"Yes."

"Who are they?"

"Etienne's son and granddaughter. Where's Jason and Joy?" asked Lauren.

"In the car, Joy's still inside Amy's body, we're about to take her to the hospital," said Renee.

"Then go!" said Lauren, Renee returned to the car and Barry pulled out the drive. "Vasteck, stay here and watch after Mom. Gloria, Mary was given a death terror, look south of here and see if you can get her to Renee so she can heal her. "

"Sure," said Gloria and she left immediately.

"Where are you going, Lauren?" asked Vasteck.

"To Amalgam, Catherine's going to need my help," said Lauren. She left Vasteck and her ethereal friends behind orbing and flying fast to the Ghost Shack.

CHAPTER TWENTY-SIX
THE BATTLE OF CASTLE EVERLASTING

Jasmine returned to the graveyard cavern where the Spirit Phoenix released the electricity surrounding the portal to transport her to the gathering plains. The ethereal bird flew inside and set the portal aflame, melting the rungs and destroying the gateway. He then ferried Jasmine to and across the Amalgam heavens by way of a network of lighting bolts. She arrived on Trinity's wicker canopy amid a legion of Amalgam's fowls organized in a Phoenix emblem and led by Gretchen and the Child Phoenix. The emblem's beak was open to the air, wings outstretched, talons spaced, and the rear guard formed a pile of ashes. Its eye was Trinity.

The Phoenix stood in the center basket, Gretchen to his right and, when she arrived, Jasmine to his left. Inside Gretchen and Jasmine's baskets were placements for their Triquetra masks. Before them were thick white clouds proceeded their advance, coverage for his aerial squadron.

"Where are we?" asked Jasmine.

"A mile from the castle," said Phoenix. "The animals have secured your tree in the Lanise crater and now all it takes to start is your mark and spectroplasm. Where are the linking tome and the djemsheed?" asked Phoenix.

"Forgive me, but Lauren escaped and destroyed the linking tome after she cut me with her mortis blade. I dropped the djemsheed and she has it in her possession."

The Phoenix was livid at Lauren, baring his teeth and hissing for losing two precious possessions.

"We must be careful of her. Follow me into the Chamber and make sure she doesn't stop me from entering the Paradise Door."

"Etienne said the angel's told your secrets to two others. What do you plan to do about them?"

"Their betrayal is futile; I'll leave them to rot forever in the Burrow of Ignominy."

Jasmine looked past Phoenix to see Gretchen sitting in her chair, crossed-legged, very relaxed with a smile upon her face. Jasmine knew she was anxious to pit her strategy against the baroness.

"HOLD!" said the Phoenix. The fowls stopped

advancing and hovered in the air. Phoenix turned to his witches and ordered them to put on their masks. They did as instructed.

"Jasmine, activate the tree's suction. I've stationed a few hundred Loyalists inside the flare. It'll be our main siege tower once the castle is lowered. Take this as well." Phoenix extended his clenched fist opening it to reveal a spindly insect that looked like an appalling imitation of a crustacean.

"This will make Devon cooperate. Place it on his head. It's self-guiding and will force him to produce spectroplasm. Gretchen will command our air support and free our centaurs while I lead the ground infiltration. Remember, we're here for the Tower of Summons, nothing more. Today we enter the Paradise Realm!"

"Deus Vult!" said Jasmine and Gretchen.

Jasmine went to her basket and cracked the reigns. Her canopy splintered as Trinity replicated and it swooped down from the clouds. Moments later, Jasmine was swirling down about the top spectral tree's trunk. The animals surrounded the expansive crater except the space filled by the discontinued Ghastly Range. The broken mountain shelf offered no hope for escape, the disgraced mountain's retribution after Catherine's decision to elevate her castle rendered the natural barrier permeable. The animals made every imaginable sound to acknowledge their leader's arrival.

"Lead us to Estoc, Jasmine, let us raid the

ghost's prisons," the animals shouted.

Trinity extended her wing for Jasmine to walk inside the tree before retracting to the original in a flash. Jasmine walked to the tree's center column stair applauded by the Loyalists inside as she descended to the prison bottom. The prison foundation was a smooth circular hardwood pit. The walls were of carved bark with no prison cells. It housed a trap door invisible because there was no crevices indicative of a panel or handle to open it. She moved to a section of the room and cast *ascentate* raising a bark block revealing more steps to the tree's gargantuan taproot.

She arrived in a sprawling dugout at the bottom of the taproot's reach into the soil created by gestalt burrowing animals like prairie dogs and moles. The cavern floor was moist with the remaining spectroplasm from the lake. The ceiling consisted of numerous lateral roots wound tightly around the taproot. The taproot's feeder chords fed into Devon. He was dangling above an altar surrounded by a multitude of Loyalists. Bound between the tightly packed lateral roots was Etienne, fresh from the gathering plains.

"Amazing isn't it, how absolute my vengeance has been? First, I'm allowed to kill or capture all of my enemies from my mortal life and then they prove useful by helping the Phoenix and I enter the Paradise Door. Truly the Phoenix is the architect of justice."

"You'll never come within sight of the Paradise

Realm," said Devon.

"One thing is certain Devon, you won't live long enough to know," she said looking up to him from the altar.

"I hope you're right, Devon," said Etienne. "I was right to kill you that night, Jasmine. You wouldn't have lived a just life anyway."

"And what would you know about living a just life? As for you, Etienne, you'll be crushed to death by the roots hunger for Devon's spectroplasm. The spell I cast on your husk will thicken it, allowing you to suffer longer. Your name should be changed to Misery; for the remainder of your life you'll be the epitome of pain."

Jasmine placed the creature on Devon's head. It quickly made way for his ear and dug inside as Devon tried to wriggle it out his ear by forcefully shaking his head. He screamed as it began to take over his mind and his ability to control his mark's magic. His body's skin began to turn gray, his muscles tensed as he produced spectroplasm. The multiple feeder roots became rigid, prodding needles rummaging his husk. He screamed as they pierced him all over.

Etienne wailed as the lateral roots became taut about the taproot. The taproot began to resemble maggot-covered meat. Jasmine turned to the Loyalists gathered in the dugout and shouted, "The battle has begun. Our salvation is nigh!" The cavern shook with praise, Jasmine touched the taproot with her mark hand and the sky warped about the broken trunk. The barrier started to weaken and slowly Castle Everlasting began to descend. The tree was pulling the castle from the sky.

* * * *

Lauren exited the Everlasting's embassy tower and flew towards Baronsguard Gate. Lauren was the last person allowed through the garden before its hedges morphed to form the protective maze and the guardian manticore unleashed. Inside Baronsguard ghosts were relaying the orders of the district representatives and Baron Catherine to the intended recipients. Selene was waiting for her by the entrance. The siren picked her up and took her to the third floor placing her before the war room door. They entered, Catherine and the representatives stood about a large round table with various mirrors along the walls showing the displacement of guards, the position of the animal ranks, and the skyscraping tree's exterior.

"Lauren, thank God!" said Catherine. All four of Everlasting's Court rushed to her for information.

"Have you discovered the secret of the phoenix?" asked Catherine.

"Do you know what's powering the spectral tree?" asked Densen.

"Where is the linking tome?" asked Names and Graves.

"Do you have the djemsheed?" asked Lion Face.

"What were the animals in the gathering plains

for?" asked Densen.

"Have you learned where Estoc is being held?" asked Catherine.

"TIME OUT!" said Lauren. "Please, one at a time!"

Catherine ordered them all to silence and asked each of their questions receiving speedy answers from Lauren.

"Do you know where Estoc is being held?" asked Catherine.

"No."

"Where is the linking tome?" asked Catherine.

"I destroyed it."

"Congratulations, how about the djemsheed?" asked Catherine.

"Right here," Lauren produced the cup and handed it too her. Catherine gave it to Densen who placed it on the table.

"Do you know what's powering Kradleman?" asked Catherine.

"I don't know. Look, give me a moment to breathe and think. I came back with Amy on my mind," said Lauren moving to the table to sit down.

"Amy? Is something wrong with her?" asked Catherine. Lauren told Cathcrine how and why Jasmine possessed Amy's body.

"Her body's badly injured and needs her spirit to heal itself. She's being held in that tree along with Nasra, Vincent, and Devon…oh my God! Devon Knight!"

"Devon? They captured him?" asked Catherine.

"I'm not sure but Jasmine mentioned capturing some useful prisoners at the Hobby."

"What about him?" asked Lion Face.

"He can create dead pools and spectroplasm with his mark. He's probably been placed in the tree's taproot," said Catherine.

"We have to free him," said Lauren.

"Free him! Seeing as how he's fueling the tree he could be helping Jasmine and Phoenix," said Lion Face.

"I don't think so!" said Catherine. "Devon may have issues with me, but he's not a Phoenix Loyalist."

"How can we be sure? After all, he's been known to wear his death rags and roam the Wilds and he never told you where the linking tome was because of his hatred for the Court," said Lion Face.

"Because I know him!"

"I trust you judgment Catherine but you have made *serious* mistakes before! And this time, there'll be no Brilliant Flash from the Judge to stop the Phoenix," Lion Face said sternly.

"If you trust my judgment, then you wouldn't question it. They're forcing him to power the tree, I'm sure of it. The taproot is our primary target. We find Devon, stop the tree's suction, and free our Court officials. Lauren did you learn the Phoenix's secret?"

Lauren relayed what she had learned from Etienne to Catherine and her representatives.

"I've never known his followers to call him

anything other than Dark, Child, or Spirit Phoenix," said Densen.

"I know Michael doesn't work," said Catherine.

"Michael?" asked Lauren.

"The Phoenix's Mortalland name. I've used it several times since he's received the mark and it's never crippled him as you've described," said Catherine.

Sigpos appeared instantaneously in the room. His cloak was red, meaning he had the highest access of any messenger in Baronsguard.

"Catherine, reports of a bird armada has been confirmed," said Densen.

"How far are they from the castle?" asked Catherine.

"They're about to fly over us."

"Damn these mirrors! They just don't work well in the sky," said Lion Face.

"Names, tell the Barrier House staff to strengthen the shield with the dew reserves. Stay there until the castle's completely protected." Names left by the room's chandelier to see it through.

"Is a gestalt lord is leading the armada?" asked Catherine.

"The Phoenix is with them, flying a bird, looks like one of his creations," said Sigpos. A screech pierced the castle walls. Trinity was summoning all ears for her master's message.

"Catherine look!" said Densen. He pointed towards a mirror of the castle exterior where darkness was creeping over the city.

"Come, Lauren!" said Catherine.

They exited the war room and through Catherine's room came to a balcony that stretched the perimeter of the third floor. Lauren and Catherine took a stair to the rooftop and there they saw the Phoenix's armada approaching. Above Castle Everlasting, the Phoenix's fowl emblem cast a shadow down on the city trying the resident's courage, now mostly Everlasting Guards. Steadfast, the guards stood in the silhouette, fearless due to their readiness for Judgment, completion of purgation mandates, and Lion Face's braver charm.

The Phoenix drove Trinity from the squadron below, nearly scraping the dew barrier. He flew just out of range of the guard's Gattling Charmers, their anti-air batteries, and shouted a proclamation to all those remaining in the city.

"To all who now stand opposed to us, lie down your weapons, throw aside your allegiance to the Court, and take the Phoenix Oath." He flew back and forth over the castle, speaking the oath to all listeners.

"If you speak it now, you will be spared from the animals and my ghosts. Your defense of this castle is futile. Flee the city while you can. My winged companions will ensure your safety to the ground where you'll wait until the battle is won and follow me to the Paradise Realm," said Phoenix. In the distance Lauren could see a few orbs flying away, spooked by the threat of war they joined the Phoenix.

A towering stream of golden dew erupted from the Barrier House. The barrier encasing the city in a golden, glistening orb became stronger offering the castle its best protection. The castle was approaching the broken trunk of Jasmine's tree. Phoenix alerted Jasmine of the danger the barrier presented to their Loyalists in the tree and ordered them into the taproot cavern. The trunk hardened and it's knife-sharp, jagged edges destroyed many skyscrapers as it erupted through the foundation.

The tree's trunk was so massive many guards on the city streets had to run for their lives as the shredded ground chased after them. The vibrations sent many objects and people flying about as the city nestled into its former home, the Lanise crater. The shockwave threw Catherine and Lauren to the rooftop and many of the guards on the balcony fell off. With the Amalgam sun, Lumi, in the morning phase the tree firmly rooted in the city center it cast a long shadow westward.

The Phoenix communicated to Jasmine to activate the spectral tree's dew vacuums. The cells of the tree's sapwood grew thick and squeezed against the bark and heartwood making the tree stronger. The roots burst through the ground and broke through the barrier, then opened vacuums to suck in the dew. The golden circle about the castle slowly cracked. Some of the hardened dew broke into shards that fell onto the city streets. The sound of shattering glass filled the city. Densen and Lion Face came out onto the balcony to receive

Catherine's orders.

"What do we do, Catherine?" asked Densen.

"Lion Face, have a regiment dispatched to the city wall immediately. You, Lauren, and I will lead them inside. Have the guards in the vicinity give us cover. Densen, you're in charge until I get back, if the animals attack sound the Horn of Olives."

"I need to get Amy's spirit out first!" said Lauren. Catherine assured her that was one of her priorities.

"Wait," said Selene coming up the stairs to the roof. "I need to be involved Catherine. I want to do what I can."

"You can take Lauren inside the tree and the two of you search for Amy and the others. I'll see to Devon."

Catherine orbed and flew to the gate. Selene grabbed Lauren and flew after the baroness. Lauren was afraid, she couldn't imagine leading a charge into this massive tree but she didn't have much time to fear because soon they were at the city wall. Arriving in formation was Lion Face's best ghost regiment.

"Make for the trees roots. Cut Devon free and it should stop that tree from breaking the barrier," Catherine said to Lion Face and the guards before turning to the guards and yelling, "*FORWARD!*"

She orbed and led the charge with four hundred guard orbs following. As they approached the tree, they could see the Phoenix Loyalists moving inside. Moments later, magic blasts barreled towards them that seemed inescapable killing numerous guards in Lauren and Catherine's company. The guards on the rooftops used their Gattling Charmers to impede the Loyalists defense. About the tree, Lion Face's regiment swirled. They entered through the prison windows, and drew their ethereal weaponry to combat the Loyalists. Selene weaved through the Loyalists attacks with skill and the baroness was flawless.

Catherine, Lauren, and Selene entered through the same window high into the prison. Lauren looked below to see the battle unfolding. The Loyalists had ethereal swords swathe around their right arms in addition to their primary weapons, allowing them to hack and slash after casting a spell. The swords were element-based, allowing for attacks of fire, ice, or devastating brilzen magic. The guards countered Loyalist spells with the opposing element and their ice shields and fire charms, defending themselves well. Catherine ordered a few guards to follow Lauren and Selene.

"Start searching, Lauren. These guards will protect you. Meet me in the roots after you've found them."

Catherine jumped into the gap falling several levels to the trunk flare bottom. Lauren took her mortis blade and began slicing the roots of the cells. She kept a careful eye as the battle, though sparsely fought on their level, was still unfolding and she had to be on guard. She cut fifteen cells before she realized just how large the tree was. Each floor had nearly thirty cells and at ten levels high, Lauren would be hacking for some time.

Urgency also filled Lauren. She wanted to make it to the caverns before Catherine. Though she was confident Catherine would try to help Devon, she knew that the protection of the castle came first and the baroness would do anything to ensure that even sacrifice Devon. As she cut the sixteenth cell, the prisoner inside flung himself out at her. He carried her off the landing and they fell until they hit a bridge beneath them, seven stories down in the heat of the battle.

The crazed ghost punched Lauren, dazing her. He raised his arms for a fatal strike but his head sprung off from his neck by Selene's razor wings. As Lauren lay regaining consciousness, her eyes focused and, looking to her right, she saw a familiar face. Selene helped her up and followed her to the cell where, after cutting the vines, Nasra emerged and tightly hugged Lauren. Inside with her were Amy and Vincent. The guards protected them while they talked inside the cell.

"Glad to see you're still alive," said Nasra.

"I'm glad you're okay. When Jasmine told me she had captured you three I was so worried."

"Were you? I thought you'd never come back actually. I thought you'd be too busy trying to make moves on Jason or chickened out and given up," said Amy sarcastically. The pink glow had all but left her except for a very small mask about her eyes.

"That's the Amy I remember," said Lauren smiling.

"*What?* You had amnesia, is that what's taken so long? I bet I'm dead in Mortalland aren't I?"

"No, but you're going to be if I don't get you back soon."

"What's the situation, Lauren? Why the rescue mission?" asked Nasra.

"This isn't just a rescue mission. We're trying to stop this tree from sapping the dew from Castle Everlasting's barrier. They're forcing Devon to power it. I'm headed down there now to help Catherine."

"What do you want us to do?" asked Nasra. Lauren paused when Nasra asked her for orders. She forgot she outranked Nasra.

"You take Amy to Baronsguard. Get permission from Densen on my orders to allow Amy to the New City and return her spirit to her body. Vincent, come with me and Selene, maybe your skills as an illusionist will come in handy."

Nasra grabbed Amy and they flew out of the tree for Baronsguard. Lauren, Selene, and Vincent left the cell, followed by their entourage, which had diminished significantly. They arrived at the prison bottom, the trap door was open, and the flashing lights inside indicated Catherine and Lion Face were fighting the Loyalists. Lauren was about to descend when Vincent held her back.

"I know an illusion when I see one, and this one is very strong," said Vincent.

"Where?" asked Lauren looking around.

Vincent clasped his hands, chanted into them,

and with a swish, revealed the circular walls to be one ring prison cell barred by thick vines. Lauren ran along the cell cutting the vines with her blade until Estoc pounced out. He stretched his mouth as if he was roaring but emitted no sound.

"Estoc!" said Selene. She got down on one knee, rubbed his face, and brushed his mane. Estoc was astonished that Selene, his old compatriot was not dead as alleged but alive and in the company of ghosts. Lauren looked above to see the battle ending. The Everlasting guards clearly the victor as the Loyalists scurried from broken cell windows and out of the tree. She returned her attention towards the lion.

"Why can't he talk?" asked Lauren.

"A spell's inhibited his speech," said Selene.

"Catherine will know the charm to break it," said Lauren. "If he can speak to the animals before they attack he'll be able to tell the truth. Come on, Vincent, Selene stay with him."

As they delved deeper under the tree, the guards from the higher levels followed Lauren and Vincent or encircled the lion and siren protecting the two.

* * * *

In the root cavern, the overwhelming number of Loyalists routed Catherine and Lion Face's guards. Catherine found Devon hanging from the taproot, giving the spectral tree continuous juice. The crustacean ran through his forehead like an embedded, energetic crawfish and he writhed in pain. His husk was dark gray as the spectroplasm left him and filled the roots.

Outside the tree, the barrier was dwindling exposing most of the city to the Phoenix's armada. Gretchen ordered the birds to take down the battlements on the rooftops. The multiple spell casting Gattling Charmers and ghost archers who would rain spells onto the animals when the barrier was down. The birds were so numerous that the sky looked like a feathered quilt. They attacked ferociously, poking their beaks in windows and snatching up ghosts. Some brazenly picked guards from the streets as they stood packed in groups. On Gretchen's command, they converged on the Horn of Olives. The guards shot the birds down with deadly accuracy, as the Horn was the second most defended place outside of Baronsguard itself.

Lauren and Vincent entered the cavern and found Catherine and Lion Face's guards surrounded. Lauren looked back to see the ghosts following them in the tunnel and realized they wouldn't have enough.

"We need more guards," said Lauren.

"We don't need more guards. It just has to seem as though there are more in our group than it really is. Lead the way, Lauren. I'll make it appear like we have infinite reinforcements."

The guards in front with Lauren gave her a waiting stare. She turned to the inside and commanded them, "To the altar! Cut Devon free!"

They screamed and followed her inside, drawing the Loyalists attention to the new arrivals. Vincent moved back up to the pit entrance and had the ghosts protecting Selene and Estoc run and swish their weapons. He then made illusions of them and streamed it into the cavern. To the Loyalists, they were the beleaguered and fled to the surface through several tunnels the tree's roots formed earlier in its search for nourishment.

Jasmine was among them, though she looked back carefully at the taproot. She couldn't protect Devon because Catherine would defeat her and she had no intentions of dying before entering the Paradise Door. Etienne, the source of her passionate hatred, disappeared under the pressure of the roots that blocked out his squeals and the sight of his agonized face. She cast a phantom of herself onto the root where she placed him and with a spectral trail, she was there.

The roots were taut about the taproot and resembled a cocoon but she forced her way into them and found Etienne still alive. Her vengeance was not satiated and she poked her staff inside to finish the job. Catherine saw her and cast *spectro sintegara* that sent Jasmine into the cavern wall and significantly drained her spectroplasm. A group of guards came to finish her but Jasmine escaped using her phantom trails charm and surfaced onto the city street.

Catherine took her sword, ran to the altar, and cut Devon down. The roots extended for his body on the floor but Lion Face pulled him away before they could resume feeding. They were too late; the tree had fed more than its share. It continued to sap the dew from the barrier until it only remained a few feet high. The Everlasting City stood naked against the animals. Phoenix teleported to the mountain cliff on the Ghastly Range and turned into a flaming column, the signal to attack.

The animals ran wildly into the city. The more limber and swifter animals were the first inside. Estoc's lioness headed for Baronsguard looking for the ghost prison followed by the rest. Hyenas pounced on the guards and gnawed their weapons to break them. The elephants congregated to form walled charges that scattered any organized resistance.

The Everlasting Guards strategy was to wait in packets of forty in the intersections and lured the animals with tempting numbers. Irresistible to the incensed beasts, the bait ghosts would unleash brilliant spells, blinding the animals. Guards waiting inside nearby buildings then shot them with immobilizing charms.

Though their wild nature was expected to be devastating, the animals were at a disadvantage. They were not prepared for the twisting and confusing city streets. The piles of rubble wrought by the spectral tree's roots effectively stopped most stampedes by the larger beasts and slowed many of the swifter creatures.

Densen stood ready to blow the giant twenty-foot horn. It was a curved L-shape and on it laid an angel with mighty wings spread. Her loving downcast gaze focused on a small dove cupped in her smooth hands. Densen gave the horn a forceful blow. Its sound was sharp, penetrating, and maddening to animals. A smooth-trotting tamed horse turned into a wild, kicking, neighing beast. Others became immobile, some fled the castle, and the birds fell from the sky.

Phoenix, however, could not have his invasion so easily defeated and he created the earless Trinity to counter the horn. Gretchen, Phoenix, and now Jasmine, who was back with them, split Trinity into three identical eagles and dove from the sky. Jasmine and Gretchen preceded the Phoenix, their eagles taking ravaging damage. Jasmine fell from her basket back into the perilous ghost city. Gretchen diverted their fire long enough for Phoenix's eagle to ensnare the horn. He took the horn to the sky while Gretchen's eagle picked apart the horn until it lain in the city streets broken in three huge shards.

"Now's the time, Phoenix," said Gretchen. "Take the Tower of Summons."

"Lead the remaining Loyalists to the docks. Have them sail for my archipelago in Jaheri," said Phoenix. "There I'll take the tower so our loyalists can enter after me."

Gretchen signaled to the Loyalists and they slyly began withdrawing, some atop the freed centaurs. They were careful not to draw the animal's attention that they were leaving before finding Estoc as Phoenix promised. Phoenix picked up Jasmine from the streets as she slew guards in her path towards Baronsguard and together they flew for the Tower of Summons.

* * * *

The Horn of Olive's resonance filtered down below. Catherine listened and heard the horn being broken. This troubled Catherine because now she didn't know how else to stop the animal attack. Catherine had Lion Face fetch Etienne from the roots and bound him with truss shackles for his trial. The baroness removed the crustacean from Devon's ear using *spectricate endodaver* spell and crushed it under her heel. Lauren, Selene, Vincent, and Estoc all approached Catherine and Lion Face.

"Take Etienne to the brig and have Devon looked at in the infirmary," said the baroness to Lion Face.

Lauren approached Devon and hugged him tightly. "I thought Jasmine may have killed you. I'm so happy you're alive."

"I had to ensure you'd make it out and it was my pleasure to delay Jasmine."

"You found Estoc!" said Catherine merrily. Lauren let go of Devon and turned her attention to the lion.

"He's been silenced, Catherine," said Selene.

Catherine raised her hand and spoke the anti-charm *sonorous permis*.

"Thank you, Catherine," said Estoc. He looked up at the cavern ceiling listening at the sound of strife filtering down. "My animals! Are they..."

"Attacking my castle, yes! They believe I was behind your kidnapping. We have to let them know the Court wasn't behind your disappearance."

"What better way to do so than you standing side-by-side with Selene and me?" Estoc asked.

"That's not enough now. The Horn of Olives has been destroyed and the fighting continues. We must see to it that the battle ends *now!*" said Catherine. Lauren quickly thought over Catherine's comments and came to a clever conclusion.

"Selene, your singing nearly killed us in the aquifer and, Estoc, your roar deafened me in the forest. Maybe if you two combined your voices it could stop the animals."

Catherine smiled after hearing Lauren's idea and wasted no time executing it. "Selene, grab Estoc and follow me," she said.

The baroness orbed and flew out the cavern as Selene took Estoc and followed her to the top of the Ages embassy tower. There Catherine ghosted to human form and Selene placed Estoc beside her. His eyes widened at the animals killing ghosts, the city in ruin, and the battle still raging.

"You and Selene can end it all right now, with the roar of a king and song of a siren or you can watch us destroy each other. The choice is up to you."

Catherine stepped back, knelt down, and covered her ears with her eyes focused on the lion. Together, Estoc released a deepened roar and Selene sang the highest musical note that surpassed the Horn of Olives and deafened every ghost and animal in the city. The fighting came to an abrupt pause. After the shock of the roar and song subsided, the animals knew their lord was free and he stood with Catherine at his side.

"It's Estoc! He's with Catherine and Selene," spoke some of the animals.

"I know you've been misled into believing that Baron Catherine captured me but that was a lie. The Phoenix ordered his witch to capture me; imprisoning me in the very tree they used to bring down the ghost's city and led you to war for his own purposes. For our transgressions, we'll be forever indebted to the Court from this day forth. Now we must seek peace with them and as your leader, I command you all to return to the Wilds. I'll rejoin you after I make amends with Catherine on our behalf," Estoc concluded.

Catherine felt peace returning as she surveyed the damage wrought to the Everlasting City. In the rumble, she spotted Lauren returning to the surface with Devon and the others by the spectral tree. Yet Catherine still heard fighting in the city. Looking behind her, she saw Phoenix and Jasmine atop Trinity flying toward the Tower of Summons.

"The Phoenix is heading for the Chamber!" said Catherine. "I've got to stop them. Selene, get

Lauren, take her to the Tower of Summons."

"I'll take you, Catherine, get on," said Estoc, Catherine straddled the lion.

He leapt from the embassy tower and landed on a nearby mountain shelf, running full speed to the summit. Trinity swooped down and wrapped her large talons over the Tower of Summons. She ripped the tower from its foundation, destroying its connecting bridge to Baronsguard and took to the sky.

"I can't follow you Catherine but I can get you up there," said Estoc as he reached the summit with Trinity passing by. Estoc leapt from the summit giving Catherine enough height to orb and reach the tower. A swarm of his eagles saved the great lion from his fatal fall and placed him safely on the ground. Selene swooped up Lauren from the spectral tree and upon flying up saw the Tower of Summons airborne.

"Selene, I need to get up there!" said Lauren. "Can you fly that high?"

"I'll try," said Selene as she flew up. Trinity faltered struggling with the load giving Selene time to catch up and Lauren a chance to help Catherine.

CHAPTER TWENTY-SEVEN
THE CHAMBER OF THREE DOORS

Selene swooped into the gaping hole of the tower's ruined foundation. Clouds raced beneath as Selene placed Lauren on the remaining groundwork. Selene's wings were in horrible pain after their arrival and she collapsed near the gap.

"Are you alright, Selene?" asked Lauren.

"My wings are tired and my strength is gone. I can't carry on."

"But I'll need your help to get to the Chamber."

"God will give you aid, Lauren. Go!"

Lauren hesitantly left Selene as she orbed to fly up the inverted stairs. Trinity held the tower at an obtuse angle making it difficult to traverse altogether. She looked down the halls, searching for a door carved with the symbol of the Three Doors to find the chamber. All she found, however, were ghosts returning to their rooms, orbs were flying about the tower, and screams of horror pervaded the halls. As she rose higher, Lauren saw a display of white and blue light coming from the highest level.

She reached the top where she found Catherine running toward a giant door at the end of the hall. Blue and white light emanated from the chamber entrance. She ghosted and tried to speak but all she could manage was a loud "Cath—" before she slipped and slid down the hall screaming. The baroness turned and waited as Lauren slid to her, stopping her as she neared. Catherine situated Lauren on the floor but at this angle, Lauren had to hold on to Catherine to stop from falling forward. Catherine placed a hand on Lauren's head adjusting her equilibrium, negating gravity, and the hall righted itself.

"Thank you," said Lauren.

"The Phoenix is in my chamber, but he'll have to wait for me. I'll need your mark and what you know of the secret to stop him!" said Catherine.

"Where is he taking the tower?" asked Lauren.

"Most likely to his archipelago."

"Why does the Phoenix have to wait for you?"

"Only my mark can open the Paradise Door."

"Then why don't you just stay away and let him take the tower wherever he's taking it."

"Because the Three Doors are inside. They're the only set given to me by the Judge and the only doors in Amalgam that can send ghosts to the different realms. I cannot summon spirits to Him without the entire chamber intact."

"And does the Phoenix think you'll just open the Paradise door for him?"

"No, which is why I'm certain we are walking into a trap. Be on guard! Are you ready?"

Though Lauren was frightened, she said yes. Catherine pushed the door inward and entered, Lauren followed closely behind. The chamber was circular with no windows, grass covered the floor that felt natural, and in the center was a large willow tree. Its crown was big and full, decorated with shimmering white beads. They shone bright in the room, the darkness hid in its glimmer.

About the room were numerous fireflies that fluttered in the air, their abdomens flickered brightly. Fifteen of these tiny bugs were carrying large oval rings that draped veils wrapped around the top. The veils blew strongly from a breeze that was imperceptible in the room and seemingly originated from the rings. There was also a fountain set off to the right. It contained an animated statue of a menacing red and orange phoenix crouched down, its feathered tail and flapping wings were aflame. Fire churned inside its eyes and its beak was open to life-like figurines of Catherine and Lauren. The phoenix wound about the two figurines with its tail blocking the way forward and the body in back.

In the back of the chamber were the Three Doors, each massive, thick and tall, exactly like the numerous representations Lauren had seen before. They couldn't find Jasmine and the Phoenix anywhere.

"I'm guessing this isn't how the chamber normally looks," said Lauren.

"No, Jasmine or the Phoenix must've cast an anamnesis."

"Like my father's message?"

"Yes but this one surely has some devious trap for us like that fountain there!"

"I thought they were just messages."

"Anamneses are ghost memories left after distressing deaths. The spiritual trauma embeds on the thin fabric separating the ethereal and physical worlds leaving apart of the soul that remains forever as a message to all who can see it. Legends have risen surrounding them such as ghosts reenacting battles, brutal murders, or rooms where spirits are weeping over dead people," said Catherine. "Some ghosts who experience these types of deaths can create anamneses at will even altering them to include deadly traps."

"So is this Jasmine's memory?"

"Yes," said Jasmine, her voice reverberating about the room as she appeared from behind the statue. Catherine and Lauren turned to her as Jasmine rubbed the top of her staff in her left hand.

"The whole room with the exception of this fountain and the Three Doors is an anamnesis of my wedding! I married Jonathan underneath this one. Mrs. Watlington and I joyously captured the fireflies the week before. It was a good time and a wonderful bonding experience with my future mother-in-law. I'd finally won Jonathan's heart and the governor's plaything was dead." Lauren balled up her hand, her fist clinched tightly as Jasmine spoke causally of taking Nasra's mortal life.

"Where is the Phoenix?" asked Catherine.

"Be patient and when he appears, cooperate," said Jasmine with a menacing smirk.

"Cooperate? Do you believe I'll assist with such appalling defiance before the Judge?" asked Catherine.

"The Judge is eternal compassion, love, not some villain like you and the representatives of your Court. I came here to find that, instead I received mandates from the very person who was supposed to be most similar to the Judge."

"Jasmine, I know you and I know the Judge. He is clear that those who go against Him will meet their end with eternal torture. How do you suppose He'll react to you aiding one of His greatest offenders?"

"Listen to you, assuming He desires to see us punished. Maybe He'll understand the way you failed to how I was murdered by Etienne, how diminished his barons have become, and how this world has failed the innocents and rewarded the sinful with control of His realm of salvation."

"Do you even know what you're saying?" asked Catherine incredulously. "You're not a crusader trying to supplant an evil oppressor. You've sent

souls prematurely to the Judge, stripping them of any hope of salvation then dare proclaim "Deus Vult!" You think the Judge will forgive you for *forcing* your way into Paradise against His commandments. Phoenix steals the Judge's mark and pretends to be the Savior thinking he'll be welcomed back in Heaven as if he's the prodigal son."

"He's crazy, Jasmine, and because you couldn't see through your own misery, you've thrown your very soul into the Phoenix fire to be consumed with him. Neither Phoenix nor any of his followers will be able to bargain for forgiveness. I'll admit my error as I'm not perfect and Etienne's actions have earned him a place in the pyre for his treachery but I beg you to break the Phoenix's oath and return to Him. Turn away from the Phoenix's madness."

"The Phoenix saw past your blindness, Catherine. He's given me justice and been truly compassionate, and for that," said Jasmine as she ignited her staff, "I defend him with my life. *Pillari cinzeré!*" Jasmine's staff touched the bird's beak and a flame burst forth, roasting the figurines that in turn, burnt their real counterparts. A column of fire erupted from beneath the two and Lauren wailed in pain as she hit the ground, yet Catherine quickly defended herself.

"Aramousghoul!" Catherine cast upon Lauren and she was no longer pained.

"I'll ask only once more, where is he?" asked Catherine threatening Jasmine with her sword.

Jasmine appeared nervous and troubled that Catherine was becoming more aggressive. In her fright, she cast a sidelong glance at a previously unforeseen fountain. Catherine smiled as Jasmine swiftly turned her gaze back though her face expressed her mistake.

Catherine glided over to the fountain, as Lauren looked at Jasmine whose eyes loathed the baroness. Catherine stood in front of a small birdbath with a fountainhead of a tiny bird with three heads. From each mouth issued water that collected in the bath. The baroness looked inside but instead of seeing her reflection, she witnessed a troubling dispute in her courtroom long ago.

"Is everything alright, Catherine?" asked Lauren while facing Jasmine, who now smiled delightfully. Catherine stood mumbling until suddenly a bright light issued from the water. It snatched up the baroness, shrinking her and bringing her into the bath and a terror anamnesis.

"*Catherine!*" said Lauren as she ran towards the fountain.

"You're not going to disturb them!" said Jasmine.

She hit the bird with another fire charm only this time Lauren was prepared with her guard spell. The burning flame appeared in a column beneath her but warped about her, leaving her unscathed as the pillar burnt the ceiling.

"So you've learned a bit of magic since you've been in Amalgam," said Jasmine. As she reached for the tip of her staff, a handle formed and she unsheathed a sword. She swished it in the air tauntingly as she approached. "But you're not a master swordswoman like me. I've been trained by the Phoenix and it will please me to slice up the new baron and the daughter of one of my victims."

Lauren materialized her sword and prepared to defend herself.

"How cute! They gave you a toy!" Jasmine raised her sword in the air to strike, but this was a feint as the witch whipped her staff-sheath around to stun Lauren. Lauren ducked.

Jasmine quickly swung her sword down to cleave Lauren in two from head-to-toe but Lauren blocked her strike. Jasmine swung her sword to split Lauren from the right side, yet Lauren defended herself by moving her sword to the left. Lauren pulled Jasmine's sword to the right, throwing her off-balance and elbowing her in the face. Jasmine reeled back and cursed at her. Unfazed by her coarseness, Lauren swung her sword to cut off Jasmine's head but she ducked and spun around to get back into an offensive stance.

Jasmine tried to strike Lauren's back, but Lauren blocked and in a flurry of quick swings and parries, she had Jasmine trying desperately to defend herself. Lauren's wrath exploded, she cut through Jasmine's defenses, slicing her arms and legs. Jasmine backed towards the fountain and collapsed to the floor. She was bleeding from her wounds and cursed Lauren in her disbelief.

"Impossible! You must have learned that from the Phoenix!"

"Being in his column seems to have been both a gift and a curse. A curse because I have to fight him and his witches, but a gift because now I have the ability to beat you!" said Lauren.

Jasmine licked one of her wounds then spat necroplasm on the ground. Her eyes loathed Lauren's sword. She was obviously thinking how to disarm her.

"I have one question for you, Jasmine," said Lauren.

"What? You want to know if your father died screaming in pain? *He did!*" Jasmine's face changed to Willem's and grew pale then she said in Willem's shivering voice, "I-IT'S SO-SOOO CO-COLD!"

Lauren bit her lip to restrain her anger before asking, "Did Jonathan ever love you? Answer honestly!"

Jasmine restored her face and her lips crumpled as if she was sucking on lemons. The truth vexed her, but she was more surprised Lauren would ask a question about Nasra instead of her father.

"No! After he learned of Nasra's death, he needed someone! I never understood what he saw in that whore but I got what I wanted. My family was elevated in society and I got the most desirable bachelor in Baker's Creek!"

"You're a sad person."

"Listen at you judging me! If you could have,

you would have done the same thing. Amy certainly did. She knew you liked Jason but she did what most people do; she made herself happy. I'm no different than her or the average person!"

"Amy's never killed anyone. You have!"

"No? Didn't she push you in front of a moving car? She was willing to do exactly what all cold souls are ready to do, what's necessary to get what we want!"

"Amy's not a cold soul and you won't make me hate Amy the way you hate Nasra. I've let go of my anger, you can't! You won't!"

"You've become a bit arrogant! You like the power Phoenix has given you, don't you? It was the same for me when I killed Etienne. If you would just join us, you could get Jason!"

Lauren was humbled. She felt she was taking revenge and learned why Catherine warned against it. It was making her just like her enemy!

"Never, Jasmine! God gave me this power. It's His, not the Phoenix's and I'm not going to take what doesn't belong to me!"

"One thing *God* didn't give you is my powers!" Jasmine raised her hand and the willow branches latched around Lauren's arms. Lauren tried to fight them off, cutting a few but they wrapped around her legs and arms. Jasmine stood erect and shot brilzen magic from her fingertips. Lauren was able to cast *cinzere voltus* to block the electric strike and used the electric fire to burn many of the branches winding around her legs. Jasmine again sent lightning and Lauren cast *flectis* and shot it back at Jasmine. Jasmine created a phantom and moved into it before the bolt struck her. Lauren cut herself free while Jasmine used the anemos element to blow the fireflies closer to them.

"*Schizenscar!*" yelled Jasmine pointing her staff and sending the charm into a nearby firefly's ring on her left.

The bolt traveled into it and bounced through the other rings so fast they all lit up before the spell rocketed from the ring to Lauren's right. Lauren ducked and fell to the floor; the spell burst a deep hole in the chamber wall. The bird blew fire again burning Lauren's figurine, setting her ablaze, but she cast her guard spell to shut out the flames. Jasmine shot a spell directly at Lauren on the ground. Lauren reflected it with the *flectis* charm.

It returned to Jasmine as Lauren stood quickly and cast *spectrogeal* at her, hoping to immobilize her. Jasmine dissolved the returned spell, and sidestepped the spectrogeal blast into the path of the bird flame. Lauren quickly cast her guard spell to protect herself from the fire, while Jasmine held up her hand and deflected the flame with *aramous*.

Blocking the fire, Jasmine pointed her staff again at the rings. "Schizenscar," she spoke. The spell leapt from her staff through the rings. Lauren stood boldly and spoke clearly, "*Flectis magnus!*" The spell raced from the rings and Lauren repelled it back through with blistering speed. The magic attack amplified three times its speed and power by the magnus charm. Lauren then cast the freezing water spell *purgen aquis* at Jasmine.

The phoenix statue was still breathing fire and Jasmine continued to deflect it. She used her staff hand to reflect Lauren's water spell, but couldn't turn quickly enough to deflect the fast returning scar spell. It hopped rapidly through each ring until it struck Jasmine in the head, mentally incapacitating her. Her *schizenscar* attack wholly destroyed her psyche and she cried out as she collapsed to the floor. Lauren used the spell *cinzeré en volpus* to destroy the bird statue and ran to help Catherine.

Lauren looked inside at the bathwater. The barons and representatives of the Morrigan nation accused Catherine of gross negligence and malfeasance. Leading them, unbeknownst to Lauren was Baron Donovan, Catherine's immediate successor, sitting behind his bench at the Gorge of Genesis courtroom. Lauren could hear their voices rising from within the vision. Catherine pleaded for forgiveness but they continued to berate her. Through the courtroom doors burst a luminous presence, Messina. She immediately quelled the court and took the baroness in her arms.

"*I'm sorry, Messina. I've failed!*" Catherine cried.

"There, there, you've done well, Catherine. Your fellow barons can't see that. I know you're strong and we can undo your great folly."

"How?" asked Catherine.

"Unlock the Paradise Door, bring those legions

of guardsmen and women back to Amalgam, and restore your army to crush the Phoenix!"

Messina relinquished Catherine and the baroness raised her mark hand. Lauren heard a door open, and as there were no Three Doors present in the vision, Lauren turned to the real doors in the chamber. The Paradise Door swung open. The room became warm, brilliant pink, gold and white, love and happiness issued from the door and Lauren felt at peace for a moment.

Cold water spilled from the birdbath onto the floor disrupting Lauren's calm when it splashed upon her feet. She backed away as the water collecting into a puddle and emerging from it was a watery being taking male shape, forming flesh and clothing, standing at a slender four feet tall. Child Phoenix stood before her looking dreamily at the Paradise door. Lauren didn't know how to free Catherine from the manipulative terror anamnesis and now, she was all that stood in his way. The Phoenix ran for the door but Lauren shouted, "PHOENIX! I KNOW YOUR NAME!"

Two totem poles carved as flaming birds sprang from the ground. Shackles and chains stretched from their beaks wrapping about the Phoenix's wrists and ankles. He fell forcefully to his knees in front of the Paradise Door.

"NO! NOOOOO!" screamed Phoenix. Lauren walked around and stood before him looking into the Great Sinners eyes.

"THE PRIZE IS WITHIN MY REACH, I CAN

SEE THE REALM! I'M GROWING STRONGER NOW THAT I'M CLOSER TO GOD! GIVE ME THAT INFINITE POWER!" said Phoenix looking into the open door. He bowed his head and heaved in frustration then spoke, "*Know this Lauren: if you give the wrong name…I'll be freed…and I'll kill you before I enter Heaven!*" Phoenix looked into her eyes and said, "Speak clearly, for you only have one guess!"

Lauren knelt down, eye to eye with him and said, "Henri Dak."

"*IMPOSSIBLE! NOOOO!*" screamed Phoenix.

Out from Phoenix's body came a large white phoenix bird, the magic of Henri's mark that flew into Lauren's mark of the Phoenix Cage. Henri turned into a Phoenix bird that screeched so loud it stunned Lauren worse than Selene and Estoc moments before. Lauren summoned her strength, raised her sword, and with one swipe cut off the fowl's head. The Phoenix's remains ignited in orange flames that engulfed the chains and the totem poles.

Lauren covered her eyes in the brilliant light as Henri burned to a pile of ashes. He lost all strength and power at the sound of his name just as Etienne said. The Phoenix's fountain caught fire and Catherine was free from his terror anamnesis, springing from the fountain onto the chamber floor. The ashes turned into the Phoenix's infamous column. It burst through the ceiling setting Trinity aflame and streaked across the Amalgam sky in flight to his archipelago.

Trinity lost her grip on the tower as she burned to oblivion. The tower fell from the sky like an anvil. Lauren and every ghost inside save for Catherine was screaming as the tower plummeted. Selene flew out of the bottom before it smashed into an island off the coast of Jaheri, not far from Jonah's city. There it stood leaning like a collapsing lighthouse, half of the foundation was obliterated by the rock, the rest submerged in water.

The ghosts in the tower tried to compose themselves but Lauren heard their screams rising from the lower levels. Inside the restored chamber, only Catherine, Lauren, Jasmine, and the Three Doors remained. Catherine closed the Paradise door and calmed herself while Lauren, fatigued, sat on the floor, stretching back, her arms propping her up. Catherine approached and sat next to her, hovering without a chair as she does behind her courtroom bench.

"How did you stop him?" asked Catherine bewildered and rubbing her head, Lauren caught her breathe then answered.

"I used the name Henri Dak. I remembered Phoenix using it in one my dreams when he introduced himself to Jasmine."

"And Jasmine?"

"Luck, training, and quick reflexes."

"Well, Lauren, I thank you. You saved Amalgam from the Phoenix and definitely lived up to the title of baroness. Messina was right about you and I'm glad the Court has your help."

Red, yellow, blue, and green cinders materialized in the room directly in front of them and hung in the air like bouncing bees. They formed her father in a blue sweater, black slacks, his slick hair, brown skin, and dark eyes. Behind him in the anamnesis were the Three Doors, the Paradise Door wide open with brilliant yellow light melting into near blinding white radiance. The room became warm again and Lauren could feel the love of God flowing from the Paradise Door through the anamnesis.

"As promised Lauren, Willem's anamnesis," said Catherine pleasantly. Lauren watched attentively.

"Dear, Lauren," said Willem gently, "if you're watching this message then you've demonstrated that you are indeed capable of completing the Judge's mandate to reclaim his treasured mark. Once Messina told me how you could aid in the restoration Amalgam I knew you could do it. I leave you now for Heaven in hopes that I'll see you again after a long life of sacrifice, loyalty, and faith in the service of the one True God. He promises your reward will be great and we know He cannot lie."

"Please take care of your mother and baby sister, Morgan. See past Anita's faults, forgive her and me, and move on as I wish I could have when I had the chance. I would have loved so much to be Morgan's father despite what I may have told your mother. Remember, I'll always be there for you.

Seek God and you'll find your path."

Willem entered the Paradise Door and it sealed shut as the anamnesis vaporized to nothingness. Lauren cried tears of joy, her father was in Heaven, and now she was encouraged to continue the fight. Amalgam would depend on her to save them from the Phoenix's great sin and ultimately God's wrath and Lauren would shoulder that responsibility. She looked forward to helping Anita raise her little sister, whom Willem named Morgan.

"You're father is a true man, he was able to let go and let God. As you can see, he's with the Father now as will you be someday I'm sure." Catherine sighed deeply before returning to her commanding nature as baroness.

"Phoenix was defeated today but this wasn't a total waste for him. He's leveled Castle Everlasting and now it's only a matter of time before he finds another way to infiltrate my city. I'll have to act quickly to reinforce the Everlasting Guard and notify the barons that Phoenix has set the board. This is the beginning of the third Phoenix war. With the Phoenix's treachery exposed, I hope that Estoc can find it in himself to reconcile the animals to us. A large army of ghosts and animals united would deter Phoenix a bit longer," said Catherine dreamily.

"We'll make sure the animals are on your side, Catherine," said Selene pushing open the chamber doors. "Estoc's personal account of his abduction and imprisonment in the spectral tree will be proof enough of the Phoenix's deception."

Catherine looked over at Lauren who was silently wiping her tears away.

"Are those tears of joy or sadness?" asked Catherine.

"Both," said Lauren.

* * * *

An hour later, Catherine, Lauren, and Selene ushered all the ghosts out of the tower and to the shores of Jaheri. Trinity's embers still rained from above and the rough seas raging about Jaheri's shore sent crashing waves against the fallen tower. The baroness froze these waves to form an ice bridge. They all crossed and Catherine, carrying the incapacitated Jasmine, led the train of ghosts to Jonah's city. A multitude of Ruin Guards aided in the rescue and protected them on the mile long trek to Ruin Everlasting, where lay the remnants of Catherine's first castle.

Lauren laid her eyes on a large twentieth-century cruise liner broken in half down to the keel and served as lodging for the ghosts of Ruin Everlasting. She saw an archaic and crumbling coliseum on a cliff to her right and the waste of Catherine's original castle to left that was still immaculately beautiful in spots. A gargantuan clock tower that's construction appeared largely unfinished stood as the showpiece.

"Well, it looks like Jonah has another

masterpiece to add to his city of wreckage," said Catherine smiling slightly.

"I'll have to take up his philosophy and put that giant tree in my city to good use. Maybe it could be a new housing unit. I'll have to find some way to transport the chamber of three doors back to my city. Without the weight of the tower, it should be fairly easy."

"What happened to you back in the chamber?" asked Lauren.

"Phoenix placed a terror anamnesis on me."

"What was it of?"

"An old mistake, the first I made as baron. One that pains me even now because of the lost we suffered for it during the first Phoenix war. Thousands of guards vanished without a trace because I had a dream and I followed it as a message from God. I sent them away and they never returned."

"Did the Phoenix send the dream to you?"

"No, although his magic felt amazingly similar. I made many enemies after that. The barons and several representatives lost confidence in my leadership and I simultaneously lost two of my best generals, one of whom was Gretchen Reis. To this day I don't know why God made me do it but I…we must have faith in Him."

Jasmine mumbled incoherently to herself and rolled her head around as if she was dizzy. Lauren saw that she was clutching something in her hand and removed it from her grip. It was a long candlestick, jasmine-scented and cool to Lauren's touch. She looked at it curiously and caught Catherine eyeing her who simply smiled and said, "Keep it," so Lauren tucked it away.

"What's going to happen to her?" asked Lauren.

"I'm taking her to Messina to get her psyche restored, her mark destroyed, and Judgment. Then I'll carry out her sentence."

As they moved closer to Ruin Everlasting, Nasra and Devon were approaching them having come through the Amalgam portal from Castle Everlasting and were accompanied by Baron Jonah.

"Congratulations, Catherine," said Baron Jonah.

"Don't thank me. Thank Lauren," said Catherine.

"Ah, the New Baron! It's a pleasure meeting you," said Jonah with a smile. He shook her hand firmly then turned to Catherine, "Next time, Catherine, leave the Amalgam portal open so that we can help."

"I was confident in our ability to defend the city but not against the Phoenix. Lauren here surprised me defeating both Phoenix and Jasmine," said Catherine lifting Jasmine's delirious, defenseless body as the proof.

"Lauren has certainly surprised us all," said Jonah smiling at Lauren. "I think we can all rest comfortably knowing Messina has sent us a capable agent. We'll have to throw a massive feast at the castle in light of your success."

"Thank you, Baron Jonah," said Lauren.

"Amy's back in the New City," said Nasra. "She's very tired; Jasmine's possession has really weakened her body. I told her to thank Renee for saving her life by patching her wound. That injury is going to take some time to heal and it will leave a scar but she'll make it," said Nasra.

"I'll tell her to take it easy," said Lauren.

"Renee also asked me to thank you."

"Why?"

"She said her mother's spirit was freed and came to speak with her before she left for Amalgam. Teresa said that the Phoenix let her go, no doubt because of you and Catherine." Nasra looked at Jasmine's body and lifted her hanging head to see her eyes spinning and her forehead tense as if she was searching for her memories.

"Poor Jasmine! I wished she had done her time in the fields," said Nasra.

"She told me Jonathan never loved her," said Lauren. Nasra thought fondly of her ancient lover and smiled but this revelation was bittersweet. She pitied Jasmine for obsessing over Jonathan, her murderous ambition to win his heart, and her coming damnation. Catherine's attention turned to Devon and she smiled to cheer up his demoralized countenance.

"It's nice to see you outside of the Wilds again, Devon," she said, finally having the chance to talk with him.

"You know why I've been in isolation, Catherine. I'm tired of warring, being hunted, and now I'm partly responsible for grounding Castle Everlasting. I'm not sure whether you're keeping me here or the Judge nor do I know the reason, but my time for summoning has been long overdue."

"So has my time and trust me, I know exactly how you feel. After all, I arrived here shortly after Amalgam's creation and been here ever since. Until the Judge summons us, we must keep moving. Otherwise, we become idle, withdrawn, and slowly but surely cold. Every day will seem like a lifetime but if we stay busy time will pass faster than you'll believe. Your powers are vast and you've proven yourself loyal to the Judge through pain and suffering. Join us at Castle Everlasting; I need a district representative to the Wilds. You can still roam free after of work."

"And become a servant?" asked Devon appalled.

"To the people Devon," said Nasra. "Better to serve someone else than yourself; that's the same selfishness that led Jasmine to the Phoenix." Catherine sighed and closed her eyes, everyone watched her. She turned her head as if she was listening to a word from the heavens. Messina was sending her a message.

"It's seems it's time you finally have your explanation, Devon. The real reason why you haven't left Amalgam is because you refused to tell the Court where the linking tome was buried. The Judge says your mandate was to destroy the linking tome, find the Mortalland Seal, and close access to the New City but you demanded an explanation first. Had you done your duty, you'd have discovered this while fulfilling your task much like our New Baron; right, Lauren?"

"Yes. I see why I need to finish my job as baroness and to whom I need to show my mark to accept the Judge's mandate."

Lauren's grail mark appeared on her left hand shone brightly. She cupped her right hand over her left, and observed it animate. The blood spilled from the cup in the graphic and trickled down to her wrist. The blood seeped into her skin there and throughout her body; she felt warmth and a tinkling sensation. She raised her hand to Devon and showed it to him.

"And I'll need your help, Devon, to complete my task. Remember, we're here to serve only God not Catherine, other ghosts, or ourselves. Be honored He allows you to be His servant," said Lauren.

Devon didn't have to think much harder after observing the mark. He was familiar with the ancient prophecy and realized that Amalgam's salvation was now at hand.

"You're right; all of you are. I'll take the position, Catherine, but I also want to help Lauren in the New City," said Devon affirmatively. "And I want my own room in that nice mansion of yours. It'll sure beat the Hobby with Vincent."

* * * *

Catherine and Lauren took Jasmine and the djemsheed to Metatron in Messina's cathedral, who promptly destroyed Jasmine's powers and restored her psyche. There Jasmine was damned to serve the rest of Amalgam's existence in the pyre for numerous infractions, but none more severely than taking the Phoenix Oath. Etienne was sentenced next, Messina read aloud his infractions and Lauren learned more about his numerous murders in his quest for fame. Messina asked Etienne if he told Lauren everything he learned of the first secret of the Phoenix from Raziel. He responded affirmatively.

Messina asked Lauren if any of the Saved survived the graveyard battle. Lauren said only Jacob and Melissa Lasitier remained alive and eternal. Lauren asked if they would lend her the chalice before it was sealed back in the treasury to offer them a choice, to remove their immortality with either the djemsheed or the mortis blade! Messina consented and they wisely chose the djemsheed. Messina had Lauren tell them that they must never to speak of what they know about Amalgam or be guilty of the Mortalland Rule. Jacob inherited Etienne's incredible wealth and he and Melissa lived the rest of their lives quietly in Baker's Creek. While in the New City, Lauren was also tasked with erasing Jason's memory for what he'd seen in the lighthouse's lamp room.

Etienne and Jasmine were led side-by-side to their respective cages in the pyre. Jasmine no longer desired to harm Etienne. Shame and the vileness in her spirit completely consumed her and brought on a deep depression. Etienne was similarly defeated having found the world he so desperately sought. He realized that had he taken his own immortality and lived righteously he could have seen Amalgam years earlier or the infinitely better Paradise realm. Only then did he realize that some of life's mysteries like what happens after death should remain matters of faith than fact.

The guards imprisoned them inside tall steel cages next to each other in the pyre. Their confines locked, and the keys destroyed in their sights. Their spirits caught fire from the ignited wood and straw underneath their cages and until the end of Amalgam, their cries eclipsed all others in the purgation fields. Lauren watched them burn from the cliff edge sad to see such a sight. Catherine joined her on the mountaintop. Having learned of their life and the circumstances that lead them to such a fate, Lauren began to weep for them.

She wondered if she'd have to see the Phoenix and all his witches share the same fate. She wondered how much more pain the Phoenix and his loyalists would bring to souls in both Mortalland and Amalgam realms. The baroness placed her hand on Lauren's shoulder to comfort her as they watched together. Catherine's palm grew warm as her mark radiated; it was time to summon souls for Judgment. She turned to Lauren before departing for Baronsguard.

"We need to resume your training to make you into a more powerful baron. When the Phoenix rises again, you'll not have access to his memories and discovering his name will take strength and intelligence. You should return home and get some rest. I expect to see you soon," said Catherine.

Lauren said firmly, "I know, we have work to do."

EPILOGUE
LAUREN'S DIARY

31 October 2003 M.R.

It's been a few weeks since I defeated Henri and Jasmine and thankfully it's been all quite in Amalgam. Estoc and Selene have managed to reconcile half the animals with the Morrigan nation. Many remain cold, but they are leaderless and scattered about the Wilds. The ghosts have been celebrating nonstop after the Phoenix's defeat! It's funny but Sigpos was right about the effect my barony would have on the ghosts of Amalgam! Numerous souls have renounced the Phoenix and returned to being faithful servants of the Judge. A number of them praise me but I know it wasn't my amateur skills that got me through; it was due to a great deal of help from Him.

I've begun training with Baron Catherine, and Renee and Nasra have often joined me. Amy is using the excuse that she's still healing from her wounds to avoid returning to Amalgam, but Catherine said she'll find a way to drag Amy back, even if she has to reinstate her as a door steward (haha!). My powers grow everyday, its amazing the things I can do! I feel so lucky and yet so troubled, I fear my powers aren't enough considering Jasmine was without her full strength for a majority of her time in Amalgam. If the Phoenix's other witches are more powerful, then it makes me wonder if I'm training hard enough.

Mom is healthy despite the scare Jasmine gave her. She continued to pester me about what she saw until I got so tired of lying that I begged Catherine and Messina to allow me to tell Mom the truth. They agreed, saying that since Jasmine revealed herself to a mortal, she broke the Mortalland Rule and allowed me to summon Mr. Vasteck in our living room while I explained to Mom most of what's happening to me (I think the distance niece stuff would have been too much for her to bear). Mom had an ultrasound today, and told me it was girl. She asked me to pick a name and I said that Dad probably would have liked the name Morgan. She loved it! So around March will be welcoming little Morgan Walston into the family.

I also explained to Grandma Betty a *theory* I had on Willem's death. She listened carefully and when I finished she asked if what I told her was the truth. I couldn't confirm it without breaking the rules but Betty sensed I was being honest and said she's content with my explanation. Betty said that if she were to die soon, she'd go peacefully now that she had some closure. Speaking of death, Mina Monroe passed from her wounds, yet I see her all the time in Amalgam. She's been developing Renee's oracle abilities from the other side when Renee's here in Mortalland and teaching her how to decipher her riddles. Life goes on indeed!

Jason's happy to be back on good terms with Amy, and I'm happy for him. I can only hope that some day soon, I'll find a guy as interesting as Jason who'll burn red for me! Thankfully, Catherine keeps me so busy I don't have time to dwell on my depressing love life. To help me cope, I think of Nasra who lost Jonathan for good and was able to move on despite all that Jasmine had done. Goodbye Jason, maybe in the next world we'll be together.

After reading Dylan's letter, I've begun my search for the sect he said was spying on the Saved. My first lead is to discover who this mysterious boy is that was following the sect and question him about this competing group. I know he'll come into my life sure enough, one thing about serving the Court is that you're bound (should I say destined? maybe mandated? No, Messina was confident!). I'm confident I'll cross paths with him sooner or later.

Jasmine's candle burns constantly upon my bed stand; it never melts. It must be magical, another device she created to help her remember dwell on the past. I'm thankful to have it, I love the scent and it's very strong. It brightens my days and settles my mind so I can rest at night. It helps me remember that I was capable of rising to the challenge and gives me the strength and courage to continue to fight. Until the Phoenix rises again, I'll keep training and hopefully I'll be ready in time!

Justin Freeman is a fan of ghost stories and an enthusiast of the fantasy genre. The Ghosts of Amalgam: The Linking Tome is the first of a seven-part series of fantasy novels combining the mysterious world of ghosts with a mixture of new and familiar fantasy elements. This novel represents the culmination of seven years of hard work to provide the fantasy genre with fresh ideas and a new perspective on the nature of ghost literature.

Printed in the United States
94122LV00001B/49-81/A